Josefu's Thousand Hills

Josefu Mutesa, British born of Ugandan parents, slowly recalls his experiences in Rwanda, 'land of the thousand hills' where he went as an UN official in the aftermath of the genocide. When UN rules continued to cause havoc by being applied just as blindly as they had been during the killings, he had a breakdown out there and was evacuated to Canada.

Now, six years later, he decides to face his past as he drives across the prairies.

Appraisal of Josefu's Thousand Hills:

"...subtle novel"
    - **Wole Soyinka,** Nobel Prize for literature 1986

"...a novel of our times"
    - **Alan Sillitoe,** on reading the manuscript

This book is dedicated to **Jane Weale** *with gratitude for her support while I wrote it and to my children* **Alex and Annie Klim** *with thanks for their inspiration and trust over many years.*

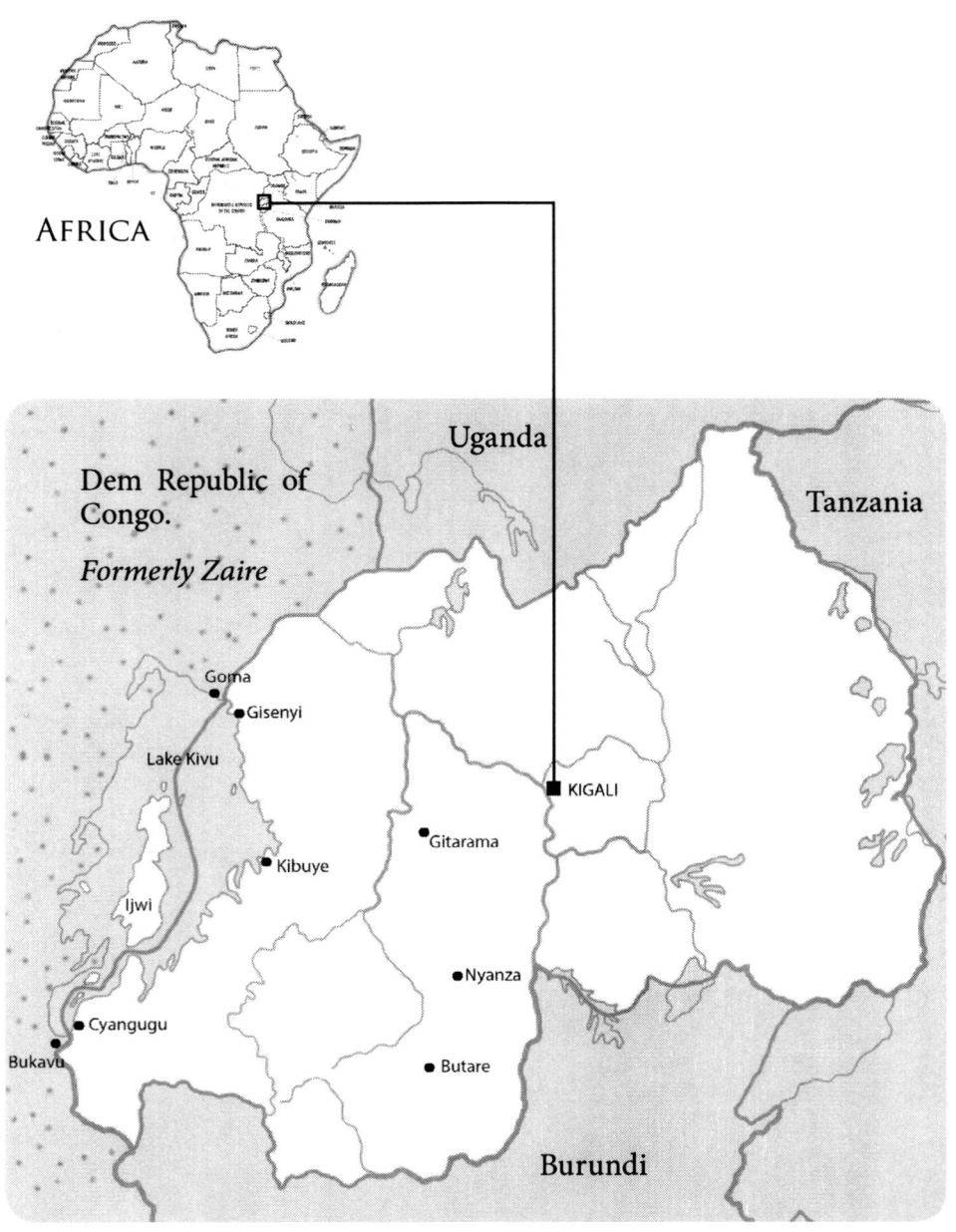

Josefu's Thousand Hills

A Novel

Tamara Dragadze

We plant a tree for every book sold

Copyright © 2014 Tamara Dragadze
All rights reserved.
The right of Tamara Dragadze to be identified as author of this work has been asserted by her in accordance with the Copyright, Designs and Patents Act 1988.

No paragraph of this publication may be reproduced, copied or transmitted save with the written permission from the publisher in accordance with the provisions of the Copyright Act 1956 (as amended).

This book is sold subject to the condition that it shall not by way of trade or otherwise be lent, resold, hired out or otherwise circulated without the publisher's prior consent, in any form of binding or cover other than that in which it is published, and without a similar condition, including this condition, being imposed on the subsequent purchaser.

> All characters in this publication are either fictitious or are historical in fictitious situations, so any resemblance to real persons, living or dead, is purely coincidental.

ISBN 978-8792632-39-5

Cover design & Layout by Whyte Tracks
Typeset in Minion 11pt

Published by
Whyte Tracks, Denmark

IMPORTANT NOTE

This is a historical novel concerning real events and locations in a fictitious context. The main character is an invented descendent of Mutesa I, whose reign ended in 1884. I believe that my choice will appear to his real family as an expression of my admiration for their ancestor, who was one of the most remarkable monarchs of modern times.

Two characters, Generals Paul Kagame and Guy Tousignant, are real historic figures, but who are described in fictitious meetings. General Romeo Dallaire and President Juvenal Habyarimana appear in visions and dreams.

Fictitious characters, with fictitious opinions, make reference to further historic figures: Idi Amin, Kofi Annan, General Bagosora, Bhoutros Ghali and Sharyahar Kahn, Professor Mugesera, Milton Obote, Mrs. Ogata, Raquia Omaar and Monsignor Perraudin. And the names are genuine of American basketball players. Everyone else in the novel, and their names, are entirely fictitious.

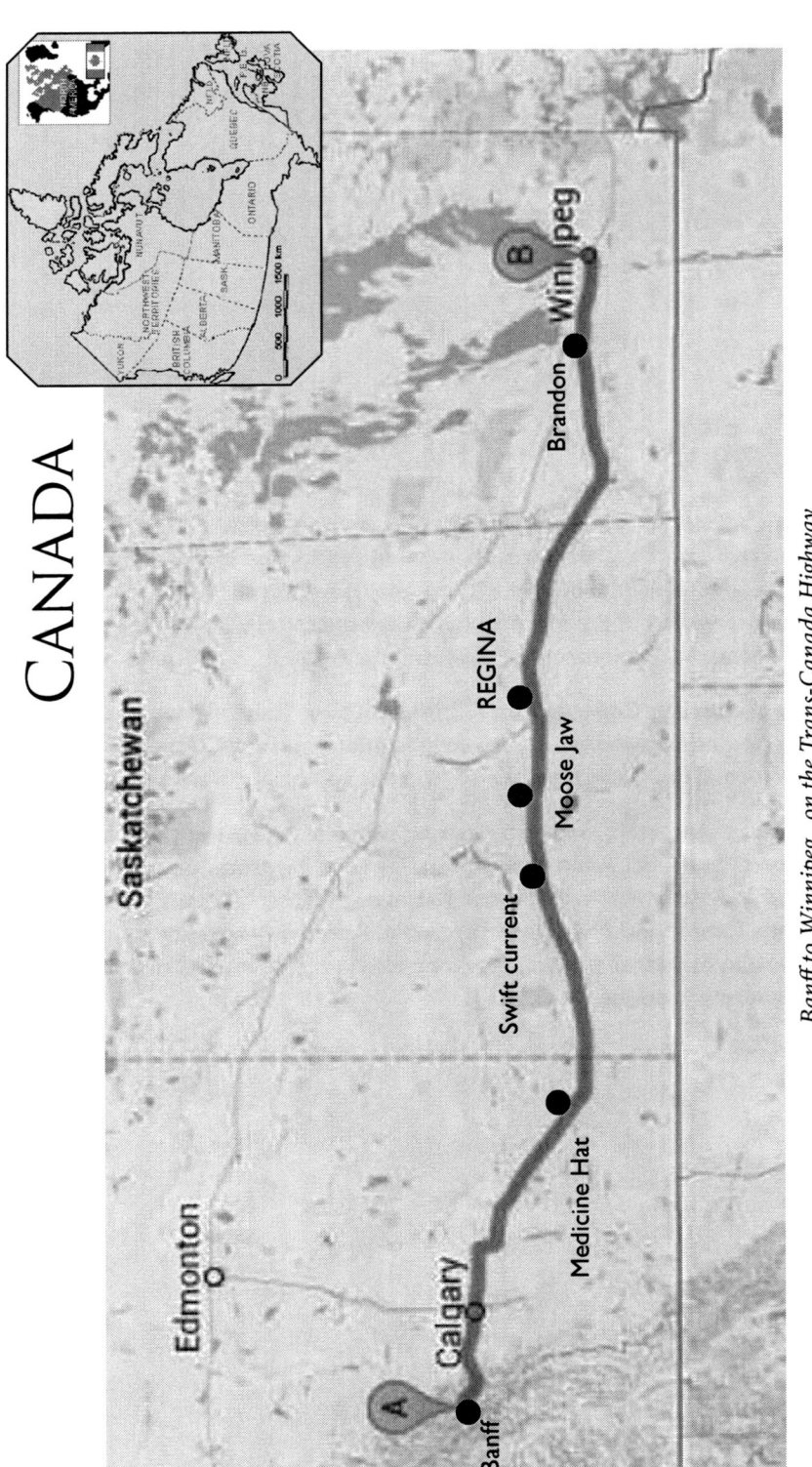

Banff to Winnipeg, on the Trans-Canada Highway

Contents

I. The Call
1 1
2 10

II. The Shed
3 27
4 56
5 76

III. Rivers and Stones
6 93
7 111
8 126
9 140
10 152

IV. The Roads
11 171
12 187
13 204
14 219

V. The Lake
15 239
16 259
17 278
18 296

VI. The Burning Hut
19 311
20 324

VIII. The Short End
21 335
22 349

Acknowledgments

Parallel Journeys

This novel is one in a group of three forming a triptych—of different characters and locations yet that are linked by an intense experience of parallel journeys.

Travelling in unfamiliar surroundings sometimes focuses the mind, voluntarily or not, on significant past journeys in a different country. Landscapes part and blend, however incongruously and each of the three works presents a variant on this single theme.

I   The Call

1

Josefu holds a jar of coffee with a red lid when he answers the phone call. Her questions chime like bells and he senses that for him, although he gives no answers, they announce across the landscape that something has broken and ended. His house is in Buffalo Street, on the edge of Banff.

"But why Canada?" she asks. "Why not somewhere in Africa?"

So she knows nothing. "Six years," he says, but she knows nothing. He dwells in mid-air, between prairie and high mountain, and she knows nothing.

He puts down the receiver and slowly scratches his ankle with the other foot, waiting, watching the spot on the floor where, so unthinkingly, he had picked up the coffee jar. Now he holds on to it, as if in fear of losing the link to the call. Her timing is odd, he reflects, to know when to ring just as he came up the drive.

Returning to the doorway, he surveys a pile of wet logs left over from winter and a large storage cabin to the side. His property is well sheltered with high trees. The sky is white, a sign of the changing season. It is the fourth day in June. He steps further out but, as always, the wood chippings under his feet unsettle him, the way they look, the sound they make. He has refused the grey stone gravel which some neighbours use, yet always moves awkwardly in his own yard.

He looks to the moist, smooth road. Four cars drive by one after the other with a sense of urgency, perhaps wanting to reach Lake Louise by the route that closes early. Usually his eyes would follow them briefly, as if to protect his domain, but now he hardly notices. There is a strong scent outside from yesterday's rain and all smells unnerve him.

The car needs better parking. He fills in the corners of most days with a long drive to Calgary and back, taking with him an empty briefcase. When returning through the Parks Canada checkpoint, the new recruits curiously inspect his Banff resident's car pass, suspecting he is some former celebrity. Josefu is black, tall and he drives a silver car. When greeted, he speaks with a clear British accent and a soft voice centred round his lips. They wave him on. Once inside the boundary, he immediately increases speed to reach his large entrance up to a house always painted dark brown.

The couple who had brought him to Banff taught him a way to defend his choice to live there: 'it was reasonable', he must say, 'solid and creative' — they were rarely lost for words and knew that 'creative' was a good option. So, except for this call, Josefu says repetitively that here, in the Rocky Mountains, his land at the rear overlooks the river. Also, he has a greenhouse. And lastly, he is a keen gardener. Their instructions are that he should not be drawn when this logic can explain nothing. After all, given the climate, there are just three months in the year for ardently tending his back garden and in the remainder he only reads about it. He has many horticultural volumes, though, and partly owns the Banff bookshop, thanks to which he has a residence permit for this restricted area. And long before Josefu settled there, Banff was a place where people came for healing.

⋮

With stooped shoulders, still nursing the coffee jar, he now goes to lean his head against the window overlooking the back garden and beyond. The swollen river threatens to part in the middle and swallow him, his legs tangled in busy, discarded branches. He prefers the heavy waters iced over, not to see the witnesses he knows they are hiding. He likes the winter snow in Alberta, the blanking out of shapes, a white screen plain and undemanding, which shields his eyes from anything to observe. It is easier to carve out paths to take and places to stop, the same each day, and then silently to rest his feet at night.

Today it is late; nobody walks on the footpath that skirts the back gardens. Along the riverbank, leafless shrubs grow in disorderly fashion. They are beyond Josefu's remit, as are the scattered stones. Out of the quiet there comes a low hissing sound. *There is no mandate, she should know.* He thinks for a moment, ". . mandate, mandate," he repeats, but quickly recoils. He turns to his lawn and sees dead leaves on the grass, out of season for the beginning of June. Dead leaves there or dead rats? "No, Alberta - the Rat Free State." "I used the wrong declension of thought," he adds. These are the wasted leaves of the previous summer. A gust of wind sweeps the brown shapes sideways and they are gone.

He trains his eyes onto the intricate, wire meshing he has carefully chosen to enclose his back garden. The impudent elk, free to roam everywhere in Banff, immediately exploit a single sign of weakness. Josefu finds them in high spirits recently, perhaps because their coats are moulting. Once someone who knows he had worked at the United Nations said jokingly that the elk are Banff's uncontrolled peace-keepers. He froze at the remark and pretended not to have heard, banishing it from his mind. The same day he intensified efforts to make the back garden impregnable. Occasionally, though, a stray elk, enjoying the shade of his openly accessible front yard, appears to greet him with a glance, which he grudgingly acknowledges.

At present, the fence is intact. The stillness overwhelms him suddenly and he leaves the window. Again, the phone call; the way she said 'Josefu' echoes in his mind and draws him into a sorrow he had no longer remembered. 'Why aren't you speaking? Josefu? Josefu?' she'd said, more and more gently. He has lost the ability to have conversations, the kind she elicits from him. These days, he listens and gives short answers. Now, though, her voice seems to enter and sear him. He begins to experience an unfamiliar anger.

He says aloud, "No! Not her, not that Ellie!" Then he sees the wooden stool placed before a television he rarely watches. He rushes and sits down, his tall bulk hunched over the coffee jar, and doesn't move till night has fallen.

⋮

Awake, Josefu hears rain outside. He goes to the kitchen and hurriedly puts a frozen meal in the oven as it is past his usual eating time. He shops for food only in the supermarket, 'Keller Foods' in Banff, and goes without if they don't have what he wants. He washes his hands carefully and sits down to eat, concentrates on chewing rhythmically the goulash and rice, sipping beer which he likes not too cold. A glance at the wall clock causes him to be grateful he has reached the end of the day. There is a tap on the door and someone enters.

"Oh - Dave," says Josefu.

Dave wears a white bathrobe just covering his knees with a large hood over his red hair. "Who cares how I'm dressed, eh?" he says, with a swift smile. "Hey, I've come about the visitors tomorrow: publishers. Arriving at noon and I suggest" he pauses, ". . that if it is raining you should not make us walk all the way up to that Hotel." He draws his cheeks into a forced smile and keeps it.

"We have umbrellas," Josefu replies, ". . and gumboots. And that is the way we have always done it."

Josefu insists that, whenever they have clients requiring his presence, they take a brisk walk up to the Banff Springs Hotel regardless of the weather. He has purchased a stock of toe rubbers for men to slip over their city shoes, gumboots of different sizes and a pile of paper bags for women to carry their shoes in, several pairs of thick socks and half a dozen umbrellas.

"You're so stubborn, you know, Josefu. With the rain, just this once, it's June for God sakes."

Josefu huffs. Dave Epstein owns the remaining third of the bookshop. Previously, he was sole proprietor, going bankrupt. He does most of the talking to publishers. Whispering about African royalty, he refers to Josefu as a mascot.

"But if I am not there, Dave, you can take them wherever you want."

"But it's good when there's you. Hey, you're still in your suit."

"I'm fine."

"Take care," Dave says, going back into the drizzle.

The whole front yard lights up automatically, which Josefu finds too bright, but the security installation was already there when he moved in. The trees are tall and towering like theatre scenery and he is fleetingly unsure of his bearings. He steps outside and stands on a stone slab to avoid the wood chippings, but quickly goes back in, knowing he can go straight to his bedroom and into the dark.

⋮

Ellie had been his first love and he had dismissed it ever since. Now in his dream Josefu stands before a dark, cherry wood desk with an open visitors' book, gold rimmed and green, ready for him to sign. 'I don't know if I can do this,' he says aloud, though unsure of who stands beside him. 'I'll fill in below: I was born in Maidenhead, in Great Britain, went to Stowe School, oh I forgot: parents from Uganda.' Then he is interrupted by an orange patched cat who jumps absurdly backwards on to the book and looks up straight into his eyes as if knowing there is a reward. 'Ellie's cat,' he says to himself, 'So simple, so utterly simple.'

But he moves away, and his feet are caught in heavy mud, making each step more painful. To find relief, he cradles his head in his arms but falls forwards and awakes with a start. He looks round and sees wet reeds behind him, a thicket of bamboo and grass. He searches for Ellie in her long woollen bathrobe, so as to explain the reason for his departure, but the bedroom reappears and he realises where he is.

He sits on the edge of his large bed which fills most of the room, picks up his white alarm clock, just knocked down, and a book with 'Shrubs and Blooms' written boldly on the cover. He is aware of being alone in the house but there is a lingering presence of other people, all nameless, all caught among thick leaves of rhododendrons, the ones without blooms.

He lies back again, a white cloud before his eyes, a small feather pillow placed lightly on his face, and he bites his lips till morning comes.

⋮

Josefu's official 'Need to reside' in Banff is that he has to be near the bookshop. Martina Patterson has been brought in, however, to be the manageress — her own chosen title — of Banff Book Shop. He has seen a postcard she had received from the group of women with whom she spends most of her social life: 'Your eyes like a legend, a goddess in your own right.' She had arrived alone in Banff, some fifteen years ago. She was widowed early, her two married sons live in faraway provinces, but she hasn't been seen dating, Dave said. Josefu follows her every order, nearly, and he knows she is aware that he appreciates her demeanour, her commanding build, luminous eyes and the heavy jewellery she always wears over her bosom.

Although his tasks are to sign cheques and entertain clients, Josefu has spare time, which he is told has to be filled judiciously. At Martina's behest he volunteers to tend the garden at Luxton House, an historic property, she said, belonging to a founding family of Banff and now bequeathed to the Museum. An extraordinary collection of one hundred and twenty three packets of seeds was discovered after the last family member died. This occurred at the time of Josefu's arrival. He weeds, he plants, and he learns as he goes, keeping meticulous records all along. It is this, even more than having rescued the bookshop, which gives the dignitaries of Banff reason to believe that they have done well to grant him a residence permit. Also, about six months after moving in, he made a donation to the Harlequin ducks research project of Parks Canada, at Dave Epstein's suggestion. "Part of my networking," Dave said at the time.

One incident had worried Martina soon after Josefu settled. Later, she told him that until then, few people living in Banff had noticed him. One day Dave invited to his own home in Buffalo Street a real estate agent known to have the mayor's ear. When asked who mowed his lawn so well, Dave answered vaguely. The man then said, "Can I have him too?"

Keen to impress, Dave had replied "Sure, I'll send him to you," and the next day asked Josefu to go. A John Deere mower was already there and so Josefu walked up, rang the bell and went straight through to the garden.

When he had finished the job, he had been handed a ten-dollar bill. He had given a slight bow in silence, slowly put the money in his jacket right pocket and turned away. But he had not felt it happened to him; there was no response he could make. He left the money in the bookshop office, neatly smoothed out and held down with a spare set of keys, always kept by the large fax machine.

A few days later, however, Martina found out quite by chance and was beside herself. "David Epstein, you've gone too far, do you hear me? David C. Epstein, listen, this time you've really blown it," she said, her gaze threatening to pluck out his bushy eyebrows.

"He didn't mind — did you, Josefu?" Dave asked him.

"Can you imagine," Martina shouted, "The owner of Banff Book Shop taking tips for manual labour! I'm going to call her now." She rapidly dialled, hardly waiting for the answer before announcing: "Hi, this is Martina Patterson, I am the manageress of Banff Book Shop but this call isn't about books. There has been a misunderstanding."

Josefu had quickly risen, gone into the office and closed the door. He could still hear her saying, "Of course he wears expensive clothes! No, he didn't rob his country…. inherited wealth from his father… and his father's brother was a king. There are several kings in Uganda," she added knowledgeably.

Then she intoned, as on several previous occasions: "Do you know what that means? What his background means? Do you understand what knowing him means?" Josefu knew exactly what she would say and bit his lips. "Let's face it," she continued, "That means there were kings and prime ministers and governments and queens and nations in Africa long before Queen Victoria. That's what it means!" Martina added emphatically: "Knowing Josefu Mutesa makes you remember: Africa had governance and office holders and Royalty of their own." As usual, she cleared her throat then kept a meaningful silence for a moment, before ending with, "That's what it tells us about ancient Africa, by knowing who he is."

Just as before, Josefu was unsure how to react, part pleased, part embarrassed. So he had taken a deep breath and at last felt he was able to surf like a balloon above the earth. He had learned to do this in hospital, not to hear or see what he didn't want to. Then he had waved to Martina who was still on the telephone and gone out, walking briskly past the grim parkade.

He came to some wooden chalets. Banff had originally been

influenced by a Swiss presence and, given the years Josefu had spent in Geneva, he valued whatever traces were left. 'There was poverty then, in the Swiss Mountains,' he had explained a few days previously, almost inaudibly, to a group of young people down from the Banff Arts Centre. 'Especially in the west of their small country. And the guides were skilled and reliable, so they came here despite the awful distance.' His fleeting compassion for the homesick, Swiss mountain guides was as close to an emotion as he could bear.

He had entered his street with a gingerly gait, hardly touching the ground, arms motionless, head erect, eyes looking straight ahead. He knew though, where each house was, including Dave's next to his.

"Perhaps he has some kind of special way of being aware," Martina had once remarked, having watched him walking from afar. "And look at that butt, like a school boy's, the way it sticks out, when the rest of him is so staid. I shouldn't say that," she laughed. Josefu had overheard her, and he banished it from his thoughts.

On the day that Dave was reprimanded, however, Martina had within hours made some judicious phone calls and used the lunch hour to make a suggestion to Josefu. "No," she had shouted as she entered his kitchen, "Stop! Have lunch with me!" He did not like his pattern to be broken. "It's an emergency. Please will you help me?" In silence he had put his food away.

"I see Dave's old bison's head is still there by his gate," she'd said. It was in a glass cage on a pole, 'for Buffalo Street, for Gods sakes', Dave had said.

Martina drove Josefu to Earl's Restaurant, which he tolerated. Waiting for a table, she said, "Aren't you dying to know?"

"No, I'm all right."

She shook back her light brown hair. "Look, I have this friend in Calgary, she's vegetarian like me. Her name is Gulshan, okay? She is director, wait for it, of the Crohn's Disease and Colitis Society of Canada for the whole of Alberta and the Northern Territories, and do you know where the main office is? In Calgary! You could go there sometimes, couldn't you? She needs help, very badly. I mean, because of your residence permit here in Banff you can't be employed in Calgary, but she'll pay expenses" They were interrupted; a table was waiting for them.

"So you want me to go there, to Calgary?" Josefu had asked after ordering.

"Yes. They need filing, a little book keeping. So? Will you give it a try?"

"Book keeping?"

"Yes, Josefu, just a bit. Please say yes."

"Yes," he said.

"Yes," she had repeated. She beamed and took his hand. "Look, it's not just to get you away from Dave, you know."

Josefu began to go most days. Rapidly Martina and Gulshan learned that he preferred to be treated like an employee, even being told to provide a doctor's certificate if he missed more than a few days. On the other hand, whenever required by Banff Book Shop, he could stay behind in Banff. Martina and Gulshan were old friends and belonged to the same Women's Whole Being Group.

As for Josefu, he started to enjoy the driving and, of this he became perfectly conscious: he could only be thankful that, what with the bookshop and being voluntary garden curator of Luxton House and the job in Calgary, he had virtually no spare time.

2.

After drinking Martina's coffee, kept over from the morning, the guests from the publishing house depart. Everyone is satisfied; Josefu is relieved it's over. He rushes to Luxton House and sits in the small garden shed for a while. It is his favourite spot at the back and when he is caught out there sometimes, people say, 'Look at that African! Just sitting there. He'll get back to work some time.' In fact, he occasionally reads his notebooks but today he just breathes quietly, his hands folded, as he had been taught in a small, white hospital room that had no windows.

⋮

At nightfall he goes outside his home at the rear, muttering. He has received no telephone calls all evening and now it is late. The rain has stopped but the smell of the wet earth prevents Josefu from venturing further from the house.

As the moonlight increases, his eye catches a large bird's nest lodged in the forked boughs of the tree that leans over from his neighbour's garden. He drags a ladder up to remove it. "All that dawn twitter," he says.

A fearless bird sits resolutely in the nest, refusing to leave the eggs she is brooding. Josefu carries the nest to a ledge at the side of the house. He holds it with both arms outstretched but the bird flaps her wings and clamours, seeming to look him in the eye.

He hears: 'Tharcisse, don't kill my children; you know them. Tharcisse!'

Josefu puts the nest down in disgust, goes back inside and wipes his brow. He cannot recall who Tharcisse could be, nor when a woman's high voice had said this before. Through the window he perceives a thin and shapeless colour before him, a haze of dark red, perhaps, or a light brown mist. He wishes there were a greater barrier between himself and the Bow River, and that he could wrap his eyes in thick crepe bandages. "Someone else would have to bind them for me, though," he remarks aloud.

Immediately walking out again he takes the nest with the bird still there, secures it back in the fork of the boughs with some twigs and grass he tears from the ground, all the time avoiding her glance. "Be my guest," he sighs, "You have as much right to be here as I do."

He dreams all night; one that he often has of being trapped in a small jewel box, containing a ring, snapped shut with him inside. He overcomes his fear and gazes into the depths of his dark blue velvet confinement. Waking, he now recalls with lucidity, that he once gave such a box to Ellie, but not to Patricia, his wife, who chose her ring herself and left the box behind. He turns over onto his stomach, his armpits wet.

Then he dreams that Martina enters his room and, fully clothed, lies on the bed beside him. He remains still, so pleased she trusted him when she had nowhere to stay. He sees that she is barefoot and wears nothing under her usual flowing skirt and he wonders whether he can touch her and how far, but wakes up again.

He moves to turn on the light to dispel the dream but finds himself driving a car without beams, trying to keep in the centre of a dark dirt road. He pulls up outside a disused, white-washed, empty schoolroom, riddled with bullets. Having entered, he sees on a charred desk an open book with gold and green leather. He says aloud, *"The Book of Days, I know you,"* but cannot remember what were the names of the places he had travelled through, which he is obliged to record.

⋮

If it were not for the sheen on the river, Josefu might have gone out to sit on the folding chair with his mug of breakfast coffee. It is early morning, 6th of June and two days after the call from when he had started counting. The chair is the one his mother used and he has never moved it. She died — it was something she did, an action, in the same way she put out her hand to choose vegetables for Sunday, or signed letters the secretary brought her, or held Josefu's head to cut his hair. She died; not a fading into absence, it was a deed. For some minutes she breathed faster, then opened her eyes and did it.

He had sat by her for six days in England, beside the metal bed, with his cousin Maria, and an uncle. She was buried in white but he recalled her only in her full Gomez dress from Kampala, the one she wore with a folded brocade gold belt, which they both liked. For all that and for the sake of all her dying, he does not move the folding chair.

He goes back in to the toilet, his eyes avoiding the mirror while he carefully washes his hands. The mornings, after showering, he smoothes his eyebrows with his head bent downwards and shaves with his chin lifted so high he can see little else but his jaw. "Things that you learn," he tells himself daily, unquestioningly.

'Who is Tharcisse?' Josefu suddenly murmurs, as soon as he has driven past the Parks Canada attendants. The question resonates near the nape of his neck. He lifts a hand to reach the spot and the car swerves. He thinks about calling Bill and Mary who live in Winnipeg and had brought him to Banff. Josefu often hears the couple being lauded, for the efforts they made when he was evacuated from where Bill and he had been on an UN mission, to get him first into a mental hospital in Ottawa and then settled in Banff, far from any reminders of what happened, just as they had been advised to, medically. He tries not to dwell on it.

Bill, now retired, says, 'You're my best friend,' yet Josefu knows he has lost that part of himself he can no longer recreate, and which Bill grieves for.

Mary let her hair go grey and even Josefu smiles when their daughter Pamela upbraids her for it. One of their sons, at twenty years old, was killed in a car accident. Josefu already knew them when it happened.

The couple visit Josefu regularly, but stay at the King Edward Hotel in Banff. Dora his cleaner told him they had said that if they asked to stay with him overnight, they'd be unsure of his reaction. But he says nothing. Mary brings small gifts including those she posts afterwards to his children. She invariably also brings a home cooked meal in a casserole which she carries onto the plane, and they all eat it gathered in Josefu's kitchen. When they are together, her hands tremble slightly.

⋮

Josefu drives slowly, glancing at the thick forest on either side of the road. Unlike so many others here, these trees were not planted artificially. He asked a Stoney aboriginal how long they had grown there but cannot remember what the answer had been. Joe Swift is the man's name and Josefu met him in Keller Foods supermarket. Joe had come up to him and said,

"I've seen you here before. I asked my father and he said that there used to be Nigger Bill here, from your tribe."

Josefu looked at him gravely and said, "Thank you."

"I like those chocolates and these cookies here," Joe Swift said.

"I'm glad you like this supermarket. I use it a lot."

"Nice to meet you."

"Nice to meet you too."

Josefu took a step back, and then regretted it.

"Hey, I'm Joe Swift."

"I'm Josefu Mutesa," he said, returning closer, in order to offer his hand.

"You buy the frozen foods," said Joe Swift and he disappeared. It unnerved Josefu for a moment but he returned to his shopping in silence.

That is how they always conduct their fleeting encounters. Joe Swift appears and they exchange greetings in Keller Foods supermarket, both standing on the tiled floor with neon lights blazing on the coloured, packaged goods. Then he is gone.

"We of the dethroned nations," Joe Swift says.

Josefu repeats the words as they solemnly face each other. They never meet outside. Josefu wonders whether he lives on the Stoney reservation in the foothills, but he does not mention him to anyone, not even to Martina or the local historian.

Every Friday he goes to the Drake Inn in Canmore, with the local historian and his illustrator wife. They hope to compile a new collection of Banff poets and painters, which could be sold in paperback, to show tourism is not Banff's only attribute. 'And then there is the healing aspect,' they say pointedly. 'Like your Mr. Luxton with the garden, who nearly died after his journey across the high seas, and never left Banff again.'

"But Tharcisse?" he says to himself again, driving faster.

The trees are dark and reproachful. He regains his composure. *Show respect to tall trees resisting time*, he searches for a Latin translation, having excelled at it in school.

His father had never appreciated all the Latin prizes. Perhaps he didn't care because of all his females, Josefu's mother had said. His father came up the boarding school drive in a silver car, and meeting him Josefu would say, "I want to return to Mama."

And his father would reply, "Here's your new Mama," pointing to whichever woman was in the passenger seat. He always laughed, until Josefu grew head and shoulders taller than him. His mother had separated, rather than accept her husband's ways. He never remarried, though, and both parents stipulated in their wills that they should be buried together.

Josefu knew it was contrary to Ugandan tradition that he should be an only child and the single heir. His father had come to England with the rest of the family when they were exiled under British rule. He had on arrival, however, made a singular but remarkable transaction in a commodities market, which brought him a large windfall. He gave a lump sum to his elder brother, the exiled monarch, and then rarely met with relatives after that. He did not return two years later to Uganda with them in triumph, and avoided all the turbulent politics surrounding his family. It was around that time Josefu was born, in 1958. By the time the others were exiled again, this time after Independence, his father claimed they had little in common, so Josefu hardly knew them.

Some had objected strongly that his father dared to choose Mutesa for him — in that part of Africa your surname was given at birth as well as your first name. It was against all acceptable norms, they said, to use that illustrious name reserved for kings alone, for their Kabaka alone, and not mere nephews. He retorted that his choice was not for any ambitious reasons, but simply out of respect for an ancestor who had remained unconquered, either by his own rivals or by colonials. Josefu had felt painfully embarrassed when he learned about his surname, but by then it was too late to change.

His father bought himself a house placed in a quarter acre of land in Maidenhead, which he referred to as a quiet suburban town between London and Oxford. Josefu remembers him coming in from a spot of gardening and sitting down with the financial pages of his newspaper. He made remarkably wise investments on the telephone through a stockbroker who later cried openly at his funeral.

Josefu's father would say, 'I have no realistic expectation of ever returning to Africa.' If asked when he would agree to go, he would answer, 'Fellow Africans, put back the extended hand, then I'll come.' There was always a bitterness in his voice.

Josefu challenged him when he was a student. "Easy for those in a wealthy cocoon in cosy exile," he'd said, to which his father replied simply with a reproachful sigh. Yet his mother refused to talk of anywhere as 'home' but Uganda; the other places she simply called, 'Where we stay.'

⋮

Josefu speeds to Calgary intending to go to work after shopping at the Home Depot And Alberta's Home Improvement Warehouse, orange and white and huge. He enters and turns sharp left to the gardening section. He seizes a trolley, abandoning the lists he made for himself and Luxton House. He sees 5-gallon canisters and picks one up.

"Water for villagers, barefoot, dispossessed," he says out loud, relieved there are no staff in the whole section to witness his wandering mind. Observing a line of axes he rushes past, pushing his trolley as rapidly as he can. He begins perspiring while throwing in several packets of large, plastic garbage bags, marked 'Sacs pour contracteurs'. Almost without touching it, he slides in a Garden Claw, with six claws, that easily loosens stubborn soil. Then he notices a large puddle in the middle of the aisle, so he turns back.

"Hi, Mr. Mutesa, how're you doing? Did you find everything you were looking for?" says the cashier.

"Fine, I've forgotten nothing at all."

Arriving in the riotously coloured Marlborough Mall, he makes his way past the Youth Club Association of Canada, up the elevator to his office.

"Crohn's and Colitis, can I help you?" Maggie, the receptionist, says down the telephone. "Gulshan? For you." Then she looks up. "Hi, Josefu, you're late."

"Am I?" he says, embarrassed. "I'm sorry."

Josefu disappears into the side office, grabs the pile of mail, knocking some envelopes on the floor. He goes through the letters thoroughly, logging each one and piling up the donations, which gladden Gulshan.

"You are in terrible pain?" she repeats on the telephone. "But you see, we are not able to give you medical advice. Constant diarrhoea? I'm here listening. Of course I care; that's why we're here. Our Society is dedicated to your suffering. Yes, especially the diarrhoea. Don't feel lost. Just ask for Gulshan. Yes, I'm the director, Gulshan. Yes, take care. Bye now."

She shakes her head and strokes back her long hair. "Ah, Josefu, you angel," she exclaims, when he comes with a pile of thank-you notes he has carefully filled in with black ink. But she is interrupted by another telephone conversation with nearly the same words.

Gulshan's husband enters, his expression lighting up when he sees his wife. They were both Indians expelled from Uganda and he is a retired local official. "I have such nice things here," he says to Josefu, lifting a black canvas bag, hints of spice filling the room. He always brings a small tablecloth to lay on Gulshan's desk. The sun breaks through and the aromas of the food caress Josefu's senses. Gulshan told Martina that although Asians and Africans had not fraternised much in Uganda, here he was like a piece of home for them. And her husband swears he had seen Josefu's grandfather.

"Shame Maggie our receptionist doesn't like our food," Gulshan's husband remarks, giving Josefu an intimate look.

"A great shame."

"Such a loss," Gulshan adds.

Then they enjoy their lunch in silence.

This evening back in Banff, he takes his briefcase carefully out of the car and, without changing clothes goes straight into the back garden and pulls out weeds with his bare hands.

He lifts his head now and sees a couple, Dave and his Lialia, entwined in the distance, and he feels resentful. There is not a single bird sound in the vicinity, perhaps it's the wrong time. The Bow River, at its fullest in June, can be heard instead, chugging and hissing in deep tones.

⋮

Josefu dials the Winnipeg number several times before getting through: "Bill, who is Tharcisse? I've had this woman's voice in my head, that he shouldn't kill her. Bill, who is he?"

After a short silence, "Oh my, oh my," Bill whispers. Josefu can hear him mouthing something to Mary. He still has the long beard he had since youth.

"Who is he?"

"This is a whole new ball game. Josefu, are you there?"

"Who is Tharcisse?"

"Do you have any idea what you're asking there? Any idea where it's leading? Josefu, oh my."

"I thought only you…"

"Can't hear you."

"Look, my hands sweat when I say the name, I don't know what's happening to me. Who is that person? Who?" Josefu hangs up.

⋮

The next day, Josefu hears one soft knock and his front door opening. "Josefu? Good morning! It's Saturday! Are you ready?" calls Martina in a singing voice.

He comes out of the kitchen.

"Yes, you see, I'm even wearing my boots." She had forbidden him to wear trainers on their mountain walks.

"I'm sorry but it's just you and me today, nobody else."

"That's fine. I've got the thermos flask with herbal tea, like you requested; beer and your spring water in a bag. Sorry but it's a plastic bag, Martina." She didn't approve of them.

"It'll have to do. Food's in the car. Johnston Canyon today?"

On their way they admire the shimmering aspen and bemoan the sight of other trees, felled for safety's sake.

"But there's a whole lot of life taking place there," says Martina, "Insects, birds, you know, all sorts of animals living in the remains of burned trees."

"Burned houses, I saw burned houses."

"What did you see?" asks Martina.

"Oh, nothing. We'll pass Hillsdale Slide soon and there's a sign that says you're standing on eight thousand years of history," he remarks quickly. "What a place for your feet!"

They come to a narrow pass and stand before a migrating waterfall, furious, cold spray spreading like steam, each year reaching higher up. Knowing Josefu would be uneasy, Martina puts her arm around him. "If you're not careful, you'll fall from higher and higher, just like this waterfall, and it won't be such a pretty sight. You've got to do something soon," she says.

Despite its deafening sound, he hears her perfectly. Turning towards her, brushing lightly against her stomach, he whispers, "You know, I can't do it."

As if coming out of the raging water, Josefu perceives Joe Swift, who seems to say, *'Today's the day.'* The image vanishes.

"Is this a special place? For the First Nations?" Josefu asks Martina, carefully watching the shadows.

"Of course," she replies softly. "It's history. You're interested?"

Everything is water and rock: water carving rock, water breaking rock, water carrying rock away. Josefu reads a plaque: 'The shapes you see in this Canyon are always changing. The rock dictates where the creek will run, but the water decides what rock will stay or go, and whether it will go now or later.'

They walk to a clearing.

On the ground Josefu lays out a tablecloth, imitating Gulshan's husband, and keeps it down with cans of beer and bottled water. They eat and drink nearly without speaking.

"Ah, that was good," Martina says and lies on her back. Josefu packs away the picnic and then stretches out beside her.

"On Monday evening, I had a phone call from Ellie, someone from university days. I'd not seen her since then and she asked me why I was in Banff and I couldn't say. I couldn't see behind me." He pauses for a while.

Martina turns towards him.

"I'm still shocked," he continues. "We had parted because I was going to Africa forever. It's I who did it. But she wanted to know about now, and I couldn't say."

"Have you called her back yet?"

"I don't know where she is; she is in hospital in London. She might have changed her name. The first time I saw her, we were three students, men, and we went to the sports hall and it was almost dark inside. Ellie had her back to us. She reached towards the basketball net, such a slender figure, long, perfect and for some reason I never understood, perhaps because I was only nineteen years old, my eyes filled with tears. When she turned, I thought her face was not as beautiful as her body, but it was alright: blond eyebrows, fully round eyes, perhaps a little puffy, and an oval shaped jaw line, you know the kind." He draws closer to Martina. "Her hair was tied back. The boys were about to whistle but I stopped them and we left."

Martina tries to observe his face; he can see she is intrigued.

"My God," he continues, turning away, "We were close. She made me speak the truth, she forced me to. We exchanged rings, you know. Even our parents met. She was a cellist, on the music programme. I learned my law subjects to the tune of her crazed practising. She had a long woollen dressing gown, she had a black velvet dress, she had some racing shoes, yes, quite a few clothes and shoes. But I started wanting to go to Africa and she jarred with my ideas of being fully immersed there. And she wasn't quite truthful to me." He looks at Martina now. "Yes, I'll tell you. She played the solo in Dvorak's cello concerto with the whole University orchestra. I didn't even play the oboe in the orchestra, I refused to, so as to support her from the audience front row."

Martina gasps. "You play the oboe and all these years you never let anybody around here know?"

"I only learned in school. Oboe and piano. I stopped." Josefu says nothing more.

Martina touches his hand and urges him to continue.

"Ellie played extraordinarily well at the concert," he says, turning onto his front. "I was convinced all that beauty of sound, and of triumph, was somehow dedicated to our union. And then, at the place when the concerto ends, she shouted, 'That's for you, John'."

"And who was that?"

"John was her dead brother. I hadn't even known about him. He had died when she was eleven. He was a little older than her and she grieved all her life. But she'd never told me. And it was I, not him, who had lived through all her preparations for the concert. I felt something had broken between us. I explained that I had to go to live in Uganda forever, no place for her. Could we remain friends, though? Oh God…." He tries to breathe slowly, reflectively. "I was living in a student house with a garden and I cooked some lunch and served it outside for us. As we were eating, she suddenly stood up and went in. I thought she was going to the toilet or something, but she didn't return. Then I found she'd left a note on the kitchen table: 'I can't swallow anymore,' she'd written. I ran after her but she refused to see me."

Josefu puts his hand inside Martina's blouse, laying it on her breast like a child. He is crying and she strokes his head. She whispers, "Like an orphan, like an African in those brochures, like I always wish I could stroke their heads." There is a long silence. "What about Uganda?" Martina now says, having waited six years to ask.

"It was a fiasco when I went there. It's very complicated, but at the time President Milton Obote had returned to power for a second time. There was such turbulence then, with many of my own relatives getting involved and in the end they asked me to leave for my own safety. I went to Geneva straight after; I was unable to show my face in England and that was partly because of Ellie, come to think of it. My father had also been very much against my trip. It was a failure." His thumb pushes Martina's nipple up and down as he speaks. He lies still after that and she continues to stroke his head.

"What about your wife Patricia?" she asks quickly.

He closes his eyes, sifting through a list of thoughts until he found the right one: "I met her in Geneva."

"More, more," says Martina.

He replies quietly after a while: "She dazzled me. She was so bright. Brilliant. Younger than me. So quick. She won a scholarship for a Masters where I was doing my Doctorate and we met in the canteen." Now he gives a short laugh.

"Afro-American, isn't she?"

"Yes, her parents both in Albany, you know, in New York State."

"I know," Martina says reassuringly.

"But when we lived on Manhattan, she was unhappy. She hated it. And she despised my work at the UN."

Martina quickly intervenes, "So you remember that?"

Josefu ignores the question. "Patricia called me a bum, but she was already two months pregnant with someone else."

"That little kid who's been here with your own two every year?"

"For the sake of justice, Patricia said. So she comes too."

There is a long pause, and then Martina says suddenly, breathlessly, "Do you remember why you left New York? Left the UN? Do you remember why you went some place else? And then, I mean, do you know why you came to Banff afterwards?"

She has broken a code of conduct maintained for years. He doesn't answer. "You know you were in hospital before you came over here?"

"Yes," he groans.

Martina clenches her fists. "You were taught things there, to handle all your stress and shock." She speaks urgently. "They taught you to live in the here and now. It's not a bad thing. We try to practice it in our Women's Whole Being group. And in Buddhism there's the present. But in hospital it's different."

"When memories creep towards you, rise above them like an air balloon." Josefu recites.

"Yes, but when you are stronger one day, shouldn't you at least try to face what happened?"

In response, Josefu moves so close to Martina he puts his leg on her.

"Doesn't Rwanda mean anything to you? I said *'Rwanda',*" and her voice trembles as she says the name.

He withdraws his hand, his body, and lays back.

Martina, having warmed to the contact, in turn gets closer and whispers, "Well, your reaction was to be expected, Josefu, moving away like that. Bill and Mary forbade me to say the word 'Rwanda', but for how long?"

"It's more than Rwanda, it's everything," says Josefu.

"Oh, so you know about Rwanda?"

"I don't know anything." He growls.

"Mary called me yesterday; something you said had worried them. They want you to go there to Winnipeg, to visit."

"I've had a bad week. It's never been like this before, you know. It started with this phone call, then voices, dreams, some 'Tharcisse' name I can't remember, so I can't take it any more. That's all." He stretches out.

Martina stands up. Josefu follows. She turns to look him in the eye. "It started in Rwanda. You came here from Rwanda. There, I've said it." He gazes at her in disbelief.

"Yes, yes," she insists. "You should take to the road, go to Bill and Mary across the prairies, and we'll all face it together, Josefu."

They drive back without a word. On entering his yard, Josefu says to her, "Please don't go." There is no emotion in his voice.

"I better take the consequences myself," she says suddenly, and follows him in. They stand apart in the living room. He moves to view his back garden and says:

"How the weather's changed. It's going to rain. Stay back, Bow River!" He realises Martina doesn't understand

She is hesitating, but then goes over and lightly kisses his neck. He begins walking. She says, "Oh I know we'll go into your bedroom, and we'll lie on your bed, but if I can give you any courage, I will."

He does not answer and moves ahead, looking back to be sure she follows. It occurs to him that if he is going to the scaffold, he should have a henchman with him.

"I'm sorry," Martina says, "I've upset you."

"No," he says softly. "It happened on its own. A moment ago, though, I blamed you."

He stoops and undoes Martina's sandals, then helps her to lie back fully clothed. He also takes off his boots and spreads himself out on the bed.

"What are you going to do? I wish I could help you."

"Listen to Marcus Aurelius," he replies softly, intimately, "There is then to be seen in the things of the world, not a bare succession, but an admirable correspondence and affinity.' It means it's natural I should be condemned. Inevitable."

"Why condemned?"

"I wish I knew. You say Rwanda. I know it's Rwanda, of course, but how? Where?" He kicks the bed.

"If you could just work it through, you'd bring yourself some harmony," says Martina. He sees she is trying to keep away from his turmoil.

"What about you? You hide too."

"I try not to. Oh I wish I could help you right now; it's your turn to see straight. Perhaps you should go to Winnipeg. Yes! Don't wait for a ticket to fly. Drive there. Take a few days on the way, in the prairies."

"A few days? How can I?" he says, attempting one last time to hang on to his protective routine, "There's the audit, the bookshop, and Luxton…" His voice tapers out.

"All the details, just details. I'll look after things. Yes, I'll have your calls diverted to me. Cheques, Dave - I'll deal with everything."

"Quick thinking! Did you know this would happen? Im letting you down." He turns his head away.

"You'll always have us here in Banff. Peace. Peace," she chants.

Now they draw together at the same time, Josefu tugging as if on a cliff edge, Martina clasping him as if to fight her shyness. The hours go by. Josefu hears a dawn bird and looks to see if Martina is awake.

"Ah," he says, "It's coming. You told me, 'Rwanda'. Yes, I sat in a burned house eating plantain. It rained and everywhere, it was dark, dark green."

Their mouths meet for a moment. Then he continues, "But I don't remember more", his face, wet with grief. "Except that in some way the fire was my fault."

II   THE SHED

3.

Josefu recalls seeing a plastic covered sheet of regulations for UN personnel in East Africa, about not driving at night, not driving alone: a first fragment. He is slowing down now at the Banff Reserve checkpoint. There is a new sign about restrictions on feeding wild animals. He waves to the attendants without looking up and presses on. Despite thick clouds, a few sharp sun-rays remind him he is tired. It is Sunday morning, and Martina had panicked, wanting to get him on his way, with a suitcase in his car trunk, out of his house and out of town. She said he had to go right now, to think and remember, but not to lose his head. He hasn't shaved, feels sick and wants soda water. He doubts he will make it even to Calgary without a break.

'Yes,' he thinks, 'those regulations, I was reprimanded. A glass with a slice of lemon was on the desk where I stood, before a woman who shook her finger at me. It was for Butare, where I broke the rules. Butare is where? From Butare to Kibuye? Name drops, sound drops?'

He shakes his head with disdain. 'The strictest rules, I remember now, they were made for protecting UN personnel, not for delivering aid. You didn't want to be reported for risking your expatriate staff; all other demands were like nothing." A newly discovered rage blocks his nostrils, "Our administration had retrenched into self-preservation, like a giant out of breath!"

Awkwardly, he looks for somewhere to stop, yet finds himself turning into nearby Canmore. "But I've hardly left," he says, smiling now, as if it were a ruse against Martina.

He sees a sign for the Pocaterra Hotel and wonders whether he could slip in there unnoticed.

Standing on the tiled floor while booking a room, he recalls drinking Mutzig beer in some hotel bar. It had yellow, cracked tiles, with black stains, a few small bullet holes in the walls. *'So that was definitely in Rwanda. In Butare. And a man was standing there, who said he preferred Primus beer. The bar in Hotel Ibis, that's its name. My God, I was drinking with a dog shooter!'*

"I said you could have Room 204," says the receptionist insistently.

"Really? You say 204?" She makes no reply. "Then I'll go up straight away and get my luggage later."

Now in his hotel room in Canmore, he drinks two small bottles of sparkling water, one after the other, and sits on the bed, repeating, 'That man, he had to shoot dogs. His paid job.' He recalls the smell of rotting leaves, 'Only worse'.

Closing his eyes he says to himself, "I had a letter: *'Meet me in Butare at the Hotel Ibis at 15:30. On the terrace, not the bar.'* It was in French, from a priest. I waited inside, by the cluttered bar, for a long time, talking with the dog shooter, keeping my eye on people at the tables outside. They looked like me, there."

Now he reflects on how rare that has been in recent years.

Head bowed low between his knees, on the edge of the solid hotel bed, he is moving in darkened circles with rough edges. There is a putrid smell, overwhelming. Three or four faceless people spin and fall on him. He shakes his head and sits up.

"This is ridiculous," he says aloud.

It might be best to go home, take a rest and be in shape to work at the Crohn's Disease office tomorrow as usual. He sees the Three Sisters Mountains outside the window; the light is bright and uncomplicated, the scenery inviting. 'If I check out, I'll take a long walk, for good measure, just to keep Martina off my back'.

There is an inescapable ringing sound, however, in both his ears and he better confront it here. He sits again on the bed and, slowly, a soft cotton sheet covers his eyes and then his thoughts and very gently he lies down and falls asleep.

"I am Père Ambroise," the man said, wearing a sun heated, dusty cassock and heavy glasses stuck together with scotch tape on either side. A thin streak of grey hair made a diagonal line across his black, short-cropped head. He was of stocky build, not very tall and had a wide nose. Out of his chest seemed to come a strength, which Josefu immediately noticed.

'Maintain distance better to observe', he remarked to himself, unsure how to react.

He was surprised by the priest's physical appearance. 'I know that he is a Tutsi, who should be tall and thin, but in fact he is neither, and could be typical Hutu — so called, who are supposed to be short and squat. That will go into my report. The briefings I was given were crap. Who in the hell wrote them? Who vetted them?'

Those questions he had asked tentatively at the time, but they had disappeared into the Secretariat building's disposal unit, overflowing with duplicated, uncontested information. *'Two physically distinct tribes fighting each other.* Rubbish! Deliberately misleading. I might be mocked as the instant expert, but at least I'm looking with my own eyes.'

Père Ambroise, his hands together, stood quietly scrutinising Josefu, who wondered whether he should bow; his mother would have told him what to do. But extending his hand, Père Ambroise tapped Josefu's arm gently with the other hand and smiled. 'In a fatherly way', Josefu thought. 'Yes, definitely! It's not going to be so hard then.'

He watched as the priest also shook hands with the dog shooter, "We know each other, we are colleagues; we protect unburied corpses the best we can," he said.

"Oh, my God," said Josefu, but quickly decided it was a bonus, so soon after arriving, to be propelled into Rwanda's ways.

Père Ambroise indicated he preferred to be just inside and less visible than on the terrace. Sitting down, he drank three beers Josefu offered him. He frequently rubbed his eyes but removed and replaced the broken framed glasses so rapidly, that Josefu did not have the time to see his expression. He seemed to be about to speak, suddenly sitting up straight and taking a breath, but then remained silent.

The dog shooter, who hovered for a while, had now gone off. The rainfall had been exhausted and there was expectancy in the air, lifting the weight of a heavy afternoon. The crumbling thoroughfare, which passed in front of the hotel and led to the market, was half-empty. Josefu looked round and then turned to Père Ambroise.

"Thank you for your note and for giving me some of your time."

"How long have you been here in Rwanda?"

"I arrived the day before yesterday."

"So you have been parachuted here into Butare, yes?"

"You can say that, yes. I arrived in Butare a few hours ago."

"Why here?"

"Our organisation needed someone here today so it could be represented in all the main towns at the same time."

The truth was that he didn't really know. The truth also, he noticed, was that by saying 'our organisation' he identified entirely with his employers and would continue to do so, as if to shield himself from the priest's gaze, lurking accusingly behind his shining spectacles. Josefu thought that it is he who should be asking questions, his mandate. But it wasn't him who had requested the meeting, so he didn't have the upper hand. He sipped beer.

"The United Nations! Your organisation!" Père Ambroise suddenly said with anger. "We cannot talk here. Can we go somewhere else?"

"To my room, if you want," and they rose. "I have nothing up there. We could take up some more drinks?"

"No, we don't need them. Let's leave." Père Ambroise spoke gently, again touching Josefu's arm and calming him.

They sat facing each other on the edge of the unstable twin beds, in anticipation.

"You have courage to have come, Monsieur. Here, you will find, people spit on the UN. Oh yes, there was General Dallaire, poor man, who did his best, sent by the UN. But in your offices out there in New

York, you abandoned him. We know that. And many of you were Africans there… Oh, by the way, where are you from?"

"Great Britain. My parents were from Uganda."

"How is it you speak French so well, then?"

Josefu smiled. "I learned it, and I lived in Geneva. I studied there, and worked there."

"So you lost no time there, and now also you are here not to lose time," said Père Ambroise, pointing to Josefu's open notebook. "In your organisation you had neglected the little time we still had, for us to continue to exist or not. Ah, look, you must forgive me." He turned away. "I am not myself. Today I learned that my dog was poisoned."

"Your dog?"

"All that was left of my home."

His voice was so quiet Josefu leaned forward to hear him.

"I have three sisters alive, three school pupils, who survived because they had been away from Rwanda quite by chance. I will live for them, yes? But we were fourteen children, and there were my parents, all in my home, and my uncles. My family, you call it 'extended family' don't you? We were eight hundred and thirty seven people. From all of them, only my three sisters and I survived. There are, therefore, four human beings remaining, out of eight hundred and thirty seven. And there was our family dog. Someone in the village kept him, you understand. But they poisoned him. Today I learned he is dead."

Josefu turned to see what Père Ambroise was looking at through his thick glasses as he spoke, but there was only a plain wall. And so Josefu waited, his tongue pressed against his teeth and unable to speak, aware his failure to respond caused a troubling void; he fought heartburn and stomach cramps instead. One or two mosquitoes aimlessly hovered before him in the heavy air.

A dank smell had filled the room. He was to share it with Bill, his Canadian senior colleague arriving later in the evening, who would ask what he had done so far. Bill had faith in his UN employers with an almost unshakable innocence, as if he had been one of its founders after the Second World War. He would be ill equipped for listening to this priest. Josefu reached for the notebook and said: "Do you mind if I make a few notes? I know it may sound insensitive. But do you know what my mission is?"

Père Ambroise faced him, contemptuous, "I asked to meet you because I was told the United Nations had sent inspectors to see if there had been a genocide or not. How pitiful! You must understand, Monsieur, I am talking as a human being, as one of the survivors. You seem to have simple manners, not to be pompous." He paused, to assess Josefu's response — which was blank. "Your face is carved in stone, Monsieur. But you represent an organisation that we now see as offensive in its arrogance. Arrogance and wilful confusion in Rwanda: claiming world leadership but then pleading powerlessness. This is what we have discovered about the UN. Perhaps not for the perpetrators, but for us survivors: it is a new discovery."

"And wilful ignorance, Father?" Josefu heard himself saying distantly.

"Yes, that too. But we have no time anymore; just look at what you are doing today! Instead of helping us bury the dead, you have come all this way to see if there are any dead at all, isn't that right? Genocide or no genocide? Use the word or not? You put too much trust in words."

"You say my thoughts. Yet someone has to do the recording work, Father, and so I am here for that, to record."

"And questions? Ask questions?"

"Ask why there were so many killings?" Josefu retorted. "At times, a thousand Tutsis every twenty minutes, they say. And why, really? We don't know really why. But this is not the time; I shouldn't have said that. Forgive me."

Josefu noticed there was a very long pause, the only reply.

Père Ambroise finally said, "My problem is that I am beginning to like you. You are frank, someone who is lost here and not afraid to admit it. Can I have your visiting card?" This time he looked Josefu in the eye.

Josefu returned his gaze, trying again to see through the glasses. "My problem is that I don't know what to say. I can only try to do an honest job here and carry out interviews. I'll get you my card," and he rose from the bed.

"You see," Père Ambroise explained, "I want to show you some mass graves and then show you how I am trying to help survivors by disinterring cadavers and reburying them. I do that as a priest. You will stand by my side a few times. You look like us; nobody will ask who you work for. You understand? Then you will see for yourself what you turned away from and you can write it in your notebook. But for us the opinions of the rest of the world have no importance any more, none at all."

As Josefu handed him the card, Père Ambroise reached up to put his hands round Josefu's neck and grew taller as he fastened his grip. Through the heavy lenses, his eyes became larger and tear-filled as Josefu gasped for breath, saying, "Why are you doing this?"

"Why should we help you in tasks that are too late? Why not die like us?"

"Père Ambroise, don't kill me, you know me, at least a little."

Now the priest's size had filled the whole room and Josefu felt dwarfed, knowing these were his last breaths, the black cassock over his face and Père Ambroise's voice saying distantly, "Yes, of course I know you, assassins always do, at least in my village on the hill."

Josefu awakes and sits up with a Canadian sun-ray straight in his eye.

⋮

Rubbing his face Josefu looks around his hotel room, conscious of a stale taste on his tongue. There is a Calgary Real Estate newspaper by the bedside lamp but he cannot see his glass of water. He goes into the shiny bathroom, avoids looking up so as not to see himself in the mirror. He rinses his mouth and spits. "Ugh! I'm sick; I'm going back to Buffalo Street. I've got some tablets in the left side of the medicine cabinet." He adds, "I'll freshen up first, get my things from the car for that."

Walking back into the bedroom he exclaims, "But what a ridiculous dream! He'd never have done that, Père Ambroise. Yes, I remember him. One of my best friends out there."

Josefu sits back on the bed astonished at the way his mind was taking off, memories thrown into the air as if they were jugglers' balls to catch, but only if you had the skill.

"Père Ambroise," he murmurs. He visualises his shoes, black lace-ups, worn heels, kept as clean as possible. He had a small cloth for that, carefully folded in his pocket, which he reached through his cassock.

"That first time we met in the Hotel Ibis, Bill entered and interrupted us. I stood next to Père Ambroise, we the two Africans, and introduced him to Bill. I could see Père Ambroise staring at his amber beard. Then they shook hands warmly, but I had the sensation of being torn between my fellow African and Bill who had come from my world outside, unsure of who would claim me as their own".

It now crosses Josefu's mind that he should phone Bill in Winnipeg to say he was on his way - just a few words. His eye catches a metal bar leaning by the television.

⋮

Josefu begins to remember walking behind Père Ambroise, past a pair of burned-out village houses somewhere, 'Oh, it couldn't have been far from Gitarama because we were about half way back between Butare and Kigali the capital, and Gitarama is just between them. I can almost see the map, it's so clear.'

'What a pilgrimage! The wooden shed, which we were going to see, stood next to what had been a school. The moist ground in the surrounding area was a deep and passionate red. It must have been shortly after I had arrived, because during that season the sky was smooth and white, not once a brilliant blue, not once. The heavy air made it a lazy, luscious time of year, when you should have been able to stretch out and drink beer, even banana beer, and lose your thoughts over the misty, thousand hills of graceful Rwanda, clad in luminous green.'

⋮

Père Ambroise walked ahead quietly, swinging his arms gently, one hand holding a small, black leather bag, 'from Paris', he had said.

'There was a Rwandan photojournalist with us, Bernard, perhaps twenty years old, too young but nobody cared. Yes, Bernard, indefatigable, with a shaved head. God knows why he shaved his head, he'd never said. He always had two cameras with him, even if one of them didn't work.'

'And there was Bill with us, promoted by the Secretariat through being conveniently faithful. And in Rwanda he was indispensable, since his presence counted for more than mine did – more seniority, more visibly a foreigner. And he was a good soul and in Rwanda everyone knew it. Bill!'

The stench was terrible, spreading relentlessly outside the shed. Josefu thought it would be disrespectful to hold a handkerchief to his nose, like the young photojournalist did, who wasn't a guest here like him.

He recalls: 'As we walked, though, Père Ambroise said: 'The Interahamwe came here — bands of armed youths designated by the government — but they seem to have run out of firearms and they even may have had only one or two machetes. So they used metal bars and wooden poles, some of them sharpened like staves. I heard it earlier from an old man here. He said these Interahamwe were all young, full of their best strength. They called it 'work', what they did'

'Following the 'sifting' inside the church — the word 'sifting' was used when the Interahamwe selected those who should be killed immediately, the men, the older women and the children — these women were taken to a shed to wait for further orders. When none came', the priest continued to explain, 'the Interahamwe had decided it was best simply to kill them in case they would be asked questions afterwards.'

The door of the shed was about to be opened. Père Ambroise was deciding who should go in first. Two middle-aged women had joined them silently, whom he seemed to know, both wearing a white headscarf with a black line through it, seen frequently around here.

Josefu looked at the men in fatigues, of the new army, who had the keys to the shed and now stood on either side of the cleric, weapons on shoulders. Their brows were high and gracefully sloping backwards, like that of his son Patrick, he thought. His child was never going to die, never. He would do whatever was needed in this world and the next. Why these trite phrases? Why was it so difficult to breathe in this sloping landscape, heaving with banana trees? Why was the soil the deep, opulent colour of an unreachable, unfading jewel? He strained to hear sounds in the air to guide him, but the women were silent and even the birds or crickets or stray goats made no noise at this time. He wished it were not broad daylight.

Standing in front of the shed Josefu remembered, very resentfully now, that whenever they had argued about Rwanda back in their office in New York, Bill had always said that everyone should keep an open mind.

Josefu now turned and said aloud to Bill, "Your face has turned so red. Can't you hide it better? Do we hide our feelings better with black skin?"

Why did I say that? How bony, how discomfited Bill looked suddenly, his clothes crumpled, all his hair moistened with sweat.

"Josefu, you know I'm just scared, you know it," and Bill shrugged his shoulders.

Josefu didn't have time to reply because the door to the shed had been opened. A gust of wind blew over them.

"Hey, you over there, come in first, I told you," Père Ambroise called to them. Josefu wanted Bill to precede him but he stood still.

"Come, you poor man," Père Ambroise said to Josefu, taking his hand. As soon as their hands met, Josefu felt his mother had arrived. She would have spoken then, proud of him, working for justice, but what did she know?

Josefu took out his notebook and tried to adjust his eyes to the dark. In the complete stillness, there lay before him the decomposing bodies of about thirty human beings.

Père Ambroise had already given him the number of fatalities, and it had been written down. The women followed, hushed and hesitant.

⋮

Josefu was afraid that if he rubbed his burning eyes, he would lose his balance and fall among the bodies. His pen was poised above the notebook. He felt the heat from Bill's body behind him. 'Silence and shadows,' he wrote down, but then put a neat line through the words.

Leaning against his right foot was half a head, the rest chopped off neatly through the nose in one blow — so there was definitely a machete here — and Josefu found himself counting the decorative beads on the hair of the remaining half of the young woman's head. 'Thirty two beads,' he wrote, then crossing it out as absurd.

Inside his own head there was a drumbeat, a slow thudding sound, which he stopped and listened to. Eventually, the light became familiar enough for him to take in the rest of the shed.

There were limbs scattered here and there, like pruned roses, he thought, a leg here, an arm there. A woman's body was lying intact, flat on her back, almost peaceful. He looked for the cause of death and could see none.

As if guessing his thoughts, he heard Bill whisper, "One blow to the head, probably, to the nape of her neck, died instantly." He too was making notes.

Josefu noticed she wore European clothing, and a navy blue cardigan with gold buttons. He counted the buttons, six of them, and wrote it down, with the comment, 'Not all clothing was looted, perhaps because there was a time limit in this incident.' He then looked at her face, eyes perfectly closed, her brow smooth, and a small and pointed nose. There was something that reminded him of Patricia, his wife who was no longer his wife, whom he now saw also as a dead person lying flat on the ground.

He despised his illicit, stray thoughts at this sacred moment. After all, his responsibility for this little planet was right here, to write down what had happened in Rwanda and wipe it with the balm of retrospective justice. 'Try again, try harder!' He looked back at the corpse, and counted the buttons a second time.

"Oh my," Bill sighed repeatedly. Josefu saw through his eyes also now as well as through his own. He knew Bill's pondering: 'How could the killers be young men, who had sisters and mothers and, some of them even, wives who were just like these women, and yet they had taken poles and staves and machetes and snuffed out the lives of thirty of them?'

"There are, in fact, twenty nine women here," Père Ambroise said just then. "These companions have counted them," he added, referring to the men in fatigues. His voice resonated as if in a cathedral. Unexpectedly, the sun shone in through the entrance. A head with a multi-coloured headscarf lay in the corner of the shed. "We will match it to the body, don't worry," said Père Ambroise.

Josefu saw a thigh, on its own, without a knee, fat and womanly. The stench was overwhelming but he accepted it. He noticed Bernard the photojournalist had negotiated with one of the women to borrow a scarf, which he had neatly tied round his face with a pretty knot on the side. His flash and camera clicked almost rhythmically.

There was one victim whose eyes were open, her mouth frozen in what must have been a scream, as if looking into the destiny, Josefu thought, of justice betrayed. She too had a white headscarf with a black stripe, and a beaded bracelet hung on her limp wrist, both of which he noted down. Then, he saw a small hand, on its own, with calluses caused by toiling with a hoe in the soil or a pole in a cooking pot during the short life of a new bride, for the hand was that of a very young woman.

Père Ambroise noticed what he was looking at. "She was very lucky, the owner of that hand. Look over there," he said, pointing to a headless body in the opposite corner, and then to a solitary head half hidden by another body. "We will put those pieces together when we consecrate her grave, do not worry about that."

'Had I worried, then?' Josefu thought. He carefully inscribed Père Ambroise's words in his notebook. He was writing furiously, to keep his distance, so that his now moist foot would not become part of the carnage and that his own head would not fall behind a bench by the wall.

"She was lucky, the headless woman over there, that she was killed immediately and not taken off to be raped," Père Ambroise continued, before turning to one of the women who had entered behind him.

After a short conversation with her, he said, "This severed corpse here, and the one with the dark blue cardigan over there, were her daughters. They both had secondary education. One was married, one was not." After hearing more, he continued, "The married one taught at the primary school, the other one was waiting for the chance to go to the University of Butare. Their mother and father both worked. Schools are expensive. The father is dead too, killed inside the church with the men, down there; we passed it. This mother here, she had been presumed dead as she lay underneath her son who was…" He asked her something in Kinyarwanda. "Yes," he continued, "Underneath her son who was seven years old and dead."

He spoke with her again. "She and the boy, with others to be hacked down, had been taken to a different outbuilding, behind the church. She lay there for about three days, probably in shock, I think. Anyway, that is how some of these people survived. The Interahamwe moved on from place to place, and the villagers who had helped them and stayed behind, they either finished their job killing any survivors or else they spent so much time taking belongings from the houses of dead victims that they had no time to spare." He gave a bitter laugh. "These villagers thought they were the great patriots of the nation."

The shed darkened and had turned into a hollow cave. Suddenly, without warning and without mercy, one of the women let out a piercing cry. Bill, Josefu and Bernard ran out into the blinding light, scuttling like rats.

Josefu felt nothing but overwhelming contempt for himself at that moment, as they stood there, motionless and wishing they could dissolve into the mud-sodden surroundings. Père Ambroise and the men in fatigues argued with the women inside, cajoling the one who screamed.

He came out after a while in a hurry. "It is the mother of the two daughters," he explained without being asked, "And I must do what I do. I must do it for her, you understand. You, please keep your notes and you, Bernard, your photographs. The bodies have not decomposed as much as would be expected now; so the photographs can be used. That has been a big problem, getting to sites like these before it is too late." He added something in Kinyarwanda to Bernard, and then said in French: "I shall contact you others in Kigali. As you can see, it will help her if I bury the daughters in a clean grave as soon as possible, but we must not lose the documentation of this atrocity. I count on you."

"The new government, you must understand, is pledged to create justice. We need the facts. And fast, because I may soon be stripped of my priesthood as my church has an ambiguous position, you can say, towards facts. Ah, you Bazungu, you Whites," he said, addressing Josefu and Bill together, "You have so much to learn. The Catholic Church here, which is my church… in the middle of all this… No, no more talk of that! We'll talk instead of these women, our sisters, your sisters, who have accompanied us to this shed as to the tomb of Christ. I must console them, otherwise I have nothing to live for."

"Your three sisters!" Josefu shouted out, a helpful challenge.

"True," Père Ambroise replied quietly. "But the Pope of Rome should allow all men to recreate their lineage."

At the time, neither Bill nor Josefu understood what he meant. Nor did they care, then. As they moved away and the smell became weaker, the impact of what they had just seen increasingly seared their senses. Josefu turned to Bernard whose cheeks were burning. He fiddled with a camera lens without glancing at it and tried to appear nonchalant. "I've seen it before, all of that," but his lips trembled as he spoke.

"Surely each time is a first time, when you see death," Josefu said softly, remembering that his father had said it once. "Come with us," he added, "We'll take you back to Kigali." He also took out some of his personal money, two hundred dollars, and gave it to him, saying "Keep this to yourself, because what I am doing is against all the rules." Josefu was relieved to have had something to do.

Bill was more practical. "We need photographic documentation. I could try to negotiate a position for you, if you want," he said to Bernard, also giving him some money. Flustered, he turned his reddened face to Josefu. "We have this matter to deal with; we won't be crazy. Oh my!" Bill had usually succeeded to keep his easy-going, Canadian prairie manner at all times, partly because he thought it was comforting to those around him and partly, Josefu speculated, because it provided a safeguard for himself. Now though, Bill repeated agitatedly, "We must talk it through, these concerns, talk them through, you and me, write them down, make something happen."

Yet, as they climbed into the Jeep with its proud UN signs emblazoned on either side, they fell completely silent, a shroud of grey light and dim forms from the shed obscuring all their vision.

⋮

Back in Kigali, the ransacked capital, Bill and Josefu had rooms at the Hotel Mille Collines, ensconced in the best and most leafy part of town. They paid the special UN rate, negotiated with the hotel owners, Sabena Airlines of Belgium. The place had been inextricably enmeshed in the troubles of the previous months, lots of killings and also lots of lives saved — both, Josefu heard. Rumour had it that one Rwandan hotel administrator should be decorated for acting heroically. But these were early days and he hadn't even been located yet; so many medals arrive posthumously.

The hotel was a nondescript multi-storey building with only the ground floor possessing any distinguishing features. The long, neat corridors with their tidy doors on each side gave the illusion that nothing untoward could ever happen there. The cleaned walls, though, had not escaped witnessing, at least in part, the same terror as the rough walls of mud and cement in all the rest of Rwanda.

After returning from the shed that evening, both men decided they would contact nobody and, if they could, keep themselves apart from other expatriates. Niether man hungry, they met for a light snack and drink by the pool. Bill, fresh in a pale brown shirt, probably ironed by Mary herself, came up to Josefu who had glimpsed him from behind a newspaper held high and of which he hadn't read a line.

Until Josefu dropped the paper Bill sat in silence. His deep-set eyes smouldered, a rarity, and he shook his head.

"Something?" Josefu asked, unnerved.

"I don't know how to say this. I was upset, so I got through to Mary. She sends you her love, you know that."

"Thanks."

"I don't know, that is, you didn't say anything so I don't know where to begin."

Josefu's heart skipped a beat while he said, "Calm down, say it."

"She called Patricia yesterday thinking she might need some support while you were in Rwanda. It couldn't be easy for her and the two kids. But well, she wasn't there. Instead, Mary got your maid, her name's Rosita, isn't it? She still comes in to clean. Her English is appalling but, well, she told Mary that Patricia and you had split up and that Patricia had left with the children to some place else in New York."

Josefu stared ahead.

"Look, I can stop. We don't have to talk, but Mary insisted I tell you this. I said I'd leave it up to you, that we were under a lot of stress here. I told her about the shed. But she made me promise I'd come out with this straight."

"Thank you, Mary," said Josefu, hearing his own irony. He repeated it, "Thank you, Mary."

"Is it true?" Bill tried to catch his eye.

"I suppose it is," Josefu said. "I haven't yet thought it over."

"Haven't you shared it? With nobody? Not your mother?"

"No."

"I had no idea, Josefu. I'm sorry."

"Thank you."

"Do you want me to stop?"

"I don't mind."

"You're making me feel embarrassed. In your own time, Josefu."

No response. After a while Bill said, "What do you think of Père Ambroise? What do you think his agenda really is?"

"Why a hidden agenda, why attribute people with a hidden agenda, especially locals? That is such typical expatriate talk," said Josefu bitterly.

"I didn't mean it in a derogatory way. You're an expatriate here as well."

"I know. But you've misunderstood. The last thing we have to think about, is a hidden agenda in this man."

"You know him better than I do."

"Hardly."

"Yes? Then how did you meet him? I never asked. Where did you find him?"

Josefu sighs. "Alright: our driver was inside some petrol station and must have been speaking with him in there. He brought out a scribbled note and told me a little about him, that he was a good priest that he knew. Anyway, that's how we met. In Butare, just before you arrived."

"Okay. Have the drivers been briefed?"

"Briefed?"

"To keep their mouths shut."

"How can I know? Why are you so suspicious?"

"Mary put the fear of God into me just now, about being careful," said Bill and laughed.

"Pathetic, sometimes, that we are so obsessed."

"You're not being reasonable." Bill mumbled something about Josefu obviously being under a lot of stress.

"I'm fine, even if I don't want to hear all you're saying." Josefu retorted.

Mutzig beer broke the uneasy quiet, much to their relief. It was brought to their table by an obsequious waiter, who reminded them several times that he could provide more if they wanted. They had both ordered the same.

A young Rwandan woman came up to them and said something to Josefu. "I do not speak Kinyarwanda," he replied self-consciously. She asked in French, with a simple manner, whether she could take the spare chair. He gestured his agreement in silence and kept his eyes down, only aware of her expensive perfume. Shortly afterwards, having eaten a sandwich, the two men rose and parted without a word.

An hour or so later Bill telephoned Josefu's room. "I guessed you'd still be awake. We didn't decide when to meet tomorrow. Eight o'clock?"

"Okay. Look, I haven't taken it in yet, about Patricia, as it happened just before my leaving. Which is why, probably, I can't take in anything else either yet. Including that shed."

"Nobody can take in the shed, not at once, anyway. About the other thing, I'd promised Mary, you know what she's like. I'm here if you need anything." He prudently ended the conversation immediately.

The rest of that night in Kigali, Josefu felt he was still on his flight from New York, his stomach tight, his hand, as usual, on his cheek while he slept, leaning his head against the porthole. He woke up and sipped some bottled water, in the night air which was cold in Rwanda. And then he saw over and over again the door of the shed being opened and the half head with bead decorations being brought out to him on a solid silver tray, a wedding present from his family.

⋮

Josefu is chilled, lying on top of the Pocaterra Hotel bed with nothing more than a bath towel. The room has the usual central air, which he detests in Canada because of the noise it always made. He remembers arguing with Bill and Mary's daughter that the sound was like the hum of a computer he was obliged to work at —constant guilt.

He rises now and goes into the bathroom, and as he puts on his boxer shorts and clothes, avoids looking at the effects of the cold on his lower body. It is too late to get very far. An entire day gone and he had travelled no further than Canmore, just down the road from Banff. He certainly would not call Martina, despite his promises to do so.

Quietly he leaves the hotel to look for stores open on Sunday evening where he could buy a bottle of Canadian Club whiskey and a snack. All the time he fears someone might recognise him, but it is difficult to hide. Bright neon lights do their job of giving metropolitan self-importance to a scattering of street sections. He stops the car before the strangely named IGA supermarket on Railway Avenue, confident that cheese and bread are available there. He remarks, "If the initials were for 'International General Assembly', that place could be more useful than the rest of the international institutions put together, at least at this time of night."

He walks quietly past the shelves. At one point he thinks he sees Joe Swift behind a row of detergents. He doesn't move, but then realises his mistake. Nobody knows him, nobody. Turning back to Bow Valley Trail, he shops rapidly in the Alberta Spirits Store and then continues on the same road back to the Pocaterra Hotel with all his purchases.

He is reminded now that in Kigali he had been surprised at how quickly commerce had picked up, the war hardly ended. Bodies were still being found, forgotten behind fences, and yet in the shops, stocks were being replenished and put on sale. If you went out of Hotel Mille Collines and turned right a hundred metres or so, there was a small supermarket on the left side of the road, with metal shelves and overpriced goods, but you could certainly buy many of the things you needed —toothpaste, soda water, yes…

Josefu tries to stop his mind straying, and also wishes he had a paper bag to put on his head, better to hide. He realises how much he had become part of this enclave in the mountains, where everyone was here for a purpose. Over six years he had anchored himself to their presence, their greetings, their paths and their calendars. It was all he had. Was this part of belonging, to be so worried that people he knew here might see him?

Why had he consented when Martina sent him on his way?

Or was it the telephone call from Ellie that had stirred him? Or was it really as he preferred to think: that he himself had decided to set out, of his own accord, staff in hand, to become a better man. Quick!

In the hotel room he sets his alarm clock, to be on the road by seven the next morning, setting goals, creating purpose. He pours out a glass of whiskey, the first in years, even though he had stopped his medication a long time previously. He toys with the glass, undecided about which side to drink from and whether to drink it neat like he had once learned in Scotland. He wonders why he had definitely wanted a Canadian brand. To make up for years of neglect of where he lived? Almost holding his nose with one hand, he swallows the glassful all in one go. "Ugh! This is tough living," he remarks.

He has a Swiss knife, one part of which he prises open to cut the cheese, eating it with plain bread. That is all he had purchased out of fear of taking too long. Unlike the picnics with Martina, what he is now doing reminds him of his boyhood, on Scouting expeditions, with clearly defined activities which he had always enjoyed. Somehow, he had not found out whether his son Patrick does anything similar, like Cub Scouts, in New York. They had never mentioned it, nor his daughter Alice with Brownies — nothing there from his own past. He considers whether he should have brought their framed photograph with him, in case he lost his life on the road, and they would be pleased to know he remembered them.

The solid silver tray that bore the head appears before him again, this time with the ugly bird from his garden. He diverts his thoughts swiftly to the poles on his fence in Buffalo Street, and worries whether they will last the summer, when elk push against them most vigorously. He senses it is irrelevant now, but wishes for anything to take his mind off the shifting shadows from the shed. He drinks another glass of whiskey like medicine. He desires a black sleep, without apparitions, without a single Rwandan hill, and that is exactly what he gets.

⋮

The next morning Josefu has the Pocaterra Hotel breakfast downstairs near the reception desk. He had checked out and has his bag beside him. He recalls that Bill and he had breakfast in the main dining room of Hotel Mille Collines, with the self-service option. It was a long meal, if you wanted to give value to the fixed price, and it made skipping lunch easy. Not one thought was to go to the hardship outside for local people. You ate your breakfast, saying you needed it to do your noble work in – after all — the humanitarian aid industry. Josefu had always felt uncomfortable, but he ate there nevertheless.

The morning after the outing with the priest, Bill had received news early and was agitated. "A pain in the butt," he exclaimed. "The office doesn't have to be so damn obvious, that we are not welcome here. I've just had a message, addressed to both of us. No vehicle for us."

"What about yesterday's driver?"

"Taken back for other tasks. There is some party coming out for the Human Rights Commission and we are to wait for them and travel with them."

"But coming when?" Josefu asked, trying to calm Bill down.

"Lord knows when. Nobody knows."

"Bill, we have our mission and it was approved, and we're going to do it. How can they stop us?" Bill said nothing. "I think it's more than just a job for you, isn't it Bill?" He shrugged his shoulders in reply. "And for me it's personal." Josefu could feel a painful smile creeping onto his face. "All right, New York thinks we can find out something they don't want, but they can't send such explicit orders to frustrate us." Silence still from Bill, whether from shared anger or disagreement was hard to tell — it could be either. "But you can see it's been weird ever since I arrived. Let's face it. And you got here the day before me and no better luck. And what were we chased off to Butare for?

"No idea."

Josefu wanted to extract their present tasks away from the authority and backing in which they were wrapped. In his mind, he removed the Secretariat labels that were larger than what they really represented. And then he sat up, his eyes intent on Bill's despondent gaze, determined to make him agree.

"But you see, Bill: we can work without their back-up. We've got our visiting cards and that's all we need out here. Providence put Père Ambroise in our path. And I have a few contacts in the new government from my Ugandan links."

Bill's face slowly lit up. "You sly man! You never told me!"

"Yes, we'll get around and do our job and show those bastards back there we were right all along."

Bill took out a piece of paper, which he quickly unfolded and smoothed out, taking a deep breath like never before.

"You're looking pleased!" Josefu said, and warmed to Bill as he often did in the morning.

"And here they are: our objectives. We have three of them. First, monitoring — a kind of monitoring. So data is being gathered by other UN agencies to show the extent of the violence here. But what goes back to New York must be accurate, okay?"

"Continue; comments later."

"We'll get to see that accuracy, okay Josefu? Real accuracy. We'll monitor it, right? Next, second: getting our own samples. We also need our own eyewitness reports, to be accurate."

"About which period, precisely, accurately, as you say?"

"The events which took place from April to July of this year, 1994. And also what's happening right now. It's not all over, right now. Right, Josefu?"

"So it's both? Then and now? That's interesting…"

"Thirdly," Bill went on, trying to contain his enthusiasm, "And here's the trouble-shooter: going back a little, we have to establish if it was possible for colleagues…"

"Our esteemed colleagues!"

"Yeah, who were out here earlier on, to have foreseen the killings the way they happened." Bill smoothed out the paper carefully again and again, adding, "Besides Dallaire. You Josefu, you always say they knew, but the story they tell is that they didn't."

"But Dallaire did."

"But did they inform New York clearly enough, clarity being that other delicate issue?"

"If they'd only wanted to, they could have written it 'clearly', as you say, just like Dallaire wrote, and so the Security Council would not have suffered…."

"Yeah? Again?"

". . the indignity of deliberately opaque information."

"Okay, okay," Bill said, impatiently." Well, here's our mission statement, all here on this piece of paper."

Josefu quickly glanced out of the dining room window towards the sky. Still thick white cloud. "And what we saw in the shed fits nicely into all those three parts of our mandate," said Josefu icily.

"Yes, it fits 'nicely'. Josefu, don't talk like that."

"It's a fact, though."

"Oh my, it's that sarcasm of yours," and Bill shakes his head.

"Look around you."

"Yes, we're all here," Bill said, his patient smile trying to hide his weariness. "So? Say something!"

"Of course we have to find out what really happened in those hundred days and especially just before it happened, so we can say: 'Now we know, there'll never be any more abandoned Rwandans ever again'. Yet I get the feeling there's still something we're doing that's wrong — the camps in Zaire perhaps? Something we, the UN as a whole or else part of it, are doing right now which we shouldn't? It's something I sense around here, especially in this spotless dining room."

"Yeah, I knew you'd say stuff about this dining room. Your eye for symbols."

Josefu put down his cutlery, not wanting Bill to be further disheartened. "That list you've made is fine, you know." He saw how instantly Bill's expression changed, almost childlike. "My reservations are not because of what you've written on that bit of paper, but about this mandate of ours. Listen: to inspect the inspectors, to inspect the inspected and to suspect the suspicious — that's what those three parts amount to."

"Quick summary, well done! A clear mandate."

"Is our mandate anything new?" Bill didn't answer him. "The usual UN mandates? Mandates?"

"I know, 'One arm tied behind your back', you always say that, Josefu. 'For the sake of the self-preservation of the Secretariat'. You always say it, when I say 'clear mandate'."

It was a verbal ritual, often repeated, a weakness for familiarity which they shared, words which could transform that hotel dining room, adorned with white linen, into their usual glass and chromium Secretariat canteen, free of insects.

Josefu waited for a while, a long while, he thought. "We've been denied operations backup so far," he said finally.

"Right," Bill replied. There's a message for us there. But even if we just work on making a record, any which way we can, I see it like this: if we show they've been as guilty as hell, I believe there could be some good changes. Definitely. I'm convinced," Bill's clear eyes catching Josefu's querulous gaze.

"This is a good breakfast," said Josefu, with another touch of obvious irony.

"So, Josefu! Plans for today," said Bill quickly. "How about we go to the Amahoro Hotel, the UNAMIR headquarters, and see the UNAMIR Blue Helmets out there?"

"How about we go by taxi?" Then Josefu went quiet, all of a sudden.

"What is it?" Bill asked, well attuned.

"I was just thinking. The day I learned that by the time we got here,

General Dallaire wouldn't be here with UNAMIR in Kigali any more, and I was so disappointed, it was also the same day I went home and Patricia told me… what she told me. Bad news, really bad news that day."

"I'm sorry. You don't have to talk about it unless you want to."

"Let's make a move. Who will telephone UNAMIR, you or me? I've got the satellite numbers too."

Bill stroked his beard. He then anxiously pulled his fingers through his thick hair, which used to match exactly his amber coloured beard but which now was speckled with grey. Josefu watched him attentively. Then Bill said: "I think we could just go along."

"Do you think we can?"

"Let's leave the protocol," Bill replied, "and appear less senior just because our secretary didn't call them for us first? Why the hell not? Yes, let's just go along."

Half an hour later they left the hotel and on the grass opposite the entrance sat a taxi driver, gaunt, anxious, even a little timid. As Josefu went up to him, he seemed afraid, but when addressed in French he smiled with relief and immediately took them down to the side where his car was. Josefu knew he would be a good ally.

⋮

Bill and Josefu reached the dilapidated Amohoro Hotel used by UNAMIR, the Blue Helmets with a mandate to observe whatever they could. Bricks in an ornate pattern decorated the walls of the building on either side of the entrance. Outside, Josefu counted at least ten white UN vehicles kept spotless by Rwandan low wage earners, who did the task repetitively as if they were cleaning their own teeth. Drivers, he knew, had been a problem recently for the returning expatriate community. Some wanted to continue employing the same people as before the change of government, regardless of whether or not they had been involved in killings in their spare time during the genocide. When survivors of the massacres congregated back in Kigali, though, there were rumours and accusations about some of the employees, which many foreigners preferred not to hear.

"Yes, who knows," a Red Cross worker said jokingly, "Your cook for the past few years could have been cleaning out other kitchens with an axe during the three months of troubles, killing all the Tutsi women in their neighbourhood who ever cooked."

"Not a comfortable thought," Bill commented.

They entered the cleanly maintained Blue Helmets' building and, in French, Bill asked a fair haired officer whether they could see a deputy to General Guy Tousignant, their new head. He answered that it was not his job to find out but, taking their visiting cards, he'd see. Bill could tell from his accent that he was one of the Canadian contingents, and they were received by another young Quebecois shortly afterwards.

Good and sensible Canadian that he was, Bill never spoke anything but French during that whole visit and Josefu followed. This officer seemed pleased with their presence, as if he were bursting to tell them something.

"Is there anything you can do? I'll be frank; I'm not the boss. Something has got to change rapidly here," he said.

"Our mandate is restricted to recording and reporting," said Bill, "But that in itself has its uses."

"Let me explain," said the officer, "The UN military contingent, the UNAMIR, was brought in with the Arusha Peace Accord between the rebels and the previous government, long before the catastrophe. 'Peacekeeping force'," he emphasized in English. "The combatants on both sides had agreed to integrate into a unified national army, with us as monitors."

Josefu took out his notebook, although he would be writing something he had known before.

"The old president was shot down as he flew back from Arusha and, curiously, within a quarter of an hour, road blocks were set up in Kigali. People are already saying it was the next day. But it started earlier. Do you know that already?"

The officer continued breathlessly: "Tutsi identity card holders were slaughtered on the spot, as if it were planned. But do you know that already?" He repeated, but didn't wait for an answer, he was so eager. "Then the carnage continued for three months. Do you know about that? Yes, of course… But the rebel forces won against the government and they seized power, anyway. Governments who use genocide for politics, whether Nazi or Hutu Power killers, they always get defeated in the end, haven't you noticed?"

The officer stood up, revealing that his khaki coloured uniform was like a one-piece jump suit. 'Probably more comfortable than wearing trousers with a belt,' Josefu thought, writing a note.

"The Patriotic Front, now ruling, are in their majority…" and the young man agitatedly lifted his fingers to sign a "T" for Tutsi, since present etiquette did not allow it to be said aloud. "The old army forces are mostly…" and he signalled an "H" for Hutu. "Already, under Dallaire, some of the old military kept to the agreed terms and integrated as best they could into the new armed forces. But not all.

"A tough mandate for you," Bill remarked.

"But here is the important point, here is what you must note: many defeated military, along with the thugs — the Interahamwe and members of the defeated government — they took nearly two million people with them, two million just as a shield and fled the country. Listen to this carefully. The humanitarian arm of the UN now runs behind all of them, murderers included, to provide blankets to them and protective plastic sheeting to them as they cross the border into Zaire where, with a fairy's wand, they are given the status of 'Refugee'. Am I tiring you?"

"Of course you're not," Bill replied rapidly.

"Forget war crimes; we only wanted to inspect the departing army personnel and confiscate their weapons. But we were told not to touch anybody because the UN had declared that they were refugees; so it was not our mandate even to frisk them. They were leaving fully equipped, guilty officers we recognised, with their armed men, leaving with weapons under our very noses."

"But are you certain of what you are saying?" Bill asked.

"Two sides to an argument," Josefu mocked.

"We even have reports," the officer tried to laugh, "of food donated to civilians being confiscated in the camps across the border by their former leaders, to sell in Bukavu and Goma markets in Zaire, so as to purchase more weapons with the proceeds."

"Bill, I told you something was going on," Josefu said in French. "What do they plan to do?"

"It's clear: using Zaire as a base, they want to launch attacks here and return to finish their job of enemy elimination. The battle isn't over yet."

Josefu slowly moved his head back and forward. "What are you shaking your head about?" Bill, red faced, asked Josefu, glancing back quickly at the officer and adding, "We're keeping what you said inside these walls."

"We've done it again: that blind application of UN regulations," Josefu said under his breath.

"This isn't the moment," Bill remarked.

Josefu hesitated but then continued: "And Rwanda isn't the right place. But we've done it again anyway, and just as blindly as ever."

"I'm not getting into this conversation any further," Bill said, "It's embarrassing."

"The battle isn't over," the young officer repeated, "And it's thanks to us, you agree, that the battle can continue. Not a pretty sight, pas tres beau a voir."

⋮

"Time to go," Josefu says to himself as he finishes a blueberry muffin and looks for his car keys. Being Monday morning, he wonders if there is a remote chance that Martina or Dave could be driving past Canmore. He again thinks of returning to Buffalo Street or, better still, going to Gulshan first and asking her to warn Martina that he was going back to his house, and to give him space. He becomes, however, more deeply resigned to the decision that he should set off for Calgary and beyond. "Bad news," he says quickly, just once.

In his rear mirror he can see the mountains clearly outlined and it increases his desolation, the further he leaves them behind. He drives steadily, past the gypsum factory, winding down towards the plains. "Oh, Ellie" he says suddenly, fighting tears.

'Nobody', he thinks, 'Once having attained a place in altitude, should ever abandon it and lose height. There is too much room for treachery in the lowlands; on the high slopes you are simply glad to have somewhere to put your feet. You keep still.' And then he adds, with bitterness, as he passes the last cluster of mountain trees before the road flattens, "The trouble with Rwanda, with its terrible hills, was that it was not high enough."

4.

Père Ambroise had informed Josefu, with a neatly written note left at the hotel desk, that the mother of the two daughters found in the shed in his presence, had arrived in Kigali and requested a meeting. He showed the page to Bill as they both stood by the reception desk in the evening.

"It's a harrowing experience, just reading it," said Bill.

"Yes," is all Josefu said. Immediately, however, he went to his room and phoned his mother, despite having previously decided definitely not to. He told her about Patricia leaving.

"Trust in God. They call God 'Imana' out there in Rwanda, my son." She implored him to pray, in any language, but his reply was that he had no voice for it. "You know," she continued, "I am proud of you being out there: you are still out there doing the Lord's work despite all the rubbish in your family. Ah, that Patricia, she brought the rubbish, but your children will be saved. Mutesa lives on. They will always have their father's name. And you are a good son. Be strong, Josefu."

The way his mother talked was also an incantation, which removed all threats from outside the door: he was now strongly immured. Ironically though, the importance she gave to his being in Rwanda led him, momentarily, to think the exact opposite. She was wrong. He did not really have a mission here. Just a show.

He looked around at his Mille Collines room, with its tidy green bedspread, grey wall to wall carpet, and modern, slightly scratched wooden regulation hotel furniture; not a speck, not a hint that you were anywhere in Africa, so perfectly duplicated was the Western standard style, except for the window that was closed against mosquitoes.

'Simplicity and strength,' he said, as if calling them to himself.

Marcus Aurelius, he remembered then, claimed he learned much from his forebears but wrote that from his mother: *'I have learned to be religious, and bountiful, to refrain not only from doing but of intending any evil; to content myself with a spare diet and to dispense with all such excess as is incidental to great wealth,'*

…or words to that effect. Josefu reflected that he himself had not vindicated his mother's strivings, since he had so few answers while a faith such as hers provided so many. Moreover, in his distress while packing for Rwanda, Josefu had forgotten to bring a book or two.

He sat for a moment listening to the crickets in the lush hotel gardens, although Bill waited for him downstairs. There was a large tree on the other side of the pool and Josefu wondered if anyone had attempted to hide in it when the killings were taking place. He would ask, he would find out, he would write it down.

"Bad news," he said to himself, "Perhaps I have a mission after all, the seriousness of it all."

⋮

Oh yes, now that he is driving on the Trans-Canada Highway, he has not packed any books either. Martina gave him no time but he wouldn't have wanted her to see his choice anyway, wary of her possible comments. He still had the Meditations of Marcus Aurelius but it was among the rows of books he had not touched in six years. Martina would have known he owned the new book on Perennials of the Prairies. He could have read it whenever he wasn't driving, but he had left it behind on the sofa. He becomes increasingly aware, however, that now those books are irrelevant in comparison to the wanderings of his mind.

⋮

After telephoning his mother from Kigali on his satellite phone, Josefu had decided to send a message back to Père Ambroise, confirming he would come, which he wrote on official notepaper. Curiously, the taxi driver they had virtually adopted — his name was Afrika — had earlier insisted, despite their protests, that he would return in the evening to see if they needed him. This proved to be handy now, Josefu realised, since Afrika could take the message immediately to Père Ambroise's residence by St. Paul's Church.

The following day at noon he was saying mass when Josefu and Bill arrived. Josefu's eyes, as if they had been affected by a magnet, rested immediately on the woman whose daughters had been killed in the shed. He recognised her, even though she was sitting with her back to them in the front row. Mostly women, the participants chanted in Kinyarwanda and a young man played an electric organ. She turned round and gravely looked at Josefu.

He shivered, immediately tucking his chin down into his chest. It reminded him of how he had fought fear at his first school away from home, as if he could smother it with his chin. As she returned her attention to the Mass, he glimpsed at Bill who had gone to sit on the edge of another bench. He had a reverent, attentive expression. Josefu envied his comforting beard, his apparent peacefulness.

They watched Père Ambroise depart into the vestry, leaving behind in the church a keen absence. Josefu knew Bill felt it also. Then, with several parishioners, they rose and waited for him closer to the altar. Josefu pointedly avoided the woman. Finally, the priest emerged wearing a dog collar and a somewhat threadbare dark suit. He spent time talking with others before approaching Bill and Josefu.

"Thank you for coming," he said, patting their arms in a fatherly way when he shook hands, and at the same time finishing a conversation in Kinyarwanda with some women. "Let's go to the Aumonerie," he continued.

Josefu sat on a wooden chair next to Bill. With head dropped, staring at his shoes, he was still aware that the bereaved woman kept her eyes on him. He had noticed that her headdress was half off and another woman tried to adjust it. Père Ambroise said nothing for a while. When Josefu glanced up at him, he saw the priest was looking at the opposite wall.

"Her name is Marie Immaculée," said Père Ambroise at last. "She wanted to see you in person, you Monsieur Josefu Mutesa. Ah, if you knew how she insisted!" Turning to Bill, he added, "I don't know why she asked, but in these circumstances we have to respect her wishes. She is very close to committing suicide. Oh, we have had many cases. The Church tradition is that we should not officiate, not bury them in consecrated grounds, but of course I do. It is grief which killed them and not their own hand. I am worried for this woman." He leaned over and spoke to her in Kinyarwanda. They both looked up at Josefu.

He himself spun round to see Bill whose eyes were sharply focused on a dent in the floor. Then Josefu turned back and gazed at his own hands, light palms turned upwards. "I don't know what to say, Père Ambroise. Tell her I feel ashamed that none of us could help to stop what happened."

After translating, Père Ambroise reported, "She said she does not want to accuse you. She says that when she saw you, she knew you could give her the answer."

"What answer?"

Now Josefu looked at her. She wore a blouse which was torn and half open down the middle, a pale pink, and the traditional cloth skirt tied on one side and then several scarves round her waist and across her shoulder, all bedraggled and unwashed. Those were her clothes. Her hands were long and thin, and she wore a small ring. He looked at her face, with a high brow, chiselled features, probably in her forties, probably good looking, he couldn't tell. Then he saw her sunken eyes, shapeless and burning. He put a hand to his throat, almost to protect it.

After listening to her again, Père Ambroise said, "She thinks you are somebody who is a teacher. It is the way you look, you understand? Ah, she said she saw you writing a lot in your notebook, a lot, you see. What?" he asked, turning to her again. Then he added, "She went to school herself for four years and she can read and write. She said that when she saw you, she knew she had to follow you for an answer. She has come all this way here because of you."

Josefu's heart was pounding. He said, "But I am here without really knowing why. Why me? What can I say to her? We are all such cowards, most of us — so I don't know what to tell her."

He glanced again at Bill, whose eyes were now unfocussed.

"Does she want me to repeat that we, the world outside, we failed her?" Josefu asked, but Père Ambroise said nothing. "Tell her I'm not one to deny it, I never did: we knew people are ruthless when they are addicts of power, so we knew what they were like, the government rulers here, and the Interahamwe, but we did nothing and tell her I know it. Please tell her that. Oh God, I don't know what to say." The priest kept his eyes steadily on him, almost provocatively. "Yes, of course, I am perfectly aware of what she wants. It's to know why she herself has been made to suffer, she personally. Isn't that her question?"

"Wait until I've translated what you've said already," Père Ambroise replied impassively, raising a hand.

The walls of the parish room were painted a deep yellow, almost ochre. The furniture was made of simple wood. Although it was daytime, there seemed to be less and less light as the minutes passed. The undulating, gentle sounds of the Kinyarwanda vocabulary flowed quietly from Père Ambroise's lips and faded.

"I don't know much about these things," Josefu continued, after a sign from the priest. "My mother could have told her more," he added, knowing it was acceptable, like in Uganda, for men to talk of their mothers in this way. "She taught me the word for God in Kinyarwanda, 'Imana'."

"Speak!" said Père Ambroise.

"She told me that Imana will always share a peaceful presence with us, when we suffer.... oh, something like that…" Josefu fell silent for a moment.

"Speak again!"

"Tell her that she'll find something to do, something to be, and then she'll know why she's still here. Oh, I'm so uneasy! It's too humble an answer."

"It isn't an answer."

"Do you have one, Père Ambroise?"

"Not for the moment. Not in my heart."

"Do you need one?"

"I'm living without it, as you can see."

Josefu glanced down at his palms again. "Well, could you at least tell her to keep in touch with us, through you. I promise to see what sources of aid are available to her and I will tell you."

"She is staying with this parishioner of mine," he said, pointing to one of the other women. "I hope she won't have to beg."

"I'm sorry, I'm so sorry." Josefu said.

Bill spoke up, "Perhaps we'd better get going."

Marie Immaculée, having heard the rest of the translation, just stared in silence at Josefu.

"She really has taken to you," Père Ambroise said. "Just as well. By the way, I have a question for you. Do you know from which of the peoples of Uganda do you come, which group?"

"Baganda."

"I knew it, not from the North, not from the West! But this woman said she knew intuitively, yes, with her intuition, you know, that your family is important. We have a few of them, important families, in our Africa."

"This is embarrassing."

"She is right", Bill said to the priest, "You know about his family, their importance." He tried to look at Marie Immaculée but then turned to Josefu. "They've played such an important role," he added with pride.

Josefu knew Bill's words were genuine, but they irritated him deeply: Bill was being defiant nevertheless, deliberately defiant, because he was well aware of how much Josefu always sought to avoid these references. Père Ambroise's keen gaze was upon him again, strong and penetrating. Whatever Bill's motives, the African's were different; it was, after all, about an African matter. And this time Josefu decided he was one of them, so he reluctantly responded:

"That role Bill speaks of was for my uncle, and now for my cousin. But I personally am without importance and my father chose to raise me far away from it all. He preferred it that way."

He didn't have to say anything else, knowing again that here, in this part of Africa, they were clearly aware of what his words implied. Père Ambroise translated and then said, "You see, we have distracted her a little. Thank you for that. I personally wondered about your surname."

"Oh my surname, I wasn't supposed to have it. I always have to repeat the same story so the name doesn't sound too presumptuous. It was just my father's whim when he chose my surname."

"Like here," said the priest.

"Yes, like here. But tell Marie Immaculée that the name Mutesa is from my great-grandfather, a king whom no colonial outsider and nobody in his own entourage, nobody, could ever conquer. He was so astute!"

"You see!" Bill said.

"Yes, I admit that it's something to be proud of, being his direct descendent. He was a strong king, a strong man."

"And Marie Immaculée must be a strong woman, isn't that so," said Père Ambroise, quickly relaying to her what had been said, with a very slight look of relief on his face. Now visibly in a hurry and anxious to wind up the meeting, he gesticulated with his arms until everyone was out in the courtyard.

After they left, Bill and Josefu neither observed anything nor spoke before they got to their next appointment. It was already becoming a habit there.

⋮

Josefu is now well into Calgary, still at the top of the morning, and he is tired already. He stops by the strip mall as he had often done recently on his way to work, but now he lays his head on the steering wheel. The sounds from the multi-coloured bustle—of small shops opening and large cars hurrying past—make the spinning in his head more intense. He feels Marie Immaculée is about to say something and he halts her, sits upright, opens his eyes wider. 'I don't want to hear it yet, not now.'

Being in Calgary, his thoughts turn from habit to the Crohn's Disease office and he feels relief to be back in familiar mental territory. It was as if he had found his old coat, the one that fitted best and was the warmest. He thinks of calling Gulshan and realises that, in all the six years in Canada, it has never once crossed his mind to own a cell phone and he has never once used a public telephone. He welcomes the excuse to divert his attention to something immediate and practical, setting off again back to the main highway with a clear head again.

He stops at a gasoline station and sees, next to some chocolates, that they sell phone cards. He notices that he has to scratch the card for his pin number. Using his car key, he finds it exciting and, without any reason, likes the number 6117. He wonders if the call would succeed first time round. Then he remembers he does not know his office number by heart. Rapidly he returns to his car and seizes his briefcase, empty except for the headed notepaper. Back at the phone booth and breathing heavily, he tries his luck and goes straight through to Gulshan.

"It's me, Josefu."

"Oh my God!" she says, "Where are you calling from? Martina said you left yesterday morning. Nobody heard anything since."

"I'm sorry."

"My dear, I knew this day would come. I wish you had told me. There is so much I wanted to say to you about this day. Where are you?"

"Calgary. I just didn't get very far. I can't go on."

"But you must, Josefu. The time came to you." After a moment she says, "But what did that girl think, Martina, pushing you out into the road? You must fly to Winnipeg, not to think too much for too long. You must take an aeroplane."

"I'm staying on the ground," says Josefu.

"Ah you, always you! But you need some food. I wish I had known, you see. But even now, you can come here and I will immediately arrange some good food, our food, you know, to take with you on your way. But on your way you must go. Without any doubts."

"I called because I don't want to leave. If I come to the office, I won't leave."

"'Leave' and 'go' is not the same thing. You go; you do not leave. Go, go!"

Josefu quickly finishes the conversation, knowing what is best for him, and returns rapidly to his car.

He tries to rise in a balloon above his slumped body, above the rustling in his chest, but it doesn't happen. He feels the echo of bereavement, a slow loneliness in a trickle, and then the raw burning of abandonment. There is nobody to obey, no safety in numbers. 'I'm still on the ground,' he sighs. 'I spoke too soon, too much. I've lost that brilliant skill of ascending into absence.' His lucidity surprises him.

He enters Calgary Downtown and sees a sign in Japanese, a Sushi bar. He forces himself back to his task—remembering Rwanda any way possible—which at this moment feels like having quickly to dig a plot of land before the rains fall. "The hand of history," he asserts, "is long. There were never any Japanese in the UN military contingent in Rwanda, for example, and probably because of the last World War. There even was a Fijian officer, but no Japanese.

The UN started doubling its troops, when the massacre was already over – the ironic bustling of Blue Helmets in defeated Kigali. Just like Bill and me, arriving late.

"Stop again! No recollections please while I'm driving in built up areas! I can't drive with random reflections." He cruises through Calgary Downtown area and feels the close shadow of high buildings on every side. 'By depriving you of direct access to light from the sky which would give you a way out, that's how these high rise edifices hold you firmly in their power,' he reflects. "I know it now."

Noticing the remnants of a Chinatown, which had preceded the Downtown of Calgary, he looks away. He anticipates an accompanying flood of memories and he shouts: "I will not, Not, not recall that meal in New York right now, oh no! Not that Chinese meal! We had heard from the Head of Peacekeeping that Dallaire's main request for permission to take pre-emptive action in Rwanda had been turned down. Several of us were there. And we were joined by Patricia and she said we should either resign in protest or shut the fuck up."

Josefu switches on his windscreen wipers, then struggles to find his bearings. "The silence then, at our table. Oh God! Please, no more of that right now."

He stretches his hand several times towards the knob of his car radio but pulls away, fearing its strangeness and intrusion. 'Not yet,' he thinks, 'not after all these years. Cripple, that's me. The Canadians call that a *gimp*. Me - a gimp!'

⋮

Marie Immaculée found a legless boy, perhaps three or four years old, in the orphanage where, as she wandered, she had gone in to hide when caught in a sudden crossfire. In small Rwanda there were several hundred thousand orphans when the troubles ended. 'Yes, hundred thousand, between two and three hundred thousand, I think I'm remembering right', Josefu reflects.

This child had survived miraculously, despite having his small legs chopped off during a massacre, stopped suddenly by the arrival of rebel troops. He was given emergency assistance by one of their medical officers. Then they themselves had come under enemy fire and fled.

Another woman had grabbed two children and since then Marie Immaculée and she had travelled together. They said their charges would be handed over to be registered as soon as it was safe. Nobody knew who they were, not even if they were Hutu or Tutsi, although most likely the mutilated one, given the time and region, was Tutsi. The women carried them, fed them what they could, spoke very little and showed them no affection. These children, however, felt the warmth and protection of the women's bodies through every dark night, wherever they were.

"You see", Père Ambroise explained, "Their bodies took the children, not their heads or hearts which are numbed. Their bodies as mothers, did it. Not all mothers are like that, though. Who knows, it could even have been a mother who cut off the legs of this child. Such things happened."

Père Ambroise had let Josefu and Bill know that once again they were being summoned by Marie Immaculée. They met her without questioning it. She stood before them, by the door of the Aumonerie, the half undressed child in her arms. She was still unsmiling, her eyes still grave, but there was a basket on her head. Without a word, she fumbled for one of the scarves tied round her shoulder and slipped the boy inside, shifting him to her hip. Then she brought down the basket and unwrapped a covered pot.

"It is banana mash, Igitoke," said Père Ambroise tenderly. "See, it is still hot. Come in, you can eat it right now." He disappeared and came back with a pair of spoons and plates.

"What about yourself?" asked Bill.

"I've eaten already. This she made for you. She insisted. May I be quite frank with you? I just don't have the energy to argue. Eat."

There was complete silence as they scraped up the last warm, slightly salty pudding.

"These are plantains, of course," said Bill. Then he whispered to Josefu, "Don't tell my Mary, by the way, you know how she worries about where I eat."

"You've lost the plot," said Josefu, "You've missed the moment."

"What are you saying? That is English," said Père Ambroise.

"We are very touched. It was delicious," replied Josefu in French.

"Delicious," Bill added, "Tell Marie Immaculée, please tell her, Père Ambroise."

Marie Immaculée still did not change her impassive expression. Then she mumbled something to the priest.

"She says that you should bring her your shirts and she will wash them."

"Our shirts?" said Josefu. His eyes moved from Père Ambroise and came to rest on Marie Immaculée. For a short instant their eyes met. 'I know her, I know her, I've seen her before, it must be so,' he thought. He was clear in his mind that she knew him too. Sensing the others were watching him, the heat of his embarrassment rose into his face. He turned away.

"She wants you to reply," Père Ambroise said with authority.

Now Josefu tried to sound light hearted. Again it reminded him of school days, needing to hide his emotion. "What do you think, Bill?" he said. "We don't have to subsidise the room service at the hotel, do we?"

"Do you know where she is leading us?" asked Bill.

"No, I don't. It's uncomfortable," replied Josefu.

As they had just spoken to each other in French, Père Ambroise interjected, "I do not think she has any ulterior motives; my experience is that it is part of her state of shock. Just look at her."

Josefu averted his eyes even further away from her, and then he said: "But she will not be allowed near the hotel and we have not yet established our office base. So there are practicalities; how will we meet?"

"Use my Aumonerie as your laundry, temporarily of course. Bring your clothes in a bag, you know, a plastic bag. She comes here to the mass at midday. To be frank, she disturbs me; there is something about her that is so uncompromising. And she is so insistent. I have already told you that." Père Ambroise turned and said something to her in Kinyarwanda.

As they walked out, he added, "And she frightens me. Well, she represents the walking dead of our country. You understand? Yet she has that baby with no legs. And she brings a pot of food for you?" They stopped for a moment under the shadow of the church building.

A group of people were waiting for Père Ambroise. "They have probably found some bones to bury," he said bitterly, "And want me to officiate. For the sake of dignity, or to feel as if people had simply died in their beds of colic, who knows." Seeing Marie Immaculée walking at his side, he added, "Don't pay her money. It would hurt her feelings. She is from that kind of family. Give presents if you want. My advice is also that you give her some soap and money just for water. The way she bought these bananas to cook has surprised me, frankly, and the groundnut oil and salt," he said, peering through his glasses at Josefu and Bill. "She has perhaps imposed herself on you? I do not enjoy being such an intermediary. If we were not going to work together, I would not talk with you so much, but we are going to work together, no? You will get Bernard the photographer and your notebooks and we will make you a thick file to take back. Where is it to go, your file?"

"The United Nations headquarters. New York," Bill replied.

"The most powerful of Metropoles, isn't that so? We in the former colonies think of your western countries in their entirety as the metropoles, your cities even more so," and for a moment Père Ambroise smiled. "We start work together tomorrow morning. I'll try to find someone else to take Mass. We'll need petrol in your car; we are going quite far, well not really that far, about an hour and a half from here."

"That's fine," said Bill, "We'll take our time and get it right."

Josefu's stomach was warm and comfortable. He thought of his mother and, for her sake, told the priest to say to Marie Immaculée that his mother's name was Rosemary and that she prayed to 'Imana'.

"Rosemary? I'll tell both of you something." He looked down and said, almost as a whimper, "My mother's name was Immaculee." By this time they had reached the road. "Don't worry," he said. They parted quickly.

⋮

Where Josefu goes now, beyond Calgary to the east, he has never gone before. While in Banff he had never gone much further in the other direction either, never west to British Columbia. Even the one time he had left Canada for his dying mother, it was through Calgary Airport. Driving out eastwards is a different matter now; the realisation makes him jumpy. He has passed 84th Street and the city limits into unknown territory.

The first item that catches his attention as he reaches the outskirts is the Prince Of Peace Cemetery. No headstones, no artificial flowers, only a marker and a flower vase allowed there. He sees small roses dotted around. Such a clean way of being dead.

The first mass grave he saw in Rwanda contained the remains of around ten thousand people; he was told others were even larger. That one was huge. "Oh no!" he exclaims, "No mass graves now; I have to push them out of my mind. So why am I driving past here, past this cemetery?"

His thoughts go to Martina, angrily. He'd get on the phone and tell her his low opinion of her reckless advice. How could he become a happier man, or a calmer one, through thinking about Rwanda? Isn't that what she said? How ridiculous to be on this highway pointing to a fine line far away. He would return to Buffalo Street. "This is a joke," he says, "A really bad one." As soon as he got back, he would lay on top of her.

The electricity poles, which he passes on his right, are like cheerleaders, urging him forwards. 'But in the wrong direction, sorry,' Josefu thinks. On his left he sees a sign that says 'U Pick Berries'.

That first mass grave he saw, you had to pick at too, like a gardener. It had been opened up and there were men, young and old, employed in loosening bones from decayed flesh and clothes. It was done to lift the bones out and lay them in rows, skulls together, and the rest separate in another line. In this way, too, you take seedlings from the earth in a nursery and lay them out ready, so they can rapidly be placed elsewhere, into deeper soil.

'But no, it's not the same, not so', Josefu remarks to himself, 'since plants here retain life and a future.' It renders his comparison, as so often happens when made with anything in Rwanda, utterly useless.

The men in rags working at the crowded grave hardly spoke. He was told it was never clear whether they would be paid for their labour. Josefu had stood to one side, trying to push his revulsion of the mass grave into lines of meticulous notes. And he tried to kill time.

Père Ambroise arrived to bless the bones, giving them form and raiment of another nature, he said, which nobody could take away. He put on a vestment folded with his prayer book in his small black bag, chanting quickly in Kinyarwanda. He ended with "Rest in peace," which he repeated in French and Latin. Josefu wrote down the words simply to stop the hardened lump in his throat from choking him.

Defiantly, blue sheeting, distributed for a completely different purpose by the UN High Commission for Refugees, was used to cover the rows of remains. Josefu remembered seeing a small boy appear from nowhere with a very large stone to weigh down the plastic. Once this was done, voices rose again and there was bantering, with men slapping each other on the back, but Père Ambroise seemed agitated and asked to be driven away as soon as possible.

He told Josefu and Bill that he had received a setback; his Archbishop disliked what he was doing, making a record of the massacres. He had asked him to leave Kigali and return to a parish in the southwest of the country from where he came.

"I am being told to live where my family was massacred and to minister to those who did it. One day, as a priest, I will be able to do that, but it is too soon now. Our church authorities are demanding forgiveness from us victims, but not repentance from the perpetrators, because that way it is easier to continue as if nothing much really happened. You can understand. These words like 'massacre' and 'killers' mean nothing for some of them personally, and their view is that to give these words a real meaning is to dramatise the situation. That seems to be the attitude that is being taken in our church." Père Ambroise appeared tormented. "Aren't you going to ask me the question?" he said.

"No," Josefu answered, "I mean, which question?"

"Ah, I'll say it for you. My superior is a Hutu, like most of our church."

"I hadn't thought of that," said Bill. "It must be difficult."

"I deny the false divisions between us, as you know. But it is hard not to distinguish between those priests whose families are alive and those without anyone left. Well, in the short term. We all end up as a group of skulls, only for some it happens more slowly, don't you think?"

"But what are you going to do? You want to stay in Kigali, don't you?"

"I'll stay. I can say I agree to go but that I must postpone my departure. Here in Rwanda I can say that every day, you know. But it's disagreeable, very disagreeable."

⋮

As Josefu drives now, some thirty kilometres out of Calgary, he looks up to discover what the weather is like. Floating like clouds in the sky he sees rows of neat skulls, all the same size, all scrubbed white.

There was a prisoner, he remembers, in Kigali Prison, a Hutu who, while participating in the massacre, had killed his best friend. When the rebels came, he went into hiding until, a few months later, he found his friend's skull, washed it clean and wrapped it in a cloth. He then went to the prison and asked to be condemned. He sat hunched in a corner, a Warden told Josefu, keeping the skull under his shirt all day, even when he ate. It lay under his pillow at night. He claimed that his Tutsi friend spoke with him all the time, to tell him what to do.

Above Josefu now, the skulls he sees in the sky are motionless. On both sides of the highway there are listless fields, also lacking in eloquence. The bugs, which throw themselves at his windscreen, however, make a clear, crackling sound as they die. His stomach turns. He rubs his cheek with one hand and slowly admits defeat: although he will have to stop the car soon, he has come too far to turn back. He knows he will be unable to leave his memories in a box at the entrance to his drive, in Buffalo Street. The lid has gone; who removed it is irrelevant. All that counts now is that he should find somewhere to get off the highway before he is sick.

Soon Josefu comes close to Strathmore, where he notices confident technology, buoyant industry. Perhaps here he can squeeze out the Rwandan mud, leave the last messy century behind and then have a clear, polished, steel mind in times to come. But it won't happen.

'Oh God,' he thinks, 'Remember the tee shirt of a small child in the first mass grave I saw, which said, *Hard Rock Café, Los Angeles*. Global Village comes to a sorry end. Yes, in Gitarama Province,

Rwanda, Africa. Oh God, oh Imana.'

The daughter of Marie Immaculée wore a blue cardigan with buttons, in that shed, certainly not made in Rwanda. It could have been China, or India, global molecules that swam towards a meeting point. Marie Immaculée herself was given a needle from New York, which Mary had packed for Bill. She had pulled his torn shirt and mimed what she needed.

Josefu had continued wondering why he felt he knew her already since it was a geographical impossibility. Père Ambroise, to whom he confided, said there was more than geography for understanding the human condition. They had drunk a few beers together when he said it, near the pool of the Mille Collines Hotel, which was becoming increasingly over-staffed.

⋮

Now Josefu passes signs, first for a Petro West Gas Station and then one he welcomes: Leroys Motor Inn at 50, The Highway. This would be the place to stay, whatever its condition, 'Until further notice, because I can't drive more and can't die either', he says to himself mockingly.

There are a couple of new buildings with two floors and a few old-fashioned motel rooms stringed together on one side, with a service station in front bustling with activity. Suddenly he sees an on-site restaurant attached to one of the buildings and tells himself: 'This is not a hillside retreat, but a spare room here will make a perfect haven'. He appreciates the surge of energy that spurs him forward, a knot coming undone, a feeling that he can smile a little.

He sees the receptionist looking at his shoes — almost new ones — and then all the way up at him.

"Hi, can I help you?" she says, narrowing her eyes behind her large glasses, a woman in her forties perhaps.

"I wonder if you have a room to spare," Josefu says quietly.

"What's that? Are you with the wedding party?"

"No," he answers, seeing a crowd of people entering all at once. "I need a room for a few nights."

He senses her looking at him closely again. "You have a credit card?"

"Yes, of course," he replies. "Do you have a room then?" he says, taking out his leather wallet with his series of credit cards neatly arranged. "I'm a little tired."

"Sure you're not sick?"

"I don't think so," he smiles quizzically, and adds, "I need a rest, you see." Now she smiles back.

"Oh, if you're looking for quiet, you'll get that here. Our family has been running this business for 25 years. The personal touch! And we've got some new buildings. Oh, you'll get rest here. Are you travelling on business?"

"I live in Banff, have done for several years. I own the bookshop there," Josefu says, reassuring her.

"Oh, you own a book shop in Banff? Plenty of money out there," she says.

"We work hard," he says. "There's an excellent manageress. And I have a partner who owns a third of the business and he's experienced; he owned all of it before I arrived."

"I see," she says, visibly relieved to have some information before her. "And you've come to Leroys for a rest?"

"Well, I am heading for Winnipeg but want to take my time. Is there a room then?" he asks.

"Oh yes, there sure is. Four nights you said, right?"

Josefu doesn't contradict her. "I'll get my baggage out of the car. Thank you."

"You're welcome," she smiles even wider.

"We'll be seeing you around." She had said something about the size of the beds in the room, using Canadian terms he hardly recognises. There are, in fact, two Queen Size beds, as they are called.

"This will do," he says aloud, taking in the rest of the room: a television, a good-sized bathroom, carpet and curtains in matching green, and no annoying Central Air. 'Yes, this will do,' he repeats several times. He has brought everything up from the car except his briefcase. There is a telephone on the bedside table. 'What if she checks me out at the bookshop and tells Martina I'm here?' he worries. 'The Banff brigade will be down here immediately on a rescue mission.'

He sees Marie Immaculée just then, as if she were standing in the bathroom doorway.

⋮

"Tell her she must accept this box," Bill had said. "It's got food in it and she can sell what she doesn't want. Josefu and I bought it in our supermarket near the hotel, you know the one, turning right at the gates."

Père Ambroise spoke agitatedly to her. "She said she wants me to give it to other parishioners here," he finally told them.

Josefu could tell that the bump, under some of her scarves, was the legless child.

"He has no name," Père Ambroise replied to his question. "But her first born was also a boy, dead now of course. He was recently married. It costs such a lot for us when a boy marries. Such an effort for the family, but he was killed and his pregnant wife along with the others. The other name of Marie Immaculée, because of her first born, would have been Mama Isidore but she doesn't want to use it. You see, I have spent more time talking with her than my other parishioners."

"I am my mother's first born, so she is Mama Josefu, because in Uganda also, women receive the name of their first born as their own. Perhaps she would accept the box if we told her it was bought with my mother's money. It's sugar, beans, and so on, well, you can see yourself."

"I'll try again," Père Ambroise replied and spoke furiously in Kinyarwanda, with 'Mama Josefu' in each sentence, it seemed. Then she accepted.

"We'll carry the box to the car and she can go with our taxi driver,

Afrika, when he drops us off. He'll take her all the way home," said Bill enthusiastically. There was a commotion after that, as she hurriedly emptied the contents into a cloth and tied them up into a bundle.

Père Ambroise took off his glasses, still stuck together with scotch tape, and wiped his brow. "Ah, now I know why she objected so much. I didn't guess it before. It was the box, not the contents, which she did not want to see. I remember now. She had told me she had so wanted to have a box and to find her last born son's little bones to put in this box, so as to bury him well. Unfortunately, his remains are impossible to find individually. All those massacred at the same time are in a common grave now. Some of the skulls in the nearby latrines have been retrieved. This boy's head was not severed. But she hoped she could have him put in a box."

Everyone was silent. The quiet was broken at last by the legless child waking up and crying underneath the layer of scarves. Without removing the covers, Marie Immaculée just tapped him gently and jogged from side to side until he seemingly fell asleep.

"Is that all he does, just sleep?" asked Josefu.

"Mutilated children do not have much strength," replied Père Ambroise, putting the empty box under a cupboard.

From then on, as long as Bill and Josefu were in Kigali, they placed their shirts to be washed in a plastic bag on a seat by the cupboard and left various bits of shopping for Marie Immaculée at the side. They also brought Père Ambroise some small presents: pens, shaving cream and some socks. It created a little routine and, in the way set patterns are able to, the flatness of the street map was raised into life, and Kigali became a home.

5.

A menu has been left carefully on Josefu's table at Leroy's motel along with an assortment of Strathmore tourist brochures. The first thing to catch his eye is that all desserts are home made—he has a sweet tooth. Today could have been enjoyable: he is on the edge of the prairie, in a festive residence, with the promise of acceptable food, in a room that should sustain the advantages of being peacefully alone. Yet instead, his head is held in a dark trap from which his eyes can barely distinguish the distant outline of the Rwandan hills. The damp smoke of war is still too heavy and too recent to see a path out. Loneliness has pushed him into an unbounded swamp. And he resents the fury of his flashbacks, revealing the hideouts of pain; the force of their derision.

Oh yes, he knows so well now, why he recognised Marie Immaculée when he first saw her: she was a mirror of himself. She had nothing left to show of who she had been before; and she had protected nobody in her family. And yet, of course, it was so African. Nothing left to show for any past beauty. Nothing achieved after so many years, even that children should be given shelter. His own children were in a split up family, like he himself had been; he had failed to protect them. At least they were alive, though; he had spoken out of turn.

'Worse,' he reflects, 'I have nothing to show for the advantages I had been given. I failed in Uganda. Ellie had shouted at me, that I was going there just because some wretched student said I was a coconut, black on the outside and white inside. I went out to prove the contrary, and proved nothing. It wasn't the language barriers. I arrived and found I wasn't just a villager out there like I had hoped. I was among my own kinsmen and they were urban kinsmen in the complex city of Kampala. And unlike them, I couldn't make factional politics my whole life. And that's what was expected of me out there, for me to be one of them, yes, among my kin. I had come at the wrong time in their history. Another time it could have been different. But they asked me to leave, for their sakes and for mine. Not my way of saving Africa. Not my way of being African.'

'But I'd try again, I thought, in a more subtle way, and so I went to the U.N. I believed in its mission then, in national dignity and collective wisdom—something like that—which would balance out African disadvantage. I really believed it. And then my time came, just once, and I failed in office: Rwanda was ignored. My defining moment and it went up in smoke, or down like a squashed tomato, or a slug.... Ugh!'

He no longer looks forward to his meal in Leroy's restaurant in a few hours time. Perhaps it's the same, when if one day he really finds the tranquillity he seeks, and it's too late. Sometimes, by the time you have mended a broken vase, the water in the tap to fill it has already run out.

He wonders where to sit in his motel room and where to direct his gaze. If Martina had not pushed him so rapidly into his car, he might have telephoned her right now, to open his heart. Instead, he simply stares at his watch ticking slowly on his cold wrist.

⋮

It had been exactly half past eleven, he remembers, when Bill and he had arrived at the UNAMIR headquarters at the Amahoro Hotel and had met the same young officer as before. He remained unforgettable for Josefu, for having so clearly vindicated his misgivings about the Zaire camps. And that his light blue eyes had shone with both fear and indignation.

"Now you have an axe to grind," Bill had said afterwards.

"That is not a suitable metaphor in this place, the way they have used axes around here," Josefu had retorted.

They had gone across the dismembered city of Kigali in Afrika's taxi. It was on that day Josefu saw how the capital of Rwanda had so little that was metropolitan. Built on hills, like the rest of the country, it spread out into a series of suburbs with no focus. The centre just was not identifiable in terms of architecture, not at all. Arguably, Josefu thought, the hub of the capital could be the area with the market and a few key streets where the density of the population was greater, that's all. There, small shops were hurriedly being reopened and replenished. It was where off-duty soldiers congregated and swaggered around.

Afrika said that after the rebels had captured the country, stopped the killings and won the war, their first impulse had been to celebrate victory. Champagne bottles had been found and opened, celebrations had begun. He explained that many of the victorious rebel conquerors were from Uganda, the Rwandans from the refugee communities that had been there for thirty years or more, and so their own immediate family members had escaped the recent massacres inside their former homeland. And returning to Rwanda was their big celebration.

Josefu and Bill listened as Africa, completely unambiguously, described how the victors had been insensitive to the feelings of the Rwandan residents who had never fled, and who were now mourning their dead. It was a miracle that these local survivors had escaped destruction and now they wanted to hold on to the little they had. Instead, they faced competition from the hordes of new arrivals.

"And what I have told you is about the Tutsis," Africa added. As for the Hutus, he said that even though many had run away to hide in the camps beyond the borders when the new government arrived, most had stayed behind.

"Afrika, tell me, are there four million Hutus left here and two million gone to the camps in Zaire?" Bill asked, to verify the figures he had received.

"I don't know," Afrika replied in a worried voice. But he said those Hutus who stayed also feared the exuberance of their new masters. "It is difficult, to watch all that triumph." Then the new leadership abruptly clamped down on festivities, even their own. "There will be less fighting that way," Afrika concluded.

The government was in transition in every sense at the moment, Josefu observed. They had not even seized their privileges yet. One matter that aroused his anger was that some Western expatriates, even young typists and attendants, were driving around in shiny four-wheel drive cars, supplied with their jobs — and it was among the very first signs that they were back in town. In contrast, some Rwandan ministers, government members devoid of funds, often had no means of getting to their meetings with the foreign institutions except to walk. Given what that represented, Josefu felt keenly awkward for them.

"If they hadn't been traumatised already, their embarrassment and humiliation would not have mattered so much," Josefu said to Bill. "Do something about it."

"Of course," Bill said.

"That's not good enough."

"What else do you want me to say, Josefu?" Bill challenged him.

"Oh, just do it," he retorted, knowing it was one of their bad moments. It was a long story: Bill had superior rank and, in affairs Rwandan, he had the advantage of being white and therefore was thought back at Headquarters to be less biased than him. That is, when an opinion and not a position was being sought.

⋮

Josefu shrugs his shoulders bitterly and glances around at Leroy's motel furniture, recalling the General Assembly seating as clearly as the first time he was shown it, four days after he had been transferred from Geneva to New York: a concert hall in the round. The Secretariat was there to serve the sitting delegates, and the delegates were supposed to serve the universe, or that part of it which had people who could evaporate into thoughts and schemes.

There are shafts of blue light before him, reflecting the UN flag. Why blue? Like a blue and sunny sky, benevolently bestowing a United Nations holiday mood across the planet? And whose happiness, then?

Josefu roars aloud, feeling his heartbeat hasten and knowing he can do nothing about it. The light blue reflections he saw are now darkening around him. He is able to shift his thoughts back:

'Let us take resolutions on poverty reduction which, successfully passed, will make the delegates dance as they leave the chamber. Long may the good feeling last...around New York, and the rest of the world can wait for a trickle effect. Yes, that's an apt example.' Josefu lowers his head and sees below him fragments of thick carpet, the ones from the General Assembly hall, muffling the sounds of strategic conversations, one national interest against the other.

"The UN is arrogant and powerless," Père Ambroise had said.

Josefu's ponderings make him spin around, his leg hitting the corner of the motel bed. 'Perhaps the UN has purpose and direction? Like the four-wheel drive vehicle it favours for working in poor countries, with a satellite phone aerial on its bonnet, strong and erect like a proud penis? And to be pushed off the edge of the world one day, in vengeance, by those to whom everyhing promised was never delivered?'

'Or what about a machine: the UN is like a machine with well-oiled components purring away. With complete efficiency? And logic? And impartiality? And then lifted up by a giant crane, operated by the betrayed and unprotected, lifted and dropped vengefully down into an inescapable scrap heap?' Josefu gives a laugh, and there is nobody to hear him.

"But the UN was none of these things in New York; only a cluster of disparate people," he tells himself, aloud. "Application forms filled in by prospective Secretariat staff requested that candidates hold a belief, shared by the Delegates, in *'the purposes and ideals of the United Nations'*. Yet once they got inside, recruits puffed away at their career prospects till the smoke they exhaled billowed so thickly that it encircled the organization's emblem. And then their first intentions became irretrievable." Josefu circles a chair and stops abruptly, exclaiming: "And the reforms had been like dentistry that took your bite away." He sits down at last.

All these years later, on a chair in a motel near a prairie, Josefu sees his capacity to reflect has returned and he welcomes it like a lost child. He can look back now, make judgements now. Suddenly, the thought comes to him that he could divide his UN colleagues into three groups.

He flinches at the number *'three'*, astonished by its suitability, although he is aware he doesn't really know why. And despite also being unable to explain to himself why all of this is so relevant to his immediate travel plans, he experiences a strong compulsion to think through this whole idea of three groups, right now. He feels a body warmth he must cool, and that he can no longer move on without working, weaving, tearing, mending his newly found concept.

He rationalises: 'a clear understanding of the issue of Headquarters' personnel provides a clue, at least, to UN failure in Rwanda.' "Yes, three groups or perhaps four," he says, again surprised by this sudden clarity.

Rapidly now, he murmurs to himself: "I know where to start. I'll start with the people who had real power in the Council and the key members of the Secretariat who knew how to operate round them."

Josefu feels he is rehearsing a speech now, for Bill. "And this", he says upstanding, hands behind his back, with slow speech and a clear voice, "This is what I declare to you, Bill. Listen carefully! During the disastrous debates in the Peacekeeping Commission of the UN Secretariat, if you remember, Bill, we were told to be mindful of the United States delegates — especially them."

Bill would of course say: "And what about your fellow British?"

To which Josefu would reply that he would not give in to any diversions Bill baited him with! He imagines he would continue briskly: "With these people, our given line in the Secretariat was to tread so carefully that we didn't even give the key members of the Security Council the latest news from the field." He'd also say: "Bill, it was not the bitter taste left by their failure to fight warlords in Somalia, which turned the Americans away from Rwanda. Rather, it was the ease with which rhetoric could be used by the ambitious members of the Secretariat for persuading the delegates to wash their hands of all Africans and their politicians' deadly machinations."

Bill would of course ask, 'why?' Josefu is enjoying this! And he in turn would say to him immediately: "Bill, did you notice these American UN members, the ones with the most power, mostly whites — okay, the French and British too — had arrived in New York, as delegates, with intellectual baggage from their own locality? And this counted, despite their denying it had any bearing on international affairs, don't you see?"

And then he'd ask him, rhetorically, "And did you notice then, Bill, that in their own localities, the majority of blacks lived in the most uncharted areas of their cities? Unpredictable. On the edge of the law! And this perception coloured — ha! — their views forever. Didn't you see?"

Bill would protest but Josefu would continue: "Outside, out in Africa, all those blacks were seen as unpredictable and lawless too. But the key word is — listen — *tribal!* So the top experts in the Secretariat whom the delegates listened to — not to me because I did not claim to be an expert — these expert advisers dismissed the Rwandan conflict as 'Tribal'. Do you know what that word means for them, Bill?"

Although alone in the motel, Josefu becomes agitated: "I don't care anymore whether you know or not!" He is aware Bill would have been hurt by the words, he'd have twisted his beard, cheeks scarlet. In real life Josefu would never have spoken like this to him.

"Alright, I'll explain," he would start again, more gently, ". . when our esteemed colleagues say 'Tribal' it is for when nobody is seen as a person in their own right." He'd stop Bill interrupting. "Because tribals are the bearers of just two imagined labels: either 'one of us and with our tribe' or 'not one of us'. 'Tribals' savagely kill the 'not us' of course! So there's nothing else to understand. It's so easy."

"Playing with clichés," Bill would probably say.

Josefu would retort: "The power of clichés is in their simplicity, their acceptability. Tribal! The password to our exoneration! Rwanda is a country of blacks and tribals, because it is Africa after all, and the experts stop any questions by declaring that we cannot understand what tribals kill for out there."

Josefu speaks even louder: "Don't you remember: 'We don't know who is killing who...' said the blond president of the United States. Yes, he said that." Josefu avoids seeing the empty chair, the single bed, the maple leaf flag on the wall that he knows are there and could menace his momentum. He closes his burning eyes: "What happened in Rwanda was because of political tactics, not a tribal dance of death."

He paces up and down his motel room, knowing that the only way he can breathe easy is to continue talking aloud: "I know where I was at: I must name the second group in New York, in the UN Secretariat, or I'm a loser and I won't travel on."

Josefu joyfully lifts his arms in the air, as if he had scored a goal. "Yes! The second group, it's them in the Secretariat: the UN career

Africans. They had cast off their own robes and donned those of the moneyed West — even Père Ambroise said it. Oh yes," Josefu adds to himself, but as if Bill was listening. "Plus royaliste que le roi! The more detachment shown by the career Africans, the more trust and approval they were able to gain from their superiors. The irony of the UN's neglect of Rwanda is that both the Secretary General and the official responsible for African peacekeeping operations were supposedly African themselves, and yet Rwanda was abandoned . . ."

Nobody is listening in the motel room, but its emptiness spurs Josefu to speak even more loudly: "I remember everyone saying, *'The head of peacekeeping operations for Africa, a good African himself, shows full objectivity, no trace of bias'*. And these UN Africans would wring their hands and claim, 'It's so complicated in Rwanda; trust me, I am an African and I know'. They wanted to keep their jobs."

He paces around the room in circles, an Alberta tourist brochure now in his hand as if it were an exhibit in court. And then, abruptly he stops in his tracks, unable to go forward. And slowly, while pulling up a chair and sitting down, he begins to understand why this whole train of thought was important to his personal progress and not only for understanding his time in Rwanda. Unless he plods tediously along with this line of explanation, he can no longer make the journey to Winnipeg in any meaningful way.

He sits and remains quiet for a long while, knowing he needs another diversion, which appears at last: "And thirdly," he smiles, ". . . the third group: they were the Bills of this world, who wanted to be nice to everyone. Those people like Bill who are faultless in their compassion, for bloody everyone. And we turned our backs on a million dead."

The light outside is changing. Josefu shakes his head, wondering how his thoughts had strayed so far? "Who said I had to spend all this effort on dissection anyway? What were the targets set for me when I left Banff? I was only to remember events, just events."

He holds a mirror to himself in his mind, right now, "No holding back!" Then he recalls with devastating clarity his crippling embarrassment and ambivalence about remarks Mary had once made, Bill's wife Mary, which now ricochet around his room.

He remembers how they had made a weekend family trip together a few hours drive from New York, to their newly found upstate haven by a lake. The landscape became poisoned, so strongly had he resented every word Mary said, especially since Patricia said she was right. It was at dinner outdoors, and Josefu had been complaining about the excessive caution of some of the African members of the Secretariat.

Mary had retorted, "Josefu, you should be more understanding, you shouldn't compare yourself with them. Even forget your British nationality for a minute here. You had much more advantages than them when they began." He got closer, to ensure he was hearing her correctly. "You have this unbelievable background," Mary had continued: "Kabaka's nephew, best private school, large home near London, universities in England and Switzerland, and you don't have to rise from anything; you don't have to prove anything. It's different for them whose struggle up the UN ladder started in some African village or township nobody knows. You should be kinder."

Josefu learned from her, later, that he had apparently looked 'crestfallen', and she had added, "But Bill tells me all that background of yours is the reason your judgement is so reliable, because you have nothing to prove, nothing you have to rise from. You're beyond all that. Oh come on, Josefu, you're special. You shouldn't mind."

Why had it taken all these years to recall her words, here in a prairie motel, why so long after? What a burden, 'reliable judgement'! And so cruel in Rwanda, to have 'reliable judgement'. So difficult to keep on going.

He tries again to refocus on the case in hand, the UN Africans, to move away from his discomfort. "Was there any real excuse for them," he remarks to himself now, "for all that caution over Rwanda among their so-called 'fellow Africans'? They always got it right about what the Security Council liked to hear. After all, it was easier — and much more popular with the decision makers in the Council — to give credence to the local regime in power, the one we already knew, than letting in a new one formed of rebels. Keeping the old usually costs less money."

Josefu leaps up and then sits down again on the edge of the hotel chair as he comments, still oblivious to his surroundings. "And me? What were you then, Josefu? The Gimp. Oh no," he says, rising and bowing, "That's disrespectful to the disabled. I was a piece of furniture of uncertain hue…"

For a moment he notices the motel room briefly, and an empty glass by the window ledge. He says to himself: "Don't try to drown all this in whiskey though there is plenty left in the bottle! And anyway, you've got the 'tribal' bit sorted. You've got a lot to sort, such a lot."

Josefu can't sit down again as Père Ambroise comes so clearly into his mind. It is the incident, Josefu recalls with detachment now, when he had delivered a sermon at the bottom of the path before they saw the shed: "If you think this was a war between two tribes," the priest had said ponderously, "the Hutu majority and the Tutsi minority, who hated each other intensely, in - ah - what you like to call an ethnic conflict, or tribal warfare, that is an even more favourite theme for you, 'tribal warfare' — then you are wrong."

Nobody had responded because of the weight and authority with which he spoke. And they had not yet known what they would see in the shed.

Everyone had stood still and Père Ambroise had continued, "It was a political war, with a political leadership wanting to get the greatest number of people compromised, you understand, to get them on their side. Blood on so many hands would ensure loyalty and keep them in power. Power, not tribe! That was the motivation of the political authorities." The priest had paused for breath, as if it were part of a routine speech. Josefu remembers it so clearly now! Then Père Ambroise had lightly lifted his hand and held their gaze. "Now I will explain: if there had been a sufficiently large number of any other group, let's say Japanese or Chinese, who knows, just any group, just any, ready to be easily murdered on a grand scale, do you know what would have happened?"

He had paused, but still nobody spoke. "The authorities then would have called both Tutsis and Hutus together, to commit crimes together against these others, on pain of death, both together against this other group. You understand?"

He presumed nobody did. "In that way, you see, it would have created an even larger number of people with total loyalty to the leadership — a loyalty that allows them to avoid punishment. I am using long phrases. But perhaps that way you can understand."

Now Josefu is standing so still that slowly the motel room surrounds him, but it is exactly like the stage scenery back at school, when he took the role of Julius Caesar. 'Why not a black one this year?' his teacher had said when he himself had queried his own suitability. But the headmaster told him he had conveyed his sense of betrayal in the end scene with brilliance. Pretty good.

"What's all that about?" Josefu asks himself, "School plays? Where was I? Where is Père Ambroise?" As soon as he arrives in Winnipeg, he will remind Bill of what the priest had taught them. He'll say he wants to die because of the way the Secretariat presented to Council as 'tribal warfare', the carefully planned massacres that happened in Rwanda. "Their facile lie was just soap to wash our hands of it all."

He'll say it all to Bill - all those classifications, definitions, explanations. Here in his motel room, he now feels exactly as he would if he had cleaned his car windscreen: the same relief, the same new confidence.

⋮

Afraid of stalling his ability to reason, he quickly changes track: "And right now I'm supposed to remember and understand what I did in Kigali the day we visited the Blue Helmets headquarters, the second time around."

But his mind wanders. 'Didn't Bill and I lunch afterwards at Chez Lando, that day? It's the young UNAMIR officer who told us to go there. I was still so disappointed then to have missed seeing General Dallaire just by a few weeks. He too had often been to Chez Lando, for dainty cuts of skewered meat and crowded but elusive joviality.'

Suddenly, Josefu sits up straight and exclaims aloud: "I know, I have an idea for my future: I want to find Dallaire!"

It is the first time in over six years that a thought concerning his future has occurred to him. Josefu rises and goes in his socks to look out of the window. He sees the hotel's other building opposite, and a damp wind from the TransCanada Highway blows around it. The weather changes so rapidly. But there is little to see out there; he is too far from the mountains now. "And I'll have to leave the prairies too," he says, "if I am to find Dallaire."

His mind travels once more, as he remembers that in New York, during the Rwanda crisis, at the end of the day when there were few people in the Secretariat building, he would drink water from the fountain in the corridor and then go to read Dallaire's dispatches. On the 32nd floor you turned a small round tap at the water fountain, instead of pressing a button, like in the rest of the building. His stomach was always full of water when he went to read Dallaire's messages.

There was something meticulous in the General's style. Josefu imagined it had undertones of sarcasm, given that Dallaire must have known his pleas for help against the carnage were falling on deaf ears.

Now he recalls that Père Ambroise had said some parishioners believed the Pope of Rome should take steps for Dallaire to be declared a Saint of the Church. Josefu had remarked to him that usually this process was put in place only after the Saint's death. Père Ambroise replied that Dallaire left dispirited and half dead already.

"Doesn't that contradict his fighting spirit?" Josefu had asked.

"No, being half dead is a Rwandan symptom. We can live with it," said Père Ambroise.

Few people had privileged access to Dallaire's missives in the way Josefu had. Yet he was unable to put this advantage to any good use. Only once, when the story went around that there had been no 'famous fax', did Josefu make his mark by producing a copy. In it, Dallaire had predicted exactly the catastrophe, which was about to begin. 'What a man!'

At that time, where had Josefu placed his own reliable judgement? Which, as Mary said, was born from a golden endowment? In New York with its undefined skies, its work environment made of chrome and glass, its dispersed light, he became unresponsive to the very space he moved in; his privileges had led him to indolence. And Josefu had become invisible even to himself.

But now he sees clearer, much clearer, so he needs to find Dallaire, even if only to touch the sleeve of his shirt. Making plans for it is something he can savour, who knows, for the rest of his journey.

⋮

Josefu's frame of mind is changing. He is getting an appetite. He'll soon be on the phone to Bill, he decides. He has things to do, people to see. "Early lunch," he says, knowing how precarious are his mood swings. He has to keep apace. He resolutely picks up the phone, menu in hand, just as the leaflet instructed, to give advance warning to the motel restaurant. He orders three courses, beginning with soup of the day, and a couple of beers, 'not too cold, please'.

For the first time in years, he glances at himself very quickly in a full-length mirror, pulling straight his shirt collar. He still avoids his face; that will be for later.

The receptionist asks him if everything was all right? He wonders again whether he shouldn't make this place his residence. 'Oh no, don't forget, you've got plans now.' They elude him suddenly, but he reaches the door of the restaurant, able to set his fears aside.

"You called already?" says the waiter, looking a little surprised.

"Yes," someone shouts out, "I recognise the accent. Give him his table."

Josefu sits down in anticipation. The soup is freshly made and he is probably the first to be served. It increases his feeling of contentment. 'Not nice, though, to be eating alone,' he reflects. 'I should marry again. So much to do now.'

He smiles at the waiter, "It looks as if the weather might clear up, don't you think? There must be nice places to walk here in the summer."

"Yes, Sir," the young man replies, but showing he is very busy.

Josefu continues to smile, to himself and at people who start filling the restaurant. He eats rapidly. 'Before I meet Dallaire, I've got so much to prepare. And so much to remember. I must show I was attentive to everything he wrote.'

He had seen Dallaire's photograph many times, but now can no longer recall what he looks like. 'Doesn't matter for the moment.'

When he leaves the restaurant, Josefu stretches, standing outside with his feet apart, hands held high and then skips lightly down three stairs. He walks rapidly without knowing where he is going until he reaches the highway itself and has to turn back.

Aware of the fragility of his unfamiliar high spirits and that, only hours previously, his despondency appeared permanent, he begins to run. A cluster of people by the motel look at him, as though he were perhaps a former black athlete, and he waves to them, surprising even himself. Inside, he finds a telephone booth near reception and he dials Winnipeg, using his 6117-pin number, which he likes. He leaves a recorded message:

"Bill and Mary, this is Josefu. I am on my way to you. I don't know when I'll get there. Might take a few days, you know. I'm fine. Bill! We'll see Dallaire; we'll go and see him. I don't know how you feel about it. Okay? General Romeo Dallaire. I'll see him. Everything's fine," and he hangs up, pleased with himself.

He knows there is more to do while his present state lasts. It is like when as a child he could borrow a bicycle only for a very limited time. Since there had always been trouble at home in Maidenhead when he was a boy, about cycling when the traffic was considered lethal, he borrowed a bike from the next door neighbour who used to time Josefu with a stop watch.

He walks more slowly in order to recall those summer holidays in Maidenhead: eating warm matoke with his father every day, mowing the lawn for him, pushing a wheelbarrow full of weeds, hearing stories of Bugandan ancestral wisdom, reading 'Wind in the Willows', and waiting for the telephone to ring.

Overseas call to be made now from the hotel: he reaches his cousin Maria on the phone in London immediately. She laughs when he asks for Ellie's number.

"Ah, Josefu! The heartstrings are pulling! You've left that Banff place and summer's in the air. Oooh! Ellie? You remember we liked her. Having regrets now? Never too late, eh? Oooh Josefu! All right, it just happens I saw her about a year ago."

"A year ago!"

"Yes, by chance, in the Residents Parking place where you get your permit renewed. So I gave her your number."

"You don't have hers?"

"No." she replies, in a way that Josefu thinks was curt.

"But she rang me from a hospital, haven't I told you?"

"She can't live far from my place in London, or she wouldn't be getting a parking permit there."

"She has daughters, she told me. Has she changed her surname?"

"How can I know?"

"But, you saw her," he retorts.

"And what say she is a married woman? And you are single, looking for romance. Uh-uh! We didn't speak for that long. It was I who recognised her."

"She telephoned me, I want to call her back. What's the big deal?" Josefu is becoming impatient and feels his good humour slipping. He had assumed Ellie was unattached as he was. In truth, he hadn't thought about it. "Maria, I want to find her. She telephoned me, don't you understand? She's in hospital, can't you see?"

Maria promises to do her best and Josefu says he will phone again in a couple of days. It is then he notices he has no diary, not since Rwanda; he had stopped using it shortly after arriving there, when plans no longer counted.

He hears loud music, probably from the motel's wedding party, but a cloud casts its thick shadow throughout his room. He feels as if he were standing as desolate and empty handed, as if his shopping had fallen out of torn bags and all that he had looked forward to was broken and dispersed at his feet.

The next few hours will be difficult alone. The phone conversation with Maria had somehow tainted a field of pure snow. But through the expanse, Ellie appears, as he liked her best, in a woollen dressing gown at the end of her college corridor.

He remembers that when they used to embrace, the size of the whole world, its perimeter and contours, were contained and shaped by their entwined bodies. The globe was not round but had their form, which also included the firmament above them and all the layers of crusted soil below.

He had never really felt secure again, or that he had a place in the created world. It never happened again. Nothing the same with anyone else. He'd forgotten it, rather than noticed it was never repeated. Isn't that clear enough? He'd been a rock then, or a fortress with Ellie on his shoulders like a beacon on a cliff. Oh yes, they knew where they both belonged then. Raining thoughts, though, had put an end to that; soil erosion had turned into a mudslide.

Inexplicably, he senses that Marie Immaculée would have understood his story. 'But I never told her. And I never pitied Marie Immaculée, I never warmed to her enough, with her hollow cheeks.' He despises himself with an ardour exceeding all he can bear, and fights only half-heartedly against the way he still fears her memory.

⋮

Josefu senses he is looking into a pool, seeing the reflection of the young officer from the UNAMIR Headquarters, round cheeks and clean-shaven, and then the faces of Bill and himself wearing sun helmets. Also the head of the High Commissioner for Refugees — he recognises her clearly. And floating along the bottom is Marie Immaculée, drowned with her white headdress slowly falling away. Whereas their contours can only be seen on the surface of the water, her presence down there is full, profound and lasting.

⋮

The light outside the motel lingers. His mind returns to the conversation with the UNAMIR officer.

"How is the operation proceeding, to find bodies still and to document them?" Bill had asked him.

"People are not always keen to reveal the sites, in case they are accused themselves."

"We visited a shed," Bill told him, "And it was remarkable that the bodies were not seriously decomposed. We obtained a lot of details."

"I have a full book of notes about it," Josefu added, remarking to himself, 'We might as well be wearing white clinicians coats; we have the required professional dispassion.'

Now, more than six years later, sitting in Strathmore, alone in Canada, he remarks that the great difference between clinicians and themselves was that they had healed nobody and stitched no wounds.

He looks down at his foot and sees the sliced half face still there, framed with curls and beads, an angel wronged, a prayer discontinued.

III Rivers & Stones

6.

The slopes on the hill opposite where Josefu stood were dotted with red lights, which came from the charcoal fires of Rwandan villagers cooking their evening meal. Everyone deserved a pot of food in the dusk, to give each ebbing day its shape and reason, a human task. It was a time when all men, women and children found their place. They were either cooking, waiting or eating. There, in gentle smoke and rising mist, reason and quiet were restored for a moment. This spread of lights was an enchantment for Josefu. From a distance they flickered with enticement, transforming human geography into an epic tale.

He had stood apart to watch the falling night; it was as if its inevitability was a reminder that some things go on regardless. For instance, he continued thinking, those stark colours that are witness to the truth of destruction; they ebb away in the approaching darkness, even in the land of a million dead. It is as if Nature knew the frailty of its own—humans and animals alike—and nightly draws a dimming cover, softly, to stem the force of stark visual effects. And even though it is then that the inner eye comes into action, he reflected, it is only for intangible dreams and they, of course have endings. After today, though, Josefu hoped he would never have to see a river again.

⋮

He rubbed one elbow, and then the other, really without any reason. He smoothed his collar. Afrika's car had broken down and he was patiently trying to mend it, after Josefu explained to him that nobody felt betrayed or angry that there was a small hitch in the old taxi. He had noticed Afrika at first had been too distressed to concentrate on the job.

During the last few days the driver had truly befriended them, impressive in his readiness to serve well. Père Ambroise had said he was a Hutu but a 'good one'; moreover one of his brothers had been killed in prison a few years ago by the previous regime while awaiting trial, accused of treason for belonging to an organisation that promoted human rights.

"So typical a waste," Josefu had remarked when told about it. "The family scraped and sacrificed to get one of their sons into higher education, just like the family of Marie Immaculée." He surprised himself for having actually been able to say her name so readily, given that he still felt such ambivalence towards her.

"Look at the case of this young man, though," he continued quickly, "Inevitably, higher education led him to the awareness of standards of justice which we at the UN, are supposed to promote globally.

"Right, Josefu," Bill said, wearily passing his hand over his damp hair.

"Yes, right! Yet although it is he who was killed, squandered, we ourselves didn't attempt to investigate it or make any attempt to prevent it from happening again, in wasted Africa. He was doing veterinary studies and would have made a difference to the people's livelihood. Our restrictive mandates are killing our conscience and killing their future."

Bill said, "That's some speech! I'd say portentous."

"Portentous? That's all you can say?"

"You go on about the spiral of failure in this continent. But you're wrong, Josefu, because there must be a way out."

"Yes, through long distance running," Josefu had replied, his mood bitter.

Earlier in the day, Afrika their driver had eaten very little at lunch, although Père Ambroise encouraged him, overcoming the first slight unease between them that Josefu had noticed. Père Ambroise intimated his preference was for the driver in Butare whom he knew. Bill explained they couldn't have that UN driver any more because there had been a lack of communication about the time of their arrival.

Père Ambroise refused to believe it and offered instead his humble opinion, he said, which was that they were going to be deliberately hindered throughout their stay, by the institution they served. This upset Bill deeply, to such an extent that Père Ambroise took Josefu aside and asked if his perturbation was genuine.

"You don't know Bill," he replied, "He is a real trooper. He cannot bear to think that his life's work should have been for an organisation which nobody here respects any more."

"But this is Rwanda," Père Ambroise explained, "And we have our reasons, don't you think?"

"Yes, but you should understand him," Josefu said.

"And what about you?"

"I am used to failure," Josefu replied.

"I admire you for that," Père Ambroise said.

Josefu did not answer and had simply looked away, still under the priest's intense gaze through the thick lenses.

This conversation took place before they drove on to a long dirt road, having asked Bill to sit behind and keep out of sight as much as possible. A lot of tension had spread about all day. RPF troops (*Rwandan Patriotic Front*) were stopping cars and people at regular intervals. The taxi with Père Ambroise sitting in front was let past. On another occasion they were halted. Seeing Bill, however, the troopers took him for a doctor and they were moved along. At another enforced stop, Afrika gave two dollar bills out of a small wad from Père Ambroise that he had been instructed to keep for such a purpose. Josefu and Bill quickly looked up at the sky. They also remarked aloud that the sun had at last broken through that day and it was warmer than usual.

Slowly, they had made their way past destroyed houses and bullet ridden public buildings, mostly little schools or the odd clinic. In this region, there were few mixed communities. Settlements had mostly been Tutsi. Therefore, not much had been left standing by the raging Interahamwe and their masters. By the time the new government troops had arrived the place was empty and they had moved on to where action was needed. It was for this reason that Père Ambroise guessed that valuable evidence of massacres was probably still available, since there were neither survivors nor new authorities to dispose of dead bodies. By that stage of the war, the killers had usually not thought it necessary to hide their deeds themselves.

The rattling sound of the frail taxi seemed to echo in the stillness. Josefu had noticed that there were few birds or insects to be heard and not enough wind to shake the banana tree leaves or any other foliage. No cows for cars to avoid, no children staggering under the weight of jerry cans of water, no women with bundles on their heads walking straight-backed, like aristocrats in films. Nothing.

Père Ambroise and Afrika were talking in a half whisper in Kinyarwanda, the driver visibly anxious. Told he no longer needed to hide, Bill now sat up and checked his camera; Bernard had been unable to join them. Josefu looked out of the windows on either side, muttering.

"You said something?" asked Bill.

"What a waste, " Josefu sighed. "What a waste!" Bill didn't respond.

Père Ambroise had then said, in a slow, reassuring voice, "Our driver drives well, and we travel well."

⋮

The car came to a bridge, a narrow and precarious crossing over a small river, made of mud and mostly broken planks. The vehicle stopped. They got out to guide Afrika in the car, over to the other side. Then, simultaneously, they all caught sight of what they were not prepared for at that moment and gasped, even Père Ambroise.

Brown, bronze, black, grey — yes, mostly grey — Grey and long, still shapes emerged in the shallow water, logs perhaps as they were nearly straight. Yet these immobile, dense forms spoke out, defiant, pulling you towards them like magnets so as to tell you they were people. Their contours pressed against your eyes, crowned your head, refusing to be distant. Halted in their flow by a boulder or by driftwood, the human bodies had piled relentlessly higher and higher, regardless of packing half way up the riverbank and almost reaching the bridge. A few seemed to lie in rows, others criss-crossed, many with their arms at their sides and some with their legs neatly together. Others, though, were missing limbs or skin, angrily showing resentment, it seemed, that animals and insects had preyed on their remains. At that moment a small object, round and compact, detached itself and started moving down the river over the rocks.

"That's a foetus," whispered Père Ambroise, "The mother is probably somewhere with her abdomen cut open." He fell silent.

Afrika got out of the car noiselessly, joined them and stood quietly. Père Ambroise put a hand on his shoulder, but whether to steady himself or to console the driver, Josefu could not tell.

Bodies were strewn all along the right bank, and some had probably flowed further downstream, as if more success was achieved by doing so.

"What is rare," said Père Ambroise at last, "is that the majority seem to have been mowed down with bullets. Look, there are not many signs of machetes. Oh yes, over there," pointing to a decapitated child's body, naked, a boy. "And yet habitually, they used firearms only sparingly, because of the cost, you know."

"The bodies were probably brought in lorries and tipped over into the river, further back," said Afrika, bringing in his expertise as a driver. He exchanged a few words with Père Ambroise who then patted him softly on the back.

"This happens, of course, that you come across such… things. I don't know what to say; it's not a scene…" said Père Ambroise, "Ah, words…I mean, this is a typical thing to see. But I did not know about it here. I cannot understand why it wasn't discovered before."

Afrika added something in Kinyarwanda.

"He says that there is no sign of a vehicle having come along here for a long time." Père Ambroise added: "You know, a cadaver always cries out for attention. That's its nature. Each one. It's always like that."

Neither Josefu nor Bill said anything. Together, almost in unison, they walked back to the car for their notebooks and Bill picked up his camera.

"It will take a long time if you try to count the corpses," said Père Ambroise, in a slightly mocking tone. "Photographs are better, go ahead, go ahead." He turned away and lifted his cassock before going down to the riverbank. They followed, with Afrika bringing up the rear.

"Is it safe around here?" said Bill, "No enemy incursions?"

"You won't die. This area is surrounded by our troops; they simply haven't come inside the terrain, that's all."

Josefu noticed the priest had said 'Our troops' when referring to the former rebel RPF. But who could blame him? Josefu was marking on one page a small stick for each body he saw, to be counted later with a margin of error added which could allow for many more.

They stumbled on stones and bracken. Suddenly an animal yelped and disappeared before it could be identified. Père Ambroise was not interested in commenting. He kept on taking off his glasses and wiping them. There were corpses as far as they could see, strewn haphazardly and giving out an odour familiar only to those who already knew the smell of decomposing human flesh. Josefu wrote the remark down. He was trying to do a job.

They came now to a point where the river widened, fuller and deeper and almost serene. It made a low and hollow sound. Although there was no end in sight to the corpses washed up on both banks now, you knew that there were even more under the water. They were either immobilised in driftwood or entangled in growths along the riverbed or else, more successfully, they had floated as they were supposed to, very far away.

Josefu continued to jot down a stick for every semblance of a body he saw. His stomach began to turn. It was at this point that Père Ambroise halted, turned to him and put both hands on his forearms. "Is it long since you were in your homeland?"

"England?" said Josefu, quickly adding, "No, you mean Uganda of course."

"Yes, where you must have eaten tilapia fish."

"Oh, my God," said Josefu softly.

"Nobody on Lake Victoria will eat fish now. So many bodies have gone there from Rwanda. My parents' bodies were in latrines, but these ones… Ah, I really didn't know we would see these cadavers here. I'll tell the authorities; we'll hold a ceremony. Let's go back. We have to move on or we will not make it to the place where living people wait for me. We must follow the Lord Jesus Christ." He began walking back to the car at such a pace that the other three men were almost running behind him to keep up.

Bill had not uttered a word. He had taken photographs but Josefu noticed his distraction, and that at times the lens would have been clearly out of focus.

One bird sang for a few seconds.

The river was busy, trying to hide secrets, making excuses for not having carried all the bodies downstream. Moment by moment, the stench became increasingly unbearable. Most of the male victims' bodies were lightly clothed, either because they were killed at a particular time of day or night or because they had been told to take off their outer clothing. The women were fewer, it seemed, and there were not many children. Just as he was observing this, Josefu saw a woman's body with both breasts cut off. He watched quickly to check whether Père Ambroise had noticed it. The priest's head was facing straight up ahead, concentrating on reaching the car as soon as possible.

Suddenly, uncontrollably, Josefu turned to the left away from the river and vomited. It was one long, strong stream, copious and forceful. 'Like a woman,' he thought. He quickly wiped his mouth and looked round. Bill had nearly reached the car with the others and was leaning, his head downwards, against the bonnet.

"This is our work," Josefu said to himself, "It has to be done."

And at that moment he remembered Patricia's words again: "Do something, stop bullshitting."

He wanted to see his children right now, out of the sky descending. He felt he had to bid them farewell. Perhaps it was for their own good he had chosen to do this job, for everywhere to be better. That's what you did for the young, made everywhere better for them.

"Bullshit," his wife had said at one point in New York, "Wringing your hands in a glass building achieves nothing."

Josefu thought how far away all that was at present, though, as he struggled not to slip onto the pile of corpses, and clambered up towards the bridge. 'That lying river,' he thought, 'that treacherous river, how I hate every river.' Aloud he added, "I'll never go home and row along the Thames again."

"What's that you said?" Bill asked in English.

"Oh, sorry," Josefu replied in French, for the sake of the others, "It's the water down there."

"Let's keep silent," said Père Ambroise, "Please, please." He seethed, enraged. They entered the car now, each in their allotted place. Afrika sat with his head and arms on the wheel. When he finally started the engine, the other passengers realised they had to get out once more to guide him across the bridge, as they were supposed to in the first place. He drove fast and recklessly, ignoring their guiding and the car screeched as he stopped on the other side to let them back in.

Josefu was sure he could hear a distinct thudding, a set of drums, a dialogue between elusive performers, a rhythm he would rather not hear. The sounds persisted but he did not ask the others about them. Worried now, he realised he had not noticed the faces of the cadavers.

"It's as if they had no faces, not like in the shed," he said aloud now.

Nobody responded, even though he had said it in French. He returned to his own musings. He tried not to blink because with eyes closed, his head would be pushed down under water. He opened his notebook, reflecting that each of the people whose bodies they had seen would have a mighty name, as he was already discovering to be the custom in Rwanda—Deogratias, Jean de Dieu, Marie

Immaculée... 'Christian names in Rwanda,' he wrote, underlining the words carefully and leaving a blank below.

Afrika's taxi bumped along the dirt road with its silent passengers. Josefu was aware of the overgrown vegetation on either side, bean crops never harvested and overrun, green bananas that should have been picked long ago, a sorrow that rose into the sky.

Josefu's sense of helplessness hung around his neck like a hangman's rope. As it tightened, he attempted to direct his thoughts to evasive action 'but in a positive direction', he added. If he found a good journalist, perhaps his observations could be put into adequate words. Patricia was a journalist but this was well beyond her, he thought contemptuously, whether poetry or international relations. 'My mind is wandering,' he sighed to himself, 'relieving itself'.

Père Ambroise asked that the car be stopped. He disappeared into the undergrowth, perhaps to urinate. At this moment, speaking in English, Josefu turned to Bill and said: "You know, I haven't got a lawyer. I mean, I discussed nothing about arrangements with Patricia, about seeing my kids. I'll have nothing left."

Bill was shocked. "Do you want to discuss it now? In the middle of all this?"

"About dying?"

"Oh, I'm sorry Josefu, I'm being insensitive. Now I hear you, I can understand. I'll get on to Mary; she'll sort something out for when you get back. You'll get to see your kids."

"Wasted, a world full of wasted moments; our time is up," said Josefu slowly, not caring whether Bill heard him or not.

Père Ambroise returned to the car. "It isn't far away now, where we're going," he said, taking off his glasses and wiping them with a crumpled handkerchief, then carefully pressing the scotch tape so that it would continue to hold them together. He asked Josefu, "What would your mother say to you about all that, all what we saw?"

"You mean about death? Death in general?"

"Yes, Josefu, What did your mother teach you?" Bill added, moving a hand away from his beard.

"I don't know what to say, really. She used to forbid everyone from saying 'So-and-so is buried here or there', but instead, 'The body of So-and-so is buried there'. It was only the body, she insisted, and not the person."

"She is right, of course," said Père Ambroise, "But it doesn't lessen the pain." There was silence again. Then he asked Bill the same thing.

"I come from a mixed background, father Presbyterian and mother Catholic, so they settled for the neutral territory of the United Church of Canada. It's complicated, forgive me."

"It is just like here," sighed Père Ambroise.

"But thanks to my wife I became a Quaker and we raised our family that way," Bill replied, "Not Evangelical, like in Kigali, the *Eglise Evangelique des Amis*. We're called 'Liberals' or 'Without a programme'. We worship in silence."

"That's very good," said Père Ambroise.

"We believe each person must find their own path and their own truth."

"That's even better. And death?"

"What my dear old mother used to say? Oh my, she was sure my father was waiting for her when she passed away. My wife Mary? She would say the same as Josefu's mother, I think, that it's only the body and not the person who gets buried."

"I thought I knew everything before. That's all gone now," said Père Ambroise. "It is as if I were a child again, having to discover, to stumble and fall, trying to understand everything from the beginning."

"So you'll learn again?"

"Perhaps yes. But perhaps not. There is a great difference from before: I have to live now – do you see it? Can you know it? — recognising that I might learn nothing, that I might not gain any knowledge. Continue to live, on and on, without knowing."

"And the doctrine?" asked Bill.

"The doctrine of the Catholic Church has died in Rwanda. It has floated down that river we just saw. Can you understand me? I am starting to obtain my knowledge all anew."

"But you said to follow Jesus Christ, back there by the river bank," said Bill.

"You should not listen to what I am saying."

"We see you say Mass, perform ceremonies, like where we are going now, in the Commune we are about to visit. Are you not sincere?"

"Why not? When I lift my hands up to God, like you see me…" he paused. "I'll say it this way: I lift my own heart up to the people I love, to those in my parish and to the dead in the river. It is an offering. Mass is an offering."

"If you say so," remarked Josefu.

"I'm alone now," Père Ambroise added.

"Have most priests reacted like you?" asked Bill.

"Ah, do you mind if we don't talk about it further now, out of respect for the corpses we just saw? Our Church is littered with corpses too. I thought you were an expert, a visiting expert. I thought you knew."

Bill retreated, apologising profusely. "You're so right; this really isn't the moment to talk," he concluded, heavily.

Later he asked Josefu what drove Père Ambroise, what kept him going. Josefu said he didn't know. "Anyway," he added, "Neither does Père Ambroise know himself, but he said he's still ready to go on that way, regardless. He said it has to be like that, not to know; and that it's a part of his loss."

⋮

They came to another bridge and got out again. Beneath them was a mere brook, cheerfully passing over dainty rocks that glistened in the shallow water.

Père Ambroise looked around and said, "I think there must be a pretty waterfall a little further back." Josefu was relieved, though, when it was not suggested that they try to find it. With astonishing rapidity he was becoming apprehensive of all water and knew that it would even be difficult for him to shower when they returned to their hotel.

"What would I give for a cool shower," said Bill suddenly. "It's so hot and sweaty."

"I don't want to know," said Josefu, "About the heat, about the cold, about the shower."

"I see you mean it," Bill replied, trying to catch his eye. "I guessed from your tone of voice. It's understandable. You know, I'm beginning to feel lonely too."

After a silence, Josefu said with a distant voice, "Call Mary tonight, Bill," and walked away. Keeping his back to the chirping stream, he looked ahead at the road they were on, which was becoming increasingly redder like the rest of the surrounding soil. It was good earth, worth killing for.

Having already driven to the other side of the bridge, Afrika walked back and with a soft voice asked each of the men in turn, all lost in quiet consideration, to get into the car again. The journey would not be too long. And at the end of the day, they would be going back to Kigali, the big capital of Rwanda, he reminded them.

⋮

A group of about forty women standing by a disused shop talked agitatedly. When Afrika's taxi drew up they were immediately silent. As Josefu had noticed on several previous occasions, many seemed to have dropped their jaw. He wondered if it was a sign of distress. There were quite a few who were bare headed, including some old women. They had been there since early morning, waiting for Père Ambroise.

"These women have nothing," he said to the other three men, "They escaped when the massacres were happening because they had been separated from their children and all the men. The children who couldn't walk were murdered right there. The rest were murdered closer to the ditch. Now they want me to consecrate a piece of land for burial. Creating a home for the dead. It happens often."

He asked for the boot of the car to be opened and that they, the men, carry the sacks of USAid wheat flour into the centre of the open space. He explained to Bill and Josefu that it was part of a one-off supply he had obtained in Kigali. One woman came forward, in her early thirties, of medium height and with high cheekbones. She had an air of authority. She looked into the distance and then, almost reluctantly, focused on Père Ambroise. She was unsmiling and solemn. A few women said something in unison.

"She is their representative. They chose her. She will oversee the distribution," said Père Ambroise.

Afrika translated that she had been a bookkeeper at the Prefecture before the war. Her husband — dead, Afrika hastened to add — had worked at the bus station in the provincial capital but they had continued to live in the village. The women had confidence in her, he explained. Her name was Beatrice. Nobody said a thing for a while.

Josefu noticed that they, the men, stood together, as if they had more in common than with the women opposite. Père Ambroise and Beatrice were placed slightly forward and faced each other. After some time, as if she had now established that her own and the rest of the women's despair had been adequately understood by the visitors, she turned and called to one of her companions.

"It is this one's husband's sister who came to Kigali and told Père Ambroise about them. So she is asking where she is and why she didn't come with us," Afrika translated. "The priest is saying that she was supposed to have left Kigali a week ago."

"But she sent the priest; he's come," Beatrice said to the upset woman, and the rest joined in with comments to console her.

Josefu began despising himself again because, for an instant, he had stood back and compared what was happening to a summer play, one of the classics of Antiquity, which his school had done from time to time, with a chorus he had learned to appreciate now. "I mustn't become hardened," he warned himself.

As often happened in this region — 'Rwanda, Uganda and so on', Josefu was being precise — there was a considerable amount of waiting around, just standing. Perhaps in this case it was the impact of grief. Père Ambroise took out a handkerchief and wiped his brow and glasses. The women whispered among themselves but did not move. Beatrice seemed lost in thought. Nobody looked in the direction of the other men.

Finally, Père Ambroise suggested that the flour be distributed, that it was just a small gift he had brought from Kigali, and that then they could walk to where the ceremony was to take place. Women undid scarves or cloths and silently received a portion of flour from the three women whom Beatrice had designated. Each then tied it into a bundle and started walking. At the edge of the village, they took a path through a small banana plantation and which then went steeply downhill. Josefu heard some of the women were gently sobbing, especially one of the youngest.

They stopped when they came to an exposed area, flat and relatively spacious, with hard soil and small stones. Afrika listened to what was being said to Père Ambroise and translated it for Josefu and Bill.

"Over there, just there," Afrika said, "the Interahamwe made a ditch and put all the bodies in it. That is how the women escaped being in that ditch too; those guarding them had become very, very drunk, that's how." After a while he added, "They are saying that it took so long to bury the people in the mass grave that the Interahamwe had to move on to another job somewhere else. That's how the women escaped, that's how. They had nothing until the next army came and said they could go and plant and eat. The RPF army came," Afrika explained. "Oh, wait…"

Then he translated: "They say they couldn't sleep, they say they couldn't live with the big grave like that. They waited for some time and then found a few old men, and a few young boys who had nothing to eat. They may have been Hutu, you know. Anything, they may have been anything, but they helped to dig and prepare another grave. Now the women are going to show us, but we will have to walk down there." They went on a few hundred yards.

An immense, flat area had been dug several feet deep, almost the size of a large swimming pool.

Bill was shaking his head, "How did they do it?"

There, in pale colours, were row upon row of bones, in different sizes, and a quarter of the area was covered in skulls. The tidiness, the accuracy of the straight lines along which the bones and skulls were laid, revealed the ardour of the women's labour. What impressed, though, was the sheer size of the grave and the large quantity of remains. Yet Josefu was reminded of a jewellery box which his cousin Maria had kept with rows of rings and a line of ear studs. He did not write in his notebook, not a word. Bill, however, took photographs standing in the same spot and very carefully adjusting the lens appropriately. Many of the women were crying now, with Père Ambroise alone among them.

Beatrice must have then said something, because they all stood back and the priest put on a robe and took a prayer book from his small black bag. He began to chant and the women, with almost infant voices, innocent and very high, followed with responses. At a signal, earth was put over the bones and skulls, using their bare hands as there were no spades. Taking the lead from Afrika, the other men joined in. At one point the task was halted, more hurried prayers followed and then a little silence, as if to absorb them somehow. Afterwards, the women surrounded Père Ambroise to talk with him.

"There has been a funeral service. A burial has taken place. Those women will have better sleep now," said Afrika, as all three men wiped hands on their trousers to remove the loose soil. "Père Ambroise is a good man, a good priest," he continued, echoing their awe.

Through his glasses, the priest looked carefully into the face of each woman who talked to him and he spoke in a quiet voice.

The other men stood around and waited pensively, for an hour or more, moving increasingly further apart. The sun beat down forcefully, having suddenly emerged as the last clouds disappeared. All of Rwanda was in high altitude but occasionally the relatively mild weather was banished for a few hours of intense, dry heat.

Bill and Josefu were avoiding each other. Afrika had a stern expression and was visibly shocked. Below them a lush valley undulated in a large expanse, opulent in the unusually clear air. From the corners of their eyes, they observed that in each other's minds, however, hovered the bones and the skulls, the silent rocks and the deadly rivers and that they could visualise little else. Finally Père Ambroise approached them.

"They have just noticed you fully, only now. You, Bill, drew their attention as you are white. I told them you would come back, like you said, when your programme is organised, to document their misfortune. I said you would tell the whole world. I said they must never feel unimportant."

"There are so many victims in the grave, though, surely more than from just one settlement. Yet there aren't many of them, of the women, I mean," said Bill.

"Don't you see, that is the whole point: there are so few survivors," Père Ambroise replied.

"They were all killed, that's why," added Afrika, "Except these ones who hid."

Although he did not say anything, Josefu wondered about their reaction if they learned that Afrika was a Hutu. It was too delicate a subject to mention before him.

"Beatrice is arranging for us to eat here. It will take such a long time to get to the nearest town."

"Do you mean us too?" Josefu said.

"Yes, of course," he replied, adding something to Afrika, who left to bring two further bags of produce from the car. "And they invited him too. I get the impression you cannot understand us, our relations between Tutsi and Hutu, however much I explain to you. Anyway, among those bones there are those of a Hutu schoolteacher who defied the Interahamwe by protecting his school class, one of our many martyrs. I was told about him already in Kigali by the woman who begged me to come here. Do you understand the concept of martyr? Can you eat now?"

Bill and Josefu could not reply to either question nor to know whether they were related, as Père Ambroise moved away.

He rejoined the women, turning once to tell the men to follow. They climbed up close to where they had first all met up. An hour later, sitting on a fallen log outside a makeshift shelter where Beatrice and a few other women were living, they ate a steaming meal out of white enamel plates. Bill and Josefu did their best to eat the mash and relish with their hands as daintily as they could. Afrika picked on his food. Père Ambroise ate every last bit, wiping the plate clean with his fingers.

For one fragment of time, the women had cooked for some men folk, although their own were dead, and had regained a familiar focus. They stood and watched on, without a word. Only Beatrice ate as well, but put down her plate after a few mouthfuls. There was a simplicity about her, Josefu noticed, which made each gesture graceful. He liked the taste of the food, eaten silently, a commemorative meal outside of the usual passing moments.

"I have told them not to worry, that the enemies will not return, but I am not certain, of course," said Père Ambroise, when he had finished eating. "The regime and the Interahamwe boasted that they could kill — you remember the words — a thousand Tutsis every twenty minutes, without automatic weapons or bombs. Is it a skill that can be lost?" After a pause he said, "But today has been marked apart. You see, these women knew that their own families were among those in the mass grave but could not tell which ones. So now they have honoured all of them. We must get on our way."

They left almost in silence, except for Afrika reminding Bill and Josefu that they were expected back again by the women another time. They drove through the region's main town, war affected, with clusters of people in rags, everyone moving at a ghostly pace. It was more like a large village, except for a few single storey municipal buildings. Josefu had forgotten how poor a country Rwanda had always been. It was shortly afterwards, back on a dirt road going towards Kigali, that they had stopped for a break and then Afrika could not start the car again.

And the evening was falling slowly. Having seen the view across the opposite hill, Josefu turned and came back to Afrika and the car.

After giving some encouragement, he moved away to lean his brow on his arm, eyes closed.

⋮

And now feeling he is immersed in the river, head under the moving water, Josefu sees unclothed bodies, one by one, come back to life and go right past him. For them not to swim into his mouth, his lips have to be firmly pressed together. He keeps still and stops breathing.

⋮

Looking around in the darkness, Josefu does not recognise where he is at first. When he sees window drapes and, more aptly, hears the drift from a loudspeaker of some Canadian country music imbued with Celtic tunes, he remembers he is in Leroys Motel and that a local wedding is being celebrated. There is not a shred of doubt about where he is now. He almost laughs aloud. 'The smallest details,' he reflects, 'provide the compass needed to direct a soft landing.'

He is disappointed, though, that stray dreams so often bring his recollections to a sudden halt. He would have preferred to pace his memories himself, but so far that rarely happens. "Bad news," he says.

Till morning comes, he lies fully dressed on his bed, with a better chance of not drowning, he thinks, if a lake or river overflows somewhere, and comes across the highway. It is June after all, and in Alberta it sometimes rains.

7.

Josefu wakes at half past five in the morning. He has the opportunity to rise early and take to the road with a realistic chance of reaching the halfway point between Calgary and Winnipeg. On the other hand, he could remove his trousers and, this time, get under the bedclothes. That is what he chooses to do, lying on his stomach beneath the blankets, hoping to get warm.

For a while he cannot sleep. Then, as he wonders how to channel his thoughts, one question forcefully fills his mind: how had the killings actually begun, the real ones, the frenetic ones? Once again, he has to halt and consider basic issues, those already dissected a dozen times before, but which he had forgotten. Now is the time to recoup, to rephrase, to re-equip. And then get back in his car and drive forward with a clearer perspective.

What was so different in Rwanda, after all, was that women killed women, children killed children, and neighbours killed neighbours. Through a belief in self-defence? Or without cause? And yet one thing is absolutely clear to him: there was nothing spontaneous. It was all meticulously planned, every kind of killing and when and how, yes, and when and how.

As he drifts into slumber now, despite his busy thoughts, he remembers once again that the president of Rwanda, Juvenal Habyarimana, was already implicated in massacres and repression for many years, long before his aircraft was shot down. But precisely on that early evening when he died, on April 6th, 1994, the new killings began immediately, many machetes—the weapon of choice—already distributed. Some analysts, the ones Josefu had liked to read, insisted the stockpiling of machetes was begun years before, and in their opinion the president himself had been involved in the bulk orders. And General Dallaire had sent those intelligence reports well in advance: 'Something terrible is being prepared'.

Josefu now turns on his side, face leaning on his hand, and sighs deeply into sleep.

President Habyarimana came down the aeroplane steps, waving to the crowd of people in various uniforms who had come to greet him. Josefu stood waiting and asked him, when he came near, if he was proud of the life he had led. They walked away together and sat down on stools, facing each other, in a simple shed.

"Can't you improve on this?" the president said, glancing round. "You know I cannot bear misery near me."

Josefu asked him to look once more at his surroundings, for now the walls had become dark gold and on the vaulted ceiling were a few rubies dotted here and there. Habyarimana smiled. He had a large mouth. "Of course I am proud of my life. Do you know how successful I was? The president of France in person, President Francois Mitterrand, he visited me. The Pope of Rome had tea with me and my wife. They were my personal guests, in Kigali, in Rwanda, and don't you think I should be satisfied with my achievements?"

"What about personal wealth in a poor country?"

"Why shouldn't a president, even in a poor country, have the display of luxuries that every head of state deserves? Why shouldn't I have had the best there was in the whole world, of which my country was a part, after all. Why shouldn't the president's wife, just because we were from a poor African country, have the same perfumes, the same fine shoes and clothes as all the other leading wives of the world? We should not be humbled by any other head of state! I was very proud and I still am, even now that I am telling the truth." His wild eyes shone. "I amaze myself, I really do."

"And the privileges you gave to your own region, were they not unfair?" said Josefu, after looking in his notebook.

"Gisenyi? In the North West? Don't you know Gisenyi? How can it be contrasted with any other area? Everywhere else there is nothing in comparison to Gisenyi's beauty, its charm—the best by far. I had roads built, the best in Rwanda; nowhere else were there such roads, good ones, to get straight from Kigali to Gisenyi. We had a limited budget, so I chose only the best and it had to be there; the best highway had to be along that route. And the people from there? How could you compare them with those from other regions? Always more intelligent, more capable, more good looking, and most of all, the most trustworthy. I knew that if I appointed someone from my Gisenyi to a responsible post, he would be totally loyal to me. And you think I should have chosen differently, with all those risks? Just look at me myself; of course we were by far the best. It was the best for the good of the nation. I always did the right thing." His hair protruded ferociously to one side, poised to grow even further out. He glanced at a golden-framed large mirror on the wall, and was satisfied with his reflection.

"But the massacres? What about the genocide against the Tutsis?" Josefu almost whispered. He felt keenly that this opportunity to ask questions was fleeting.

"Genocide? What a word! Genocide is used for human beings. So tell me, do you think they were human, those traitors? Do you?"

Josefu wanted to reply 'Of course they are human' but his lips were stuck together.

"You see, even you cannot answer! What you call 'genocide' is an operational adjustment to the demands of the time, that is, for authority to succeed. It always is! An operational adjustment, with emotional overtones. All of the Tutsis were traitors."

Still, Josefu could not comment; despite the African sunlight in the room, the coldness in those words had frozen his face, ice splinters cutting into his cheeks and jaws.

"Let me tell you, in my early days when I seized power I was criticised for speaking the truth about them, so although you will have difficulty to believe it, when I first became head of state I pardoned a few Tutsis, gave them some nice positions, just to some of them. But in their view that was not enough. They refused to forget their feudal past, or how they had dominated us, the Hutu, when the Belgians came to power here in this part of Africa. So now they should continue to pay for their past errors but they never want to. That is the arrogance of the Tutsi. No repentance, or at least not enough. The fact is they are cockroaches rather than real people. Just look at them, those cowards in Uganda, the ones who started the war against me. They fled this country about the time of our Independence and for thirty long years they couldn't settle down there. Cockroaches do not want to stay where they are; they can't stay still!" Habyarimana looked at Josefu convinced he would be impressed with that last comment.

Josefu was aware that this was the crux of the matter, the answer he had been so curious to learn about. But he feared he was losing his hearing and strained not to lose the thread.

"They…them… they asked to return to Rwanda but I told them there was no room. There are geography experts who are whites writing that Rwanda has too large a population for such a small country, so why become more crowded? Too many complications and, anyway, how could I trust them? And was I not right? Instead of busying themselves with their cattle, they meddled in Ugandan internal affairs, yes, their hosts' internal affairs. That is the right term, the right word, I tell you."

"What do you mean, then, since you have the right word?" Suddenly Josefu could speak again.

"You ask all the wrong questions. You can't think of my country or its president without always asking about the Tutsis. Why don't you, for example, ask me about my ability to have stayed in power for seventeen long years? Do you know how hard that was? Do you know how I wanted stability for my country, even in my last years when I became tired, and that I still remained in power?"

"I see," Josefu whispered.

"You are interested in the cockroaches who bit the hand that fed them: they sided with Museveni, a dissatisfied Ugandan rebel who went into the bush and then overthrew the government in Uganda to become president himself. So ungrateful! Now I tell you, with the Western governments who gave us gifts and loans, we were always having conversations about power sharing, the word they love so much. But who would power-share with that rabble in uniform? The Popular Front, they called themselves. Thin little officers, tall perhaps but still so thin. I was such a saint to sit with them and negotiate peace in Arusha. I think the Pope must have known."

"Why did you kill innocent people?"

"Do you know how many times I have been asked that since I arrived here, in this place where one must tell the truth? Could you not think of a better question?"

"Repetitive though it is, I must ask it again. Forgive me."

"I tell you, the Tutsis really were not people. How could they truly be people if there was a chance they would support the invading rebels—do you know there were even Hutu among the invaders whom those Tutsi sorcerers had turned into degenerates!

If they threatened my authority, then they were not human. Why did we call them cockroaches if there wasn't a reason? What do you do with cockroaches? Or any other insect? You have a family yourself, so you know: you exterminate them. I believed in the hygiene of my country."

Josefu tried to write it down but struggled with the spelling. "Can't you say something else instead?" he asked.

"Oh, all right, I'll tell you something else as well: we needed loyalty from our real supporters, our people the Hutu, so we put them to work for us, so we would feel we were one people, all doing together those things, even the cruel things, needed to protect our country and its president, and afterwards to protect the successors in the president's family. Not all of our people agreed to work in this way, but the young Interahamwe indeed did want to do as we asked them. Till then they had nothing in their lives, nothing. We made them the exalted elite, the most importantly feared cadres in the whole nation. Do you not understand?" His face shone, the look in his eyes was clear and proud.

"What exactly you are proud of? The tactics?" said Josefu bluntly.

"I was prepared. I want you to understand the necessity," President Habyarimana said, somewhat lowering his voice. "So it was all prepared. Ah, we told some machete exporters in Europe we needed those large orders for our sugar cane. We have very little sugar cane but nobody there minded much what they were told. That is how they do business out there in Europe. Our army was not well endowed. The French helped us but not enough. So we made plans the best way we could. And we achieved our aim. You think of women and children being destroyed, but they were dangerous if they survived because they would have been untrustworthy. So it was a necessity: they all had to be destroyed.

I did what was needed to survive. And even after my death, my followers did what was needed in my memory. That is when the greatest work was done! And Rwanda will never be the same again. No, I have no regrets."

"Your people are not in power now," Josefu said with irony.

"But they will be again soon. They love me, you see," said President Habyarimana.

"So you are happy with what you did in your life and what happened in your country?" Josefu asked one final time.

"I have no regrets. I am proud of myself. I had crowds in the Stadium praising me. I will never forget it. I had a very good life. I thank God for that. And the Pope blessed me."

He remained seated as Josefu rose and turned to leave, slipping immediately on a broken jar of honey which lay on the parquet floor, and cutting his chin.

⋮

Josefu's mother hugged him as he cried, sitting on her knee. Even when he was distressed like this, he loved her warmth. She disappeared in a flash.

Then he grew to a man's size, nursing the onset of age with an aching shoulder. The door of his half empty New York apartment was ajar and he thought Ellie was in the corridor. When he went to look, it was Martina standing with an old English picnic basket. His first impulse was to shut the door but then he followed her to the elevator, which they entered together. They sat on the floor and ate, going up and down, from the 32nd to the Ground floor, Josefu anxious that in the meantime his apartment door might slam closed. He was in a white bathrobe and did not have the key. As his arm stretched, becoming longer and longer like a cable till it reached the entrance to his home, he worried that he would not find a shoe to wedge the door with. Thinking he had found one in the outdoor cabin from Buffalo Street, which now had been positioned on the apartment balcony, he returned to place the shoe at an angle, only to find it was merely a sandal. Martina put a strawberry in his mouth and touched his groin, asking that he hurry with that door thing because she didn't want to wait any more. He smiled pleasurably, helplessly, but rolled alone in the elevator down the shaft into the basement.

⋮

Josefu was surprised that down here, on the riverbed, such a delicate, reed-like, straw-coloured plant should stroke his face. Small fishes blew on him like a cool breeze. He knew that it was important to remain lying flat at the bottom, but there was warm, soft sand providing comfort and space. Above him, people's bodies swam by, all black skinned and well oiled, clothed in Olympic swimwear including caps with numbers. Although they were difficult to see from where he lay, Josefu knew that all of them would come first in the race. The tranquillity was beautiful and the knowledge that even the smallest child swimmers would receive prizes gave him a quiet confidence, which he hoped would never leave him. It was mid-afternoon and the sun filtered through to the riverbed, making it luminous and luxuriant. Interestingly, the passing bodies cast no shadows.

⋮

Josefu slips out of the bed onto the carpeted floor, pulls his legs up and leans against the bedside table. Almost awake, he hugs his knees, head kept low. His mind is perfectly blank and he is aware only dimly of being in a hotel room somewhere on the outskirts of Calgary. Slowly, though, the fluidity of the dreams freezes into ice lumps that fall like rocks on his shoulders. 'I could do with a better day,' he thinks.

⋮

Abandoning all plans, though, he drifts back to when he was turning the car key for Afrika, who peered into the bonnet of his broken down taxi cab. A sound like a small explosion caused both of them to jump. Bill came running up but not Père Ambroise who, Josefu could see, was scribbling something on the back of an envelope.

"You're nearly there, Afrika," said Bill encouragingly. This time Afrika wriggled under the car, astounding the others with his agility.

"I'm sure he'll get it right, although we could spend the night here if we had to. There's the protection of a locked car," said Bill to Josefu, who couldn't quite decide if it was meant to be humour. Out here, Bill was becoming more complex, perhaps because he did not have Mary to sort out his thoughts. Their eyes met momentarily, solemnly.

Afrika emerged with a triumphant smile. "I found it, the fault, I'm sure I did."

This time Josefu successfully started the car for him and they all laughed loudly with pleasure, even Père Ambroise, in a way which they would have found unthinkable only hours before.

Bill and Josefu sat in the back, and Père Ambroise, who said he had just written some words for a sermon, chatted to Afrika in their own language. There was a sense of celebration and relief in the car, because Afrika had mended it and they were on their way to somewhere better.

After a while, Bill leaned over and said, "How is it, Afrika, that you speak such good French?"

"Does that interest you? I studied in Bujumbura, capital of Burundi. I was doing well, but then there was this trouble with my brother in prison so I had to come back. My mother was losing her head. I was his follower, the next one born after him, you know. So I came back, that's why."

"And you couldn't continue your studies here?"

"Yes I could have; it wasn't that complicated, engineering mechanics, but I began working with my taxi, another one. But this one I had to take to Bujumbura to have it painted the right colours because it was cheaper there."

Bill looked fleetingly at Josefu as if seeking approval, but said without waiting, "And what about the ethnic difficulties there?" Josefu turned away, embarrassed.

Père Ambroise intervened, "In Burundi, in Rwanda, in all these countries, you come from outside to talk about our ethnic difficulties but forget about the politics of corruption and greed and ambition and vanity and how it is then the people who pay the price."

"Yes, yes," said Afrika.

Josefu realised he was not very keen to pursue a conversation which would lead to discussing Tutsi-led governments in Burundi who chased Hutu and vice-versa too.

Bill simply said, "I admire your language ability."

Afrika warmed to that and answered, "I speak some Swahili too, although it is not a language of our country. And I have learned a few words of English now: 'I tek you var? Ma nem is Afrika. One, two, tree…' My accent is how?"

Bill laughed, "You speak like a perfect Frenchman!"

"It's the colonial survivals," said Père Ambroise. All four men chuckled.

A large group of soldiers appeared on the dirt road out of nowhere and stopped them, a whole company, Josefu estimated. Two officers said sternly, gesturing with their arms, that they must get out of the car and Afrika had to open the boot. The soldiers were ready with guns and rows of bullets. They seemed to have new uniforms. When they saw Bill, however, the officers waved back the soldiers who had begun to crowd round the car menacingly.

A conversation took place with Père Ambroise, which Afrika translated quietly. Probably because of the ambivalent attitude of many RPF members to the UN, Père Ambroise was saying merely that Bill was seeing how to help groups of women survivors, without specifying for which organisation. When the officers said something to Josefu in Kinyarwanda, it was Afrika who intervened. Josefu was intrigued to know what had been said because they patted him warmly on the back and spoke in English, saying 'Good, you are good.' Afrika then took out his car documents and discreetly laid a few dollar bills on top, "for cigarettes," he said, shielding an officer who was able to fold them quickly away.

When they finally drove off again, Père Ambroise turned to Josefu: "You see, both officers came from Uganda, and they returned here to where their parents had come from; they speak no French. How was their English?"

"Fine, fine," Josefu said, slightly bemused.

"We were lucky, we could have been held back for two or three days, the time it would take for them to check us out." The priest, not one to criticise them, explained that the army was very worried about surprise attacks from across the border and they could have thought we might have useful information. They also hoped to prevent further guilty genocidaires — as the killers from the previous regime were beginning to be called, Père Ambroise explained — from being spirited away by foreign charity workers, wittingly or unwittingly.

"They certainly felt they had been cheated by the UN Refugee Commission, whatever it is called, and the other humanitarian bodies who insisted on treating everyone wanting to leave Rwanda the same, on principle."

"Exactly what a serving UNAMIR officer told us in Kigali," said Bill.

"At the Amohoro Hotel," added Afrika. "Yes, you were there for a long time, there inside, with UNAMIR."

"We drank no beer there, believe me," Josefu teased, not quite knowing what Afrika had implied.

"If you know how to talk to the military and to the police, all will go well for you," said Afrika, who smiled at Père Ambroise.

Josefu thought, 'Change of mood. Relief, relief, the car works, the soldiers have gone, we'll soon be back in our comfortable hotel.' Indeed, as they emerged at a junction, they suddenly saw a half effaced sign pointing to Kigali.

⋮

Now Josefu sees a woman kneading pliant dough that she stretches out and pats together again. Noticing her hands are white, he looks more closely to see where she is standing and realises it is in the cavernous kitchens of his preparatory school where he had been sent with several other small boys. She says, "Up and down, in and out, like your mood. And yooooooo," she adds, looking at Josefu, "You miss your Mum, I hear. Well, you'll forget that when I've finished with you, because you are going to eat my cakes, and my buns, and my scones and my fritters. Up with you, up with you, little man, up with that smile."

He turns and sees a hand by a switch on the wall. The light goes out. He finds himself now in an open space, all alone, and his face is carved in stone. An axe is raised to break it and Josefu, become a statue, falls flat on the ground.

⋮

He feels some blood trickling on his face and sits up, realising it was from knocking his head on the television stand and that he is in the motel in Strathmore. Going into the bathroom, he immediately notices in the mirror that the blood is pouring copiously. He quickly dresses sufficiently to run downstairs to Reception.

"You could have called us, Sir," says the round-faced woman at the desk.

"I slipped and fell," Josefu says, knowing it sounds better than to say he had been dreaming.

"You always spout a lot of blood if you cut your head, Sir," she adds. "You don't have any disease, do you?"

"I might need a stitch, I think," replies Josefu, not quite understanding her. He notices the towel he clutches is increasingly more blood soaked. He closes his eyes, trying to duck out of panic's way.

"For God's sake sit down over there," the receptionist says, "And wait. You'll go to our Strathmore and District Hospital. It's a good hospital; or do you want to go to Calgary?"

"Oh, no, not Calgary."

"You got something to hide?"

Josefu is distantly aware that he shouldn't say it is because he worked there. He struggles for words and they come, as if from somewhere else: "Not where my late mother was, not that hospital."

"Oh, I'm sorry, Sir, I didn't mean it that way," the receptionist says.

Josefu remembers little between that moment and lying in an ambulance with a green interior, overhearing a young man say, "He's a Banff resident; he's got insurance, it's okay. Alberta Health Care, the usual. He's okay. Not Canadian, but he's got a valid credit card to pay for the ambulance if he isn't covered by some other scheme."

Later he becomes aware he is in another place, with a bright light overhead and a woman says through hospital mask, "We're shaving some of your hair; you'll be needing stitches. Then we'll take some X-rays and keep you in overnight. Do you know what 'concussion' means?"

"Yes, I do," he murmurs.

"That's why we have to keep you in, just to make sure, okay?"

"Okay." When he is asked for next of kin, he pretends he can't hear and keeps his eyes closed, and his fists.

⋮

"These appear to be revenge killings," said Père Ambroise as they surveyed the freshly bleeding pair of bodies on the wayside. "Two young men here, perhaps Interahamwe; what do you think?" he said, turning towards Afrika.

The driver was trying not to get too close. "I cannot stand the sight of blood," he said, "Even of animals. My wife prepares the skewers of meat. And blood, when its from men…" His voice tailed off.

"Forgive me," said Père Ambroise. He stood straight, unsure of what to say next. Then, lifting both arms towards the sky, he chanted in Kinyarwanda for several minutes. He opened his small black bag and took a bottle, emptying what must have been holy water over the two corpses before saying more prayers. He turned to Josefu, not to Afrika, and asked him to help tear some branches from a nearby tree, which they piled on the side of the road. "This way, there will be a sign for when people look for those boys. We'll stop at the next village. Ah, it's so tiring, all of it," he sighed. Josefu could smell the blood, even after the car drove off. Bill was checking his camera; he had, after all, photographed the scene. Afrika looked embarrassed, Père Ambroise morose.

"It's human vanity," the priest commented, "Always wanting to be the judge of who has the right to live. Here in Rwanda, we have had very vain leaders, including the deceased president."

"I know," said Josefu. "And he had many friends."

"I'm bitter" said Père Ambroise.

"We understand you," said Bill.

⋮

"Josefu, I understand you." Waking in the evening light in a hospital bed, it's difficult to believe that the voice is Dave Epstein's.

"No, it can't be," says Josefu.

"Yeah, it's me, Dave." It's the cascade of red hair.

"You know, I keep on thinking: Père Ambroise, he still sprinkled holy water on the two corpses we found on the wayside, even without the usual throngs of pleading women. But do you know why?"

"Hey, Josefu, I don't know. It's me, Dave."

"What are you doing here, in Kigali?"

"What's that about? It's me, and you are in the Strathmore General and District Hospital in Alberta."

Now Josefu tries to sit up, realising where he is. "Uh, Dave, sorry."

"What's up? I'm scared shitless. By the way, I've come alone. Martina doesn't know. Last night she left because of an emergency with her son, no—the grandson, a baby—and she's flying back tomorrow. She told me to take every call; something might be there for you, she said. Do you hear me?"

"Yes, of course. This is bad news."

"I mean I was just sitting in the bookstore and the phone rings. It's a doctor. She says you're there in the hospital. Then she says something about a concussion. And there I was just sitting there. Do you hear me? Geez. This is scary."

"Dave, can you get me a glass of water, without ice, please?"

"Let's ask if it's allowed."

"Sure, I'll check his chart," says a young woman in nurse's uniform standing at the door, listening, and she brings water in a small plastic cup.

"I hate these cups," says Josefu.

Dave laughs. "Ya, I remember! Josefu, we miss you. And everyone's blaming Martina. I asked her how she could let you drive off like that; you've never gone further than Calgary! She said she couldn't stop you."

"Did she say that?"

"It's true, isn't it?"

"Well, perhaps I wanted to, you know, find out more. Remember."

"We didn't talk about it, that thing in Africa, right? Medical instructions. But I always thought that if you would come over and relax in our Jacuzzi, it would just flow out one day. I mean float away."

"Down the rivers. Children, women — women like mine — men… floating…"

"Hey, Josefu, what's up with that? And Martina's done this? Man, the grief she's put me through, the aggravation, over all these years. You come on back to Buffalo Street right now, partner."

"No. I must find out more. I'm feeling sick." Josefu tries to get out of bed.

Dave rushes out. The young nurse reappears. "We'd rather you didn't move at the moment, Mr. Mutesa." She gives him a bowl and a bedpan, nods her head.

"Are you Irish?" he asks her.

"How did you know? And you speak like an Englishman."

"I want to tell you something," Dave says darkly, interrupting, while sitting down and looking around. "The doctor who called me, she said she used to work in forensic medicine. She said you were lying to her, and that you couldn't have fallen the way you said. So something's going on. So I'm taking you back to Buffalo Street."

Josefu puts his hand on Dave's arm.

"Those pink fingernails," Dave says. "Hey, I miss you."

Josefu wants to reply but tiredness overcomes him.

Dave breaks the silence. "What's up between you and Martina, hey?"

"Don't change the subject."

"Me change the subject? Me?" says Dave.

"I've got the need, now. This journey. It's myself. I mean in two words: my self. My moi-meme, as Père Ambroise used to say," Josefu chuckles.

"I don't know him," says Dave. "You really are deep into that thing."

"Deep. Buried. Not risen."

Then Josefu sees out of the corner of his eye that as Dave leaves, he is writing notes on the back of an envelope.

'I wonder what the sermon was about, that Père Ambroise had scribbled in preparation?' Josefu asks himself. The priest appears before his closed eyes, unsmiling.

"I am writing about the secret life of humble people, those without vanity, how they carry their sorrow and hopes. Yes, what you feel deeply, asking for Imana to bless your loneliness — that customary thought."

8.

The next morning, in the calm of a very sunny day, Josefu is confidently discharged from the Strathmore General and District Hospital. He walks alone to the front exit, from a place that for him had neither form nor face, his echoing footsteps on the tiles embarrassingly self-important. But he was told to rest a day or two before continuing on his journey and to remember that the stitches need removing. "Some day," he had suggested.

"No, not some day," the doctor said. "I've already talked to your, ah, business partner. He will remind you. Your cab should be waiting outside right now."

The wide faced woman at Leroys Motel comes out from behind the desk when he arrives, and smilingly says, "There are fresh flowers in your room. Your friend sent them. And yes, we'll give you room service. You had an accident; we understand you need individualized attention. We can do that, we're running a family business after all."

Josefu wonders what Dave had told her, probably the usual glamour, but he is past caring. Before going to his room, he becomes distinctly aware that the receptionist is dialling a number and has begun to talk about him. 'Probably to Dave,' he thinks. Slowly a map is emerging, with pointers to places he knows like Buffalo Street, and from there a line of dots right up to his room here off the Highway. A name for his left foot and for his right one to stand on, even if his head floats up towards a thin, unsheltered line of motionless mist.

He has barely entered his hotel room when the telephone rings.

"It's me, Dave, of course," he says. "Hey, you've got us all worried."

"Who is 'us'?"

"No, Josefu, I did not tell Martina. Oh boy, you won't believe this. Martina is seeing someone! Yes, she came back from the airport and they were holding hands, and he kissed her. They kissed for real, right in front of the bookstore." He sounds excited. "Why don't you say something? Speak! Hey, damn it, did something happen between you in the end?" Josefu still doesn't reply. "Okay, I'll talk to you later.

Listen, I'm leaving Banff at four o'clock again and driving over this evening."

"That's ridiculous; it's a five hour journey there and back, or more. I'm really fine here."

"I'm not happy with you out there. I mean, this should never have happened."

"But Rwanda happened, uncomfortable, but it did."

"Rwanda? Gone there again? Don't you think, in your state of mind, you shouldn't be out on your own? I keep on saying the same thing, I know."

"Yes, you do, and Dave, I've been where they tell the truth, an endless kind of place."

"You've never talked to me like this before."

"I'm telling you the truth. I want to drive now, and remember in movement; it's easier, flowing over field and river."

"Rivers? You hate them. Bow River at the end of your garden and you never said one positive thing."

"Yes, Dave, yes. But I do care about you."

"Are you out of your mind? And you've not said that before. Thanks, I mean."

"My mind wanders."

"Like what?"

"Do you know, the whole time I was in Rwanda my kids were with Patricia and I didn't know where she had gone."

"Did you love her? Your wife, I mean?"

"Because she was my wife, I loved my choice, yes."

"We all do that. Don't you think I did?"

"Yes, Dave. I'm tired. But I can't blame Martina. Dave, are you there?"

"I'm here. I just can't believe it's you talking. Did you fuck Martina?"

"I can't say anything to that." And then Josefu realises, with dismay, that he himself hardly knows.

"Is there someone else, I mean in your life?"

"Yes, a girl I'm looking for." That, Josefu is clear about, a light in the window.

"Josefu, I almost forgot. A woman from England phoned you. She called the BookShop. Martina set up the call forwarding for you, and so I spoke to her, okay? Very English. The accent." There is silence from Josefu. "Did I say something wrong? Listen, she said she would call again."

"Didn't she give her full name? Didn't she say where I could call her back?"

"She mean something to you? I'm sorry, she didn't leave a number. Oh yes, your cousin had been to see her in hospital and thanks for the flowers. Hey, Josefu, flowers all the way over there?"

"Maria! Trust Maria, that's my cousin. Oh, I'm saved, she'll have the number now. I wish I could leave right now, and find her. But I cannot abandon Marie Immaculée, she's about to reappear. And also find Madame Dubois, the UN organiser during our tour in Rwanda, you know, Operations and Support."

"Yeah, yeah, I know. Not really, but I'd sure like to know where you are coming from, Josefu."

"It's where I'm going. Dave, I appreciate all you've done, but please don't try to drive here, or stop me. I never thought I'd really depend on you like this."

It is Dave's turn to be silent.

"Did you hear what I said?" Josefu repeats it several times.

"Yeah, I'm just wordless, sort of feeling I didn't know you before…I'll call you again," Dave says, and hangs up.

A minute later the receptionist telephones: "Your friend says you need a light lunch, and then dinner at six-thirty, is that correct, for at least two days?"

"If he said so, it must be right," Josefu answers.

"We're sending a menu up to you. We're doing this as an exception. Mr. Mutesa? Do you prefer 'Mr.' or something else? Your friend didn't say."

Josefu doesn't reply.

Marie Immaculée is standing at the end of his bed and he almost jumps. With eyes closed, he thanks the receptionist quickly and puts down the receiver. Then he returns to watch the silent figure in front of him.

"Can you tell me where Ellie is?" he asks.

"I was given a goat today. Just a little milk will go a long way. It's a better day."

"Glad for you, Marie Immaculée. Where is Ellie, though?"

"She'll speak with you while you are still in this room. But, now if you could just help me with my papers, to stay in Kigali. Père Ambroise forgot. Ask the white man to talk to the soldiers."

"I'm thinking about myself. I'm sorry." He looks at her, eyes sunk deeper than ever into her skull, burning like charcoal, unblinking. Her shoulders are pulled back. She is quite still. Her clothes are immaculately clean, her headscarf shining white. On her narrow, wrinkled feet she wears flip flop sandals and they are a pale green. Josefu notices all these things and sits up. "Marie Immaculée, I'm so sorry, I'm so sorry," and he begins to weep. "I showed you fear, I showed you indifference, but I didn't mean it, Marie Immaculée, I didn't want it. I'm so sorry."

He cries loudly, rocking back and forwards, shaking his head in pain, and does not answer when there is a knock on his door.

⋮

Père Ambroise was dropped off first, at his request, when they returned to Kigali from their trip across the river. Among the people waiting for him, probably all day, was Marie-Immaculee with her charge, this time held on her hip and the other woman was there too, with the two children she looked after. Afrika opened the boot of the car revealing three sacks of charcoal they had managed to buy from a wizened woman standing on one of the rural roads. Père Ambroise asked Marie Immaculée, in person, to supervise their distribution among those who wanted some. Afrika took a cloth from her, however, and put coals for Père Ambroise himself and pushed the bundle into his arms.

As the driver took the others back to the hotel, he said, "I've seen where he lives, Père Ambroise, with some priests who are very old. He shaves them every morning, helps them. One of them cooks, as the nuns have gone. You can see how empty the town is, still."

"Are the priests survivors, like Père Ambroise?" asked Bill.

"Oh no, they are all Hutu, except for him. Me, I'm Hutu. I feel bad, sometimes, you know, that I have all my family, all my cousins, my brothers, my sisters. Only my one brother who was killed. And because of him, the RPF do not hate us, and because of a Hutu relative with our Parmehutu, the Hutu Power people, that side didn't touch us either."

"Weren't you pushed into working with the Interahamwe?" asked Bill, calmly.

"Perhaps some of my relatives did, and some of them I don't know. Perhaps they did. Many of us were afraid of being asked. Many of us went away to hide. I told you I was studying in Burundi. My father has relatives and we all went there in April, driving in my taxi. I did four journeys to the border and we had special letters from someone in the army. My father's cousin-brother was a colonel in the army of the government of Rwanda, the government then. He had been with some French army teachers too. But we also had a copy of the newspaper which told about my brother whom Habyarimana had killed, in case we were stopped by the RPF. It is complicated," said Afrika, softly.

"I know, I understand," said Josefu.

"In Uganda, is it the same?"

"Yes, in many ways."

"But you never lived there, you escaped from Africa," the driver said.

"My family, my father left. At first it wasn't voluntarily. Later, they simply decided to stay away. But I went back when Milton Obote was in power for the second time."

"Obote! Obote. Yes, I remember," Afrika said triumphantly, "I remember President Obote of Uganda."

"So you know a lot about the politics of the region," said Josefu. "Well, I didn't want to remain in Uganda at that time because it became too complicated with the situation of my relatives and the politics. I wanted to stay, but my family said it would be worse for them if I stayed." Josefu felt he was explaining his guilt.

"You talk to me, like friends talk to me. We are friends," said Afrika boldly. They had reached the Hotel Mille Collines.

"I hope we are friends," said Bill.

"I shall ask Père Ambroise his advice. I would like to ask you to come to my house." Bill's eyes lit up. Josefu's heart throbbed. "Yes, I would like to invite you. I would like us to have a conversation."

"It would be an honour for us. Can it be soon, though, before our official program starts, when we may even have to leave Kigali," said Josefu rapidly.

⋮

The telephone rings. "It's reception here. Do you see the menu? It's pushed under your door. When you are ready, please call me."

Josefu rises and collects it obediently. His stitches hurt when he bends down. He has made some promises, to himself and to Dave and to the doctor, to maintain some form of stability. He'd have an omelette for lunch. Fish for supper. *Cake for life. Biscuits for heaven.* The receptionist says she'll have his meal up for him in the room in twenty minutes. He once thought he'd drink spring water forever and ever. He has actually ordered a beer, not too cold, of course.

⋮

The best days in Rwanda, really, were those first days, when they were able to enjoy the freedom of being virtually incognito, not even recognised by their own organisation. Bill said they could continue that way, but it was not correct. He made it part of his easygoing nature to avoid complications, by always keeping to the rules himself although he sometimes overlooked it in others. The head of the UN Mission, he said, was Sharyahar Khan and they would pay their respects, by telephone, if that is all right with Josefu. Right?

"Right? Right?" Bill said impatiently as Josefu had remained silent.

"You know we're doing a better job our way, Bill. You know we'll be hampered as soon as we get caught up in the wheels of the organisation."

"But we aren't paid to do the job our way, even if," and Bill laughed, "...even if it is more efficient."

"Let's delay it, though. Anyway, the unceremonious way we were received by that Madame Dubois doesn't warrant what you'd call 'precipitate action' from us," replied Josefu carefully. He knew that Bill, upon arrival had not been met at the airport, although he did get a lift with the UN Military in whose plane he had travelled from Nairobi. Josefu had taken the same one the next day. Luckily they had known the name of their hotel; Bill's secretary had booked the rooms from New York since he was already becoming a little suspicious.

Madame Dubois claimed provenance from Luxembourg, but Josefu thought it didn't ring true, and which of the French speaking bordering countries she really came from, was anyone's guess. She had grey hair, owl-like glasses, and her build was so wide, she barely fitted in her office armchair. Her skin was completely white and unexposed to the sun, Josefu noticed, or perhaps it was pale pink with a down of white hair. He also observed she was the kind of person who permanently smelled of urine, or it may have been ammonia.

Although they had sent their visiting cards in, Bill and Josefu were kept waiting for some time in a corridor outside her office, overhearing her conversation, in fluent English with only a tinge of a French accent.

"So, Jeanette? You have diarrhoea? How many times yesterday? Oh no, every half hour? Twenty minutes? Was it brown or yellow? Yellow? You should be evacuated! No, not with water, with an aeroplane. What sort of pain? Like many knives? No, I'm not busy at all here; it's dead. Just some people waiting in the corridor and there is nothing to tell them. Nothing is programmed for them. You can ask your cook to make rice for you. You can ask your cook to make tea. Rwandan tea? I'll visit you later. I'm afraid of nothing." It sounded as if she put the receiver down several times.

She called Bill and Josefu in, oblivious that they had overheard her.

"I have to disappoint you. We do not know you are here. We do not know that New York sends you. We do not have a program." She was looking in her handbag and the men leaned over, hopefully. "No, it's not for you," she said, addressing them like children. "I have to warn you. Everyone's lips get dry here. Oh perhaps not yours," she added, turning to Josefu. "Ah, I have it. My lip salve." She stopped talking to apply it. "Nothing for you," she continued. "I have nothing for you."

Bill could hardly contain his anger. "I'm sorry," he said, heading for the door, even his hands had become red.

"Out here you don't leave like that! This isn't New York," shouted Madame Dubois. "Without thanking me for receiving you, not even that!"

Josefu gestured to Bill to wait, turned and said calmly and in his perfect French: "Madame, please understand we are extremely surprised. You cannot think we would come out here unauthorised."

"I tell you, there are no documents."

Bill called Josefu to come away, but he continued: "There may have been an error of communication from New York; surely you must have experienced it before."

"We experience it every day," said Madame Dubois. "I have worked in Cambodia and a hundred other UN missions. I see you are reasonable, Monsieur, wherever you come from."

"Great Britain. My parents came from Uganda."

"How did you get your French?"

"At the University of Geneva and many years working for the UN there."

"You charm me. I'll tell you what. There is a car and a driver and it is going to Butare. The person who was supposed to go, does not exist. There is some chaos here."

Josefu noticed with pleasure, the look of surprise on Bill's face as they left.

'But that', now thinks Josefu, 'Is how we met Père Ambroise, because of the UN driver who knew him, was the one who took us to Butare. And when the UN driver was removed from us, we found Afrika — stars and stars pulling strings and strings.'

He lies back carefully, placing his head slowly on a pillow, and wonders if it is time to take a couple of painkillers before lunch, as he has a couple of things to do.

⋮

"Bill, this is Josefu," he says on the telephone, nursing his head.

"We've been worried, like everybody else. Mary's out right now. When are you arriving here in Winnipeg? We're waiting for you. That Martina was crazy."

"Do you remember Madame Dubois?" Josefu interrupts.

"Dubois?"

"You remember, her glasses, enormous glasses? Where else had she worked besides Cambodia, before Rwanda? I mean, I was thinking about how she went from mission to mission, always setting up the same desk, the same lip salve."

"Lip salve? You remember things like that? You've lost it, big time. Yes, she was helpful when you were leaving."

"Can't you answer my question?"

"What, besides Cambodia? Somalia, Angola, I guess the usual…I can't remember such details," says Bill.

"Fine," Josefu responds, "Thanks. I'll speak to you later," and he hangs up.

Next task, next phone call.

"Maria," he says.

"The whole world is worried about you, from country to country. If Mama Josefu were alive…"

"How's your own mum? It's so long…not seeing my father's sister Narubaga, … I miss her," he says.

"This doesn't sound like you at all, Josefu. Anyway, if it's love, then I've seen her. Ellie. Yes, Ellie. Having an operation. Privately done. Cromwell Hospital, remember? Why are you calling me? Oh, here's the number for the Ward Sister. Write this down." Maria has a slight impatience in her voice.

"Thank you. What's wrong?"

"Wrong? It's you who are wrong. We haven't got the money to fly out to you and so you go your own way, lock yourself up somewhere on a Highway. I phoned and got that Martina who only told me where you were heading, but Bill at the other end didn't know either. I've done nothing but run around for you, Josefu, but you, you don't even bother to have the courtesy to tell me where you're ringing from. You're always off into the clouds."

He ignores the tirade and says, "Do you remember my Mama had a mkoo in Kampala, a brother-in-law, her sister's husband? I was closest friends with his nephew when I was there. His name was Musisi, remember I told you about him?"

"The one in the Army?"

"Yes, he came from Mbarara to visit me when I was in Rwanda, you know. It was great. He stayed for one day and had to go back."

"Why are you telling me this?" Maria asks.

"I thought you might remember. I thought you might still be in touch."

"No, perhaps you should do some looking around yourself."

"I'm sorry I annoyed you," Josefu whispers.

"Perhaps Ellie can knock some sense into you. Yes, she hasn't got a husband anymore. Just the right match, if she comes out alive. Josefu, stop playing hide and seek."

"You don't seem to understand."

"That's always easy to say."

"I'm journeying."

"Journeying? Go and stay somewhere safe or do something better than what you're doing. I don't know what it is, but don't do it."

"Maria, I can't go on now, but I promise I'll phone you. Thanks for everything you've done to help."

"I got flowers for Ellie."

"Maria…"

"Oh shut up, Josefu. Stop messing around, like you've done since you first went to that Canada!"

Josefu says a hushed farewell. He knows that if he hesitates another moment he will never make the next phone call, so he begins dialling.

"I can give you the direct number in her private room," says the nurse, "…but she's still recovering from her operation. She may not want to talk." He dials the second number, almost feeling it was not himself, neither in the hotel room nor by the telephone.

"Josefu?" Ellie says in a distant voice. "I knew you'd telephone, that I'd get to talk with you."

"I've been thinking of you and didn't know how to wish you well, for the operation."

"No results for a while, you know that, don't you," says Ellie.

"No, I don't," he replies, but with a strong conviction which invades him, almost overwhelmingly, that he should not probe any further.

"Mmmm," she murmurs. "It's nice. Drifting after the anaesthetic, with you on the telephone the other end."

"Ellie, give me some time ... I'll see you," he says.

"Yes, nice," she replies, and gently puts down the receiver.

Josefu begins to shiver, rocking gently from side to side, his knees hunched up on the bed. His head throbs rhythmically with his heartbeat and, surprising himself, he says aloud, "Find your feet, Josefu. Both your parents are dead."

⋮

Père Ambroise, Afrika, Marie Immaculée, all the Rwandans he met in his first days, changed their attitude towards him when Josefu's relative arrived from Uganda. If in their view having relatives must be intrinsic to being a person, then perhaps he had not really been considered fully human before. And so he became even more despairing about the recent carnage: some Rwandans as a result had no relatives at all. So would they, in their own eyes, ever be human again? If only he could share his own relatives with them!

Josefu had met Musisi as soon as he had arrived in Uganda. His mother made great efforts for him to meet her side of the family, perhaps in part because she was aware of the dangerous politics in which his father's side was embroiled. His father, in fact, so disapproved of Josefu's decision to go to Uganda that they were barely on speaking terms. Josefu had worked with an Oxford plumber all summer to pay his own fare and expenses.

Musisi and he were the same age, barely a month apart — Josefu was the eldest and teased him. Another advantage was that Musisi lived in a vibrant Kampala township. Kamwockya was always teeming with activity from early morning till late with candlelight. Josefu attracted no curiosity there, and by keeping his voice down and staying close to Musisi, they eyed girls, and walked around in the mud. Josefu really felt he was in Africa, in the way he had imagined it. The best part, he had thought at the time, was that he never saw a white face. This made him glad that he had left Ellie forever and his whole life in England, which had kept him from his true identity.

The fact that he spoke not a word of the language and had an enthusiasm for poverty, which nobody there understood, did not deter him from believing he fitted in perfectly.

Today, though, Josefu wanted to remember Musisi in his later apparition, in an army uniform, when he travelled across the border to find his relative in dangerous Rwanda, with bags full of food, some of it cooked. Josefu was not expecting to see him when Reception called him to the lobby of the Hotel Mille Collines; they had ceased corresponding shortly after he left Uganda. This was because Musisi had joined the rebels in the bush, which later brought the present Ugandan government to power. Before Josefu could even focus on who stood by the desk, his visitor said, "I am Musisi, remember? Remember?"

"Kamyocka," Josefu cried out immediately. They embraced, both as tall as each other, the hotel staff looking on bemused. "You've got grey hair," said Josefu.

"And you have only two grey hairs, Josefu!"

"Musisi! Do the girls still admire you?" They both shed fifteen years and almost danced around each other. But then Josefu was still and blurted out suddenly, "Oh God, Musisi, you have no idea what it's like here." His cousin said nothing and bowed his head.

"Come, let's go to my room. And then you'll have to meet my colleague Bill. What's that you're wearing? Army?"

"Yes, rank of Brigadier, in fact. And I know many of your new Rwandan officers here; we were in the bush together."

Josefu recalled that the current President of Uganda had been helped to power by Rwandan supporters from the refugee camps. It had then been payback time for him when the RPF invasion began into Rwanda. Bill would be so pleased that through Josefu's relatives, they could expand their government contacts much more than through official UN channels. Then Bill would see Josefu as more of a local himself, with all its advantages.

In the meantime, the arrival of Musisi immediately gave Josefu a sense of delirious relief, following the strain of the lugubrious experiences of the past days. Despite his abhorrence of extravagant behaviour, Josefu insisted that, with Bill, all three of them should drink excessively, exorcising ghosts, reclaiming the African continent. He thought they could bring each plant to life there through careful recognition and place each star at a slant appropriate to the clear night sky.

⋮

   Josefu knows he needs one more night in Leroy's motel. Although he ordered only two beers, his head spins as he lies back to contemplate what appears before him. Ellie is in African dress, for the first time in his experience, and he is unaware of and uninterested in the colour of her skin. She belongs to him. He knows where to find her whenever he wants. His mother is in the room too, in her golden traditional dress, as also is Marie Immaculée in hers. These women are so beautiful, and he beams at them. To one side, both Père Ambroise and Afrika talk with his father who carefully empties a meerschaum pipe. Only Bill looks alone, in another corner, hunched over a dog, the one they heard General Dallaire had killed with a pistol in self-defence. Josefu would hide it from his own son and daughter. He'd get them a dog of their own. They too needed to be here for this fortunate reunion. As his telephone rings and he leaves it unanswered, as the light fades behind the green curtains he has not yet closed, as the motel furniture sways from side to side, Josefu believes he might be dying. Since he has one foot in Rwanda for Musisi's visit — his only experience of being happy there — now could be a fitting moment for him to depart this world.

   He finds it unfortunate, though, that he has to rise to go to the bathroom first and, by the time he returns and lies down again, under the bedclothes, he falls into complete oblivion, the kind you feel when you drown in the deepest part of a very slow river.

9.

Josefu aims for Swift Current, but thinks he might only reach Medicine Hat. The vast expanse of the prairie, the intensity of its spaciousness, hits him in the face, on the mouth, so strong is its impact through the windscreen. He intends to drive as fast as the law permits. But the impression he feels, of being on an ocean borne ship, has the effect of slowing his foot on the accelerator.

For him there is no silence yet, since the sounds of an earlier conversation still orbit round his head. Warned by Dave that Martina was about to set the police on Josefu's trail, he had quickly called her just before he left.

"I'm so well, Martina, and even more so if you are okay too," he had said, trying hard to be sincere.

"I felt really bad, you know, that you didn't call. Angry. Used."

"Did you?"

"Well, it's in the past. It was therapeutic, you and me, yes? Some liberation from my fifteen years of hell. No, 'hell' isn't the right word. But I am seeing someone, do you hear? He's been after me for years and there he was. A flick of my finger. Don't you care?"

"I'm bewildered," Josefu had answered, wishing his compulsion to tell the truth was not so strong. "You're a fast mover, it turns out."

After a long pause, Martina said, "We're having a conversation, you and me, not just a series of confessions! It's like I'm talking to a different person!"

"You're the best judge of that. But I couldn't telephone you after I left. I couldn't talk with you. You see, I'd have probably returned to Banff." But after a pause he said to her, "Okay, I'm glad about what you've just said, your news. Don't be burdened with me anymore. I mean sending the police on my trail, what an idea!"

"Yeah? That Dave, he told you? What do you expect, Josefu? You're a bastard for not calling."

"Martina! Strong language? What would Gulshan think? All the 'Wellbeing' people?" He smiled. "I'm on my way to Winnipeg, and if you don't hear from me, don't worry, don't."

"You just take care of yourself."

"Take care."

"Take care."

"Take care," Josefu had said it last deliberately, and they parted.

He wants to carry some of Martina with him, like a picnic basket of food he can nibble at until satiated. She could be seeing someone else but he feels entitled to some part of her.

Suddenly now, though, as the flat landscape surrounds him, he wishes his car were roofless so he could stand up. Who wants any possessions when the freedom of the green and yellow fields, and of the grey and white ones shimmering in the distance, formless and borderless, takes you right out of your skin and into the middle of creation? Here you are at the centre of all the galaxies, at the hub of time itself. Josefu gives out a loud roar, a very piercing sound.

The fields are rolled out like priceless rugs, and it is a fearful thing to walk on treasured textiles. Perhaps he should stay in the car and never get out, until Winnipeg. Increasingly now, Josefu's ears become blunted with the absence of sound, but still he refrains from using the car radio. He hopes to be able to continue driving. All his focus is on the limitless presence of the prairies before him. He trusts he is moving forward, but cannot be sure, his senses at all angles. Yet here, at last, is the respite he had yearned for, the chance to be woven into a bland fabric.

And yet, although he'd expected to be absorbed into oblivion in the prairies' infinite horizon, he notices how much activity around him is jostling for attention. In fact, as he passes along the highway, there is eager movement all the time. Sometimes it is the telephone poles – the cheerleaders. Sometimes it is a railroad track trying to beat the road in a race. Silos and barns, although abandoned, are relentless in their wish to outlive their former owners. And occasionally, oh so rarely, Josefu thinks, a vehicle passes in the opposite direction, far on the other side of the wide central verge. He will never fall asleep at the wheel here, after all.

Sometimes in Rwanda there had been a great roll of a valley, like a sign of opulence. In England too, there was the occasional large expanse of flat land. Here in the prairies it is different, though: whereas elsewhere the landscape itself stirs before you, here only human intervention halts the unchanging stillness. Josefu feels a great sense of purpose now, to act, to mark the planet.

For starting this day productively, he will try to recall some momentous event as he drives.

⋮

Kagame—Paul Kagame—it was said he had been 'the strong man of Rwanda' after the war. Had he come to these prairies, he might have found a balm here, out in the open, for the austerity of his intensely unbending soul. Who knows, thinks Josefu, who had met him shortly after arriving in Kigali, whether his constant vigilance could have been laid aside for a few moments while he contemplated the quiet and unthreatening fields?

So why not begin with Kagame this June morning? It is reasonable to do so, and he could say to Bill: "I reasoned, I analysed, I dissected my reminiscences, I prepared a memoir. Memoir or memorandum? Which sounds better? Typed or word-processed? Hand written or dictated into a tape recorder? 'Recollections by Josefu Mutesa'." But then he notices, 'God, my stitches on my scalp hurt! I mustn't let them influence my judgement'

With a short cough, he begins aloud: "At the top of the morning, moving towards Medicine Hat —no maps needed— I recalled meeting the Chief of Defence, the then Vice President of Rwanda, the embodiment of recent history, the leader of the rebel forces who took power. Yes! And Chairman of the Rwandan Patriotic Front. And people shouted it, his name, and they wrote it down, again and again: Paul Kagame. And we met him when we had hardly been more than a few days in Rwanda! Such an achievement for us, damn it! Why did our headquarters not acknowledge that?

"On the cusp of August and September in 1994, Paul Kagame was the most sought after individual in the country for the donor country representatives to meet. I must clear my throat before I continue," says Josefu, driving now with only one hand on the wheel. "While his compatriots inside the country wanted to obey his every command, foreign visitors for good measure and to feel safe, wanted to prove their worth by giving him unsolicited advice. Kagame was also chief military commander in an unfinished war."

Josefu takes a breath. He remembers the awe the leader's remote manner elicited: everyone described him as looking remote. That had probably been his style since school days, to impress with burning eyes, but few words.

"And how did we get to shake his hand?" Josefu chortles in a youthful way. 'Thanks to my Musisi, my relative, the mkoo, the brother-in-law to all my mother's family. The priceless Musisi. What a hangover we woke up with, though, on that important morning, ugh!"

⋮

There were twin beds in Josefu's room at the Hotel Mille Collines and so they had spent half the night talking, boy to boy, man to man, flipping back the years and spreading them forward, then returning to the present. They had also phoned Rosemary, his mother. 'Mama Josefu', as Musisi addressed her. She was woken from her sleep but laughed and joked, chatting for a few moments in Kiganda, their own language. Once again, Josefu felt her voice brought into the confines of his room a further kind of respite from the turmoil of recent days.

Josefu exclaimed, "It's so good you are here, Musisi, so good! I've seen so much since I arrived, the bodies, the cruelty."

"Cruelty," Masisi said reflectively, "It's a word you use; you used it then, I remember, when you visited our Uganda."

"And you don't... But it's what I see."

"And I see."

"And I don't know what to say. And I don't know how to hold back and say I'm not really from Africa. It would be easier, you know, to feel less ashamed of what I've seen here."

"I'm a soldier," Musisi replied, "And driving to Kigali we passed many fatalities like you had never seen in our country, in our Uganda. But we are all human beings, the Bazungu, the whites, and us Bugandans — you and me — and them, the Bunyarwanda, the people of Rwanda. We are people, all of us, and we kill each other because it's what people do. But I wish you had not seen this thing here."

Josefu experienced a sense of urgency, to fill all he wanted to say into this one visit, because Musisi would be departing the next day. So he even told him, as they lay on their beds like they used to long ago, about Patricia leaving him and taking the children to live with another man. He saw that Musisi began to cry.

"Mkoo," he said to Josefu, "Why you? Why were you with a woman who has no respect for her husband?"

"It's true, you know. She stopped respecting me. Do you know the word 'bum'? That's what she called me. I say it over and over again and nobody will believe me, even Mama. She said I was a bum because of the Rwanda thing. Because I was angry with the UN but did not resign and fight from the outside. You see, Musisi? She said that if I had some guts I'd have denounced all of them in the UN by name and by country on CNN television. And she said, 'I spit on your dignified silence'."

"Dignified silence?" Musisi repeated, pondering. "But perhaps that's the way we do it. I stay in the army. I don't like what our army's doing in the North of Uganda. We fought against the North against Obote but now it is a different situation and I disapprove. Yes, I disapprove. But I do not resign. I move up in rank and then I can take more of my own decisions. That's another way of doing things. But you've lost so many women, Josefu," he laughed. "By the way, that woman, you know, whom your uncle wanted you to marry, she stayed in America. She never came back. Your cousin brother saw her. And instead you married this woman here." Josefu did not comment. "You know, I'll tell you perhaps this woman, she said to you 'Rwanda' and 'disgrace' and all that but she was already being paid by the other man."

"Paid?"

"Paid. Anything. She is rubbish." Musisi got out of bed and dragged Josefu up and led him in a dance, singing,

"I Love you, Baby Touch Me".

"Hey, by Taby Lay!" Josefu laughed, joining in, the tune and words readily coming back to him. Wagging their hips, they both turned in the space between the beds and chanted the words in a mixture of English, French and Lingala, the musical language of Congo.

"The best!"

"The best!"

Now Josefu repeats the song again as he looks at the prairie insects splattered over his windscreen. Without experiencing too much disgust this time, he uses the car's window spray and wipers to clean them away while freshly dead. He chants, tapping on the steering wheel, "I love you, Baby touch me!" This time he puts a hand to his head, simultaneously remembering the following morning's hangover in Kigali and today, in Alberta, the persistent throbbing of the awkward, insoluble stitches.

Although Musisi was fractionally shorter than himself, Josefu thought he cut a striking figure. It was so rewarding, so enjoyable, having such good memories of their time together.

"Let's have a council of war," Josefu had said when dressing and shaving. "Let's decide about Bill."

"I think we should take him, Mkoo. It will help you always, when the boss sees what your relatives can do."

"Perhaps Kagame will be hostile if we aren't alone, and not receive us at all."

"He will receive us. He will receive us," Musisi grinned. Josefu sunned himself in Musisi's laughter. A lump came into his throat, though, because of knowing they would soon have to part.

Kagame received them within minutes of their arriving, either because of sheer luck or else because he had good memories of Musisi. He was a soldier's man, probably, and respected the bonding between veterans of old.

They had gone in Musisi's jeep to the military headquarters where Kagame spent most of his time. Afrika had run up as they came out of the hotel but when he was introduced to Musisi he beamed at him, patted Josefu on the back, repeating pleasurably, "Your relative, your relative," and made a dignified retreat.

Josefu recalled the darkness of the room where they met Kagame. As the door was opening, Josefu noticed he was in full uniform, crisp and well ironed—-by his wife or a subordinate soldier? Here a wife would iron. Patricia never ironed a single shirt. The effect of the hangover kept Josefu's mind wandering. This changed as soon as Kagame saw Musisi. The austere, almost impenetrable expression of a moment ago vanished as the two men walked towards each other.

"Eh, Musisi," said Kagame as they exchanged greetings warmly and spoke in Kiganda.

Musisi turned to Josefu and said, "You see, he knows a few words of our language," and laughed. Addressing Kagame again, he said: "I am based in Mbarara, you know that. So I've learned a little of your Kinyankole, your Lutoro, from where you were a child in Western Uganda, but I speak no Kinyarwanda because your people have all followed you home. That is good. You have done your dream."

"Brigadier! Congratulations," said Kagame and they warmly patted each other on the arm again and laughed.

"This is my mkoo, Josefu Mutesa," and Musisi added something again in an Ugandan language, which Josefu guessed was about his father's lineage. Kagame did not make eye contact but he smiled gently when they shook hands.

"And this other one?" asked Kagame in a low voice, referring to Bill.

"My colleague from the UN," said Josefu, giving Bill's full name.

Kagame returned to his better-known remote manner and shook

hands a little curtly. Musisi added that he was from Canada, and Kagame muttered a reply nobody heard.

Bill was awed by the meeting, and it elicited a kind of compassion in Josefu. They were asked to sit down and were given some soda water, which Musisi poured, laughing at the same time. "We nearly died together, in the bush," he said to Josefu.

Every sinew of Kagame's almost emaciated body was taut; his intensity was imposing. He hardly moved, the hallmark of authority, Josefu thought. His deep-set eyes burned, but his slim fingers were placed on the desk neatly, like small birds perched on a telephone wire.

Bill took a deep breath and spoke. He was on a mission, after all.

"I want to tell you, Sir, that not all of us in the UN Secretariat think alike. Each decision on Rwanda was discussed with passion and several of us had radically different views to those taken at the top, at the time." As Kagame did not react, he began again: "Both of us work in the UN Secretariat, Josefu Mutesa and I, and we didn't agree with the decisions which resulted in further help not being sent in time. Many of us recommended that things be done differently. So perhaps not the whole UN should be condemned."

Josefu realised that nothing could stop Bill from defending it whenever he got the opportunity, and so he smiled benevolently at his incorrigible colleague.

Kagame sat up, folding his arms over his stomach, breathing with difficulty, his nostrils and face carved in rock. "A day will come, believe me, when we will see Boutros Ghali, Kofi Annan, Mr. Boh-Boh, and we will say they should have listened to Dallaire when he asked for help to stop the killings. And we will say much more."

"Don't worry," said Musisi patting Bill on the forearm, "Don't worry. He will do everything."

Josefu intervened. "We have come on a fact finding mission. You have not been informed yet because we were not expected till next week. I'm sorry."

"Is that so?" said Kagame. Josefu could see that he was suspicious.

"We do not even have an official car yet, but we are using a taxi. We accompany a priest who is helping survivors."

"A priest in a taxi?" Kagame said, cynically. "Though that way, you will discover more of the truth, probably. With your official four-wheel drive, you will be prevented by your own organisation."

"Thank you, for helping my mkoo with advice," said Musisi.

"The world outside, your internationals, put UN personnel here, to stop us coming from Uganda to save our people here. Which Arusha peace accords could be respected when all of Rwanda was being asked to kill us, asked for on the radio, in every open place, to kill us and all Tutsi? Who could want the Arusha accords when they were disrespected? For peace? For transition to justice? For all Rwandans to be equal? Hutu moderates, yes, they had been killed too." He cleared his throat sharply, "But tell me, what about now? We want to be on our own, solve our own problems. But your UN has tried to take that out of our hands by accompanying people to the camps in Zaire. We will get our people back from your camps in Zaire. We have a military situation because you have not let us finish the war." Kagame spoke with a crisp voice and Josefu was almost relieved that he did not set his piercing eyes on him or Bill but looked into the distance, as if he were addressing many others.

Nobody replied until Bill almost whispered, "I'm sorry. What I have seen so far...I cannot forget."

"There are a few good Canadians," said Kagame. "But we really need to be allowed to act alone."

"He doesn't sleep at night," Musisi said to the others, "Mr. Kagame, General, he still must continue with the army to repel the enemy attacks from outside the country, from Zaire especially."

"Ehhh," Kagame confirmed. He looked at Josefu. "Please let me know if you need something. Your mkoo is my old friend." Josefu was pleased when Kagame then tapped him on the shoulder as they left. "When your mkoo returns here, I hope I'll have more time and we can meet again."

Afterwards, they were told it was rare for him to have shown such affability.

They all rose to leave, but Kagame asked Musisi to stay for a moment. They rapidly exchanged information which nobody else could follow, presumably about the military situation. Kagame returned to his desk and wrote a note, which he handed to Musisi.

Josefu looked on from a distance at the thin and pained figure who had taken the yoke of Rwanda onto his bony shoulders. He could not help but think that, even when young and at school, Paul Kagame would have already learned his tactics, of reserving judgement and then acting with decisive ruthlessness, a well-developed habit now. Yet he envied men of that inclination and destiny, who swam knowing where they were going and then, on dry land, had goals to achieve both day and night. In contrast, those who had been carried adrift by failure and self-restraint, however, could only float downstream along rivers that were shallow and which divided without reason.

In the corridor Josefu turned one more time and saw Kagame on the telephone giving instructions in a clipped voice, and thought, 'He cannot stop, he can never step back'.

Several doors closed behind them. Josefu's impression of the meeting, though, stayed with him so forcefully that nearly every day in Rwanda, in his probing and increasingly isolated mind, he sought to find Kagame and to assign him a leading role in his thoughts.

⋮

Josefu had considered inviting Musisi to his wedding in New York but he'd felt constrained since it was Patricia's parents who organised it, American style. Now both his own parents are dead, he will have to rely once more on Maria to help him to trace Musisi. Or else he will find him on his own. In this large expanse of prairie, distance is so manageable that going to Entebbe airport and into the heart of Uganda does not seem at all a daunting idea.

⋮

Musisi had been persuaded to meet Père Ambroise before leaving to cross the border out of Rwanda. Josefu, with Bill's full agreement, was keen to bask in his relative's reflected glory. Till this visit to the parish, however, Josefu had not appreciated fully the mark life had made on Musisi in the intervening years since they had been together.

When they all met Marie Immaculée in the parish doorway she was holding the legless child on her hip. Seeing her, Afrika, who had followed the jeep in his taxi, rushed up to interpret.

She lifted her head and looked into Musisi's eyes slowly, penetratingly. She whispered something to Afrika.

"She says he is a good man, to come and show that Monsieur Josefu is not alone, that's what she says, because he is a good relative, that's why," Afrika said in French, which Josefu promptly translated into English for Musisi.

Knowing already from Josefu about Marie Immaculée's background, Musisi gently took the child and held him up affectionately. The infant gurgled and smiled when the Brigadier chanted a little rhyme.

"I remember that song, I think," said Josefu.

"There were so many orphans when we were in the bush, around the Lowero Triangle and in other places. It is a terrible thing." He handed the child back to Marie Immaculée carefully and very slowly. "Often we were the first to find them. Tell the priest, in French, that we people in Uganda have had our orphans, our deaths, and it is terrible."

Père Ambroise, who had watched Musisi carefully, said to Josefu: "Now I see your relative, you no longer surprise me. I can see who you are. It is difficult when you meet someone who is alone without kinsmen, to understand them." Josefu did not respond but repeated for the priest what Musisi had said about the orphans and killings in Uganda.

"We say many of the same things, that colonisation in Africa created enemies," Père Ambroise continued. "Also that poverty created perversion. Those are epic words. Yet really there is the fact that it is so easy to kill, especially little ones. This child was going to be killed."

Josefu translated quickly. Musisi flinched and nodded silently in agreement. Afrika had carried into the courtyard the baskets of food and produce brought by Musisi and which it was thought prudent not to leave in the heated hotel room.

"He is a fine man, your general," added Père Ambroise, taking off his glasses for a moment.

"He thinks you are a general," said Bill.

Musisi laughed. "No, never. I just like to do my job. Brigadier is enough. Ehhh, I have to be going!" He took Bill and Josefu aside. "I am concerned for you because Kagame's main preoccupation is that the war is unfinished." Then he added, "You have not seen that there are land mines everywhere and you are riding around. Please tell your driver. And your priest."

Josefu felt thankful that it was at St. Paul's parish that they were parting, where he could go with his sadness back into the church to linger for a moment.

They had never met again. Musisi may not be alive. But he must find out now, even from Canada.

"I want the truth," Josefu says aloud. "And the truth is always short," he adds, looking at the length of the highway before him.

10.

General Tousignant had obviously been in the open air when he returned to his office; he was wearing a blue beret worn at some formal event. 'Mmm… He looks like someone who may not take these serious ceremonies too seriously,' Josefu mused. 'And yet he probably knows, yes, that such formal affairs are indispensable, with their ritualised dress and gestures, with their connivance in creating for the participants a sense of importance. In a desert or a jungle, they create an ordered space, and that allows everyone to dance.'

And yet the absurdity of that thought dispirited Josefu and so he remained immobile, silent. He let his eye wander: the whole Hotel Amohoro headquarters were in need of repainting, this office room too, but it didn't really matter, not today.

Measured and efficient in gesture and word, General Tousignant channelled the impression of being energetic directly where he wished. On this occasion it was into his handshake, which was perfectly timed, Josefu noticed. After greeting him, Bill spoke in elaborate French, which elicited a smile from the General. He wore no glasses except to read a note left by his telephone. Josefu was surprised at how clean they were, and only wished that Père Ambroise could have the same.

'All in good faith, ' remarked Josefu to himself, 'Père Ambroise, he struggles to see and General Tousignant, he sees by right. Not technology but faith gives vision, though. I still use the naked eye alone, yet what I see in Rwanda is increasingly blurred, never to be corrected because I don't know where to look.'

"I learned you were here, Messieurs, quite by chance while playing tennis yesterday with Sharyahar Khan. It's what we do every evening, good for our rapport, he being the UN Special Representative and I Commander in Chief of the UN forces, you understand. He is very supportive. As for your presence here, there must be security arrangements made for you."

The two visitors exchanged glances. They wondered whether he knew about Madame Dubois' outburst.

Josefu drives past a huge metal grain elevator, next to a compelling, Alberta speed limit sign: 110 kilometres, it says. Mercifully there is no noise in the air. In contrast, he remembers that Madame Dubois' whole office had shaken when she rose to speak, a deafening siren of war. Josefu tells himself that before remembering more of Tousignant it is important first to turn his thoughts to Madame Dubois. "So am I getting a little better at organising memories?" he remarks to himself aloud.

"You are not here," she had said, "Officially we did not know you were here. Since you knew that, we thought you would not leave the hotel. Then you come to my office now without my asking, and you calmly tell me that you have been outside the city several times. Was not that trip to Butare enough? No, you rode without knowledge, without authority, around the whole country. And with no written mandate, you even presented yourselves to the vice-president of the country! Yes, that is the one thing we heard about without your telling us yourselves."

"He is a friend of Mr. Mutesa's family," said Bill with pride.

"Ha! You're an African," she remarked, turning to Josefu. "But that can be an even worse peril, you know, to look like one of them. May God preserve you! Though you show no respect for regulations."

"We have come here to ask when we will have our programme, our vehicle, and our interpreter?" Bill asked.

"How am I to know? So many of us suffer with our stomachs. We have other things to do. And don't go complaining to Sharyahar Khan!" said Madame Dubois.

However, Bill had already spoken with him on the telephone, who endearingly, reassuringly, told them both to be patient. It happened that he often said it to people on missions in Rwanda.

⋮

Now it is time at last, Josefu thinks, to return to that first encounter with Tousignant again. He taps his steering wheel, lightly, kindly.

The meeting had been brief. If Tousignant knew about their

whereabouts during the past few days, he did not mention it. He only said, "It is I who am responsible for the security of all UN personnel; I do not want to lose a single one of my men or women."

'Madame Dubois?' Josefu wondered again. 'Has she already complained?'

"Obviously, when I know your programme I can see what security can be organised. We keep as tight a rein as possible on organisation. And discipline, you see. Have you socialised here? Have you met people? We have a little reception planned in a few days time. A few more of my officers are leaving and we are replacing them with others. More are arriving, more and more."

"We are aware of that," said Bill. "You will not suffer the near martyrdom of your predecessor, General Dallaire."

Tousignant looked slightly embarrassed. "My predecessor did a magnificent job," he said.

"What is your most immediate priority?" asked Bill solemnly.

"Priority? Right now we have pressed for the departure of the French contingent and we are securing the Zone."

"The Zone Turquoise," said Bill. "Our Rwandan friends were uneasy about it. There is not much love lost between the French military and the present regime, I gather."

"Of course, you have seen Kagame," said Tousignant, turning to Josefu. So Madame Dubois must have spoken.

"He did not discuss it at all," Josefu replied briskly. "But the exodus of so-called refugees, aided and protected by the international community, he did mention that, very disparagingly, although we were on a social visit. A social visit," Josefu emphasised twice. From working in Geneva he was even more aware of protocol than Bill.

General Tousignant's face lit up, however. "Do you know the camp problem too? Just between us, the decisions taken by the humanitarian organisations and our military priorities are diametrically opposed on the issue of the camps."

"We will support you on that," said Bill rising. "Whether anyone will listen to us is a different matter. Your position is perfectly clear."

"Perfectly clear," Josefu echoed, as they shook hands.

A white envelope arrived a few days later, at night, with a hand written invitation to the Meridien Hotel.

Bill said, "I know Mary would tell me to go to this party, but I'm not in the mood. Those two corpses haunt me, you know, perhaps because they were fresh."

"You took photographs," said Josefu, "You did your job well."

A few nights later, having been to the reception, Bill said: "Did you see me talking with Tousignant? You know how you can start out in life one way and end up outside your plan. Tousignant finds himself head of UN forces in Rwanda, in this tormented place. But at military school he had wanted to join the infantry, to be un fantassin, but the army claimed he was flat footed. Knowing us Canadians, perhaps they just needed a few more of the others and so he became a logistics man. And now he's here."

"And alone. But you're both heading towards retirement. I'd forgotten because neither of you look it, that's why."

"Thanks! Flattery will get you nowhere," Bill laughed.

"But does Tousignant's dream, which he had as a recruit, match up now with hoisting a blue flag over these smoky Rwandan hills?" Josefu asked. "Doesn't he see it that way?"

"It's a big effort, I guess."

"And he's lost one battle already. A mandate on human life, a principle of thought," Josefu added.

"You say a battle?"

"Of course, Bill, a battle. I see on one side all of Tousignant's troops, arranged in ancient lines, bearing banners of honour. They think they are there to save human lives. But if they have to kill while disarming the killers who are fleeing, some of them, it's just the acceptable cost. But our bosses, yes, our bosses, they didn't take it that way at all. And they blatantly supported the opposite side."

"The opposite side?"

"Yes, the opposite side — Bill, why do you keep repeating whatever I say? On the opposite side are the ranks of the humanitarian industry. And they have stood their ground too. Not only holding firm with little difficulty, but with a louder voice."

"The ones around here?"

"Yes, and their position is the exact opposite: human life itself is the principle, not human lives. There is no higher interest for them than human life for its own sake, and for them there is no such thing as expediency. No such thing as guilty or innocent. All have the right to Life — killers, mutilators — and it is better to agree to their demands rather than see a single person perish."

"They think they've got a point there."

"But security is not their concern, not their aim, nor is anything long term. I'll say something…"

"You always do."

"We're here for the genocide but it's already happened. So what about what happens afterwards? That's another story. You know what, Bill, I think that will be our story—the aftermath."

"Reconciliation, democracy, state-building, peace, that's the story. That's what we say, anyway. You know that."

Josefu couldn't tell from Bill's expressionless face whether what he was saying was meant to be ironic. "But Bill, an enemy just outside your borders enables even the most democratic political leaders to become despots, so who knows what could happen here in Rwanda next? That's what all our blunders and stubbornness, however well intentioned, are helping to create. Tousignant has been thinking of the future; the others who opposed him don't. Tousignant is in the thick of it, Bill. A battle that should have been fought in Manhattan, using plastic coffee cups."

The stench of decomposing human bodies was imposing. So different to other smells, even that of excrement which it most closely resembled; it seemed to cover Kigali and the roads that led out, like a hellish ozone layer. It penetrated your nostrils even when there was no visible source of provenance. It had lingered for over a month already. Josefu had not once used a handkerchief over his nose, feeling it was disrespectful to the dead. However, he began to dislike all strong odours, not just rotting flesh and excrement, but even the smell of barbecued meat or fried peppers in the hotel's restaurant or in the streets. All the sensations he had been so alert to, he now wished to blunt and harden: no more sniffing spices with expectation, gazing at the greenness of lawns or the contours of women, or hearing the acuteness of his oboe well played.

Here in Rwanda the captivating aromas in the Maidenhead house seemed so remote, he reflected, as well as those in his mother's various kitchens as she moved from place to place in London, where dishes were still cooked the African way, for hours and hours of patient bubbling.

Boots, sandals, bare feet left their imprints where killers had run, their minds spinning with plans and explanations — their lofty thoughts. Josefu suddenly realised in a way that shook him, when it was already too late, that Musisi had not mentioned once the names of any of their formerly youthful relatives and companions, and perhaps it was because some of them had died in the Uganda fighting. Neither had he explained why he, a flirtatious, exuberant young man had decided to join a guerrilla movement and, after their victory, been transformed into a thoughtful, measured army officer.

Josefu was always aware of a great chasm between his relatives and himself, isolated from his origins, and he was reminded of it once again in Rwanda. He had been brought up in Europe with verbal politics, while his relatives in Africa were raised with armed rebellion as an acceptable political option. There you marked your vote by laying down your life. The stakes for winning a place in government were exalted and all encompassing in those countries: the privileges were seductive and exclusive and coarse. It was a different political world when you had spent your childhood barefoot, perhaps, and saw the chance of flying in the sky.

Bernard, the young photojournalist, arrived at the Hotel Mille Collines when Bill and Josefu were in the foyer, waiting for Afrika who had invited them to his home. The young man attempted to appear full of energy, but there was something drawn about his expression which Josefu noticed immediately. His face had lost the gentle shape of youth; it was hollow and almost beaten into angular shape. He flashed a smile, which only had the effect of showing a row of exceptionally large teeth.

"So, how are you, Monsieur Bill? Monsieur Josefu ? Eeh, Mze !" he added to Josefu, 'Mze', being a local title of esteem. "So, Rwanda is good to you? Our country of a thousand hills?"

"We thought you had disappeared. You didn't come when we expected you, and not a word," said Bill, trying to smile as well.

"Ah, I'll tell you everything. Everything." Turning to Josefu, he said, "I had no choice; it was a good job I was offered."

"I'm sure it was," said Josefu, almost whispering, trying to catch Bernard's eye.

"Goma! I got the chance of accompanying a German journalist to the camps, with all the correct press documents, everything, all the laisser-passers. He had a lot of money and paid for everything. And he paid me everything too. I couldn't lose such an opportunity."

"Of course, of course," said Bill. "You're forgiven," he added with a laugh.

"It was terrible there," Bernard said, not knowing how to begin. "Yes, of course I'll work with you."

"We understand," said Josefu, again in a low voice.

Bernard then looked him in the eye. "There was so much happening. So many humanitarians there! The camps have given a lot of jobs to the whites. I have a question for you: would they have jobs anyway, without the camps?" Not waiting, he turned to Bill and said: "There were television cameras, a group of them together, from ABC, from CNN, from the British BBC, some were women and some were men, with very large amounts of equipment. As they were about to film a little baby who was dying, his mother put him down on the ground. I think she had lost her mind." Bernard stopped talking.

"Well, well?" said Bill. "What happened?"

"Two men from different humanitarian agencies rushed towards the baby in front of the cameras and crashed into each other. One of them fell on the baby. They both wanted to be seen with the tee shirt of their organisations on television. Probably the one who didn't succeed would lose his job immediately and his organisation would be closed down. I had that impression."

Josefu looked accusingly at Bill. "Will you listen now? Not always two sides to a story. Bernard saw it himself."

"I'm listening. It's not our job, but I'm listening," Bill sighed, giving Josefu a sideward glance, being patient with him, at his wife Mary's request.

Bernard continued: "The man who had fallen on the baby was closer, so it was he who won the fight, because he took the baby as he got up, you can understand, no? Then he crouched down, with the baby in his arms, next to a woman and you could see his tee shirt and its name very clearly.

I want to tell you that I photographed him too. Only he was not beside the woman who was the mother of the baby. It was someone else. I think the baby was dead by that time. The defeated white man, in the meantime, put his arms round another woman and started consoling her, loudly, so the sound would be picked up, but she was not the mother either. I photographed everyone. Then I asked the mother —I had seen her— where she came from. Cyangugu, she said. I asked why she hadn't gone to Bukavu camp, which was closer than Goma, but she said her family had first gone to Gisenyi, President Habyarimana's province, thinking that it would be good there. But the local leaders then said they should leave for Goma. All of it, you see, all her troubles, her child ill, all her running she told me…and the humanitarians were just wiping the dust off their clothes because the cameras had moved on."

"Bernard, this is terrible," said Bill. "What did the TV people do when it happened? Did they shoot it?"

"I don't know," replied Bernard, "I wasn't looking at them anymore."

"What do you think happened?" Bill persisted.

"They did not film the two men lying on the ground over the baby," he replied, embarrassed. "I think they filmed only the victorious one on his feet again, with the baby in his arms. But they also went on to film a different child, one who was alive; I watched that, because he was fighting with another boy, like children used to fight when they went to school. So they filmed a little normality in the camp. Voila."

Josefu was shaking his head. "This whole thing doesn't surprise me," he said. "The camps make good film footage, manna for the charity organisations."

Bernard moved away, looking for a light for his cigarette.

"Josefu, stop being cynical," Bill remarked in English. "It disgusts me too, that story, but in the camps there is plenty of suffering anyway. Let's not forget that. And there are folk who are helping out."

"Bill, you always want to see the good side. But you know we never seem to get it right. That sounds over simple, but it's true, we never get it right."

"We?"

"Yes, 'we'. We, the so-called international community, call it whatever. We rarely get it right. We have to think about that."

"There's too much in Goma", Bernard interjected, having returned with a cigarette he flicked ash from nervously. "You know, before in Kigali there were some American missionaries, who spoke perfect Kinyarwanda, perfect. They spoke with an accent, though. Well, I tried to use their same accent, because that is good for a photo-journalist. They thought I had flown to Africa from another country. Don't you think I was right?" Bernard asked Josefu.

"Yes, it was a good tactic," he replied.

For the first time, Bernard gave a genuine, unforced smile. "I'll continue telling you, then. Do you want more?"

They both looked at Bill who quietly said, "Sure."

"There was this Interahamwe who was very tall; you would have thought he was a Tutsi! I asked him what he was going to do in the future?"

"Excellent question," said Josefu, warmly.

"He said that they were going to win the war, against the Tutsi, against the new government, and come back to Kigali very soon. And then he was going to be thanked for all his work, all he had done, and he would fly in an aeroplane to Paris. I asked him, 'Why Paris?'"

"Yes, why Paris?" Bill said.

"He answered that he would buy a television there in Paris and bring it back. And when I said he could have taken a television from any Tutsi rich household in Rwanda, he said he had taken at least three already, but in Paris he could get one where he could see himself and his friends and all his family. Strange, such an idea, don't you think?" said Bernard, slightly baffled.

"He'd need a video camera and a video player for that," said Bill.

"But why in Paris?" Bernard repeated.

"It's the great metropole of francophone Africa; ask Père Ambroise," said Josefu.

"I'd give anything to visit Paris too," said Bernard.

"If you work hard," said Bill.

"I will. I'm looking for a Belgian journalist now. My German man went to Burundi. He was looking for transport. I didn't know about your taxi," said Bernard.

"Our taxi is for us," Bill remarked, "Until we get our own vehicle."

At that moment, Afrika came up to them and greeted Bernard, tapping him on the shoulder. "He has got thin," he smiled. And they spoke to each other in Kinyarwanda, and Josefu could not guess what they said.

"I invited him to join us," said Afrika, "But he says he is busy," he added with a wide smile.

Josefu found that curious, because he had wondered, knowing the inevitable invitation was going to be made, about the nuances of Tutsi Bernard going to Hutu Afrika's home.

Bill touched Bernard's shoulder," Come and have breakfast with us, Son, tomorrow at eight." Bernard almost ran out of the foyer.

"I invited him," Afrika repeated, "But these young people, they are always in a hurry, always going somewhere else," he added with a laugh, but Josefu had the feeling he was relieved, for whatever reason.

They drove across the town, and then started to climb a hill, past a mosque, past a fence where Josefu was sure he glimpsed a corpse with a red tee shirt, past a deserted café bar, and then into a wide road where a small cow grazed in a corner. Opposite was a large iron gate. Afrika hooted and a barefoot, short young boy of about sixteen rushed out and opened it.

"Who is that?" asked Bill with a tender smile he usually reserved for enquiries over young members of a family.

"Oh, he's our 'Boy', that's who he is," said Afrika, using the English word. "He works for us. He comes from a village."

The boy was unsmiling, and kept his head down.

They went up some stairs and entered what seemed to be a relatively new house. Bill realised he had to take off his shoes like everyone else, and without Josefu having to tell him. When Afrika tried to prevent them, Josefu said, "This is just like home."

The whole family had gathered. Afrika's parents stood side by side. His father had white hair, about the same medium height as Afrika, and his mother was only slightly shorter. Josefu recognised her eyes heavy with bereavement; that never changed, when your child died, your son alone in prison. This was a world in a strange and badly odoured dream, where the loss of one child was comprehended immediately but where Marie Immaculée's case could hardly be acknowledged, so intangible was the extent of her loss.

"Oh God!" Josefu shouts out.

He passes a sign for agricultural machinery, the best in Canada. Rubbing his eyes with one hand he tries to see what time it is, but forgets as soon as he looks. There are bales of straw in the fields on either side of the highway, left over from the previous year, it seems, waiting to have something done with them, to be taken away. Josefu reflects that likewise there are events left over from many years ago, still waiting for him to come and load them onto his life.

The road imposes itself now, almost coming through the windscreen as—unexpectedly—it undulates along some short, green hills. He begins to drive the car more slowly, strapped in firmly with his seat belt, resisting the urge to close his eyes as he feels the movement of passing ground beneath him. Remembered faces dim, and disappear behind the shrubs. His thoughts, like thin cloud, turn into wisps in the sky. He is alone and voiceless, and although aware he has passed Gleichen, even without his mislaid map, he is unable to give it any significance. He knows that he should look for landmarks to dignify his route with reason.

Now he begins to regret not having sought advice from Joe Swift for his voyage on the highway but, like his bearings, he has left all companions far behind. He was right to have invoked him, though, because road signs indicate that to the right of the highway the Blackfeet, the cousins of the Stoney people, have a reservation nearby.

These reservations are perhaps lost causes, Josefu muses, or mere flags of convenience hiding deregulated history, but they provide nonetheless a resting place for people who seek simply to survive behind swellings in the earth. Everyone else has been left just to roam, like himself and Joe Swift. Likewise in Africa, there were signposts indicating that the roads were bad, but some led to places where both the killers and the maimed hid between the mounds along dried rivers. They called those places home, though, which others left behind and mourned.

At present, Josefu longs for a cup of coffee, to take with a couple of analgesics provided by the Irish nurse in white. His craving has an urgency that undermines his yearning for pure wilderness. Besides, his dashboard indicates the car will soon be out of gasoline, a kind of wake up call he welcomes.

There had been certain customs that Josefu recalled from his youth and which in Rwanda allowed him discreetly to gain favour. He had debated what to take to Afrika's party. Then he negotiated at length with the hotel administrator and afterwards with the chief barman that he should be allowed to purchase a whole crate of Primus beer. He presented it to Afrika as a fait accompli, knowing it would be appreciated. When Josefu saw how many members of the family had gathered to meet him and Bill, he was glad there would be enough beer to go round. Given that the father was present, they would drink with restraint, Josefu reckoned; later, Afrika would still have plenty left.

"What a wonderful welcoming party," said Bill, "There are so many of you," he added.

Afrika's father and mother, her sister and brother-in-law and both sets of children, daughters-in-law and grandchildren all stood in line, ready to shake hands with the visitors. They had gathered behind the father who said in perfect French, "You are very welcome here, Messieurs."

"He used to work at the Post Office that we passed when I pointed out the Caritas bookshop, remember?" said Afrika. "Now meet these persons in my family."

All of them smiled, some demurely, others as if it were a huge joke. Afrika said, "We are all here together in this house because it is still not safe in our country. Neither side will attack our home because everyone knows it. So my aunt and her family are here too, that's why."

"It's impressive, to see the whole family together, about thirty or more of you here, I see," said Bill.

"More, more," said Afrika. "I'll tell you their names," and he began to enunciate them, like a litany, solemn names like Theophile and Theogene, Epiphanie and Elizaphan, like Deogratias and Damascene, and others. Josefu refrained from taking out his notebook to record them, but as they were said he repeated the names aloud, hoping to retain them. He noticed that since he had started recording first names, he had gathered over fifty.

The visitors were asked to sit down in large armchairs and a sofa surrounding a series of low tables where eventually food and drink would be laid out. Afrika's mother spoke in Kinyarwanda to Josefu, patting his forearm as he sat down.

"She's saying you are a good man," Afrika explained, and he added, "She says that you and Bill are teachers and I tell her you are not. I say to my mother that you have come from America to see what has happened here to our Rwanda, and that you are writing it down in your notebooks. She is interested."

At this moment many of the women left the room and Josefu could hear them giving orders in the courtyard. Food would appear shortly, he thought. Beer bottles were opened. "Next time, you will taste banana beer here," said Afrika's father. "Now everything is chaos. Everything like that is difficult," and he sighed.

They went outside into the courtyard to wash their hands under the one tap but there was no water so it was scooped out of a bucket in reserve.

"That's rain water," said Afrika, running up to them, "It's straight from the sky," he added.

Josefu felt genuinely reassured, given his new fear of water carrying the aftermath of floating corpses. He saw in a glance that Bill had not caught the nuance of what Afrika had just said and explained it in English to him rapidly.

"You think of everything, Josefu," he responded irritated.

Returning to the main room they both saw that the low tables were weighed down with food and a large pile of plates. "Take one and make a tour, that's it," said Afrika. "You must taste all of it, that's how, with us here in Rwanda."

There were large bowls, as big as washing basins, filled to the top with steaming food. 'Just the sight of it is festive', thought Josefu. Dishes of puddings—maize, wheat meal, plantain—and fried green bananas piled high, stews of chicken and of beans, steamed pumpkin, steamed bananas, and a salad of chopped avocado pears.

As for Bill, he was speechless until he said, "I've never seen anything like this in my life." Everybody laughed.

Although several family members were in the room, it was only Afrika and his father and uncle who joined the two visitors to eat at the same time. The uncle was small, with a wasted look about him, preoccupied and unsure. They ate almost in silence. Urged to take more, Bill helped himself to more avocado salad.

"He's a good man," suddenly Afrika's aunt said, from the corner of the room where she was standing near a door. These were the words that were translated.

"I thank her," Bill replied. Josefu sensed a hushed suspense filling the air.

After some arguing, in which the old father intervened too, Afrika said, "She asks if you will be going to Goma."

"Ehhh," said the father, "Let her explain. Mothers are like that, women!"

Josefu guessed what was going to be said. But he reflected: perhaps Afrika is wondering if he'll keep his job now as he forces himself to interpret.

Afrika began by flashing an anxious smile at both visitors, and then said, "Her son is there in Goma, one of the sons." He paused and said, "She told me to tell you that he took drugs, that he was always running around, nobody could keep him inside their house. My aunt and her house were in Kicukiro, a suburb of Kigali. We can go there, I'll show you. A lot of people were killed there, you know."

The father intervened. "Many people were afraid, we the Hutu. The boy, he was with his gang of friends and they were poor, their families had much less than us. I worked at the Post Office; it was enough. We had relatives with land on the hills that we all cultivated. And my brother-in-law here, he drove a bus, a taxi bus. You see, Afrika watched him, to drive a vehicle like him. But those boys were gangsters, an American word, 'gangsters'," he added, trying to smile.

Afrika continued, "They took him with them. They would kill him if he did not go. We do not know what he did; we have not seen him since the 6th of April when the aeroplane of the President was shot down. But we know he has gone to Goma."

"Goma and not Bukavu, not anywhere else?" asked Josefu almost in a whisper.

After exchanging a few words with the uncle, who kept his head down, Afrika said, "They know it is Goma because relatives of the other boys of the Interahamwe who were gangsters, we told you, well they said it was Goma, that's why."

There was a long pause. Bill said, "Yes. I think we'll go to Goma or Bukavu as part of our program."

Afrika's father said, "Me, I stood up and said: 'We are leaving this place because we will not participate in killing with the Parmehutu'. And I said to my son 'Afrika, you will take us to Burundi.' I thought we would lose our house and everything in it, but a neighbour whom I knew from the Post Office also, he was a great killer, he killed many people, I know. He looked after this house. Nobody dared approach him. When the RPF won the war he ran away and all his family with him. Then, there was a miracle," he added, his eyes lighting up.

"What is that, my father? Tell them," said Afrika in a clear voice.

"We had a Tutsi neighbour before, born around the same time as one of Afrika's brothers. Emmanuel, where are you?"

A young man appeared, thinner and taller than Afrika, in his late twenties.

"You see? The Tutsi neighbour and this one, they went to school in the same class. That boy he went to Uganda and joined the RPF. When he returned he came running, to see his house. It was completely emptied and it was damaged, not one window left unbroken. His family had left in April running, running, but whether they were all killed at the road blockades I do not know yet. I am still waiting. This boy told his RPF comrades, pointing to our house with his finger —this is what I was told— that it was the house of my other son who was killed in prison by Habyarimana our former president, and nobody was to touch our house." He cleared his throat. "This is the miracle, that nothing was gone, not one plastic bucket, not one light switch. That Hutu neighbour and the Tutsi neighbour, you see…. It's difficult to talk," he said, lowering his head. Again, there was a long pause.

The aunt said something several times over. Everyone looked at Afrika. "Will you find her son in Goma?" he said quietly.

"We'll take his details, of course," said Bill, "We'll try, we can't promise, but we'll try, won't we, Josefu?"

He didn't reply. Other members of the family were now entering discreetly and filling their plates and going out again. 'These people are like a cluster of trees, providing welcome shade if you get close enough,' Josefu thought. 'Fine trees,' he added, 'Beautiful trees.'

Anger then welled up as he said to himself: 'Which evil storm swept through this land? At knot speed. How hard hitting and putrid smelling was the wind that blew the killers along, trees killing trees, stones thrown against stones!'

"We like patisseries, in our house," said Afrika. "But at the moment, in Kigali, there are not the ingredients. Perhaps tomorrow there will be. My mother, my aunt, my sisters and sisters-in-law and my wife wanted a better dessert for you," he said as he handed round sliced oranges and mango pieces.

"This is the best," said Josefu, confirming that the previous conversation had ended and that a truce was called in the battle that could have engulfed them.

Talk evolved into exchanging information about children. Bill as usual, did not mention his son who was dead. Josefu did not say that his wife had just taken his children and moved in with someone else. Afrika, having pride of place in the family on this occasion, paraded his four children—three boys and a small girl —standing in a row while his wife was bashful and only stood at the door laughing. She reprimanded her daughter, however, for not removing a thumb from her mouth, at least this is what Josefu guessed. One of the brothers pulled it away for her, she hit him and cried, the eldest picked her up and the fourth child led them all away in procession. Everyone seemed relieved, though, that both Bill and Josefu started laughing.

"Children will be children," said Bill, shaking his head, then looking up to see if he had said the wrong thing.

"Here in Rwanda, we like to have many children," said Afrika. A hush descended, like soft rain. He then urged the guests to drink more beer and the afternoon grew gentle, bearable and slowly became timeless.

⋮

"Your coffee will be on its way," says the waitress in a red and white uniform at the highway stop Josefu had entered.

"I think I'd like to make some phone calls, first," he says to her. "Please forgive me. I'll be back shortly."

"You're welcome," she answers, slightly puzzled. He can see that she stares at him when he walks out.

"Ellie," he says, "It's me."

She laughs quietly. "Again? You know, my daughter just left, the eldest, just a minute ago."

"How are you?" he whispers, suddenly choking.

"A little better. I've had something to eat today. Why do you keep phoning?"

"I don't know," he replies.

She laughs again. "It's strange, really, given the way you could hurt me all those years ago. Where are you?"

"Still on the road. I'm still in Alberta. I'm in a roadside café."

"You sound perfectly clear, as if you were next door. But why do you keep phoning me?"

"I want to know how you're getting on. I want to see you," he pauses, "...to see that you are all right," he adds.

"It's strange, though, after what you did to me before."

"Do you think about it? I mean, you telephoned me first."

"It wasn't vengeance. I just wondered about you. And Maria and I had met quite by chance. I'm ill, after all, now, I'm ill."

"I'm sorry. What happened was long ago."

"How is your journey going?" she asks.

"Fine, fine. It's very complex."

"I'm tired, I've got to go anyway," Ellie says.

"If I don't phone for a while, don't worry."

"I won't. Bye," she says.

The taut stitches pull at his head. He had not observed where he had turned off the highway to look for a phone box and he'll soon have to make his way back. The bright neon lights inside the café and its casual, almost dismissive music underscore his confusion. Perhaps he will stop calling Ellie; perhaps it would be better that way.

'Let's remember instead', he thinks to himself, 'the food at the first official reception I attended in Rwanda, given by the UN Military'. He moves a plastic chair back so as to accommodate his tall frame, and realises the waiter is watching him. 'Get back to the story', he urges himself.

The catering at the reception had been frugal but impressive, given the circumstances in Kigali at the time. 'But no,' he almost says aloud, rushing outside. 'This is false! I cannot use memories of Rwanda as an escape from the stitches in my head.'

The realisation is a warning. "But I can survive," he exclaims.

As he looks out, however, at the quiet gasoline station, the pale green field beyond and the trucks and tankers passing slowly by and far apart, he becomes increasingly uncertain that this is the case.

IV   THE ROADS

11.

"It isn't poverty," Bill called out, running down some stairs into the foyer of the Hotel Mille Collines. "It isn't poverty that counts. Think, Josefu!" he added, making sure he could see him. "Oh my, Josefu, just think of the German Einsatzgruppen in 1942, those German officers who killed women and children in Byelorussia because they were Jewish, just think. It just isn't about poverty."

And Josefu was astonished by this breathless cascade of words coming down towards him. Bill was dishevelled, driven, and unstoppable.

"They aimed real close, eye to eye. Did you hear me, Josefu? They didn't use machetes. But just they first made those women and children strip, who knows why, before they stood them in a ditch and opened fire. Perhaps being naked makes them look less human? Oh my God!"

Josefu resisted Bill's whirlwind, or rather he struggled to resist it.

"And then the commandos waded in among the corpses to kill at short range, with neat pistols, anyone they had missed before. I've seen two photographs of it, can you believe it? Someone took photographs!"

Josefu could not respond to his unrecognisable colleague, who was so ardent, so oblivious of his surroundings, his brow so deeply furrowed.

"Did you know, Josefu," Bill continued, "...that at first the Einsatzcommandos were told only to kill their most dangerous enemies?

That meant just all of the men and male adolescents—familiar strategy! But then, they slid effortlessly, no problem, into their new orders to kill the women and children too. No trouble at all! Do you know what my point is?" Bill didn't wait for a reply. "Not hunger. Those Einsatzcommandos were not short of food, not short of land. Germany was no Rwanda with its Goddamn excuses. Yeah, they had everything right then, but they still shot the women face to face, right close up, like I said, face to face." Bill was swinging his two pieces of luggage with both hands.

Josefu was baffled. Trying to gain some distance, he said as quietly as he could, "What's all this about? Bill, can you hear me? You were talking with a man in the bar yesterday blaming poverty in Rwanda. Is that what you're continuing here, right now?" Then he added, "What's the use?"

Bill put down his bags and came so close he had to look up at Josefu who was taller than him. He said, "You yourself said a hungry hollow in the stomach makes dreaming more intense, that people wish for more and more, when they're pushed by hunger, right? And that they're willing to go to extremes to get what they think they want. In politics, yeah? The followers, okay?"

"Okay, Bill," but Josefu still tried not to be drawn.

"And yesterday's Belgian economist with his high population density figures for Rwanda, remember, and which he used as an excuse for murder, okay? Well, it's all bullshit. It's not hunger. It's not overcrowding. It's something else, isn't it?" He paused, eyes unfocussed again. "Admit it, Josefu. And so what is it about these people, these Rwandans, or is it about all people? Admit it: you don't know!"

Josefu was taken aback. Bill had never, ever, raised his voice like this before, anywhere; he hadn't ever made history… Josefu wanted just to watch him silently but, after a moment's forced reflection, he replied, "Look, Bill, we hungry Africans are not a different kind of species to the rest."

"You're not a hungry African, Josefu," Bill said mockingly.

Josefu was relieved to see him returning to form. "All right, Bill," he smiled, and spoke more slowly, more patiently, "…what I mean is that the Rwandan murderers, just because they were hungry, were not a different species from other people–other, more fortunate people—who weren't hungry. I mean, you can't say that hungry Rwandans are dogs and that those with enough to eat are cats. You can't say their behaviour differs because of the presence or the absence of hunger, can you?"

"But hold on there, aren't we on the same side then? Haven't I just said that?"

Though aware it wasn't the time or place for this argument, now Josefu felt intensely driven to continue talking regardless: "And then, you get the Germans, like you said, Bill, like you said, with their Goethe and Schopenhauer, stomachs becalmed with all their tinned meat and biscuit rations."

"Becalmed!"

"That's the food they had to eat then, I know it, Bill. But they mowed down women and children whose breath they could feel, yes, you're right, they could hear them, see them, as if the women were in those very soldiers' sitting rooms."

"I get the point, we're on the same side, Josefu," Bill replied, but only half believing it.

"Aimed their pistols at women who could have been sipping coffee with their wives, eating strudel."

"Spare the details, Josefu."

"No, it's all in the details. The Japanese were soothed with delicate tea and ceremonial geishas but the camp commanders still decided to torment their prisoners very slowly."

"Now you stop that."

"And the UN was going to stop it happening, straight after the last World War. But of course there's been more of it, more of the same. The hot and the cold, everywhere in the world, the contrasts." Josefu wondered where his own thoughts had strayed.

But Bill said hoarsely, impassively, "Get a move on! Say it! Make your point, Josefu."

"About massacres with machetes? The comfortable way they feel after they've done it? Ugh! What a portentous conversation we're having again, don't you see?"

Both of them stood immobile, staring at each other.

"That's the way it's likely to be Josefu, 'portentous', as you say, when getting to the crux of the matter, right?" Bill responded, more desperate than defiant. "Serious. How else? You know what we're talking about."

"Why here? Why now?"

"Because why in the hell do this trip, then? I'm going nowhere until we finish this portentous conversation. The crux of what we are investigating." Bill spoke so slowly now, as if he were defining their mission, not like someone about to snap.

Then Josefu closed his eyes and let his arms go limp and lingered for a moment.

"No, you're not going absent! This thing, got to know it," Bill ordered.

"The crux of the matter, you say? Why did it happen? It's the perfidious capabilities of the human mind, that's it."

"Oh, God!"

Josefu breathed deeply as he spoke. "The power of those capabilities of the mind can bring us to our ultimate humiliation," he added, opening his eyes but looking nowhere. "That's what being human is about," he ended, in a whisper. Now Josefu paused for effect, and turned to watch Bill who rubbed his bearded chin with nervous, rapid strokes. But then he continued, "The other point Bill, of course, is that we're all the same species, all of us, we humans. All of us are humans who are not dignified with the good sense of an animal. You can't say to a dog, pointing at a cat, 'That isn't a cat, it's a mouse.' The dog knows perfectly well that it is a cat. You see, don't you? But with humans you can point to a person and say 'That isn't a person, it's a cockroach, a witch, a poisonous tree,' and the chances are that you'll be believed. Don't you agree?"

Several people began to gather round them, porters, other hotel staff, and a couple of journalists with cameras. The two were oblivious to them. Bill held Josefu's gaze, who took a step backwards and continued: "You want to know why they did it? I'll tell you what, Bill, I'll end with this. The Rwandan Hutus who massacred Tutsis were all supreme intellectuals. Don't you see? That's because they used their mental capacities to the extreme, you know, just the way all we humans typically do—fantasising, inventing what we see. Being able to call a dog a cat, and to see a human being and call him a plant or an insect, and then go and stamp on him, dismember him."

Bill said nothing. Josefu thought he looked as if he were recovering from a blow. A potted cactus in the hall cast a shadow on his face.

"Don't you see?" Josefu repeated, "Hungry or satiated, Bill, literate or not, or German or Rwandan," he paused for breath, "...we humans can all point to a child or to a woman and tell ourselves that they're different to what our own are, and squash them into the earth like beetles, and–listen to this—believe they really are insects. Oh, and that they'll eat our crops if we don't get rid of them."

Bill's frozen gaze imposed itself on the dialogue as if he had spoken again, but he said nothing. Josefu added, almost to himself, "The grisly miracle of the human intellect"

He'd sometimes thought of this before, fearful, alone. Now he turned away, dismayed like Bill by what they'd been saying. "Well, that's all."

But he knew it wasn't all; it was the reason they were here.

He noticed, just then, the deer-like young woman he saw the first evening by the pool, who had taken a chair away. She was standing and staring like the others who had formed a circle round them. As he walked towards her, though, she moved also until they were within inches of each other. He touched her hand and was shocked by the instantly soothing and embalming effect. They looked at each other and he drew away, unused to the sensation and somewhat embarrassed by the public way they had just met.

"I spoke to you the other evening," she said in French, her voice even softer than her skin.

"Yes, yes. I remember," Josefu answered, a little shy now. "Are you alright?"

"Yes, thank you. Are you leaving? Why are you and your companion so angry?"

"No, it was not a dispute, just a discussion."

"A conversation?"

"Yes, a conversation." He wished she were his sister, his wife, his friend, that he should not lose her. "We're leaving for a while. We'll be back," Josefu added, moving towards Bill at the reception desk.

He was relieved, however, when next turning round, that she had gone. He was spared the need to find out who she was with the subsequent complications of encountering her again. Yes, the subsequent complications.

Soon he was also pleased that Bill had inexplicably recovered his good spirits, talking so fast to the bespectacled Rwandan receptionist that his French Canadian accent thickened by the minute. Josefu had observed in the last few days, that despite their increasingly prickly arguments, Bill was buoyant most of the time, because he was back in his element: in the thick embrace of his employers' organisation.

They had been some time in the capital Kigali now, 'within the orbit of the air-conditioning,' as Josefu's mother had said on the phone. Unlike Bill, he found it frustrating to spend most of the day talking only with expatriates, and pass the evenings inside the hotel for security reasons. For Bill, though, it was 'real life' again, at last, to be following the pattern of most of his fact-finding tours–fully accompanied, fully time tabled, collaboration fully defined, at least on paper, between the UN organisation and the locals. And all facts —all data—only received value in Bill's eyes when other expatriates had acknowledged and approved them.

For Josefu, however, perhaps because of the very imprecise way this tour in his ancestral continent had started, it had awakened a selfhood that was stressfully divided. As a result, he strained against the formal part of his mission, to the extent that on two occasions he had slipped away alone, simply to stand at the back of St. Paul's church during midday mass, and there he had endured the relentless gaze of Marie Immaculée.

Now they were leaving Kigali to go to a town that had been in the Zone Turquoise.

"It's by request from New York," Bill said.

When they had first arrived in Rwanda, he had concurred with Josefu, deliberately to refrain from cabling reminders to the Secretariat. Finally though, Madame Dubois summoned them to announce that their documents had arrived. And then Josefu had felt she was issuing them with equipment for outer space. What she gave them seemed so incongruous in this bullet ridden, half-abandoned land: plasticized badges with their photos on it, and in neat typing, stamped letters of accreditation in shining folders, and walkie-talkies as if they were breathing apparatus.

She exclaimed, however, that in the parcel sent to them from headquarters, there was no lip salve, no anti diarrhoea tablets or many other essentials, but what could you expect. She said General Dallaire had asked for torches for his men to see at night but when at last they had arrived, there were no batteries; it was a useless consignment. "And that was for real danger," she added.

Then they displeased her again. Earlier she had warned them that no interpreter would be available, and so now they insisted that Afrika come with them. They presented her with a Certificate authenticated with an ecclesiastical stamp from Père Ambroise stating he had worked as an interpreter already. Through a letter from Josefu to the Vice President's office, they obtained a government affidavit as well.

"But I know who he is," she protested, "The taxi driver. And he is Hutu."

"Hutu, as many UNAMIR local employees were before, and continue to be," said Josefu promptly.

"Ah, you've heard! Despite the problems, we apply multi-ethnic principles, here," she added.

"Well, we rest our case," said Bill, beaming at her. "We take Afrika or else we call off the whole mission and see your budget cuts go through."

"That's impossible," cried Madame Dubois. "Ah, you are giving me such a terrible pain in my small intestine, I can feel it there."

"Afrika is our interpreter," Bill said mischievously.

These were moments Josefu remembers well, of annoying her like schoolboys. He hardly heard her admonitions, watching instead her large, round glasses slip down her small nose.

Then they had followed her into the next room and joined the rest of the UN staff, all sitting on rows of folding chairs. Again, Josefu saw how glad Bill was to be part of a group once more. He wore a linen suit, a dapper look. But Josefu preferred their raggle-taggle team of the first days, perhaps because it was more of his own making.

Madame Dubois had stood before them and began the session with a list of regulations, while waiting for General Tousignant to arrive, since Sharyahar Khan was unavoidably absent. This she repeated several times, explaining that he should have been there, because he was the special representative of the Secretary General. Josefu was reminded that he and Bill, to add pomp, were both grandly appointed as envoys of the UN Secretary General in person, and so were all the other field officers. It was as if the Secretary General were a large, glutinous amoeba from which they had split and, Josefu thought, they had all become such curious entities!

His mind had wandered. Precisely at that moment and in perfect synchronicity, Bill and he both noticed a young woman in khaki clothes at the end of their row, whom they soon discovered was called Gabrielle. A typical Third World aid worker, Josefu surmised, she had slightly tinted glasses, no make-up, hair tied back, a large wrist watch, a top with several pockets and she was wearing strong, sensible sandals. She was from Syracuse, New York State, she said, telling Bill that was not too far from Canada, and gave them both a vigorous hand shake.

'Strong grip, but without meaning, not like Tousignant's greeting,' thought Josefu, admitting his comparison was odd. He couldn't understand why he hadn't yet warmed to her already, instantly. He was irritated with himself because of it.

"I'm going to Kibuye," she added.

"But we're going to Kibuye, Josefu and me," said Bill, pleased to have company but surprised they hadn't been told.

"Strategy evaluation. I've come over from Haiti to do it. I'm not UN staff; I'm on contract. I'm on contract to the UNDP. I get hired out, like to Haiti. It's just the job I do. That's after Afghanistan and before that Guatemala and, oh, there's more," she said with the characteristic understatement of international professionals. "I just go in there." They sat down again for the General's arrival.

Madame Dubois stood and frowned in their direction. An Australian in regular military uniform joined her now. He stood at ease before them and spoke exceedingly slowly, giving great reassurances about the excellent medical back-up available to them and the good communications network in case of trouble—for them, the staff, alone. Precisely: the non-local staff, of course. And Josefu remembered that in April, while the fluffy pets of expatriates were being evacuated with great compassion, Rwandans who worked for UNAMIR or the diplomatic services were left behind, mostly to die. For lack, naturally, of a mandate.

'If a song is ever written about the lack of mandates, I'll sing it every day to my children,' Josefu thought, realising only slowly that they would not be with him daily ever again. 'There will be world championships for mandate songs,' he continued, 'Yes, love songs, protest songs, mandate songs, mmm... the new genre.' His mind would not keep still and when the Australian made a joke he laughed politely, but hadn't heard it.

At least Afrika would be local staff now, temporarily, and have a steady income for a while. 'Appearances deceive', Josefu reflected. 'It looked as if there was so much food at the lunch party in Afrika's home, but what was served up in those steaming basins was all they had. When the guests had eaten and the rest was divided up among perhaps thirty souls, it didn't make more than half a plate each, something like that.'

He had learned by now that most of the produce had come from outside Rwanda. Here the country was so ravaged that nothing could be harvested. 'Appearances deceive,' Josefu repeated.

General Tousignant arrived, wearing several nametags: a metal one on his wrist, a plastic one on his buttonhole and an embroidered tape above one of the many pockets on his uniform. He took one look at the waiting audience, took a breath smiling and began by saying he had not been very long in the country but had already seen great changes and that the international organisations had contributed greatly to improvements. Josefu saw Bill and Gabrielle were listening very earnestly.

He admired Tousignant's tact, but his thoughts strayed yet again. How many of the people present had been invited to the homes of humble Rwandans? Would they even say they had the time? Once Bill and he had integrated formally into the mission system, the number of working dinners and improvised receptions had increased, nearly all at the same Hotel Mille Collines, as if the sense of siege added to their importance. Social occasions were marked by enthusiastic discussions about the demarcations and rivalries between the various UN institutions. The most prized information concerned the destination of every memorandum. It captivated the mind and eye, while the sun faded unnoticed behind the hills.

Now his ears pricked up. Tousignant talked of his own military endeavours, to complete taking over the Zone Turquoise. Josefu had been told by the young UNAMIR officer whom he had met again briefly, that the French personnel had cut the gas and electricity lines as they were leaving. Of course, it had not been in their mandate to bequeath them to UNAMIR, who had so unceremoniously requested their departure.

The question of mandates, once again, had its rules. A game of backgammon, relying mainly on the luck of the dice, was being played with the mandates on an imported game board placed on Rwanda's head. The country was asked–please—not to fidget any more until one of the players had won.

:

Josefu wants a short-term aim on the highway and it is to get to Brooks and there isn't far to go. He drives past fences arranged to streamline cattle so that they can easily be loaded for transport to the slaughterhouse, for the great North American meat industry, for the work of the righteous. He eats meat, good beef, so why complain. Alice, his daughter, does not want animals to be slain but doesn't realise graphically the relationship between meat, especially hamburgers, and animals of any description.

Josefu reflects, though, that in Rwanda he saw no fences for channelling either cattle or humans to places where they would be out of public sight. No indeed, there were none of the transport networks of the Nazi German empire and people were not furtively herded into trucks and trains, heading for the push-button gas chambers hidden from view. In Rwanda nobody, no observer, was pushed away, nor victim concealed. At crossroads and bridges, wherever it had been convenient to stop humans to check for Tutsi among them, you saw the traces of heavy blood where people had been pushed a mere few paces away and hacked to death in full view, with a few strokes. And there were even leftover signs where the killers had sat and rested between their vigils and their murdering: upturned boxes, discarded cans and empty bottles, cigarette stubs… For them, the heroes, their debris was worthy of indulgence.

Josefu had said to Père Ambroise: "I cannot understand how nobody felt the need to conceal what they were doing, not even removing someone from the pavement to kill them, in Kigali or Butare, in the largest towns where there were so many people around."

The priest put his hand carefully on Josefu's arm and whispered, "It is called impunity. That is a great sin, impunity. It is the end of human dignity. Impunity pulls down the whole edifice of all human culture, all it accumulated from century to century, from land to land, all of it."

The sign that says 'Welcome to Brooks' stands just after a line along the highway of maidenly trees celebrating their own greenness, no doubt in honour of the month of June. Once his daughter had pointed at a fruit tree in full blossom and said, almost in shock: "What's that,

Daddy?" He remembers so clearly.

He'd replied, "That's a tree wearing her dress for the May ball."

"And when the tree has only green leaves?"

"That's the way she dresses only for a tea party, Alice."

When she told her mother, though, Patricia said, "That's cute, Josefu. It's the story old-fashioned English gentlemen tell their black kids in New York City. Can't you think of something that's more in tune with life around here, huh! Even if they do live in pretentious, stupid Manhattan?" But he was embarrassed and felt a magic moment had been trampled on. Patricia thought it was a battle for reality.

⋮

These rows of trees in the highway, which have appeared suddenly, cut across the lines of resting train coaches and of double glazed mobile homes for sale.

Josefu notices that the exit speed is 80 kilometres, realising he has been oblivious to the need to check how fast he drives. He is made aware by another billboard that there is a 'Brooks Greenhouse' which invites him to come exploring. He needs the toilet, and he senses that the absence of plants to touch has made the skin on his hands feel dry in the last few days. He rushes inside the huge store, attracting the attention of several staff who immediately come up behind him. His heart pounds in his ears and he has difficulty focusing as he sees rows and rows of potted plants, thickly green and without flowers. They are identical, all potted rhododendrons, and he crouches to examine each one, as if looking for a particular feature. "Hutu or Tutsi or Twa," he repeats several times, "Or Banyamulenge" he says aloud.

"Can I help you?" asks a young assistant in blue dungarees.

"Sorry," Josefu replies," I was looking at them. They are very much the same. The same species," he says.

"Yeah, right," she says. "Do you want me to get someone who knows?"

"I know. It's all right, I'll take that one," he says, pointing at a slightly smaller one at the end of the row. "It'll probably have to live in my greenhouse for quite some time before it can be transplanted," he adds, taking out his credit card at the till. "Do you sell MacKenzie seeds?" he asks.

"Yes, Sir, right over there. I can hold these here while you check those out?" says the cashier.

"Oh, I've changed my mind, no time now."

Only when putting the plant on the car seat at the back and seeing his travel bag does he remember where he really is and wonders what he will do with his new purchase now? He feels calmed, though, by having seen the rows of potted plants. Normality brings an appetite: it is time to eat. The array of coloured signs on the road confuses him. How do you avoid poison? 'Aeneas!' he recalls, and slows down his car to recite:

> '...the snake now, dragging its gradual
> Length among the bowls and polished wine-cups, tasted
> The sacramental meats, then harmlessly went back under
> The burial mound again...'

Translation from the Latin, never to be obliterated! What a snake it must have been, though! And like Aeneas I'll never know whether it was my 'father's familiar, or the genius of the place.' And who am I to worry about the consequences, when I see Rwanda so far from the original now, and what that country had to say is so incompletely translated, without rhyme or syncopation.

He sighs and draws up besides a Wendy's Diner, who is hiring day and night crew, till 2 a.m. He bows his head towards the spotless table, uncomfortably alone. Nearby, an ambulance team are resting and eating. He has come to the right place, after all, he muses.

⋮

The first thing Père Ambroise said, when Bill told him he and Josefu were going to work in Kibuye, was that Marie Immaculée would be devastated. She was inside the parish house, he told them, with their washing, and she had brought another warm pot of igitoke. She handed both in silence to Josefu and stood back. Père Ambroise looked at his shoes and announced the decision to her. She said something as if she were spitting.

"She says that she wants to know why you are unsatisfied here," he said.

"You know that's not true, Père Ambroise, can't you explain?" said Bill.

Afrika came in and stood by the priest, talking to Marie Immaculée in soft tones. Turning to the others, he said, "I told her you work here for a big boss and he has sent you to Kibuye, that's why."

And then Josefu went up to her and said in English, "I'm sorry, I'm so sorry," his eyes smarting. She raised her eyebrows briefly in acknowledgement, as people in Rwanda did, and simply watched him.

Père Ambroise put a hand on Josefu's shoulder, "I understand you, my friend. Ah, poor man, you don't know how to take us."

"Monsieur Josefu has refused," Afrika told the priest in French, "To accept to travel in the helicopter which that general, that head of the UNAMIR forces offered them. Monsieur Josefu wants to go by road," and then he looked at Bill, knowing his displeasure.

"And Josefu wanted me to fly on my own, Père Ambroise, but I can't," Bill said. "We've been friends for a long time, not just colleagues." He sat down on a bench and leaned on his elbows. "I lost a son. Yes, my second son died."

"You never told us that before," said Père Ambroise, immediately translating to Marie Immaculée.

"He rarely speaks about it," Josefu contributed, and suddenly lifting his voice he said, "Mark was a fine young man."

Bill said, "Josefu and his wife, former wife—sorry, Josefu—they stood by us."

"What has this world come to?" asked Père Ambroise. "Evil killings are, in a way, more straightforward to explain, at least they used to be before all the recent killings happened in Rwanda. But until then, I used to find it so difficult, when good people, really good people, lost their children through illness. Illness—such a wanton way of dying. I was not a good priest, you know." He repeated it all to Marie

Immaculée in Kinyarwanda. She raised her eyebrows a few times but did not comment.

"It was a senseless motorcycle accident," Josefu whispered slowly.

"Yes, senseless, yes. When the sun sets," added Père Ambroise, "Behind the hills, I sometimes think I have understood something, but it never lasts till dawn, never. You understand me, don't you," he said specially turning to Josefu, who then closed his eyes.

"Please, Father, tell Marie Immaculée we will not be parted for long."

They ate the plantain in silence, their spoons clanging against Père Ambroise's enamel plates, and Josefu thought how completely separate they were here from where they were going next—to a UN briefing with a cocktail, supposedly to boost their confidence. It was always the same story, these contrasts out of place.

⋮

Close to Brooks, Josefu drives past a sign pointing to 'Bassano Dam', Italy in the prairie, an evocative name. In Uganda at the source of the Nile there was Owen's Dam. Eventually, though, these foreign names blend into the landscape. He had told Bill that the names of aid agencies were likely to become integrated into Rwanda in the same way. It was their only national income at this present moment, he remarked, and nobody right now could know whether the export of tea and coffee would ever provide a significant alternative in the future.

Having parked, now he walks out into the warmth–the air-conditioning in Wendy's has impressively chilled him—and the bright neon lights in front of him, redundant but insisting on attention, make him wish for Joe Swift to arrive and explain how to live when all is out of place. 'Put one foot in front of the other'. That's Ellie's words; she's back, Josefu acknowledges, resisting the urge to find a telephone.

⋮

Josefu now remembers how travelling in Rwanda had always led to realignments among colleagues; the moment they left Kigali, an unmistakable sense of irritation was felt inside the car. The new driver clearly disliked Afrika, although they exchanged civilities in the usual traditional way. Gabrielle, who was travelling too, had very little French and so she insistently pressured them to translate into English, all that Afrika said, which Bill did more obligingly than he.

Even though this journey had barely started, Josefu felt his strength had already begun to be eroded. He was losing his fitness because of being unable to jog, unwilling to run past lurking corpses, and so he was uncomfortable and stiff. He disliked constant company and missed not being able to walk to work alone, as he had done in New York always, after parking the car near the children's school for the nanny or their mother to collect later. All those things had their place back there, but his household would be gone when he returned.

He thought Bill talked too fast when speaking to Gabrielle and this sign of attraction irritated him. He himself did not know the name of that young woman at the hotel. Nothing was important. It was stupid to look out of the window at the face of Rwanda–the beggars, the lame, the lost and the frightened, and all the devastated crops across the hills, such a sorrowful destiny.

They rode by cautiously.

12.

What happened was unexpected because the Commune of Gitarama had been taken over by the new government relatively early on. Mopping up operations should have been over by then. The new authorities had established control there and everyone assumed that the reckless remnants of the previous regime had already implemented their policy to herd their own people, as they referred to the frightened Hutu among them, as human shields while travelling towards the camps in Zaire. Nobody supposed there were any stragglers still left behind.

At exactly the same moment, both Josefu and Afrika saw two children alone in the roadside and shouted at the driver to stop. His first reaction was to refuse and he continued forwards, but on their insistence he halted and reluctantly reversed. Then Bill got out as well, while Gabrielle looked on from inside, Josefu now recalls.

A girl of around ten years old was trying angrily to coax a younger child, a boy of about eight, to continue walking. Blood spilled copiously out of his mouth as he coughed without ceasing and his tee shirt was covered in it.

"Oh my," said Bill, "Ask them where they're from."

The girl was visibly cross with the younger boy. Afrika interrupted her and soon translated, "They are brother and sister. They're going to a camp, she doesn't know where. The relative of the man who used to be the local prefet came and told them all to leave their village or they would be killed, that's what he said. They are Hutu and they were living in the same village as before the war. She says that her family was moving ahead and they told her to look after this boy here and to follow them and she says that he kept on coughing and making them late."

She sounded exasperated and gave her brother a push. He was crying and coughing desperately. Afrika continued: "She's fallen behind with him, that's what she says and she can't see her parents in front of her anymore."

"Neither can we. Where does she think they've gone?" asked Josefu.

"She doesn't know. They went down this road."

"When was that?"

"Oh no," said Afrika, after asking her. "This is a big problem. I cannot understand. She says it happened yesterday. This is a big problem."

"Well, what are we waiting for?" said Josefu. "We will have to drive them to the group, or there must be some Refugee station somewhere further down, or the soldiers might know. We certainly can't leave them here."

"No, obviously not," said Bill.

"You are good people," said Afrika.

Gabrielle had joined them by now. The driver, a monosyllabic tall and thin man called Celestin stood by in disdainful silence. The little boy had been crouching as he coughed but now he fell on the ground and his crying diminished. Josefu stooped down and grabbed him. "What is the girl's name? What is her brother's name?"

Africa answered: "She says his name is Hercule."

Josefu was on his knees now, the Hercules of Rwanda in his arms, only a little older than his own son, smaller in size perhaps. "Smaller than Patrick, don't you see?" he said to Bill.

"Should you be getting so close?" said Bill, "I mean you don't know what it is he's got."

"Hercule, Hercule, don't cry, we'll take you to your Maman and Papa," said Josefu, holding him closer still. Afrika translated, getting down too. The sister, suddenly realising she was surrounded by strangers, stopped her angry rebuking and became silent and shy. Josefu cried out again, desperate now, "Little Hercule, at least don't weep," and finding a folded handkerchief in his trouser pocket, untouched since he was in New York, wiped the boy's face. The child looked up, beyond Josefu, somewhere far, somewhere rapid. A slight shudder, discrete and delicate, overcame his body but his gaze did not change, it was so intense. It never changed. He was silent. Josefu held him against his chest, already knowing what had happened, and then lay him gently down, still continuing to cradle his head.

Afrika bent over and with tired expertise, he sighed, "He is dead, that's what he is. We won't tell the little girl yet." He talked to her, whose name was Amandine, and then exchanged a few sharp words with the driver.

"I say that we cannot stop too long or we will be late getting to Kibuye before nightfall," said Celestin in French to the others.

Josefu was on his knees on the dirt wayside, keening, despairing, trying to straighten out Hercule's body with one hand and holding his head with the other. He closed the boy's eyes and held his chin, without thinking, the gestures of domestic death, learned he knew not where, perhaps from the movies. Yet here was the Holy Child from a Christmas Manger, one Père Ambroise would recognise beneath a guiding star. Whether it was for birth or for death, here was the most sacred child on earth; of this Josefu was certain. He looked around without seeing his travelling companions, only the red earth side-path and the deep green of unclaimed trees. Here, on the road to Gitarama, he paid his last respects to the brave soul of Hercules of the thousand hills, dead of disease, fallen while his parents and protectors were forced to follow the selfish and the deluded.

"Josefu," said Bill quietly, keeping a little distance. "It has happened so fast, what are we going to do? Do you know?"

"We can't leave him here, it would frighten the sister too much. And we have learned enough from Père Ambroise," Josefu said reproachfully, "We can't have the gall to leave this corpse unburied and without honour." He said it loud and clear.

"Oh no, you don't," shouted Gabrielle, "We're not having a corpse in our car. We are not expected to do that, it's certainly not our mandate to have a corpse in our car, oh no!"

"You've got no choice," said Josefu. "It's not your problem. It's not your decision."

"How dare you," she replied, and turning to Bill she cried, "Don't let him do it, Bill. Tell him this is a UN vehicle. He's African but he ought to be taught we can't do that. It's against regulations. No, tell him I can't, tell him to go away. We can't have a dead kid in our car," she screamed.

"Shut up, Gabrielle," said Josefu, surprising himself. He gathered the child's corpse in his arms and stood up.

Afrika said, "I've told the girl he is very ill."

"What's he said? That damn French, I can't understand. Tell him and the driver we can't have it in the car, that thing. I'm not riding with no dead kid," Gabrielle shouted. Bill kept silent.

"Let her sit in front," said Josefu. "You, Afrika, take the girl in the back, you can talk to her in her language. Now you get in the middle, Bill." He had rarely barked out commands before, but his voice resonated. "And you, Celestin," he said, returning to the driver, "You will drive us to the first collection point we see and forget about when we get to Kibuye, the hour is not that important."

"It's the light," said Celestin. "The United Nations regulations state we are not to drive at night."

"We'll deal with that later. Now let's go," said Josefu, easing himself and the child into the back seat next to Bill and closing the door with difficulty.

"I'm not travelling like this ever again," said Gabrielle, in a low voice. "This is too far out."

Nobody replied. Afrika spoke softly to the girl. Josefu could feel the child's body hardening and getting colder. He thought, practically, that hopefully they could lay him to rest, at least temporarily, while the corpse still had enough heat to be shaped and laid flat with dignity. As the skin cooled, he tried to detach himself from its contact with his own body. He was oddly reminded of creating a distance with an attractive girl he was forbidden from pursuing. Part of him, though, wanted to lavish affection on the boy so he would not feel he had died fatherless; he wanted to hold him tight and tell him he was a great child and had a wonderful name and tell him the story of Hercules the Great, until they reached some shelter with an open fireplace, where they could roast some marshmallows, read a story book and finish the tale, oh God, oh God.

"Bad news," he said aloud.

"You can say that again," said Bill who hadn't moved once.

The driver gathered speed, bumping furiously over the potholes in the road, looking attentively for people as he had been asked, and muttering unintelligibly to himself. For the first time since they had arrived in Rwanda, Josefu felt his own tears falling and they were ice cold.

⋮

Now Josefu wishes he hadn't stopped to eat lunch outside Brooks. He is combating stomach cramps, and draws up about ten miles forward, signalling a right turn although there was nobody to see it. He steps out onto the prickly grass. 'Bad news,' he says to himself, 'as ever there was bad news: you cannot walk barefoot in these prairies. From a distance, though, you would have thought they were endless, soft green lawns'. Crouching, he looks across into the distance at the unbroken view of spider-like insecticide sprayers as they crawl across the fields.

'Are they necessary?' he asks himself. 'Preserving the crops at any cost?' Ignoring a hissing sound, which he thinks could be a snake, his ideas wander away:

'The radios across Rwanda had competently sprayed their words around, their rallying cries to kill the Tutsi insects, to kill the President's enemies. People had wondered: how far was it between the voice of a radio in the air and the voice of a spirit? Not far. So how could they ignore it? And therefore the authority through which commands were relayed could not be questioned. Even when the messages were said to have been sent in code from radios in the refugee camps outside the country.' Josefu strikes his fist on a green and jagged tuft of grass.

Yes, little Amandine said to Afrika that her father had asked the former prefet's relative, "Were you told on the radio that we have to leave our village?" and he had replied 'Yes, the radio said it.' So there was no choice and they had all started walking.

Josefu, as he remembers the incident after all these years, no longer sees the fields before him and once more loses his usual reticence as he keens violently from side to side. "Yes, death sat on my lap," he recalls, "I held it skin to skin."

The shock waves of the memory cause him to quiver. There, on his knee, had been small Rwanda itself, fragile, exquisitely shaped and mindlessly wasted, dead as it was beginning, although so beautifully named. And Hercule, who would have moved a thousand hills, was betrayed and forgotten. "We all did it," he reflects, "We all brought Hercule to his end." Josefu had rarely felt such anger—against the human species, himself included—as at that moment.

Now, stepping forward into the prairie he sits down, although the grass is wet, and clutches his knees. He feels the moisture seeping into his boxer shorts and little does he care. Noticing a small stone, he carefully picks it up, throws it out into the greenery.

⋮

The earth had been quite tender when they dug it, finally to bury little Hercule. They first found a garrison and some soldiers pointed them towards a Red Cross station. There the Swiss officer in charge looked at Josefu in horror as he stood with the dead child slumped against his shoulder and hastily explaining that they had to be discreet because of the vulnerable little sister.

The officer said there were at least eight hundred unclaimed children, recorded in his sector alone, but he would process Amandine immediately and see whether he could identify the group her family was with. As luck would have it, a Belgian journalist, a woman with red hair tied back neatly, entered the building and told them that she had crossed a small group of refugees being escorted by UNHCR officials not far from Butare.

"It's worth a try," said Josefu.

"We cannot go all that way just for the sake of one child," the Red Cross official said, "Although she is a sweet little girl," he added, looking at Amandine whose hand Afrika held tightly.

Josefu had insisted that Bill also come into the building, given that with foreign aid a white presence always meant less explaining. His expression was blank, but after glancing at him briefly Josefu said, "We will bury this one first, then take our chances with the refugee group."

He saw that the Red Cross official did not want the journalist, who was there trying to find another Belgian colleague in the region, to realise the boy was dead and he led her away. Fellow Europeans so highly sensitive, the official probably assumed; they had to be protected. Missed opportunity, Josefu thought. A good journalist worth her salt could have made much of this incident. A moment of irritated silence followed.

When the official returned Josefu asked for someone from the Red Cross team to accompany them, so as to complete the paperwork on the spot if they found the girl's family, and that they would drive the staff straight back.

"I am very reluctant," the official repeated, "Just for one child. Anyway, first let us deal with the other one and as you know, it is against all regulations, what you are doing," he said, resentful that to make eye contact he had to lean his head so far back to look up at this tall, black UN official. "There is a place we have a hundred metres from here, where dead people have been buried," he sighed.

"We'll be getting a priest," said Josefu, "Not now but later, we'll definitely be getting one."

"They are not liked much in Rwanda today. A lot of people don't like them, thinking they even helped to organise many massacres," said the official.

"That's something difficult to face up to, for the churches, but we're making records," Bill said quickly.

"And there is no rule, of course," replied Josefu. "The priest we have worked with is exceptional."

"Nothing surprises me anymore," the Swiss official said, "Do you know that?"

They started to walk outside. Afrika said, "I'll take the girl away now, back to the car, and say that you are taking the boy to the doctor and that we will call their parents, that's what I'll say."

She rushed up to her brother, however, and held on to his ankle. Josefu stooped and with one hand gently pulled hers away. "Afrika, tell her she better go away with you now or she'll soon cough like him."

"She says she must stay with him, that's what she says," Afrika commented, pulling her away more forcefully now. And after speaking with her again in an agitated way, he added, "I have told her that her father said she must go with me, and look, she obeys her father," and he rushed her away towards the car.

Bill with Josefu, still carrying the dead boy on his shoulder, walked solemnly behind the local assistant whom the Red Cross officer had assigned to them, and who carried two new shovels. He helped Josefu lay the small corpse, unwrapped, unprotected, in the grave they dug deep into the earth. The soil yielded easily. Josefu found it difficult to let go of the body, to leave it there.

"Can you say a prayer? It might help all of us, you know," Bill said to him suddenly.

In English, Josefu half whispered: "Oh God, oh Lord," and louder, "Oh Imana, oh You Whom we have betrayed, Whom all mankind has betrayed, and oh You Who also have betrayed us, give rest to this child, to the Hercules whom Rwanda will never know, whom we will never acknowledge, whose feet we never worshipped, and whose footsteps we never followed."

Bill stood close, pale and bent over. His chin shaking, he said quietly, "Rest in peace, with all the other children too."

When they got back to the car, Afrika was visibly agitated. Leaving Amandine inside he called Bill and Josefu aside. "I cannot continue like this. When I returned with the girl, the driver was talking with some people here and said it was because the children were Hutu and I was Hutu that we were doing all this. I cannot continue."

"This is terrible," said Bill in English, turning to Josefu for help.

"Afrika," said Josefu, "We know you. We know your family, we know you, we know you. What others say is not important at the moment, however stupid their remarks. We know their words are stupid. We have some important work to do and we need your help. Please, Afrika, will you help us?"

"Ah, Monsieur Josefu," he replied after a long pause, "You say such things so we have to listen to you."

Even more cramped now, with the Red Cross assistant in the back of the car as well, they set off. The driver's sulking was matched only by Gabrielle's heavy silence.

By late afternoon a little miracle occurred, as Afrika said, because they found Amandine's family, with a large convoy moving on foot behind two foreign aid vehicles. The parents had glazed eyes and at first could hardly speak, as they slowly acknowledged what had happened to their son Hercule. But both turned and pulled Amandine towards them with relief, and now she began crying like she never had before. All of them bewildered, they continued walking, unable to leave that fearful dream surrounding them and leading them forward.

"It's difficult to speak with them, that's what it is," said Afrika.

Josefu had then insisted that the pace of the exodus be halted for a moment so that the parents could step aside. "Tell them," he told Afrika to interpret, "Tell them many times over how Amandine did everything within her power to protect her brother but that it was too late. They must praise her and be proud of her," he repeated several times, insisting that Afrika translate each time separately. He also said that they had covered the burial site with branches, that they would get a priest and later make a good grave.

After the Red Cross assistant had written down some details and moved away, Afrika slipped a few dollars into the father's hand, as instructed in a whisper by Josefu. By the time they had dropped off the assistant, who had hardly spoken at all during both journeys, back at the Red Cross office in Gitarama, it was too late to continue cross-country to Kibuye. Josefu suggested they travel again in the direction of Butare, and try their luck there at the Hotel Ibis. There were protests from Gabrielle and the driver, who said that it was a waste of precious petrol.

"You saw that our very small effort for the girl was well rewarded. Your attitude now is going to crush you," Josefu said in a clipped voice to Gabrielle.

"Bill, do you hear how he talks to me?" she exclaimed.

"I'm sorry, I don't want to be caught in the crossfire between you two," Bill replied, too irritated to make a joke of it.

"We have to pull together," said Josefu more gently. "Can't you see?"

Arriving at the Hotel Ibis, Josefu was pleased to see the place where he had met Père Ambroise for the first time. He thought that their prayers now would be more similar.

He ensured that Afrika, the driver and Gabrielle each had separate, single rooms although it meant that Bill and he had to share the only remaining one. There had been a large delivery of beer that morning, imported from Burundi, and even the surly driver made his peace for the evening with the rest of their group.

The sudden death of Hercule was not the only reason he remembered the event so clearly, though. It had marked a strange turning point, when the rest of his companions there, including Bill so many years his senior, and grudgingly even Gabrielle, started to wait for him to give the lead, to take the initiative, to make comments. It could be that he was becoming a teacher, albeit a reluctant one.

⋮

Since the taps in Hotel Ibis were not working at that moment, Josefu scrubbed his scalp twice and then the rest of his body with water specially brought in a bucket for him. He had carried Hercule in his arms but had felt the weight was around his head, like a thick, stiff scarf, the sort he would have worn in an unkind desert wind.

Then he had gone downstairs and listened.

"Here in Butare..." the cropped haired, squat, Canadian UN military observer was saying—Bill had contacted him immediately and he had volunteered to join them. Several beers had already been drunk. "Yes, in Butare," he repeated, checking that there was no stranger listening in to their conversation, "We have seen many terrible things, so they've been documented, carefully. Of course that Africa Rights woman, she's been doing it already, Raquia Omaar, do you know her? She'll make history, that woman. But we've got to get it all in place in our way too. And so do you. Well, that's your job so you are very welcome here. Here in Butare is the place where there was the hospital where, look, the doctors killed their patients who were Tutsi."

"Why doctors? Why would they have done that?" asked Gabrielle.

Immediately Bill interrupted the officer, to conceal her lack of knowledge. "You have the details?" he asked and started making notes.

"Oh yes, we have those details," he answered. "And here, in this Butare here, is the seminary where priests killed their seminarists who were Tutsi. Here, in Butare, is the University where the professors killed their students who were Tutsi."

Josefu leaned forward, then side to side and finally sat straight, and with an unusually vibrant voice he intoned: "Butare, in Butare there was no city dweller, no doctor, no teacher, no priest… Nobody who could be recognised according to whom they had been before. Neither killer nor victim! In Butare, there were no human rules, there was no human understanding. Human, I said, human… Don't you see?"

The others looked puzzled.

"Honour went into hiding," Josefu finished.

Then he rose before continuing, so that his startled audience had to crank their necks to see him.

"It had started so well in Butare, with the only bourgmeister in the whole land who refused to participate in the carnage. He stood up to the monstrous cyclone, so that Butare could be an island defying a hurricane. But he was swept aside, trampled on and murdered, and with him every human right still standing."

"How do you know?" asked Gabrielle.

"How do you know so much then?"

Josefu held up his hand, indicating silence, and pointedly translated into French for Afrika what till now had been spoken in English, adding, "It would be more courteous, given that we all speak French, if we switched for the sake of the only Rwandan among us." And then he said in French, "I read all this in the dispatches that came to the 32nd floor of the Secretariat. Intelligence was excellent, from Dallaire downwards. And now for you, Gabrielle," and stopped himself just in time from saying, '...because you are so poorly prepared'. Criticizing colleagues in public was not the UN style Bill embraced. Instead, he took a deep breath and repeated his speech in English, word for word, pacing away and back again to the small coffee table between them. Finally sitting down abruptly, he repeated, "Now we shall continue in French, please." The officer exchanged glances with Bill who simply gave a sigh.

"Let me give you a security briefing for travelling tomorrow," said the military representative in French, and slowly he began to smile.

As he emphasised the importance of testing the radio equipment in their car, Gabrielle showed her annoyance by rapping her fist on the table, because she was unable easily to follow him. Bill leaned towards her and whispered a few translations, breathing in the scent of her hair. Josefu, who had not overcome his reservations about her, conceded that she had remarkable hair, a beautiful texture that he would have liked to touch.

Butare showed every sign of a war of conquest and of heaven lost. The officer said, "Nobody can come to terms with what happened here, worse than in Kigali. I mean the whites can't get it."

He paused, again to check whether any bystanders were listening but they were alone; the place was nearly empty. Afrika had just brought more bottles of beer from the bar.

"All the investment," said the officer, "All the years of teaching, of sending lecturers out to do courses in Quebec or Brussels or Paris, bred and nurtured by our universities and our churches. Nobody wants to believe that their protégés were capable of being monsters. So it's going to be hard to bring people to justice, I think, especially back home, where some are already heading as refugees," he added, looking at Bill.

"You're not saying Canada!" Bill quickly remarked, looking to see if Afrika had heard. "I see… it's 'yes'. Oh my…"

Gabrielle reminded him instantly to translate and he obediently complied.

"That's it. Butare is weird, but safer than Kibuye where you folks are heading."

"What a thoughtful person," Bill said of the officer, when he left, "Very thoughtful," he added in French.

"He's really too young for the job, it's too harsh," said Josefu.

"It shouldn't be like this," said Afrika, "Coming to Rwanda should have been something pretty, something agreeable. Ah, what they did, what they did…"

"What we all did," said Josefu. "We all did it."

"What's he saying now? What's Josefu saying?" said Gabrielle. After Bill told her, she added "No, that's stupid. I had nothing to do with it. I'm not a savage. Don't translate that. But I didn't know what was going on, I did not! April to July, I was on home leave. Then at the forestry and natural resources conference. Then New York, then Haiti. Don't drag me into it."

"Josefu doesn't mean it that way," said Bill.

"Then tell him not to get at me."

"You're not the centre of the world, you know. And you're no different to the rest of the human population on this planet of ours," whispered Josefu.

"I'm not responsible for the damn planet," said Gabrielle.

"Why are you quarrelling?" Afrika asked Josefu, worried because Celestin had just entered the Hotel Ibis's crumbling restaurant where they sat by the terrace.

"I'm getting too nervous," Josefu said to Afrika, "I'm sorry."

"The food here is not very good, here in Butare, not any more," said Afrika, "That's why you are nervous. Madame Gabrielle also; tell her that's why."

Josefu smiled and tapped him on the back. "Food in Butare is okay, Afrika. And I'm sure Butare was a beautiful town before. It's just now, with everything fallen down… And though I try, I can't listen to my companions; I left my head buried under the earth with that little Hercule."

"Ah, yes, the little boy. Other people say," continued Afrika, turning to Bill now, "That we Rwandans don't give a big price to our lives, that's what is said about us. But it's not like that. We lose people early or we lose them late, each one, whom we were close to, each one we cry for, when they die, that's what we do. But we have to continue to work because of having to eat. So it looks as if we are working and not looking to our poor dead, that's how it looks. But we cry a lot here in our hearts, not in our eyes which people would see." He saw Bill and Josefu listening attentively. "We keep our faces clean, we show our teeth when we smile, that's for the others. And our thoughts are full of our work, that's what they are. But in our hearts we cry, in our hearts made of stone. Made of stone, or rocks. Rocks, perhaps, they are bigger than stones, aren't they?" And he went silent.

Josefu had sat down and listened with his eyes closed. Without opening them, he said, "Gabrielle, I'll translate carefully for you."

Having listened, she said, "You know, it's too much poetry around here, getting out of hand."

Opening his eyes, Josefu immediately saw Afrika looked upset, something that had to be stopped. When Gabrielle rose with Bill following behind her, Josefu stood between them and put his hand gingerly on her shoulder. Bill backed away rapidly, his best option. She turned to Josefu, saying, "Well? I'm not scared. I know my rights, my mandate."

"Can I just have a word with you? It's terribly important."

"You talk like an old colonial, Josefu," Gabrielle said.

Alone in a corner, he stared at her and slowly spoke: "Gabrielle, we seem to have started off on the wrong foot yet we have to work as a team. We can make an effort and not get into a rut, you know." He had to force himself also to make a commitment to that, he thought.

"Ah, the leadership skills, Josefu, I see you've got it all under control."

"It's not that easy, being here."

"Those children were none of our business."

"Would we have set a good example if we hadn't stopped?"

"Well, you looked cute, I suppose, with that tiny kid on your shoulder. A kind of gentle giant."

"The boy was dead. It's not easy, for anyone."

"Okay, okay. You seem to patronise me, Josefu, the only woman and you don't like Americans."

"Americans?"

"All this crap about speaking French."

"French?"

"Yes, Josefu, you set it up, that whole thing, against me. You know I don't feel I need to know the French. Even in Haiti I can do without."

"But do you feel comfortable?"

"I'm not a Canadian, you know, with their bilingual scene."

"But in Rwanda it's a delicate subject too. The incoming authorities from Uganda speak English, the local ones who never left speak French. The masses speak Kinyarwanda, of course, which the officials speak among themselves. But do we? Afrika, who speaks French, is important to us, not just as our interpreter. I want him to feel at home with us. We're in his country, after all."

"You're so sensitive", said Gabrielle trying to force a smile." I know what you're saying, I guess: let's work together. But I just want to get my job done and I want to get out of this place in a hurry."

Josefu bent down and kissed her cheek. He knew that Bill was watching from a distance and thought, 'He must have misunderstood'. Josefu turned, waved lamely and then walked out alone into the street to stand in front of the hotel terrace.

⋮

Josefu sits on the edge of a plain, throwing stones at a thistle. He wants to keep a vigil, never to move, not his foot, not his seat, not his eyes, and nor his head with the taut stitches. The loud hooting of a stationary truck forces him to turn round. The driver approaches and simply asks whether he is all right and whether he needs any help. It is a husband and wife team, he guesses, both with hair tied back in a knot. He thanks them, says he is fine, but then glumly moves off in his own car.

He is tired, with a long way to go yet if he is to reach Medicine Hat. Within the hour, however, he sees a road sign for a place to halt again. He buys an ice cream. There is a telephone and he calls New York.

"Patricia? Is that you? Oh, why? I'm on my way to Winnipeg. What do you mean, have I left Banff? Yes, temporarily. It's a long story. I want to talk with Patrick. I know his birthday is in August and now it's June, and I know it's not Sunday but I just want to talk with him. And Alice. And Emily, of course. For God's sake, Patricia. I'm going through a lot. Yes, talk with Patrick." His ice cream is melting. During a pause he quickly bites into it and gulps down the rest as fast as he can.

"Hello. Patrick? My mouth full? I was eating an ice cream. I'll ask Mama to buy you one or you ask Dada, okay? Yes, of course it's me, your own father. Josefu, your Dad, Daddy, what you like calling me. You live with Mama and Dada and then there's me, who am calling you. I just wanted to know what you did today at school. You had a fight with whom? Leroy? I stayed in a big hotel called Leroy's Motel. It's good because you want him to like you? And that's why you fight? Buy him an ice cream? Yes, you can do that too. You say Alice and Emily are watching TV? You don't want to go there because they throw cushions? What is all this? I love you too. Bye."

There is an entombment in the telephone booth, a burying of rights:

Patrick has left him; Alice is busy. Here is another urge Josefu has: not to move. And because he has lost his voice he cannot call anyone else. The sun is suddenly blinding, indifferent to its injurious effect. There is a menacing noise of nearby trucks on the highway to his left, and to his right, the nagging train coaches rumble loudly on the railway line behind this gasoline station, which also sells ice creams. Trapped between sounds, which he cannot identify and appropriate, he fears for his life. He drags himself to the car and drives off, his eyes half closed. Mercifully, the road is almost straight.

13.

"Responsibility should be something nobody welcomes," Josefu says to himself, "Yet so often you extend your hand, palm downwards, and pull responsibility towards you like a luxurious rug."

He begins to worry about the potted plant in the back seat of his car suffering from heat in the drive towards Medicine Hat. Too much effort is needed for an insignificant plant. He could give it as a present to Bill and Mary; would it survive till then? But now it is his responsibility.

He also wonders whether the thermostat in his glasshouse is working and whether he should telephone Martina to have it checked and double-checked. The weather is definitely getting warmer and plants in a glasshouse are unused to variations.

Gabrielle had been so impervious to the need for improvisation before they left the capital; Josefu reckoned it would have been better if she had been vacuum packed until arrival, to be opened in an air-conditioned, fax operated reporting chamber. And it would have needed to have automatic good news air filters, with just enough cracks for her to stay in her job which, after all, was to reflect on poverty.

He had stood on the empty road in front of the Hotel Ibis, reflecting on contract workers like Gabrielle, and her kind of professionalism, devoid of sentimentality, which, who knows, achieves more at lesser cost? Getting on with her was his task in hand. See where she's coming from. Wonderful hair, it must mean something, for Bill, for himself, or even Afrika, who can tell?

Josefu had begun to notice the rapidity with which the sky acquired its shiny night-time appearance, when Afrika came up beside him. "You should not be here alone. You never know what can happen," he said.

"That's not new, Afrika."

"Monsieur Josefu, so you know, but you standing here as if you did not know."

"We must each fulfil our duty."

"And what is your duty, Monsieur Josefu? To look around you, to write in your notebook. But you could be killed very easily, just through some little misunderstanding. That's what happens, these days especially, the misunderstandings."

Josefu looked at Afrika whose head tilted slightly to one side, his eyes down, out of modesty, he thought. "I know it isn't easy for you to tell me that but, Afrika, I do listen to you."

"You listen, Monsieur Josefu. And I know you feel you have a stone in your heart. There is madness here. It is we Rwandans who did it, that's who. Why should you worry so much?"

"I worry, yes. But not just about my job; it's that I don't like being who I am, a human."

Afrika gave him a puzzled look out of the corner of his eye. "But you aren't one of us Rwandans who lost our heads."

"But I'm like any Rwandan, I am! I too can create a lot of disorder, because that is what we humans do: seeding plants and then tearing them out, building cities and pulling them down, running in circles instead of in a straight line when we are thirsty and there is a deep well clearly in front of us."

"I think I understand you, Monsieur Josefu. We see water over there and we run over here. We Rwandans, we do that, but not you who come from far away. You have so many riches; you must have known how to make clever decisions. So you live at a high standard. You know, there were two Norwegians working for a charity and they washed themselves with mineral water. They were so rich they even had this money to choose their water."

Josefu laughed, "And you think that is a sign of intelligence, Afrika?"

He smelt the beer in his own breath and his mind wandered, until Afrika said abruptly:

"I told Père Ambroise about these two, and he was not happy! We had a conversation, Père Ambroise and me. I told him what was in my heart, my fears. There are many fears today for everyone who is

Rwandan, if you are Tutsi or Hutu or from the North or from the South or from Rwanda or from Burundi or from Uganda. Ah yes, or from Tanzania. And from Zaire." Afrika suddenly looked round and said, "We are having a conversation, you and me, in the middle of the road here in Butare. I had wanted to stop your sadness. Would you like to go round the corner, to the place where you can hear the sounds coming from? Listen! It is a place with many Rwandans."

Josefu heard the buzz of talk, of celebration, wafting temptingly across the still evening.

"Shall we go?" asked Afrika.

Josefu quickly glanced backwards and thought it would be simpler not to say anything to his colleagues inside the Hotel Ibis. He tapped Afrika on the shoulder and they walked briskly, their gait increasingly good-humoured.

The Café des Pres Verts was over-spilling with Rwandans revelling.

"Amstel beer from Burundi," said Afrika expertly. "Now I'll tell you who's here," he added.

"I can see there are RPF government officers," said Josefu spiritedly.

"And soldiers. Look, the soldiers have no money but the Burundi Rwandans are paying for their beer. And food, look, look."

Josefu did not look; he preferred not to see where the strong smells were coming from.

In a corner was a family group, several women and children sitting with men of all ages. One of them beckoned to Afrika and Josefu.

Afrika said quickly, "They are saying we should sit with them and they have money. They have sold their house in Burundi and have come back to their Rwanda. They are Tutsis who left before, before, long ago before. They lived there in Burundi after leaving here. They had houses there. Them, they lived well there. But I know, Monsieur Josefu, that not all lived well. Some were very poor there. Ah, Monsieur Josefu, they want to know why I am speaking so long with you."

"Let's not wait. We'll join their table," and Josefu resolutely walked up to them with Afrika following behind. Afrika was telling them he was from America, while Josefu recklessly shook the hand of anyone who offered it, nearly the whole café, including the waiters and the owner. When he finally sat down in a wicker chair, Josefu closed his eyes for an instant, adjusting to the festive air. He had chosen a place next to a grey haired man who had beckoned to him vigorously.

"My name is Auguste," the man said in very clear French, shaking hands again. Josefu noticed he was very tall but frail. "Rwanda is beautiful. It is my country and I am happy to be back. We are having a happy time."

Josefu tried to imagine his father returning to a reformed Uganda he would have approved of, but realised immediately that he would have tolerated little festivity, given the terrible losses the country had endured so recently.

"People have paid a great price for the conditions to be created for your return, don't you think?" whispered Josefu in the man's ear, just loud enough for Afrika to hear too, who was watching anxiously.

The old man rested his hand on Josefu's arm. "There is a lot of misery here, too much misery. So we are told not to show our happiness at being back in our own country. Kagame, you know who he is, he has said that at the weddings of officers in his army they must not serve alcohol. I am a person who has been very lucky. My brother remained here when my family left thirty years ago. We are Tutsi. But by chance this brother came to Burundi with his family three days before the President's plane was shot down, just three days! And this brother's son is here, who is called Dignity, look in that corner." Josefu saw through the crowd a slim man in a pale blue shirt, short-sleeved, spotless. He was clean-shaven and smiled very brightly, listening attentively to some young people of student age. "He is my nephew and he is a full professor of geology. He helped the RPF a little, you know, a bit here, a bit there, because he knew how we suffered, having had to leave our country and live in Burundi. With the RPF, people like us can come back. My nephew, he has now been called by the new government, to look at the University of Butare and to tell them when it can be opened again."

Afrika told Josefu, "They are calling him to come up to us. This time, we will tell him who you are."

Professor Dignity shook their hands keeping the same bright smile, and sitting down he looked Josefu straight in the eye. "You have a visiting card? Your name is what? And where are you from?"

Afrika intervened: "I present to you Monsieur Josefu Mutesa, of Ugandan father and mother, born in England. He has British nationality and a special passport. He lives at present in New York in the United States of America, that's why." He said all this in French. "And his visiting card…" Turning to Josefu , he whispered, "You must give it to him," and smiled back at the young professor.

Josefu came in on cue: "I work for the United Nations but am very concerned about what we have failed to do."

"Some of you are ashamed, yes?" said the professor rapidly, his light brown eyes shining. "You could have respected General Dallaire, given him troops."

"You're right, but we have come here to make enquiries on the spot."

There was such a din in the cafe that Josefu had to shout, making what he said sound pompous and empty. He felt a surge of irritation, which flushed his cheeks. Besides, the odour of burnt meat and other scents began to overwhelm him. Although not as obvious as in Kigali, Josefu was aware of the stubborn reek of death in Butare, which exacerbated the restaurant smells. He was about to rise when Afrika gently held him down by the wrist.

"Listen to the professor, he wants to tell us something," Afrika said soothingly.

"I have made an inspection today of the University of Butare, Messieurs," Dignity said, addressing Afrika and Josefu together. "It is very strange, but although the place had been pillaged, and terrible killings took place, the library is completely intact. And we looked at the rooms of the professors there: even the handles of their doors were stolen, but the books are on their shelves, just as they were before."

"And the National Museum of Butare has been left intact, outside the town," added Auguste.

Josefu buried his head in his hands.

Afrika shook his arm and whispered, "They think they have said something to make you cross." After commenting to the others in Kinyarwanda, he added: "I told them you are very sad about Rwanda. But here there are festivities. They are so happy to be back in Rwanda."

Professor Dignity tapped Josefu's other arm. "You should not judge these people who are feasting," he said, a little irritated.

"It's not that, it's not that," replied Josefu. "It's what we all are capable of; we can recognise something like a shelf of books and leave it intact, because of the thoughts we have when we see them, but we rip out the guts of our fellow human beings for no reason except... our strange thoughts."

"You've lost me there; I'm a geologist," Professor Dignity said smiling again.

Grabbing a freshly opened beer bottle, Josefu said, "Don't worry, I am lost myself," but his heart pounded and Afrika whispered to him that he could see the veins on his temples were beating.

Yet there was also something gratifying for Josefu, to be drinking in the Café des Pres Verts in Butare, among people who looked like him—if only that. After a while, he turned to Afrika and said, "It's a long time since I had news of my two children."

After keeping silent for a while, Afrika said, "I know, because Père Ambroise told me. A misunderstanding with their mother. We also have troubles. And with the war, some of our women went to a lot of different places."

"What are you saying?" asked Professor Dignity, smiling again.

"Monsieur Josefu says it is like being with his family here," said Afrika in French.

Auguste held out another bottle of beer. "It's good beer, it comes from Burundi. We are bringing a lot of things here to Rwanda so that those of us who can afford it can eat and drink. What can we do! We are happy to be here and we can make a good living here, bringing all the produce Rwanda no longer has."

Josefu drank in silence. The fusion of merriment and mourning was disconcerting. His feet had been buried half way into the soil with Hercule only this morning; just a few hours separated him from the hole in the ground and the Café des Pres Verts. He felt he would never walk with ease again, never run, never jump. Now he feared the merrymakers could start dancing any time now. He wished he could close his eyes but with new willpower he tried to focus his gaze on the smoke of a cigarette stub which had failed to be extinguished, acknowledging to himself that momentous events can be so easily crowded out by the minutiae of unreflective living.

A long time passed, perhaps, as the beer was drunk without further comment or control. Afrika finally said, "You are tired, Monsieur Josefu," and began exchanging farewells.

Professor Dignity and Auguste stood up and barked commands, which brought at least a dozen young men out into the street. With this large escort, they walked Josefu and Afrika back to the Hotel Ibis, "For safety," Afrika said gratefully, "These days, you never know."

"Yes, you never know," repeated the young professor who walked close to Josefu. "We will meet again, in Kibuye since there is no more Zone Turquoise, or in New York."

"Please, do keep in touch," said Josefu bowing.

"You suffer for us Rwandans, that's good," said Professor Dignity.

"That's good," repeated Auguste. "Where is your father?"

"He is dead," replied Josefu, suddenly finding it hard to believe.

"May God rest his soul."

After a silence, Afrika said, "We will say Goodnight."

Soon they were in the hotel corridor by their rooms and Afrika continued: "They thought I was a Tutsi, you know. There were two or three Hutu officers there, I recognised them: one has a high rank in the RPF army. Hutus who were already in the opposition and joined the RPF rebels, you know about it. Everyone loves that café. You were surprised by the laughter there tonight, but before in Rwanda often it was like that. It was often very beautiful. Very friendly."

"So why do we humans do what we do, then? It's a question I ask out of habit, but it's so tiring a question because it won't leave me."

"We are all different, Monsieur Josefu, that's what we are, all different."

Josefu suddenly noticed Afrika was very weary; it was as if the leaves of trees, that were centuries old, had fallen on him. "But it's very difficult, Rwanda is difficult," and Josefu detected a few tears in the corners of his eyes, secrets opened by a few bottles of beer.

"You have beautiful soil here, on your hills, and if you push your roots down deep into the earth, you'll find water, and somehow you'll survive." Josefu said, as if repeating words whispered in his ear. Embarrassed now, he shrugged his shoulders.

"You teach us beautiful things," said Afrika, looking away.

"Go and rest," said Josefu, "We'll work things out."

He waited for a moment outside his room, guessing that Bill might be in there with Gabrielle. He heard her voice:

"But they aren't like us, Bill, they are savages. Don't worry, nobody's listening. They never invented anything. In Haiti it's the same; they live on handouts and fight over everything. Hello! We didn't kill anyone in Rwanda; they killed each other. Why do I have to say the same thing?"

For maximum effect, Josefu threw the door open, knowing it was unlocked. Both looked embarrassed but he did not utter a word.

"Where were you? 'Round the corner', we were told, but you went without saying," Bill whispered, sitting on the edge of his bed while Gabrielle perched on the other.

"Somewhere, for, err — hell! — Natives only?" said Gabrielle staring at him.

"I don't have to answer that question," Josefu said as softly as he could.

But Bill panicked and said, "It's late, it's late. Let's all get to bed. It's been a difficult day and Celestin wants to get an early start. He's disappeared, of course, somewhere in this town, but he'll probably be back."

"And sulk a little less," said Gabrielle.

"It's late," Bill repeated. "Let's call it a day."

Josefu did not move. Gabrielle slipped past him and out of the door. Once she was in the corridor, she shouted, "This is a shit hole," and walked noisily away.

"Leave her alone," Bill urged Josefu, "She's stressed out."

Josefu didn't reply. He got into bed in his boxer shorts and closed his eyes, flat on his back, as if he were doing some relaxation exercise in a gym session.

Bill continued to fret, tossing from side to side, then he said: "You're not being fair. I know you're awake."

Josefu sighed, "I'm just not preoccupied with Gabrielle's likes and dislikes or even her human rights, right now."

"You're being sarcastic again, all over again."

"I'm not. Isn't even a savage allowed some sleep?"

"She wasn't talking about you," said Bill wearily.

"I don't even care."

"You're being aggressive," said Bill softly.

"I don't have your Quaker equanimity. Okay? I'm not angry. I just want to sleep. I love you. I love the world. Have I said all you want me to say now?"

"Yeah, yeah. I guess I'm tired too," and Bill gave a slight, reassuring laugh and lay on his side.

Trying to sleep, Josefu was aware that nearby, people were revelling in the adventures of a recently regained homeland while others gaped at their entombed lives and vanished possessions, in cycles and through hoops. In his dream, he slid down a slimy, moss-covered hill into autumn cold and brown decay.

⋮

Josefu shakes his head as he nearly falls asleep at the wheel. He can smell the dank scent of the plant in his car and impatiently seeks out a garage to stop.

With the sign for Suffield, he knows from his memory of a map studied earlier that the far edge of Alberta cannot be too distant now. He notices that the fields on either side of him are amazingly dry and a pale green that is almost sand coloured.

The absence of sound, which contrasts with the din of the Cafe des Pres Verts he has just remembered, should be soothing him, but instead it increases his unease and his car is swaying dangerously. He steadies himself and the wheel, and thinks of his responsibilities, above all to get a message to Martina about the plants in the glasshouse. His awareness of the triviality of his concern irritates him and the car swerves again. As he wearily straightens out and catches his breath, he realises he'll have to stop soon.

"You're getting married, Martina? Say that again?" Josefu asks, when he gets through to her from the booth in a diner.

"That guy I've told you about? It's thanks to you, Josefu, that night, it freed me, it opened me, thanks. Thanks," she chants.

Josefu feels he is at a bus stop, and although he put out his arm to hail the bus down, he is left behind.

"Why aren't you saying anything? Don't worry about the bookshop; he's agreed to live in Banff."

Josefu scratches his eyebrow, then his nose.

"Can't you talk?" asks Martina. "What's wrong? I mean, it was therapy between us, wasn't it? We helped each other."

He still can't talk, but mumbles to himself inaudibly.

"Hey, come on, you can't do this to me. Everybody is so happy for me. I don't understand you sometimes. You can be really hurtful, you know."

"I'm just surprised, it's so fast."

"Well, sure, but you never worked out your feelings for me."

"Did you yourself, Martina?"

"Oh, so you are interested? Look, I'm marrying someone else so it's all in the past now, it's history. But I thanked you just now, and that's why I hoped and prayed, do you hear me, I prayed, that you would call me just so that I could say it."

"I'm glad for you," Josefu says, adding a final greeting as he hangs up.

He never wanted anything from her, but she is part of his world, at its centre, the only world left to him. And now she'd share it with others—a diffusion of focus, which is always too noisy.

His coffee arrives with the colourfully advertised doughnut he ordered. He finds the loud din of the background music not conducive to his startled mood. 'She's not rejected me as a black, surely! But it had never occurred to me to propose to her.' He is irritated with himself for experiencing a sense of rejection. 'Ridiculous.'

He returns to the phone booth and dials Dave's cell phone.

"Hey, Josefu, you've heard the news," Dave exclaims. "Wait a minute, I'll tell these folks I'm busy…I can tell from your voice you've heard. We might at last get the place to ourselves, the bookstore just for you and me."

"Dave, she's staying in Banff. Nothing's changing."

"That's what she says, but with time, who knows. She's been fine, though, and you guess this: she even had a conversation with Liala on her own. She'd always refused before. That's how much things have changed around here. Josefu, come back. We'll run things our way."

"Yes, I see, it's your wanting power that's driving you. But earlier I was thinking about how it was this wanting power which inspired people to organise the killings so meticulously. There's a power in wanting."

"I guess."

"And power was bequeathed, that's the word, bequeathed by the State organisers over to the last wheelbarrow pusher they recruited, who promptly turned executioner, to savour power over life and death. Yes, I can see all that now, I can see so much clearer,"

"You talking holocaust or genocide? I mean Hitler or Rwandans?"

"What difference does it make?" asks Josefu.

"Yeah, we can talk about all these things; I'm Jewish, remember. You see, we'll have more time now, when you come back to Banff. Why did you call Martina anyway? Why didn't you call me first?"

"I needed to tell Martina about checking the thermostat in my glasshouse."

"That's fixed?"

"No it isn't; I didn't get around to telling her. I was surprised how she hadn't pondered, didn't think through her decision. Transistant society, in Banff, in the Western hemisphere, transistant society. It's my own word, as far as I know: not 'transcient' but 'transistant'."

"Yes, very theoretical," Dave remarks.

"Could you ask Martina to check the glasshouse, get the electrician from the museum, the one who did some work in Luxton House recently, I remember him. He should know how to check the thermostat."

"Sometimes I hate you, Josefu, the way you ask Martina for things which I could do myself, because I am your neighbour, but you block me out."

"I showed her how the thermostat worked about a year ago. But I can see your reaction just now! You want territory just for you, and to cultivate it, don't you see? And Dave, for those who do ethnic cleansing, it's all about good plants and the weeds which must be eliminated in that same space, and it's all in the mind."

"Josefu, you've left me out! Martina should not have let you out on the road like that, with all your thoughts! She acts like she's the Earth Goddess but she's impulsive."

"She's fine. I'm fine. I'll call back. Don't forget my thermostat." Josefu hangs up and goes back to gulp down his coffee. Returning to his car, he opens one of several chocolate bars bought at the gas station. Perhaps they will provide him with the stamina to move forward.

⋮

When they rose the next morning in Butare there was a mild smell of decomposing bodies, which mingled with the crisp early air. There had been rain in the night, probably at dawn. Bill had used his satellite phone to call home and Josefu didn't want to hear the news. He too was able to make calls but had nobody except his mother, whose anxiety and plain speaking unnerved him. His new domestic situation accentuated his sense of isolation on the Rwanda mission; his irritation grew. He, who had despised power seekers, hated his own sense of powerlessness because he did not know, and it was so humiliating, where to telephone his own son and daughter. He would easily have assaulted Patricia if she had been around right now in Butare. He took a breath. 'I am here for the sake of Human Rights, everyone's, even my enemy's. And yet I could cause my own damnation in an instant! A biblical parody!"

The son of the owner of Hotel Ibis was out on the terrace with a coffee at an empty table. It looked as if it were part of a routine. 'How strongly people hold on to the set patterns they make in the middle of devastation,' Josefu commented to himself.

Celestin arrived smiling, and it was immediately noticeable that he had been drinking with agreeable companions the previous evening. He even greeted Afrika who told him to sit down to drink tea imported from Uganda.

That did not assuage Josefu's irritability, however, even if he attributed it to lack of decent sleep. He looked out to Butare's empty road and beyond. In his mind's eye, he saw all the rest of the shaken and crushed country whose gardens had to be husbanded and brought back to life. 'But plants don't grow where there's anger,' he thought.

⋮

Josefu stops again, after driving barely half an hour, and buys some cans of coca cola and he drinks one on the spot, standing by the door of the anonymous highroad station, with billboards larger than itself.

"Do you have a telephone?" he asks the drinks seller.

"Round the back," yawns the vendor, who nevertheless stares intensely at Josefu.

"Ellie, I know it's early," Josefu whispers down the phone.

"Josefu, what's the matter? Luckily I'm in a hospital where I can have my own bedside telephone."

"Are you sorry I've called?"

"Don't be silly. It just amazes me."

"Ellie, I'll work things out. And so will you. Everything is going to be okay."

"Do you know who you're talking to, Josefu?"

He smiles; she sounds so much like in their student days. "Yes," he says, but had wanted to reply: 'My own Ellie'.

"Look, I don't want to spoil any of this, but have you worked out why you're saying all this to me? I'm very vulnerable at the moment, you know. I can't play games."

"Don't say that, Ellie! I was always open with you and always shall be. I'm just frightened right now, seeing this thing through, this thing of mine. And you're there, you see. Do you see?" he says, wishing he knew what was urging him on, into her presence on the telephone.

"But do you have any friends, Josefu? I mean out there? I don't really understand what's going on."

"Yes, I have friends." Now he can think again. "It's just that since your first phone call I've wanted to clarify my position, my thoughts."

"About me too? I shouldn't push things but I'd really like to know."

"I'm finding out. But I was speaking to a friend from Banff earlier today, and reprimanded Western society for its trivial attitudes to decision making!"

"Sounds familiar! I wonder if it isn't all some kind of a dream, this phone call, like the after effect of some medication I'm taking or something. God, I must sound cold, don't I?"

"No, not cold. I'm really sorry, you know, if I disturbed you."

"You sound awfully lonely."

"Yes? I shouldn't be, with the friends I've got here. You couldn't wish for better. They have their own lives too, you know. And I've got my task ahead."

"It's a bit of an odd task. Maria said: crossing flat Canadian prairies to see Rwandan hills."

"Something like that."

"Rwanda obviously meant a lot to you."

"I suppose it did. I suppose it does now too. Look, I better go," says Josefu.

"Please take care," Ellie says in a supplicating voice, which stirs him.

"And you rest well. I'll call again if I may."

In an instant the weather has changed and clouds seem to be appearing out of nowhere, pushed by a brisk wind. Josefu rapidly wipes off the prairie insects, which have met their death on his windscreen, and he jumps back into the car, driving onto the TransCanada Highway and nearly breaking the Alberta speed limit in the process.

14

Celestin the driver made an announcement, standing with shoulders back and his arms straight in military fashion, just as they were about to load their overnight bags into the car. He swallowed and took a deep breath and slowly said there was insufficient petrol to take them back to Gitarama and on to Kibuye.

To find your bearings without a map, you had to remember that from Butare you had to drive back towards the capital Kigali and shortly before reaching it, at Gitarama, you turned left and westwards to Kibuye. They would still need spare petrol once they arrived there, until Celestin learned what supplies were available locally. He dismissed Bill's reassurances that UN vehicles would get fuel through its military wing if necessary.

"General Dallaire could tell you how little petrol they had sometimes," he sneered, "In the middle of the crisis."

Everyone was surprised, however, that Celestin was actually engaging in conversation.

"Do you know what happened to him then?" Josefu asked rapidly.

"Even before April, they had to measure their petrol at UNAMIR. I was there, not with UNAMIR but in my old job and we were few Tutsi drivers but I had a good job with the UNDP, they liked my driving," and he gave a little laugh.

This was a new Celestin, they all remarked as he went off. Where had he been last night? Nobody complained at the delay. Even Gabrielle said, "I guess we have to trust him."

"What he says is true, that's what it is," said Afrika with authority.

"Shall we go for a walk then, look around Butare?" Bill suggested.

"Oh no," Gabrielle said, "No more dead bodies lurking in the alleyways. Let's stay safe."

Afrika looked around, greeted an armed guard who stood in a corner, and sat between Josefu and Bill on the terrace. "Ah, we are so tired, you know," he said spontaneously.

"We should be able to rest when we get to Kibuye," said Bill.

"No, I meant to say it is us, the Rwandans, who are tired, that's what we are. You see, you come here now and think our troubles started in April of this year. But that is not true. Those bones that Père Ambroise buried for the women, remember Beatrice? After the river with the cadavers, remember? They were not from the killings of April to July, not all of them, because they would not be in that state of dryness yet. They would still have had flesh on them. Some of them were from a mass killing long ago. Then they added the more recent bodies, those women did. They cried in their grief and some people cleaned the bones so that they would all be the same, bodies killed long ago and those killed later. It's like that. If you go to the hills, you will hear how tired we are, all the population, Hutu or Tutsi, it's the same. We're all tired."

Bill whispered a translation for Gabrielle, who immediately said, in English, "Wait a minute. How many people were not too tired to kill anyway? Bill told me and I read some, about what happened. Killing was hard work, and they weren't too tired for it."

Afrika looked embarrassed, when Bill hesitantly relayed it to him in French.

"Continue what you were saying," said Josefu pointedly to Afrika in a clear voice.

"Stop telling him what to do, can't you see he doesn't want to speak, it's bugging him," said Gabrielle.

Josefu ignored her and repeated himself, this time nodding his head in emphasis.

Afrika looked into his eyes seeking help and then sighed, looking downwards. "Some people killed, maybe, to stop the tiredness, to change things."

"Is that an excuse?" asked Gabrielle.

There was silence. Bill said, turning away, "Perhaps we shouldn't talk about all this, first thing in the morning."

Yet Afrika continued, "We are tired in Rwanda. We had the revolutions in all those dates, you know, when the Belgians… Did you know it was them who brought identity cards to Rwanda with Hutu and Tutsi written on them? The Belgians are called our colonials. While they were still here in 1959 those Tutsis ran away, houses burned here, houses burned there, on all the hills. And in the towns also. The Belgians turned their faces away, and they were glad to see our King go – the King of all of us go, and the Tutsis go. The Belgians said of the Tutsis, when they went to Uganda : 'Let them go to the English and leave us in peace.' There was supposed to be a fête for us Rwandans when our country had independence, and did it happen like that?" Afrika asked rhetorically. "Eeeh, many houses were burned. Then one president, Kayibanda, stood up and people were killed and houses burned. Then another president came and stood up and people were killed and houses burned, this one Habyarimana, our president who died in the plane."

"Wait right there," said Bill, "So I can tell Gabrielle in English."

Josefu reflected on Bill's great sense of fairness for which he even risked drying up a conversation.

"Eeeh…Our houses," Afrika said, trying to remember where he had stopped, "You know women: they put a little thing here, a little thing there, they clean, they cover with cloths, they make photos smile on the walls. In the towns and in the villages, everywhere. And if you are on the hills in the huts, it is the same thing, believe me, each person has their things, each woman cleans their home and puts something in it, some decoration. And children, in their home, even when it is a one room hut, they have their hidden places to hide their treasures. Yes, and the women. Even when there are no roads, just the banana trees outside their huts, people sometimes have flowers growing." Turning to Josefu, he added: "You plant and you look. One leaf comes up and you look. Then a little bud and you look. Then there is a flower and you look and you wait while it lives. Yes, you see poor people on the hills with one flower which they look at. All that and then…people come and burn your house. Eeeh, the poor peasants on the hills! It is frightening for people who have no more house."

Having heard what he had said, Gabrielle remarked, "He should work for Mrs. Ogata, head of UNHCR, yeah, and tell it to the world."

"Is that all you have to say?" said Josefu furiously.

Bill said to him, "Don't start. It's early morning still. This conversation was a mistake."

"I have a job to do," said Gabrielle.

"We all do, and one of them is to listen," retorted Josefu. "You know, that is one of the problems we have: so many of us doing our job without listening. We might as well work from home. Most of the time we would do better to leave places untouched rather than do our jobs, as you say. Do you know, with our charity donations we actually fed the warmongers in Ethiopia! That was the paradox of doing our job and refusing to listen when remarks were made about the side effects our supplies were having."

"I embarrassed you, it didn't fit, so you want to change the subject," said Gabrielle.

Afrika started to rise, "I said something that Madame became angry about and my father says I should not speak so much. But it is the defect of taxi drivers, we speak too much, that is what we do, too much."

"This is ridiculous," said Josefu, "She wasn't talking about you, just whatever goes through her own head." Bill did not translate it.

After a moment watching Josefu, Afrika decided to resume: "We are very confused, we Rwandans. And in 1990 with the war starting, every day people were being killed. People who did it said everyone was killed because they did it too: 'Here they did it, they. There they did it, they.' The fear was everywhere, like rain falling on the hills. Eeeh, our poor hills, that is what they were, all the hills, our poor hills, our poor country. And then all the guns were given out to people in our villages to make fear, to obey the orders to make fear, you know, to create fear. And each used the guns for themselves, you know. I'm speaking too much."

"Continue," said Josefu sharply. Bill whispered the English to Gabrielle.

"One of them would like a woman for the night, yes a Hutu woman even, no difference, and he used his gun. It was the first fear for all the people who had sisters, or daughters. All the hills were tired."

"Afrika, do you think," said Josefu in a low voice, "There was hope for all those who were tired that if they became killers themselves, there would be calm again?"

"Hope, Monsieur Josefu? That there would be order again once and forever? Yes, they thought that there would be a better world, that is what there would be."

And then Afrika beat the table with both fists and put them back quietly on his lap. He said: "But those who killed, they killed because they were killers."

"They were killers?" Josefu repeated softly, folding his hands. He noticed several of his nails were too long. Bill listened without translating.

Afrika said, "People who kill are killers. There are those who did not kill."

"Before it happened, could you tell the difference?" asked Josefu.

"Yes, perhaps I could."

"Even among children?"

"Perhaps I could," Afrika repeated.

"Do you think people are born like that?"

"No, Père Ambroise says they are not. I never spoke so much with a priest before, and I say what he says."

"Is it good, what he says?"

"It is good. Sometimes you have to lie, but he does not lie very much. Eeeh, you know, he is very tired also. We are all very tired, here and here and here," Afrika said, touching his heart and head and arms and legs.

Celestin came just then and beamed a victorious smile at all present, even at Afrika. "I have found petrol. A Burundi man is selling it."

He looked at Bill and then at Josefu, to whom he put out his hand, "Give me the money."

"Give it, give it, Josefu, we'll work it out later," said Bill anxiously as Josefu discreetly did so.

Afrika sat hunched on a chair, staring ahead, muttering that everyone was tired.

Josefu's eyes filled with tears when he met Afrika' s gaze.

This did not go unnoticed by Bill who said, "Careful Josefu, or you'll crack up."

⋮

A few raindrops fall on the windscreen of Josefu's silver car. The telephone lines, the pylons, the insect sprayers and an abandoned wooden house cut into the sweep of the prairies and sky. Josefu himself, he reflects, would have otherwise melted into oblivion. His shoulders ache. He mourns for all the tired of spirit. As he cries, removing his now redundant sunglasses, he imagines Ellie as a white rock on a windswept, winter beach and that he could lay his head on that rock uncomfortably but thankfully. His thoughts wander again towards the encroaching grey clouds, advancing like waves on a high tide. He is approaching Medicine Hat and decides to stop there and go no further.

"People kill because they are killers," he thinks, repeating Afrika's words. "Is that a saving grace for us here, a standard to use for separating the sheep from the goats? That's bullshit, as Gabrielle would have said, but anyway, it isn't what Afrika meant." Now he realises, though, that on that point he had never properly understood him. "But, of course, it is the real issue, for knowing what happened in Rwanda or, for that matter, any genocide."

In his student days, naming unfathomable questions had been a pastime delightful as an excuse for sighing and getting drunk or stoned. Ellie had been bad company then with her stringent, matter of fact comments, which filled that otherwise enticing void. Now he could ask her opinion again; this is not an intellectual leisure pursuit, and she has a place in his life, so where is another phone booth? He pulls back and reflects on his own trivial approach to a relationship, the very behaviour he had criticised in Martina. For the first time in that context, his mind wanders to his former wife Patricia, aware that until now he had avoided making any appraisal of their interaction.

The rain is becoming heavier.

Patricia his wife had been too combative, he realises, for him to have wished to discuss the issues which really interested him. Perhaps it ran in her family, that they all induced his unwillingness to exchange ideas, or to debate, or to tease. She had reproached him for not embracing her large family in the way she expected. Some of the summer barbecues in Albany had brought fifteen or twenty relatives together, and all had greeted him as warmly as they did each other. He had tried to imitate their gestures but could not change how he spoke; and sound had more bearing than appearance. To give special significance to their sharing the same skin colour would have been unprincipled, anyway. But again the 'coconut' taunt, from his student days, returned and set him shamefully apart. He never had nightlong discussions with any of them, nothing that could have brought them closer. They had been thoughtfully silent, like both Patricia's parents, or else had argued so forcefully that Josefu always pulled back.

And suddenly, it hits him now like a rainstorm—he had had a spectator's attitude, yes, at all those barbecues where Patricia had tried so hard to impress him. He had been a spectator and he had remained consistently, heartlessly aloof. From his very first encounter, he was filled with a sense of unreality. The men of his age group reminded him exactly of the Black American basketball heroes of his youth—the names, like Wilt Chamberlain and Oscar Robinson and Karim Abdul Jabbar, and Bill Russell, and Julius Erving—such a collage of posters on his school locker door. These were the band of heroes he begged his father to embrace as his own people even if they were not Ugandan.

His father would reply: "How can I if I don't know them?"

And there was Maria to thank forever and ever when she brought him a special basketball vest from New York for his fourteenth birthday, and all that and all that! Josefu is breathless now. Then his mind returns with a jolt to Patricia.

Her young relatives talked exactly like his sporting idols. But it was this dreamlike quality itself that turned their barbecues into a distant spectacle for him. Welcoming, warm, self-sufficient, Black American weekend get-togethers, where he should have embraced their familiarity, he instead retreated into an observation tower. Cringing with remorse now, he wonders how he could have been like that! Patricia had watched anxiously, hoping he would merge into her world. Instead, he never expressed any affection towards either the people or the habits she embraced, but instead he had stepped aside and watched them.

How clearly he sees himself now as he drives in the flat landscape.

He had definitely been so awe struck that he had not allowed himself any familiarity, but why? Was it perhaps because these young men had struggled out of their burdened history to create a hero's world? In comparison, he himself had done nothing; he had not even fought against colonialism like other Ugandans, or for a better government for themselves. He was nobody at all and, for that not to be discovered, he had treated Patricia's gatherings as if they, and not he, lacked reality. So he had convinced himself that there was no need to relate to a dream show, whatever its proximity. The car swerves as he feels his shame.

'Poor Patricia,' he thinks, 'I never really tried, nor let their voices reach me. But I lowered their sounds, like turning down the volume with a knob to watch silent TV instead. I indulged myself, by keeping from them the same distance as a cinema seat from the screen, to be a better spectator. How deeply insulting, the frustration I must have caused them! That's how I wounded Patricia. Our marriage died in the space I kept between her family and me. Fuck! Hell! Oh hell, letting our family die with my hands behind my back instead of clasping theirs. I breathed so thinly through my nostrils then, I stood so damn still. Fuck! And my own two children now, torn in all directions, also fading slowly. I myself caused it.

And where in the hell was Afrika, then? Where was his gentleness?'

Josefu wants to leave the highway, signalling rapidly. He could take the car into a ditch, but he does not deserve an easy death, one not long enough to be painful. "All hell's broken loose and there's probably much more to regret in that cracked earthenware container I have, full of worms. I myself have dug them out, one by one, from the loose soil of my life's path."

While finding a roadside turnout, he reflects that he might never make it to Medicine Hat, never, although he had passed a sign saying: 'Welcome to the Gas City' and another saying 'Great Food in Two Minutes'. He would tell Gulshan about that, and she would tell her husband, telling and telling. Good food should be fresh and so it takes longer than two minutes to cook. And here is a tip: a real oven brings out the flavours more subtly when you reheat pre-frozen food than when you use a microwave oven. How many of these packs had he left in his freezer? He'd have to check somehow.

As he brings the car to a halt, Josefu recognises how trivial thoughts are like the insects on your windscreen, which mar every idea you hold of a clear view. Integral to the environment you have entered, however, insects have as equal a right to existence as the spectacle you wish to see through the glass.

Perhaps the reason why Mankind continues to survive, despite the plagues of single vision and predatory willpower that swept across centuries and landscapes, is because the crumbs of incidental, trivial thought provide that nourishment which more substantial ideas have destroyed.

⋮

Out of the narrow ditch that forms a line in the flat, brown expanse along the edge of the small slip road, where Josefu sits with his head down, appears a young seventeen-year-old boy. He is tall, black, and characteristically lean for his age. He wears a white, ragged tee shirt, khaki coloured shorts and trainer shoes which, although soiled, are neatly tied with a double bow. He looks expectantly at Josefu who says to him, with a pounding heartbeat, "But why Canada? Why not somewhere in Africa?"

"But you know me, Monsieur Josefu, you know me," he answers reproachfully.

"Ah, you are from Rwanda; it's only there they called me that," he replies.

"Yes, I am a Tutsi in Rwanda. But from my hill I went to Kigali, to my aunt there and I saw television and I saw the basketball players from America and I learned their names on that television. They are: Shaquille O'Neill, Michael Jordan, Charles Barclay, David Robinson, Larry Johnson, Karl Malone—isn't that a lot of names? And then I got my shoes. I had worn flip-flops always, always. Then I got my shoes, my basketball shoes, des basquettes, you know which ones, Monsieur Josefu. I bought them in the market after I carried water for the neighbour in my village every day, every day and every day. Mummy said I could keep the money in her special rag and then I went to buy the shoes. They had two holes, look, one here by that toe, and one here by this toe, but they had all the laces and they were long laces. So I had my basketball shoes. I had no ball and no basket on my hill, but I jumped and jumped and went higher and higher, jumping with my friends. There was the son of Tharcisse, the one who led the team that killed me. His son could not jump as high as I could. He could not remember the players' names like I had seen on television. I knew all the names. Please Monsieur Josefu, remember I told you that and the names were right, please, please."

Josefu shakes his head vigorously to stay dry eyed, but loses his voice. Finally he murmurs, "Of course, Son, all the names are dead right."

"You know my story, you know how I went to look for my little brother who was with our cows, not knowing he had already returned. Then I found a tall tree and I jumped very high in my new shoes and so I was late coming home. That was the problem, I was late. Ours was the first house in the row of houses, and that was the other problem. I didn't see what had happened in our village. Just as I called my Mummy when I found my home empty, I heard Tharcisse's son cry out, "There he is, Ignatius, I knew we'd find him," and they came, the Interahamwe I did not know, and other boys I knew from my hill."

The youth continues: "I called 'Hey, where's everybody?' Did you know it, Monsieur Josefu?"

"No, I didn't know," he replies, tightly shutting his eyes.

"In one go, they came at me. I was afraid and shouted for my father. But you know they had all been taken away, all my family, towards the church, except that I saw my neighbour's child dead on the ground by the first banana tree on the right side of my house. Then I was even more afraid, and I asked them what they wanted me to do. That is when that boy who took one of our chickens a long time ago came towards me. I was about to fight him when several others took my arms and broke them. It hurt terribly and I wanted to cry. I asked why they were doing this but there were too many of them. Together with the son of Tharcisse, they broke both my ankles and then took my shoes. Then he returned and cut my legs off below my knees, hacking and hacking with an axe. When they cut my head off with a machete I did not feel anything any more. I heard them blaming each other because the blood I had caused meant that our yard would have to be cleaned before their people could use our house, as was their plan.

A neighbour, a girl called Aline, another Tutsi, was dragged towards me. She was only small, perhaps like my brother who had just started school, and she was screaming and her urine had gone down her dress. She was told to pick up my feet and my arms and take them to our latrine. They hit her head and she obeyed. One boy who was a really good runner when we ran races, from the other side of our village, whom I saw nearly every day, Monsieur Josefu, he was there and he was told to carry my head. He started to cough and someone I didn't know who might have been from a town I do not know, one of those Interahamwe, he picked up my head instead and then my body was quite heavy so two of them threw it into our latrine. Then they took Aline and cut her neck so she was dead in one blow. One of the men was older and he did it very quickly, he knew how. Aline's body was thrown on top of mine into our latrine. Then it was quiet. Then she and I decided what to do. Why don't you use your shirt to wipe your nose, Monsieur Josefu? You are crying but you aren't afraid, isn't that so? I was very, very afraid when it happened, my end. It was the pain in my first arm that hurt most, but not as much as being afraid. I was old by then and I was ashamed that I showed some fear."

"Why do I know you?" asks Josefu.

"Because my mother was Marie Immaculée."

⋮

Just as Josefu winces and hoarsely shouts out the name he's just heard, rain comes pelting down onto the prairies. The effect on him is instantaneous: he sits completely still, conscious nobody else is there now, and that he shouldn't move until he is soaked through. He feels the tautness of the stitches above his temple and wishes to pull them out. He wants to shed some blood. Close by the ditch he notices an abandoned metal hook, probably from a farm implement. As he is about to rise to reach it, Joe Swift's voice says from behind him, "Don't touch!"

Josefu slowly uses both arms to squeeze his scalp, despite his wound, trying to head off the apparitions, and he draws up his knees. "Great God," he repeats several times, "This is such bad news."

The sound of the busy rain, though, slowly begins to provide an increasingly companionable presence. He notices the clarity in the strength of this downpour. "And I acknowledge, Joe Swift, that I am in your domain right now. But why do you bother talking to me in Keller Foods supermarket or here in the plains? I'm not even Canadian. Oh my God, is anyone else like me?"

He raises his head and sees walking along the horizon the stooped figure of General Dallaire, who begins to mingle with the rain, growing larger till he fills the firmament.

⋮

Josefu returns to his car. He is cold, shivering, and he must urgently push ahead. Driving past gas pipes and reservoirs, he knows eventually he is sure to reach Medicine Hat, an industrial oasis that waits stoically in a slight valley. He had noticed, just before, that a few slopes broke up the level fields, which till then had met the thundering sky in an unbroken line.

⋮

Glancing at his dashboard, he recalls his first helicopter ride over Rwanda. Earlier, he and his team had been going by car from Butare towards Kibuye, the heat unusually strong. They had already turned into the road off Gitarama, the surface pock marked but relatively smooth. It had been macadamised through the privilege of leading towards the previous president's home town. Dramatically, radio contact was made with the car. Celestin immediately stopped and beckoned to Bill. As Josefu translated from the English for Afrika and Celestin, they learned from Bill that they were to return to Kigali because some unexploded mines had been discovered on their route. General Tousignant was adamant that these orders be respected and they would rendezvous with a helicopter, kept back especially for their benefit, on its way to the former Zone Turquoise where Kibuye was located. The General was aware of Mr. Mutesa's reluctance but unless they wanted to delay their mission by a week, a helicopter ride was the only way to reach their destination. "But we're starving," said Gabrielle, interrupting a torrent of discontent voiced by Celestin as he turned the car, pulling his cap lower to shade his eyes from the sun.

"Now, you don't know General Tousignant," said Bill mischievously. "You don't know what he has given us," he added, requesting that they stop when a new government military patrol straddled onto the road. "Ask them if they can provide some firewood and protection while we heat the bottled water we have here," he told Afrika.

"Bill 's the Boy Scout forever," said Gabrielle.

"And it's commendable," said Josefu emphatically, as he slipped a few one dollar bills into Afrika's hand for the soldiers.

There were four of them and they all spoke English. "From Uganda," sighed Afrika, exchanging a meaningful glance with Celestin.

Given that there were likely to be few vehicles, if any, and in order to avoid other dangers, within minutes a little camp fire was lit right on the tarmac. Bill excitedly poured bottled water into a canister, which he proceeded to heat with gleeful precision, holding it with a wooden stick. After a while, he asked Josefu to take over. Afrika and Celestin watched on, bemused and silent. The soldiers had taken up their positions, to guard them with rifles cocked and ready.

"I wondered what you had been sneaking into the car," said Josefu with bonhomie, when with great care Bill opened a neat cardboard box.

He produced, with the flare of a magician, five vacuum packed US Army meals. He remarked that the two Chile con Carne were for Afrika and Celestin, because Tousignant's aide de camp thought they would like them best. "They think of everything, my Canadians," he said proudly.

"Bullshit," said Gabrielle. "Anyway, it's from my country, not yours," she added laughing.

Uncontrollably, Josefu began to shake.

"What's wrong?" she asked, faking patience.

"My former wife's favourite word, 'bullshit', and I don't like it," he said.

"For Christ's sake don't spoil the fun. This is America, you know," she replied, shrugging her shoulders conspicuously.

"Stop, you two," said Bill. Briskly grabbing the stick from Josefu, "I resent you for this," he whispered.

Gabrielle rummaged in her luggage and shouted, "I'll let it pass, just this time, fuck you, Josefu, because you're crazy. Anyway, I've got the best in town here," and she waved with both hands a heavy, outsized bottle of Jack Daniels.

All the men began to laugh, Afrika and Celestin because of her dancing, Josefu and Bill at the incongruity of the whole event on the eroded tarmac, near the edge of Gitarama.

Josefu said ruefully, "Well done Gabrielle. The best in town."

"The way you speak, Josefu, is unforgettable. So far, in this whole trip, the one thing I'll always remember is that voice of yours. It's deep like Africans and Afro- Americans have, with something soft too. But your British accent, it's so unreal, so like something out of a movie."

"Is that a compliment?" Josefu asked, and turning to Celestin, he said, "I hope you like this food from the American Army of the United States." He did not say the supplies were remnants from Operation Restore Hope in Somalia. Nor did he say that the US led mission in Somalia had failed, and that it was their key reason, though flawed, for not intervening in Rwanda, the key reason.

"We eat simply here, and before we did not think food was very important," said Celestin. "We Rwandans are not like our neighbours". The rest all listened, surprised to hear him again in conversation. "In the old days," he continued," If a man had guests they would drink beer, but he would never eat before them, or they with him. So his wife would call and say a child was being naughty, you know, needing discipline." He paused for breath. "He'd rush away, quickly swallow his food and return, complaining about the children," he laughed. "Or he'd even pretend he was going to the toilet, but never talk about eating. That was a long time ago, even before the Belgians. Do you know, my grandfather was a Tutsi who said he was surprised to see these Whites eating with strangers. He thought it best to do it in private."

Bill indicated they should sit in a row and he placed a tin foil dish before each of them with a plastic white spoon and fork. Nobody spoke as they ate, as if it would break a spell.

Finally, it was Afrika, when they had all finished, who said first, "How good it would have been if Père Ambroise were here with us."

"He sees people, many people," said Celestin.

"We can't visit him now in Kigali," said Josefu. "We are going straight to the airport without stopping."

"You're resigned to the helicopter flight now, aren't you," Bill affirmed wearily, talking to him in English

"No harm done in having attempted this journey by road," said Josefu, "At least we saved Amandine."

"But not her brother," said Afrika, when Josefu translated.

"Dallaire had plans to save many people," said Celestin.

"Do you want me to comment on that?" Josefu said, taken aback.

"Dallaire did not trust his drivers," Celestin volunteered. "Those murderers, those murderers," he now said with both hands off the wheel, "The government's army killed many Belgian soldiers, to frighten all the whites so as to make them leave. Dallaire passed one of the Belgians in his car as he was dying, but his driver would not stop. Everyone was in fear. But if this soldier had been saved, the whites would have stayed. So Dallaire, that is what they say, what we drivers say, declared that he would drive himself and never have a driver again. But by then it was too late because nearly all the white soldiers, of UNAMIR, left the country as the killers had planned, and only Dallaire remained with a few soldiers, who were from those countries that had no money, and who would not fight. He knew all that and so he drove his car himself."

"Yes," said Afrika, "That's what we drivers say, we who know Kigali, who know our country, who saw things that Dallaire had to do." And louder still, "Everything Celestin has just said is true. He is very right about it."

Celestin looked rapidly in the rear view mirror to see Afrika's face and then seemed reassured.

When Gabrielle heard what had been said, she commented, "There may be other explanations. Generals are usually individualistic and self-reliant, or they wouldn't be where they'd got. That's what my Dad said, and he should know. He was Army. Tell Afrika, tell Celestin, about my Dad."

Josefu conveyed the contents of her remarks word for word. Time was passing rapidly and they were soon approaching Kigali. He preferred to look away from the window, and rested his eyes on Gabrielle's thick hair. She sat directly in front of him and he could almost touch it with his nose if he leaned forward. Suddenly, he longed for the elusive woman he had met by the swimming pool at Hotel Mille Collines and as he closed his eyes, he felt her presence as strongly as if it were telepathy. He knew for certain, however, that he would never see her again. As he pondered at length and in silence, he must have dozed off, since next he abruptly heard Celestin announcing that they had reached the place where the helicopter was waiting. Celestin drove off rapidly and mysteriously as soon as they had unloaded their belongings.

A group of Canadian soldiers rushed them onto the aircraft, one of them giving a note to Josefu from the commander of the British forces who were based near the stadium. As he read the invitation to join him when he was next in town, and that there was an officer who had been at Stowe School too, who hoped to see him, Josefu's cheeks flushed enjoyably. He had not expected that his Britishness would be acknowledged in this way and for a reason he was hard pressed to explain to himself, it was very pleasing.

He felt uncomfortable in the helicopter, however, at being so entangled in advanced technology travelling over the African continent, even more so in this airborne mode of transport than in the four-wheel drive jeep. That sentiment of his, he recognised, was the romanticism which had condemned him in Uganda and set him apart from his relatives and those who shared his origins. It was something he now was helplessly unable to correct.

The noise of the helicopter, even with earphones, was damning, but he looked out at the Rwandan hills and although realising it was with the passion of an adolescent, he wept at their beauty as for a betrothed, he thought, in all her finery and whose hand he was denied.

⋮

Having resolved, for safety's sake, to stop over in Medicine Hat, one large signpost catches Josefu's eye among the myriad that impose their presence with brash exuberance that is 'typical of North American landscapes', he tells himself. It is a notice for the Imperial Hotel in Medicine Hat and, to him, it sounds familiar and safe. Names may count for little, but he easily finds the large building not too far from where he had turned off and has no hesitation in bringing his vehicle to a halt.

"I got caught in the storm," he says to the female receptionist, thin and tall in a black suit who keeps a deadpan expression. "I'm sorry I'm wet. Can I have a room, a single room, or a suite, I don't care, for one night. Or perhaps two," he adds wearily.

Keeping her eyes down, she says, "Credit card?"

"Yes, of course. Do you have a room then?" he asks, noticing her eyes were now fixed on his pink fingernails as he takes out his soft leather wallet. Each receptionist had been different. What a journey!

She lists all the considerable amenities the hotel possesses, including an indoor dining room, which interests him most. He asks her again whether there are any vacancies.

"We've got lots of rooms," she says at last. "What do you want?"

"A room away from all the noise, if possible. I'm on my own, but I don't mind what I have. A suite if that is quietest."

"You don't need a suite for that. I'll give you a good room, and you can look out of the window during the day. Are you Jamaican?"

"No, my parents were Ugandan. African. I was born in Great Britain."

"I thought your accent was a bit different, interesting. I went to university in Edmonton, our capital, you know? And I was going to travel to Africa, but I didn't because of my boyfriend. Did I do the right thing, who knows?" She looks up at last.

"No, you didn't," replies Josefu, "But it is never too late to mend mistakes."

"Do you really think so?"

"Where would you like to go?"

"I'd like to go where it's safe and where I'm needed. I'd like it to be Africa, not India or somewhere else that is poor."

"That is poor? Well, you have a point. Have you heard of Rwanda?"

"Sort of. Isn't that where that Canadian General was? He had some kind of syndrome after being there? I think I saw that on TV last year."

"General Dallaire? Last year in the year 2000?" says Josefu excitedly.

"I think that is the name. I remember that it was a country in Africa. There are some things I don't forget. Sorry, Sir, I better help you with your room." She looks at the card he filled in. "Mr. Mutesa, that's a nice name and it is very African. Well, here is your key and have a nice day." She goes into another room, for whatever reason, perhaps to the telephone. On this journey, attention reserved for him alone—he has almost forgotten the experience—is meted out in small measure only, something he begins to regret.

Josefu looks around and decides to fetch his luggage from the car. He enters his room, with white walls, maroon upholstery and curtains, and with a weary déjà vu sensation. 'This has been my choice,' he reminds himself, 'And so I have no grounds for complaint about any aspect of my travels,' and he salutes the television set, military style.

He sits down on the large bed and closes his eyes while running a hand along the smooth bedspread. And yet his disquiet does not leave him. Is it because there seems to be no sound coming from elsewhere in the hotel? Purposefully, he stands up and slips out of his still wet clothes. He is relieved to find he has some cotton pyjamas with him. He would order food up to the room, a bit later.

Now he gets into the bed, attempting to tuck himself in like a child. And then it appears clearly against the opposite wall, distant like on a postcard, but resounding with a low and persistent hum, trembling with the majesty of blue colour and the grace of its serene outline: Lake Kivu as he had seen it for the very first time.

V   THE LAKE

15.

It occurred two mornings after their arrival, when they were looking for suitable accommodation. Unlike the others who had glimpsed it from the air, Josefu had closed his eyes when the helicopter landed in Kibuye and had kept his head down until they arrived, in a military jeep, at their shelter for the first few nights. Then it happened:

Lake Kivu came into Josefu's sight.

It was, without hesitation, the woman of his life: he was winded, smacked on the lips, eyes fixed and, even, a hardening in his trousers. Somewhere, in the back of his mind, he recognised a similarity with the first time he saw Ellie in the sports hall or when Patricia first smiled at him in the Geneva cafeteria, events now nameless but forever immobile.

The lake was dressed in the shimmering blue of royalty, of such intensity that it stopped you in your tracks. But you couldn't bow to pay homage, because its contours moved like those of a maiden dancer. He held both his hands to his head and stopped himself reaching out to temptation. Large local trees were studded like casual jewels along the banks. And there, like a discarded veil, in the middle of what was visible of this immense body of water, lay Ijwi Island, beckoning to be touched.

Never had he seen a lake like this. He stopped hearing sound; surrendering his will and powers to observe, he yielded to its beauty. Perhaps he had reached his destination, an aqueous gate with his own nameplate. One step forward into the water and his union would be consummated. Josefu was close to delirium; he was clearly aware of it.

The next moment though, he began to recoil, at first without concious thought but then with anger and disgust; he let out such a strong, low pitched cry that Afrika ran up to him, Gabrielle following behind.

"This lake is a liar, a beautiful cheat," he shouted. "There is no serenity, it is full of murdered people and it smells."

"Monsieur Josefu!" Afrika exclaimed, to whom Josefu repeated his words in French.

But Josefu continued: "And it doesn't take much imagination to tell that over a hundred thousand bodies have been thrown into Lake Kivu." He was almost yelling. "Reports are usually much higher than that, you know," he added, in both languages. "But look at it! More of a visual deception could not be conceived, by Nature or by whomever," he spat.

"No, Monsieur Josefu, this lake is our lake, of Rwanda, of Zaire-Congo, which God gave us to enjoy, but we humans abused our wealth here."

"The lake should not hide our crimes like that," said Josefu, "But this one does with its miraculous allure. It is too terrible."

"Too terrible," Afrika repeated, at once appearing frightened by Josefu's shouting.

Bill shook his head. He too looked at the lake, his shoulders stooped, cowering. Then he remarked, "You're right, Josefu, we must know what's there. When we get closer, the traces of all those massacres will still be there for us to see, we already know that... And it's a question of time before they disappear."

"A question of time," Afrika repeated.

"Is that so?" Josefu said, "In time, some kind of deep water oblivion?"

"What a mission for a lake, though," Bill remarked, "to bring about that kind of oblivion, what an assignment!" Then he added calmly, "I understand your thinking, Josefu."

"I hate this place," said Gabrielle. "Josefu's right, it hides too much."

He rose to that, however, and hissed, "It's only here at this lake; it's only here that Nature has joined in the task of hiding it all away, like Bill said." The others drew back a little. "Everywhere else, the dead were left out in the open, all those bodies in the roadside that you complain about in the towns, Gabrielle. Do you know why we're here, Bill and I? The whole point of our mission is for rules to be drawn up, some sort of agenda, to punish such impunity. It's a new word, 'impunity', with a new meaning from Rwanda. Did you know that? Gabrielle? Bill?" He paused. "And that is what must be punished, the very impunity of the killers, their entire lack of shame, who made no effort to hide their crimes."

"So you think Hitler did better? Because his people hid their murders better, were more discreet?" asked Bill.

"Quiet!" replied Josefu.

The thin surface on the lake of the water, now tinged with silver, and with its alluring, blue sheen, caught his attention again. It inconspicuously separated the broken spectacle of grey and solemn, floating cadavers away from the closer, luxurious serenity for tourist appeal. A quiet shift of focus.

By now the group had walked nearer to the shore, by the former Kibuye guesthouse, a diving board still visible. The lakeside had long been a playground for the aid workers and staff of accredited donor agencies. Priests and nuns came here too, relaxing from their expatriate, daily toil. Rwanda had been judged a success story. Perhaps they had believed God's reward was the creation of this lake, and that His gift was in anticipation of a final blessing.

"What nonsense, what stupidity," Josefu said aloud, again in both French and English. He saw the others' puzzled expression. "Sorry, I meant my own thoughts," he explained, almost managing a smile, "Sometimes they wander. And sometimes they're stupid." Turning to Bill he said, "I'll talk to you later."

"You're still young, you know," Bill said to Josefu. "You're in your late thirties and I'm nearly twenty years on. Sometimes it makes a difference."

Josefu was angry again. "Why do you always change the subject?

Whom are you being fair to now?"

"You should calm down, you've got a job to do," and Bill walked away.

Josefu vowed he would never look at the lake again, a promise he knew he would not keep.

⋮

It had not been on the day of their arrival that they went to see their surroundings and the shores of the lake bordering part of Kibuye. If they had, then Josefu might never have completed the preliminary paperwork and other administrative necessities, with all the accompanying ponderings he could never resist and which slowed him down.

A few days after reaching Kibuye he was holding the registration papers of his team while he stood by a broken window against the fading light, on the ground floor of their stopgap office. He was preparing them to present at the makeshift prefecture. This was an act of faith, since the former Zone Turquoise was still in such a transitional state that the new government was little more than symbolic. There was hardly anyone around in the local administration whenever he went to look. From the first day, however, Bill next door composed dispatches; he tried to tame the precarious nature of their mission in a situation of moving sands. Josefu was helping him; he read over and over again the spelling on the list.

There was Afrika Ndemeyimana, whose name apparently meant 'I accept God'. It was pronounced without the 'd' which, in the great intricacies of the Rwandans' language, remained silent. Celestin Karangwa's name was there too. The surname meant nothing at all or it could be 'The Indicator'. It was now difficult to imagine how they had managed without transport before his arrival in Kibuye. When he came as soon as the mines on the road had been cleared, he was greeted like a long lost ally. He never spoke much, but his aloofness had disappeared for good. Then there was the cook and domestic chief of staff, Marie Immaculée Musaniwabo, whose surname signified that 'she resembles her own'. Père Ambroise said the name was a poetic thought. Josefu had made a special trip back to

Kigali to regularise her position officially and bring her to Kibuye as an employee. She came with the woman companion from whom she would not be parted, and rightly so, he reckoned. The friend was not official staff; it was a private arrangement with Josefu.

He felt mildly impatient, however, nearly every day: he would have liked to appoint Père Ambroise Sebatware as their chaplain, and have his name first on the list. They worked for the United Nations, however, so it was inappropriate, he joked lamely. The Tutsi surname meant 'father of noble princes', a curious theme, Josefu decided, to be discussed when they next met. Instead, they had Bill Macpherson for dispensing guidance and gentle reminders that he, as head of mission, would like them to be fair to all sides. And he also used his mother's maiden name Riveau, and he said it was good French Canadian, hoping to impress the ubiquitous UN military staff of the same Quebec origins—bilingual in French and English and therefore indispensable here.

Gabrielle was not on the list; she was not UN staff and did not belong to their section of the mission. She was meant to be contracted to another team of UNDP workers. Every day she stated that she just worked on contracts for them, just some job, she'd say many times over, almost—Josefu remarked—as if she was convincing herself that it helped maintain her perfect detachment. But they were caring for her because the contractors' backup had not appeared as planned, typical of course for Rwanda at that stage, she was told. 'So let's think coolly', Josefu told himself. Whose list should she go on? She was sharing their abode by default, as well as some of the envied UN support operations from which they benefited. It simply happened that way.

Surprisingly, Gabrielle declared, however, that she needed more time than planned. She said it was because of the difficulty of finding an English language interpreter. At first she refused a Rwandan soldier from Uganda who was offered to her because she couldn't understand his accent, nor one from Tanzania either. Then she tried the first one out again and decided that if he spoke very slowly she could half guess his words. He was immediately released from the army and given a suit of clothes and a badge. In this way, Gabrielle discovered the local costs of building materials and other essentials to base her cleverly calculated estimates of how much spending was needed, in U.S. dollars, for the region's reconstruction and development—her mission and mandate.

Josefu promised Bill not to bring up a favourite debating issue with her, which was the meaning in reality of the ideas of 'reconstruction and development', of what could be included, and where they stopped. Here in a discussion, if you were told to go to hell with your arguments, it was risky: you could take a few paces backwards and fall straight into that lake.

Josefu checked the list again, glad that he had the practicalities of their mission under control. Thus, with their names emblazoned on plasticized identity cards (which nobody read, preferring to look only at the photograph), they all shifted from side to side in the silent roads of Kibuye, like ants along an open wound.

⋮

The attempts Josefu and Bill made to follow UN procedure by engaging with the local authorities were difficult with so few on the ground. He knew why: it was a tricky place to be in. Tousignant had warned him and Bill. "Kibuye?" he had said, quickly sketching a map on a stray piece of paper. "Not your decision but made in New York? It's in the former Zone Turquoise."

He had spoken dynamically, his tone providing a boost Josefu wished to take away for himself. When the French forces left, who in effect had supported—let's say 'tolerated'—the previous government, Tousignant had insisted that the UN peacekeepers' contingent should arrive first, on their own, and that the new Rwandan government and its new army should follow later. He said he worked hard to get his view accepted but spoke with Kagame, who took those decisions, general to general, in terms he understood. There was mutual respect there. Bill said he was proud of Tousignant: Canada at its best.

"And Rwanda too, at its most reasonable," Josefu retorted. "And long may it last."

But nobody knew what would happen in the former Zone. Josefu and Bill were told Tousignant took the decision so as to reassure the local population left behind. These people had been loyal to the old regime or were tolerant of it, and simply in virtue of being alive probably meant they were Hutu. And some of them had already fled across the border, with dire future consequences. Tousignant had reminded Bill and Josefu of this manmade danger yet again. As for the local Tutsis, they had all died, except for a few still hiding in the forests. Ethiopian UN troops–whom Tousignant appeared to have particular affection for—wearing their UN blue berets, searched for Tutsis in the forests, knowing they were there, because infants had been found by them, stillborn or barely alive, abandoned in the night.

Josefu and his team's first overnight stay had been in a building vacated and scrubbed clean by Senegalese troops who had been left behind when their French commanders departed and whom Tousignant had rapidly coiffed with blue berets. The new Rwandan government wanted them out, a request taking a long time to be processed.

Now Josefu noticed that Tousignant's helicopter was somewhere in the region nearly every day, the only predictable element there was in those parts.

"What a shambles here in Africa at the edge of the century!" Josefu said to himself when he first heard the aircraft. "To begin with: African buyers of weapons, rotund and fat thighed, arrive at the best hotels in the metropolitan world, turning and turning through bright, revolving doors. Oh God, my head is spinning." Josefu had scratched the back of his neck. "And then," he continued to himself, "They return to the gluttonous games of their masters back home in Africa. Hot saliva runs, houses burn and plants are trampled. Can anyone hear me? And corpses fill forgotten lakes."

After a pause, he had reflected, "Then some photojournalist—a man, my Patricia says with sarcasm, because a woman could be disbelieved—turns the whole spectacle into newsprint. And then the experts come here fresh from the canteens of international buildings, thanking God they have a job to do. And I'm among them, and I find my bearings through the hum of a UN flight path going to places where native drums have ceased to sound."

Josefu's bedclothes remain cold and his body is chilled; it is not warm today in Medicine Hat. He turns over and hopes for improvement.

He reflects that Patricia had retained his surname with which she had already made her reputation as a professional journalist. Her present husband, who was apparently very easy going—that was his advantage, she claimed—made no objections. So when she telephoned Josefu in Banff, a year or so ago, he told her it was fine when she requested permission for her new daughter Emily to use the Mutesa surname like her half-siblings, making it easier at school.

He pulls over another pillow, thinking clearly: Nobody has a smile like his wife, Patricia' s. It was the most adorable he would ever know; Ellie had no such smile, none of its sweetness, really. However much Patricia brooded, her sudden smile was that of a genuine rainbow, the smile that was a semi-permanent landmark in a really magical dream, those words precisely. 'Oh God, it's come to me in a flash; it was that smile which ordained that only she could be the mother of my children. I'll have to win her again, adopt Emily, forget everything, claim back what is mine.' He buries his face in the ample hotel pillow, hiding his sudden shame at this sentimental futility. He sobs, also in fear, because he definitely has swallowed the waters of Lake Kivu, sometime in his travels.

⋮

Josefu awakes from such deep slumber that he feels some chains have been broken at last, that he can cover greater distances in his recollections with greater speed. He is now determined to recall the town of Kibuye, come what may, as his team discovered it when they had first arrived.

⋮

"What's that sound?" Josefu asked, stopping Afrika and Bill in their tracks as they walked slowly past a row of abandoned villas. "O my God, it's a Saraband! One I used to know!" From behind an overgrown hedge and a broken down gate floated the timid, melancholic piano sound of a piece of classical European music. It was played with a certain amount of hesitation.

"Yes, the piano, I can hear it now," said Bill.

"It's the saraband in Bach's first French Suite! I used to know it well. It's one of several pieces I prepared for an exam. But then I switched full time to the oboe in secondary school. Bach in Kibuye!" Josefu marvelled.

The melody was repeated, hesitatingly and with some notes missing, perhaps because of broken strings. It seemed only the beginning bars were known to the player, leaving the piece unresolved, but gripping with its sadness and simplicity. Josefu was tearful again. Bill noticed it and patted him on the arm.

"There's only one thing we can do," Bill said, "We will have to follow the music."

Afrika looked nervous but led the way. Inside the gate, it was soon apparent that they were in a compound, which had probably belonged to a religious order. There was a cross at every corner, above the door and in the entrance to the cool, dark house. They heard a short gasp, that of a young girl, but when they found the room with the piano, there was nobody there.

"She's hiding," Bill said with a patient smile. Afrika indicated that they should stand still, but nothing changed.

Josefu went up to the small, black and upright piano. Its yellow keys were worn, the music stand rusted. It may have come to the Belgian Congo many years ago, then brought across the lake. He moved the squeaking chair back a little and sat down.

With his eyes closed at first, he began slowly to play the same saraband. He had never performed it again since he was a schoolboy, but the notes flowed into his fingers, almost involuntarily. Not knowing what they were to be till he played them, he was in trance. A noisy wasp buzzed around the almost empty room, as if life should have returned to normal, that there should have been fruit on the table, set times for meals, and cleanly scrubbed children in a peaceful town somewhere in a country where the sun shines regularly, that's all.

Josefu continued playing till the end of the piece, his tall frame bent down towards the piano. As he struck the last chord loudly, majestic in its sudden major key, Afrika tapped his shoulder and discreetly pointed to the doorway. Opening his moist eyes and following Bill's gaze, Josefu saw a young girl of about twelve or thirteen in plaits, standing there.

Afrika said, "I told her not to be afraid. I told her you were a teacher," he added to Josefu.

"How do you know this piece of music?" he asked the girl, Afrika translating, as she took a step forward.

"Sister Geraldine taught me."

"Did she really?"

The girl grew bolder. "She said to me that she knew I loved the piano. I loved music more than anything."

"Can you read it?"

"Only a little."

"This is a very difficult piece. Did you ever play it to the end?"

By this time the girl had come right up to the piano and Josefu moved so she could sit down at her seat again. Bemused, Afrika and Bill watched in silence as he dragged a folding chair next to her. She ran to a floorboard on the other side of the room, which she lifted high enough to pull out a plastic covered, small stack of music books. Afrika said something to her as she had looked at him in fear.

"I told her I worked for you foreigners and I think she believes I am also a stranger like Monsieur Josefu, although I speak the language."

"Oh Lord," said Josefu unbelievingly, "Edition Peters, Number 4594, the German edition—by far the best! We had them all at Stowe, I mean at my school. Where was she from, this Sister Geraldine?" He rose from the chair.

"She was from Ireland," Afrika said.

The girl was nearly crying now. She said, "Sister Geraldine gave me this music. When she taught me that piece, she said it was the best thing she could give me in the whole world and in heaven."

The three men now stood around her, silent and still, in the graceful orbit of the nun's gift, as if resting on a journey, but no longer in any given place.

Finally, Josefu whisPèred, "Yes, the nun was right. You can't lose music like you can lose your faith. Nobody can take it away from you."

After exchanging a few words, Afrika said, "This child's name is Epiphanie. She says the nun did not want to leave. Some of them were not bad people. And this one loved music."

"Let's play again," said Josefu softly. "She and I deserve this one." Epiphanie was timid, but Afrika cajoled her.

As they sat together at the piano, Josefu put his right arm round her. "So, Afrika, she thinks I am a teacher!" he laughed quietly. "So ask her if she knows that the lower notes give the music its main strength," and Josefu played them with his left hand. Now Epiphanie joined in with her right hand, giggling a little with shyness. They repeated the opening passages she knew of the saraband, as a duet, several times over. When they stopped, Bill applauded softly.

"Play the end bit," the girl said to Josefu. "Sister Geraldine knew it but never finished showing me." She had long tresses with ribbons, a flat nose and round cheeks. Her eyes were captivating, Josefu thought, so large and expressive. He played the entire piece again.

Suddenly, Bill looked agitated and was about to leave the room.

"I'm sorry," he said in French. "Josefu, you remember Mark played the cello. And lots of Bach. Oh my God, oh I'm sorry. It's a memory, you know how it is," Bill added, "But why here in Rwanda, in Kibuye?"

"Bill, it's all right," Josefu said, touching his arm. "You see, even here unexpectedly people can bring things, intimate things to you, to your own memories—some good, some bad." Then Josefu explained to Afrika, "Mark is the name of his son who is dead, who played music like this."

Afrika looked worriedly at Bill. After a while he lowered his eyes and whisPèred, "I did not think you lost your children in your countries, like we do here." Nobody commented. He then said, "Ah, Monsieur Bill, may God have his soul."

"He does. He does."

The girl, interrupting, turned to Josefu and said, "Can you take me away from here?"

"Where, Afrika, does she want to go? Ask her. It's always the same request," said Josefu, despairing and shrugging his shoulders.

"She says she wants to go where it will be like it was before," Afrika replied quietly.

"All was really good till Sister Geraldine left," the girl explained, "All that war, and now my father who has been taken to prison. We were going to Goma, but once he was taken away by those new soldiers, my mother said we might as well stay here. But there is nothing left. I just come in secret here."

"Ask why her father has gone to prison," Bill told Afrika.

"She says he killed a lot of people," he replied. "He worked at the prefecture and got many rewards. It was the Tutsis he killed, that's who and she says the old prefet said he was a good man. He worked well. Ah, she says he helped in Bisesero. He helped the owner of a tea factory who came with his workers to kill Tutsis. Everybody respected him. But now he is in prison." The girl was crying quietly. "She said she wants her father to come back home and Sister Geraldine to return and everything to be like before. She wants to learn the rest of the music. Or else she wants to go away." Then Afrika fell silent too.

"Did she have any Tutsi friends, ask her," said Bill.

"Ah yes, Monsieur Bill. But she says her father said that they all had to be killed because they had diseases, and that if they stayed alive her baby brother would die and yes, she says her father told them they brought war and disease and thieving and that they burned houses. He was doing a good thing to kill the Tutsis, he told her, that is what he said, Monsieur Bill." Then Afrika turned to Josefu and said, "Perhaps you could tell Monsieur Bill that I can't speak anymore. It's too embarrassing for me."

"I understand," replied Josefu, "But it is not your words, just a translation of what someone else is saying." Turning to Bill abruptly, he said, "Isn't that so Bill?"

"Of course, Afrika, you're just doing your job."

"But I do not like to move my lips in that way," remarked Afrika.

The girl asked if they would come back tomorrow for some more piano. She was told it would be another day as they were going to be travelling for a while first. Josefu requested her to play the one piece she knew a last time. They stood listening reverently, a stillness enveloping the whole room. And they lingered there for a long while.

When they were back in the hushed, empty street, Josefu thought aloud: "Did Bach, did Sister Geraldine, did Epiphanie herself, did anyone know the answer, why this piece of music played by Lake Kivu had not brought its listeners to forgiveness, to a place of rest?'

"Well, you know, perhaps those claims of art being universally appealing are mistaken, the same old story," said Bill.

"Perhaps. But was the attempt to play Western music importations a kind of damnation, though? Despite the claims of all composers that they are immortal and universal, could it have been the first step to damnation? I mean local damnation? Instead of playing the gracious music of the region? I'll ask Afrika."

"All music is good," Afrika said, suddenly cheerful. "I like that piano. I like the electric piano too, like in our churches. We like our African music, our drums, our songs, but especially Lingala from Congo Zaire, on the radio. And music of the whites too. It makes people happy. President Habyarimana liked music. But with politics nothing can stop the killings, nothing."

"You know," said Bill, "Ever since I've been here, I keep on wondering why the beauty of this country, which strikes you so forcefully, didn't simply swallow people up into some kind of peace?"

"Well done, Bill," said Josefu, "You're asking the right questions."

"Bill?" says Josefu on the telephone. "Just checking in. I'm at Medicine Hat. I wanted you and Mary to know."

"We were kind of expecting you today," Bill replies.

"Well, I've not left Alberta yet. Maybe I never will. I'm not ready."

"That's a lucid judgement, Josefu," Bill laughs.

"It's no joke. I know I have to stay here a while. But I'm not looking forward to it. The hotel is fine. But what a way to live, from hotel to hotel, prairie to prairie!"

"Are you going through the whole mission, from when we arrived in Kigali? I'm curious, you know. And you've got everybody worried. By the way, your cousin Maria called Winnipeg here, yesterday."

"I know."

"How did she find you?"

"I called her myself. Bill, do you remember what became of the registration papers we were ordered to hand in to a non-existent prefet in Kibuye? The silent successor to a real butcher of a prefet… Do you remember we found a cache of Wellington boots near the old prefet's office? For when you're ankle deep in carnage?"

"Where are you? Can I call you?"

"Leave it. I can't discuss it any more. Bye!"

Josefu puts down the receiver and he knows that Bill thought it prudent not to attempt to ring back.

⋮

As he lays a tray of Room Service dinner on the bedside table, the young waiter asks Josefu if he plans to go to the jazz evening later on, the best in Medicine Hat.

"I do not come from a jazz tradition," he replies, "But curiosity may get the better of me."

"Enjoy your meal," the young man says, noticing the tip inserted with the signed bill. It is a relief to Josefu that he does not have to say another thing and he waits for the door to close again.

⋮

Celestin excitedly told them he had found a place in Kibuye where imported beer could be drunk by the lake. Josefu had gone along only because, otherwise, Afrika would have insisted on staying behind too. At first Josefu had attempted to sit with his back to the water shore but then he rose from his seat and walked towards it, resentfully, hypnotically.

They had stopped at a curve in the shoreline, which offered intimacy and seduction. A fecund avocado tree grew further along and a clump of palm trees waved nonchalantly a few yards away from the edge of the lake. He wanted to throw his beer bottle into the water, to pollute it even more, to make it depraved.

One of the main tasks of the new government was to complete the removal of dead bodies that had been washed up. 'Such decisive action', Josefu remarked to himself, 'still won't hide, for years, the presence of cursed foreboding. That is because it lurks immediately beneath the lake's surface.'

He noticed someone beside him. A white haired man greeted him in French. He stood with his shoulders pulled back, his black face shining. "You are not Rwandan like us others," he said. "I hear you are on a mission with the United Nations who replaced our friends the French. We liked them here. They knew the truth."

"The truth? I'm interested in that." Aware that his words are nearly Biblical, Josefu says: "What truth is it that you speak of?"

"You must not believe what you are told, Monsieur, that's all." He pulled himself even straighter. "There are a lot of enemies. They are enemies of Rwanda. They claim to be patriotic but they are not. They harm Rwanda. They do not count the cost."

"I wonder who you are referring to?" asked Josefu, with a blank expression.

"I shall tell you something completely true," the old man continued. He wore a clean tee shirt under his jacket which had a few holes but no buttons missing. Josefu keenly took in these details. He was of slight build, his hands had some traces of arthritis, but his nails were neatly cut and clean.

"Not one single Tutsi has been killed. It is all a big lie that they invented," he said.

Josefu wanted to shield himself from this serpent in a tree. Only another snake, one plucked out of his own father's garden and hurled at him, would nullify what he was saying. Josefu bit his lip; he should remember his occupation, his mandate, and not think of his own survival. It was simple. As quietly as he could, he asked the man, "Whose are the bodies in the lake?"

"Hutus, of course. The Tutsis, especially those from Uganda, they killed Hutus all over our country and brought them to Lake Kivu and threw them in. That's why there are so many, because we are many Hutus and they killed half of us."

"But I have seen burned out houses, even in Kibuye, which belonged to Tutsis who have been killed. Who did it?"

"They, the Tutsis, did it themselves, to blame the Hutus for it afterwards. They wanted the whole world to turn against us. Now we are being chased out of our own country. That is why so many people are in Goma, in Bukavu, in the camps on the other side of the lake, in Zaire. It is all lies. The Tutsis tell many lies."

"Aren't you afraid of staying here?" said Josefu, adding softly, "With views like yours, you could be arrested."

"The Tutsis have taken power. They are thieves. But I am not afraid of them. I am an old man and if they want to kill me I am not afraid. I will tell them I know their lies."

Josefu forced himself to look at the old man again. "What did you do here, during the war?" he asked.

"I did my work as a pensioner."

"What does that mean?"

"I was a state employee before, at the office of the Bourgmeister, a great privilege, before I was pensioned off."

He won't say what he did, Josefu thought.

"Of course," the old man continued, "I have not been paid for a long time. I am indebted to my family. My sons are now in Goma and I hope they will come back, but the new government might want to kill them."

"Why should they want to do that? If they are not guilty of any crimes, then they should have no problems," said Josefu, "At least that is what is said by the Rwandan government."

"Which government? Ours or someone else's? Or that of the RPF, those who say they have won the war and come to our Rwanda?"

"Aren't the new authorities also Rwandans?" said Josefu, feigning ignorance. He hoped Afrika would not join them, obliging him to be more sincere.

"But Monsieur," said the old man, "I do not know which African country you are from, but there are too many liars on our continent."

"My parents are from Uganda, but I come from Great Britain and I live in America."

"You are not among those we trust. We only trust the French."

Josefu lowered his head. "What about the Belgians?"

"We only trust the French. They know the truth."

"Which is the truth that they know, please tell me, I know so little. You see, I am not French," said Josefu, almost mockingly.

"The truth is, Monsieur, that we had a good president. He was killed and it was terrible. His wife is a good woman and her family tried to protect all of us. But the Tutsis told so many lies: that we had committed murder against them and destroyed their crops and killed their cows. Imagine! Who would want their cows!"

"Do you think all Tutsis are liars and bad people? I was told that Hutus and Tutsis even married each other and were good friends," said Josefu very slowly and clearly.

"Some Tutsis are good people. I cannot say all Tutsis are bad. But the liars are bad. They wanted to destroy our country. And they have succeeded because of how they lied to all of the world. And Rwanda, look how it is now: in ruins. It is all their fault."

"Would it have been better, in your opinion, if all Tutsis had been eliminated? Would you have preferred it if Rwanda had no Tutsis?"

"The Tutsis are not Rwandans. They have their own home. They are from Ethiopia."

"Who told you that?"

"A great professor, on the Radio. He had studied somewhere else, Canada or France or somewhere like that. If you could understand that he was a very learned man, then you would know what he said was true."

Josefu knew that a certain Professor Mugesera was known to have said this in public a couple of years before the genocide, a provocation which the entire foreign community chose to ignore. He even had suggested Tutsis should be returned through a shortcut, as dead bodies floating in a river back to Ethiopia.

Part of the team's mandate was to establish the facts about this famous speech. Josefu did not ask for the old man's name; it might have been imprudent anyway right now. With beating heart, he said, "That is a very interesting viewpoint. Do you agree with the professor?"

"I do not, in fact, agree with the professor, that they should be sent away," the old man said ponderously. "They didn't bother me, the Tutsis. If they had kept their heads down, nobody would have noticed them. But when they wanted to destroy our country, kill our president, make a genocide of all the Hutus in Rwanda, we had to defend ourselves."

"'Make a genocide', did you say?"

"Of course. You should not believe all the lies. It is they who wanted to kill every Hutu in the world."

"All Tutsis wanted to kill all Hutus?"

"Ah Monsieur, you are very demanding. I do not think all Tutsis wanted that. The good ones, those who were quiet, they wanted nothing except to lead their quiet lives quietly. But we in Rwanda have many enemies. What can we do?"

"Are you asking me? Is killing lots of people a solution? Look at this lake, isn't it terrible to have it full of dead people?"

"You want answers from me and you think I need none from you. You ask a lot of questions, Monsieur. I know the truth and you may perhaps not know the truth. Not one Hutu killed one Tutsi. We Hutu are innocent people. We had a good government; a president who loved us and his family loved us afterwards. And we have suffered unjustly. We are a poor people." The old man stood straight and looked out towards the lake. He pointed to Ijwi Island. "That island should belong to Rwanda, but it belongs to Zaire. The president of Zaire is a clever president, very rich, his name is Mobutu. He was very friendly with our old government and so he might allow our people to use the island to fight a return back into our land."

"Why do you say this? Why are you telling me this?"

"Listen to me," said the old man coming closer. "I love my Hutu people. All Hutus love their people. I cannot admit that we are monsters the way many people say about us. We are good people and we do no harm to anybody."

Josefu rapidly looked for a mental label to pin on such thoughts: deep denial, for example. But he recoiled; it was too frivolous, too insular, too predictable and not to his liking. Lifelines are precarious and few when you are drowning in muddied waters.

The man stood looking out to the lake in anger.

"And if I die because of what I have said to you, I am not afraid. I am an old man. Many Rwandans do not say the truth. I prefer to die than not tell the truth. My hope is out there, on that Ijwi Island. Perhaps I can die there, with my hope."

The sun went down more rapidly at times, Josefu thought, than at others. Tonight it sank with the weight of a lost cause. Walking slowly back to his colleagues, burdened with a testimony they had not shared, he felt alone, weary from a journey into another's mind which led to a dead end. Josefu took off his jacket and threw it over his shoulder deliberately, hoping the increasingly cool air would chill his diffused thoughts and alert him to further pitfalls.

16.

Nobody in authority was pleased that Bill and Josefu were going to Goma, Madame Dubois told them on one of their return visits to Kigali. The UN Refugee Commission, which ran the camps there, preferred not to be asked to receive them. She blew her nose and said that probably they suspected Bill and Josefu were too close to UNAMIR, especially the General, with whom the UN camp people were at loggerheads at the moment. She said moreover there were rumours—unfounded, she knew—that Tousignant had been especially attentive to them both since Bill was Canadian. Was it a fatuous judgement, she asked? Was it the sole basis of his approval? Wasn't there more, and that they admired the General? Agreed with him? She looked up at them, putting down her handkerchief.

Neither Bill nor Josefu answered, Bill out of principle. And Josefu, for some time now, had decided to cut short all commentaries about the infighting in their Organisation, "out of respect for the dead," he added. They thanked Madame Dubois for warning them, but she did not demonstrate in any way that she heard them do so.

Now back in Kibuye, with a pile of appropriate documents, they prepared to drive to Goma, immediately inside the Zaire border on the other side of Lake Kivu.

Gabrielle was not coming on this first trip. Josefu had watched her climbing into another jeep earlier that morning, to visit the remains of Kibuye Hospital. 'There are two types of women's behinds,' he thought to himself, 'shaped or blurred.' Hers was of the blurred and overspilled variety. 'Room for exploration,' he mused.

He was anxious to press ahead with their own departure to the other shore of the lake and to get the visit over with. He did not look forward to walking in the ashen camps of refugees, which he was convinced were wantonly created, and were being misused by a government in exile with blood on its hands.

Yet he knew Bill would treat as good colleagues the unabashed, unrepentant international staff who, in the name of universal principles of tolerance, were hosting killers, giving food and shelter to those who rearmed and plotted and mocked... Bill discreetly told Josefu that if he could not be professional and polite, then he better not come.

Afrika had kept silent, with his head down, when he heard Josefu first had refused to go on the trip. He said, "Monsieur Josefu, I find it difficult to translate what I do not like to hear. When you are there, I feel you teach me, because you can understand me." He cast around nervously and added, "And then there is Celestin who is careful when you are there, whereas Monsieur Bill is too kind and cannot realise what Celestin says to me. You do not understand our language but you see with your eyes."

"Does Celestin still worry you? I thought he had changed."

"He is alright. I have no more problems. But you never know the future. We Rwandans are complicated."

"Not more than anyone else," replied Josefu patiently.

After a while, Afrika almost whispered, "It is dangerous in Goma for inside our heads, that is what it is. So if you are not going, then I do not want to go, that is what I do not want," he said, more agitated.

Josefu then relented, although reluctant to accept the responsibilities, and so he promised Afrika to travel with him, across the border, into an unpredictable, smoke-filled situation. Afrika now reminded him that his young cousin was among the Interahamwe, presumed to be in Goma. He himself could be recognised by other fellow Hutu, he said. Yet he was going with an UNAMIR escort, which was seen as hostile by those running the camps. Josefu now began to appreciate that Afrika had only talked about his dislike of interpreting words he disapproved of, and never once had he mentioned his own vulnerable position. This strong reticence to draw attention to the risks he was under himself was something Afrika showed time and time again, and it increased Josefu's affection for him.

Now as they waited to depart, Josefu's legs were unpleasantly heavy. He had hardly slept the night before. He had found the day too hot, the evening abruptly cold, two small reasons in September for wanting a change.

Bill had followed him into his room at bedtime. "I don't like it when you speak of leaving our mission," he said.

"But you know what I'm thinking, don't you?" said Josefu, "Why shouldn't I want to leave, so as to go to New York and work out something with Patricia, or at least find out if she's still there? Not one word about the children since I've been here in Rwanda. And do you know what? I can't even phone my mother because, frankly, I'm scared of what she'll say has happened to them if she knows. I'm being honest with you, you see."

"That's good. False pride will get you nowhere. Perhaps I could get Mary to do something more for you. She didn't want to intrude, you know. Yeah, you're under pressure; and you can't do anything from here. Kids matter; you can't get away from your own kids."

"Patricia accused me of being obsessed with Rwanda."

"Be honest again. Your work alone didn't drive her away. And it's a worthy obsession. People murdered here in Rwanda were a thousand every twenty minutes, your worthy obsession. Look, I'm repeating your own words. What am I doing here anyway?" And then Bill added, "Talking to you, I mean."

"But I want to talk."

"Okay, Josefu, what is it now?"

"It becomes part of the national flag, doesn't it, those numbers, 'a thousand Rwandans killed in twenty minutes'," Josefu remarked quickly. "In Cambodia, natural beauty, or traces of grace and high culture, all of them were there. Yet for most people it became, 'Cambodia—two million dead in the Killing Fields.' That became the conversation piece."

"Yes, I'd forgotten, you made your name working out there monitoring the elections. You got collaboration from our awkward customers like nobody else," Bill laughed, "And it got you a promotion too."

"Yes, yes. But why do you always have to change the subject, why? I was saying, you raise national flags and the numbers fall out like storage dust: a million dead in Rwanda, Cambodia two million, Germany six million, bells ringing, ding dong, dead." He took a deep breath and said, "Except that numbers count for nothing. By themselves, that is."

Bill closed his eyes, impatiently. "Can't you listen to anyone but yourself?" he said.

"When will the thousand green hills of Rwanda take precedence again here over the dead?" Josefu said in a low voice, "But for whom, for whom in Rwanda?"

"Are you talking to me?" There was no reply. "Josefu, can you hear me?"

"Oh, God."

"I mean," Bill said, "you saw Vice-President Kagame again when you went up to Kigali for Marie Immaculée. What did he say?"

"Hadn't I told you? He said he doesn't yet control the situation. And he said that since we, the international community, are allowing the others, their enemies, to regroup across the border in Zaire, it's going to lead to a war throughout the whole Great Lakes Region. It is 1994 right now, so let's see what happens, that is, if any of us are destined to live on and see." Josefu threw a small pebble in his shoe against the wall. "And your Tousignant said exactly the same thing."

"Are you using your mosquito net?" asked Bill.

"That strange thing like a tunnel over the bed? So far I don't find it necessary. I'd use one of the old fashioned sort that hangs down, though."

"I promised Mary I would use one, but if we see the other nets in the market in Goma, let's buy some. It's going to be great, getting out of this land of ghost towns for the day."

"Yes, Bill, all in a day's work."

"Josefu, I can hear you, you and your sarcasm," he laughed.

"I'm not in a joking mood. I'm dreading Goma."

"Everyone's point of view, we must listen to everyone, our mandate. You can get drunk afterwards. Yes, I've seen you and Afrika attacking the beer."

"I've seen you and Gabrielle with the liquor," Josefu retorted.

"It's run out now."

"Yes, she told everyone. You'll find something in Goma for her, undoubtedly."

"Stop that, Josefu. See you tomorrow," and Bill walked out, shuffling quietly.

Josefu fiercely threw another piece of gravel out of his sock, then folded it carefully with its pair, for Marie Immaculée to wash. He looked at the satellite phone by his bed and wondered whether he shouldn't use privilege and phone the maid in New York or else try Maidenhead, where his mother now lived since his father died. He lay back, hands under his neck, with the sensation of being covered by a vengeful wave of water. Because of the way he cried now for his children, his head began to throb insistently.

Soon, he was sitting on a rock, surrounded by limpid, still water and he gazed down into the deep. Out of the lake rose the old man he had met before, offering to help him ashore. The man's hair had somehow lost its crinkle. It hung, white and wavy, around his shoulders like a Father Christmas's. His eyes grew larger, every time he blinked with kindness. His brown and pink fingers were long and delicate, like those of a concert pianist. He beckoned and turned around, clockwise, several times. Josefu felt he was being swept by a gentle wave towards him, his legs wide and ready to curl around the old man's waist, better to be carried out of the water.

He said, "What a relief, what a deliverance—so, really, nothing happened, no crime, no guilt, no suffering. I might have just had indigestion before."

The old man looked triumphant. "You see, it isn't so difficult to recognise your mistakes. Open your arms and be at peace."

Josefu hesitated one last time. "What shall I do with my blue plastic folder, full of these incriminating documents? I mustn't get it wet, you see. It was entrusted to me with my mandate, this folder, even if it contains no true facts"

"Prove that!" came another voice from behind him.

"I was only being diplomatic," he turned and answered into the dark, "not to hurt the old monster's feelings."

The lake receded.

When he awoke, his first thought had been to acknowledge that the conversation of the previous day with the old man by the lake, had actually taken place. In Kibuye recently, his dreams were more real than the waking day, as if his experiences attained validity only when translated into the accusing visions he saw at night.

⋮

Josefu sits up and draws his knees towards him, surprised at how clearly he had recalled a dream from years ago, whereas now in a dark hotel room he is somewhere he cannot remember, except that it is already far from Banff. Without turning on the light, he reaches for the television remote control, placed comfortably by his bedside, and switches on a station at random. It is an adventure film with two men struggling on a cliff side. Josefu turns it off immediately.

'I must get back to Kibuye, people are waiting for me there,' he says to himself, settling down with his arms round one of the pillows. 'And it's less lonely than here,' he adds, with a mocking laugh.

⋮

Nothing went to plan the next day, following Josefu's dream of the old man, the day they were going to Goma. Bernard the photo-journalist, who knew the town and camp well, had not yet arrived as promised. This was a setback, because without him it would be difficult to move around there independently of their official hosts. Bill remarked, however, that they would be making more than one journey, so objectivity could be achieved gradually, if that was Josefu's concern.

"I don't know what's got into you lately, as if you were afraid we will all be hoodwinked in Goma. Where's your confidence in your own independent mind?" Bill added.

Josefu refrained from replying that Bill himself was more likely to be misled. "It would have been better if Bernard were here," he sighed. "Let's delay departure by one hour."

"I guess we can wait anyway since the UNAMIR escort isn't here yet."

It was then that Josefu decided to take Afrika aside and tell him about his encounter by the lake, the day before.

"I saw you, I saw you, with that old Rwandan man," said Afrika, "But Celestin was speaking with me like a friend, so I stayed. You did not call for me."

"He spoke French. He does not believe a single Tutsi has been killed by a single Hutu."

"But that is the way we wish it were. No war, no dead. And nobody to blame. He must be from the north, from Gisenyi, perhaps, where the president came from, even from the same hill, perhaps, that is what it may be."

Josefu closed his eyes and saw a snake in a tree again, something like a pomegranate tree, or a plum tree.

"Monsieur Josefu, you are tired," said Afrika.

"And I wish Père Ambroise were here."

They heard two vehicles arriving at once in front of their building, one a jeep with the UNAMIR escort of blue helmets: three Senegalese and a French Canadian. The other had an African driver with Bernard in front and at the back an unknown, thin faced, slightly built, white skinned man, under thirty years old, Josefu remarked. He was introduced as Jean Pierre, a Belgian journalist representing the organisation 'Reporters Without Borders.'

"Doctors, lawyers and journalists without borders; it's a shame arms dealers have a borderless trade as well," remarked Josefu as he viewed Bernard and Jean Pierre, who went and sat on the bonnet of the car like two birds on a line.

They soon all sped northwards to Gisenyi, the graceful, lakeside resort from colonial times. Josefu kept his eyes averted from the car window.

Celestin was excited. "I've never been here before," he explained. "It is the town of President Habyarimana. Now it is hit by the war, but it was beautiful before. I heard that on the radio."

"I do not want to see it, just like Monsieur Josefu who holds his head down, I have remarked how he turns his head away." Afrika spoke slowly. "I do not want to know how beautiful was Gisenyi."

"Bad news, bad news, this whole trip," Josefu mumbled. He sat in the back with Afrika, Jean Pierre and Bernard, his tall frame increasing the discomfort of being so crowded. All were nervous. They had insisted that Bill sit in front, his seniority and whiteness making the importance of their mission plausible to anyone who cared to check the vehicle.

Before long, however, and with remarkably little fuss, they had been ushered across the border and into the outskirts of Goma.

"Out of Rwanda," said Bill, "For six hours."

⋮

Josefu looks at his watch. It is four o'clock in the morning, Daylight Savings Time, and his hotel room is still dark. He observes himself looking for he knows not what, and yet without any hesitation, he picks up the phone beside his bed and dials Martina's number.

"Are you alone?" he asks, in a driven tone of voice.

"Where are you?" she whispers.

"In Goma. I'm quite clear about what you wanted me to see."

"Where's Goma? Have you left the highway, are you still on Highway One? Did you turn off? Are you all right?"

"I want you here. By my side. I haven't left Alberta."

"What? Why don't you let anyone know what you're doing? Where are you? I mean not in your head. Where are you, with your feet?"

"My feet are on a bed."

"Where on a bed?"

"In Medicine Hat on a bed."

Martina sighs with relief. "So what can I do for you, now? I'm taking the phone outside, hold on."

"He's next to you, isn't he?"

"Josefu, you know I would never lie to you. I thought you were happy about it, and happy for me."

"I cannot bear it alone here."

"This is unusual for you to be so truthful, so open, Josefu. I like it."

"Some kind of priestess, you are, pronouncing! Concluding!"

"What's bugging you, Josefu?" Martina asks.

"You have no idea about truth, beneath the surface. I'm out here, surrounded by water, sinking into a murdered lake."

"I thought you said you were in Medicine Hat. And no doubt in the best hotel there? I know you'd get the best hotel."

"You pushed me out of Banff."

"I did not. Come back, if that's how you feel," Martina adds.

"It's too late. I'm not leaving the prairies. I need the open spaces right now. The hills are too encircling, the emerald green too overpowering."

"Where are you, Josefu?"

He hangs up without another word. He goes to the window, to punch a fist through the glass wildly, but a potted plant below suddenly catches his eye. Then he remembers the one forgotten in the back seat of his car.

A young night porter jumps up and says, "Sorry Sir! Can I help you?"

"The plant, the plant! It's suffocating. I have to get it. Can't breathe, can't drink. I'm such an idiot," he replies running outside. On his return, struggling to hold the pass key to his room when his arms are full, he continues saying to the young man, "It should never have been neglected. I must take it up to my room." The porter's whispered reply is unintelligible.

He puts the plant down in the bath and runs the shower over each leaf patiently. This meticulous attention will perhaps atone for what was described in the black leather covered Book of Common Prayer given to him at Confirmation, as the sin of omission.

⋮

The serious problem in the Goma camps was the volcanic rock, so hard that you could hardly dig the ground. By the time of Josefu's first visit, the cholera epidemic had just about been contained. It occurred in part because the earth was too unwieldy to dig latrines and drains. And yet there had not been any natural disaster to bring about the misery in Goma. It was fantasy and greed that had raised up the hands of human sorcerers, who lifted people out of their emerald slopes high into the deceitful smoke, who swallowed them and spewed them out, so they drowned in ashen mud. And several cadavers had slid down into Lake Kivu, like so many poisoned victuals at her ruinous feast.

⋮

The baobab trees outside the property cast a fragile, lazy shadow through the front window into the waiting hall of a large villa, a few miles down the coast from Goma. Josefu knew he was the cause for the delay to be received. Jean Pierre was in another room persuading their host, a deposed member of the previous government, to receive the whole party, despite Josefu's parental link with Uganda, a perceived enemy.

"You do not want to be accused of being a racist, after all," he overheard Jean Pierre, speaking with his strong Belgian accent in French, followed by a loud guffaw from the former minister.

The door opened and a sturdy man, in an immaculate light grey suit and silk tie, swaggered out with a wide smile despite the stern look in his eyes. He had smooth black skin a shade lighter than Josefu's, not typical for a Hutu perhaps, and high cheekbones. He held each man's hand for a moment before shaking it limply. Then he sighed, as if not having found what he was looking for, Josefu observed. Their host asked them to follow him.

They came into a vast room, with what seemed to be marble flooring. There were armchairs and sofas of white leather at one end and a set of ornate, white brocade covered furniture at the other, towards which they were led. Josefu quickly imagined the map of Zaire and how far all these objects had to be transported. There were a whole series of luxury villas along the shores of this side of the lake, mostly owned by Mobutu, the ailing dictator, and probably a few others belonging to his circle of cronies. It was all very well to say that they only imitated their former colonial masters—the Belgians had favoured the area as a resort. Yet now the effort put into building and decorating imitation follies in an increasingly impoverished country was macabre, Josefu thought.

However, the Rwandan former government emptied the nation's coffers, taking every form of currency with them into exile to distribute among themselves. They now presented the privileged Zairians with a lucrative source of patronage and income. Josefu realised he was thinking with detached lucidity.

Because of the large patio windows and the lack of curtains or shades, the whole room they were in had an almost blinding glare. Everyone appeared with a hazy outline and one that could only be glimpsed from time to time.

Aware of their host's gaze on him, however, Josefu bowed slightly, before sitting down, without a smile.

"We were committed to democracy and the abolition of feudalism, but that does not mean we were against kings in other countries, nor against all princes," said the former minister to him, "But that is yet one more calumny said against us, you understand. Your country does not respect our independence."

"If you mean Uganda," replied Josefu in a quiet voice, "I was only there once, and hardly more than a few months. I regret it, of course."

"Yes, yes, I know your story," the former minister interrupted, glancing at Jean Pierre. He turned towards the far door and shouted. A bodyguard with a Kalashnikov appeared briefly and then faded away. There was a moment of silence, and the minister smiled. He had fat thighs, Josefu noticed.

"We appreciate your taking the time to receive us," Bill said.

"We are indeed very busy," the minister replied, before indicating to the bodyguard who had returned with a tray of cold drinks, to leave immediately. The young man moved away, returning his weapon to his side from behind, with a minimum of noise.

'The polite manners of the violent,' Josefu reflected.

He hesitated out of principle to accept hospitality, but the host gave him a bottle of coke first, in a deliberate manner, before turning to Bill. Josefu wished his father's tamed snake could test the drink for poison and that all deities would forgive him for supping with a man he condemned. He watched the minister again, who served Afrika last, by simply pushing a bottle in his direction.

Men in silence, men of the world with their cold drinks.

The light was almost blinding. Again, the host looked severely at Josefu, then furrowed his brow and said, "You understand me: it is difficult for us here in exile. Rwandans want to live in their own country, not anywhere else. We each have our hill and we want to live there quietly."

"I see," said Josefu in a whisper.

"How long do you think you will have to stay before returning?" asked Jean Pierre with a journalist's typical gravity.

There seemed to be a long silence. The minister said, "Why do you put such a question? The answer is very simple: it shall be very soon." He took a deep breath, as if stoking up energy and said, "We love our country. How can we sit here doing nothing and watch it being taken over and ruined by those irresponsible RPF boys? They have no experience and they are thugs and you expect us not to try to save our country? We had good friends but we were betrayed. Look, your UN Secretary General, Bhoutros Ghali, he was a long time friend of ours; he visited us in 1983, can you imagine how long ago? When he was Foreign Minister of Egypt, he sold lots of weapons to us, to our government, not to those ruffians in foreign camps who are in Kigali now, but to us. We defended ourselves well. We were respected and understood."

When he paused, Josefu suddenly closed his eyes, as if hit by lightning. Nobody had ever told him in New York about this aspect of Bhoutros Ghali's past. No wonder it was a much more tortuous path for him to acknowledge the murderous nature of Rwanda's former government which he had known personally in better times. Until now, there had been no explanation for the strange hesitations, the way he had allowed information to be sifted so that only some of it went to the Security Council… The uncomfortable nature for him of Dallaire's fax, his best one… Yes, mislaid, yes… Bhoutros Ghali's efforts, finally to come to terms with the new reality in Rwanda, might have been really tough for him. He was a Secretary General who, after all, was merely a man who also had a past.

Feeling Bill's hand on his arm, Josefu opened his eyes and noticed, despite the sun-drenched glare, everyone was looking at him. "Excuse me," he said hurriedly.

"Do you want me to continue? Do you want me to say anything?" said the former minister.

"Of course, of course," Bill and Josefu exclaimed together.

"There is nothing but calumny said against us, false accusations and here we are, suffering outside our country."

Josefu was aware that this man before him was known to be a close ally of General Bagasora who was accused of masterminding the genocide, right down to the most minute details of tactics and timing, and of supplies. Given his high rank, this former minister's ears must have heard the massacre plans and his lips must have been used to pass on orders. What those narrow, slightly bloodshot eyes must have seen, one could scarcely imagine. Josefu saw his bodily form, clad in a suit that seemed to turn to silver, shimmered in the sunlight, changing size constantly, challenging the very elements of which this earth was made. Realising the pause in conversation was long, Josefu added in a quiet voice, although he was trembling, "We very much want to hear your story."

"You want to set me a trap?"

"No, Minister, our mandate is only to investigate as openly as possible," said Bill, looking quickly at Josefu.

"Do you want another drink?" asked the host.

"No," replied Josefu.

"Thank you," said Bill.

"We are fine," said Jean Pierre.

Afrika and Bernard said nothing.

"General Bagasora had taken up his retirement and had a quiet life already. But his patriotism was stronger than anything else. He was called upon to save his country. We all had our moment of history; it was the crisis for Rwanda. If you have an invasion of enemies who want to destroy a peaceful country and annihilate a hardworking, honest people, you have to face them with courage and eliminate them. Why do we stand accused, when we were simply defending our country, like any government would do and any army?"

"Your government is accused of attacking Rwandan civilians inside your own country, that is the real problem for you," said Jean Pierre.

"Ah yes, the famous accusation of genocide, that General Bagasora and myself and all of those who remained till the last to defend our country, were Hitlers who arranged a genocide," he laughed bitterly. "Ah, it makes me angry, that kind of accusation."

"How do you explain," said Bill, "What we have come to see in Rwanda and have found time and time again—mass graves, cadavers floating down rivers, cadavers being eaten by dogs?"

"And here in our camps, did you not see the misery of our people who died of cholera, cadavers being taken away by French bulldozers and also buried in mass graves, thousand upon thousand?" the former minister retorted.

"We mean inside Rwanda," said Josefu half whispering.

"If you met Madame, the unfortunate widow of the president, she would tell you how much the entire people loved him. She herself is the best witness. She too comes from a distinguished family," he said, looking once again at Josefu. "Then you would understand what it is to see the anger of a people. There is no shred of doubt in anybody's mind that the RPF, those insects, those criminals who respect nobody, not even innocent life, that it was they who shot down the plane of our president, without any thought for the whole region, since they murdered in this way the President of Burundi as well."

"So the deaths that we have seen are the result of mass anger?" asked Jean Pierre.

"Of collective anger, yes," answered the former minister. "Each peasant went out and took revenge on the villagers who supported feudalism and who waited for the arrival of Rwanda's enemies. It was spontaneous, spontaneous," he repeated. He then looked Jean Pierre in the eye, defiant, but Josefu saw it was like a dead man's gaze .

"The genocide was meticulously prepared, Monsieur le Ministre; roadblocks were set up within forty five minutes of the plane being shot down. Arms and machetes were distributed long before. What is spontaneous?" remarked Jean Pierre trying to look innocent.

"If you know everything already, then why have you come to talk with me? I am very busy. I wanted to help you by telling you, as intelligent people, the truth, but if that is not of interest to you, what is it you want?"

Jean Pierre looked anxious and unfolded his legs. He had a frail waist and wore a thin and elegant belt. His slightly pointed cheeks were flushed and red, as far as Josefu could make out with his present difficulty of vision.

"No, no, no, no, no…"

Bill broke in, "Monsieur, the Former Minister, we value your testimony. I repeat, our mandate of enquiry is that we listen to everyone, regardless of the content of what they say. Regardless of whether or not what they say matches our own eyewitness inspections of massacre sites in Rwanda. We represent the United Nations, not an interested party."

Josefu could tell, however, that there was a good deal of irritation in Bill's voice, despite the calm tone. 'I know him too well,' he reflected.

"Ah, Monsieur, you, the Canadian! Let me tell you that General

Romeo Dallaire insulted us," said their host.

"Insulted you?" asked Bill, solicitously.

"Yes, he insulted us. Do you want to know why, or do you know everything already? I shall tell you why. He treated us and the RPF as equals, trying to arrange ceasefires between our armies as if we were equals. Yet we, we represented the legitimate government, recognised in the whole world, represented at the United Nations, at his very own United Nations. Our army was the national army of our legitimate country with a legitimate government. Yet he treated us on an equal footing with those rascals, those little men with no legitimacy, who were rebels, bandits, people who represented nobody."

"I see," Bill whispered.

The former minister saw everyone was attentive. "Look," he continued, "According to his way, all you need is to get some tramps off the streets of any town, any so-called refugee camp, grab them from beer stores in miserable villages and give them guns and then give them the grand title of 'Rebel Army'. They were no army at all, just a band of criminals and marginals. And General Dallaire expected us to accept his attitude towards us and them, that we were all among equals. The French knew the difference, but not him. We always treated Dallaire with every politeness, of course, but really we despised him, for his lack of judgement. He should have respected us more," he concluded, raising his voice.

There was a long silence. Josefu, still dazzled by the glaring light, could no longer see him. Some of these words were part of a set script, exactly as reported by people like Père Ambroise. To hear one of its creators repeating these sentences verbatim, however, had a menacing tone. He struggled to adjust his sight again, this time more successfully.

Josefu suddenly noticed that their host, who was now tucking his tie more neatly inside his jacket, had a habit of licking his lips with his tongue whenever he stopped speaking. The tongue was small and pink, like that of a kitten.

Here before them was a known mastermind of mindlessly cruel acts, of ruthlessness and terror, which would soon fill the archives with records of the highest crimes known on earth. Yet his tongue was dainty and vulnerable, pretty, a delicate pink and with the sweetness of movement of a fresh and endearing kitten. Or of a small child, perhaps, the way he had been before? Until when? When did he change? Using his wide lips to issue commands for murder and then licking them with his delicate, rose pink tongue. What are human beings, what are they?

The former minister focused his attention on the two whites, Bill and Jean Pierre. "You don't want to accept that the people, the majority, the Rwandan people, love us, their real government. Look at what is happening in the camps here in Goma! They demanded of the High Commission for Refugees that the organising inside the camps must be done by us, whom they trust, right down to their bourgmestres and their prefets."

"The UNHCR on principle promotes the concept of 'community leadership' be ing recreated in the camps so they must have been pleased with the demand," Jean Pierre said, looking sideways at Bill and Josefu to express his sense of irony.

"You don't understand," the former minister contended. "The people wanted us in charge, they wanted us! They wanted to be reminded of how things were before, that is what reassured them. Let me tell you another thing. They have suffered so much, the whole people here in the camps, yet they donate part of their relief rations to us representatives of the only government they respect. They donate! They give what they can for us to sell, so we can use the money to rebuild our means to rescue our country for them, away from the hands of those insects who call themselves human beings."

Now he nearly spat. Nobody commented further.

Bill looked round, as if waiting his turn, and then asked slowly "Do you think all Tutsis are in favour of the RPF and therefore they are all your enemies?"

"They can't help it, you know, they have been fully persuaded by irresponsible propaganda from the RPF. All of them now have poisoned minds. They have no future in a free Rwanda. I assure you, Rwanda will soon find its dignity again. And we will, you know, we will! There is justice, and the rule of law will always prevail over chaos. We are stronger. We are legitimate. Montesquieu was not the only author to write about the spirit of the law, you know."

It was then, as Josefu rubbed his burning eyes to relieve them, that he noticed how close to perfection was the Minister's French accent.

Nobody else spoke, so the Minister continued: "There are too many insults against us, too much scandal. Tenez, Messieurs, let me give you an example. One person among the group of our leaders now accused of murder and genocide, he was formerly at the Rwandan Embassy in Germany. He is a very accomplished artist, a musician who has played the organ in Kigali. He also directed a wonderful choir there, and everyone listened and marvelled at the beauty of his music. Now you tell me, how could someone of such sensitivity, whom everyone loved, with all the Whites who heard him play the organ, all the educated among us, all the refined who admired him, how could he go and commit such terrible crimes? I repeat it: how could someone who is a musician who plays the organ wondrously, miraculously, then become a genocide mastermind? You see, there is only calumny, and you want to believe it. You like having enemies. You Whites, you made Rwanda poor and yet you still want to have a clear conscience. So you choose our people who are even more accomplished than yourselves, to vilify and tell stories about."

"Minister, is it possible that this former diplomat, this accomplished musician, ordered the killing of all Tutsis because he really believed he was saving the nation?" asked Jean Pierre in a small, high voice.

Despite the dazzling light, Josefu now tried to see Afrika, and saw that the veins in his temples were throbbing. He had barely touched his drink. Feeling his gaze, Afrika sent a furtive, anguished look in Josefu's direction.

"An interesting question," said the former minister, licking his lips quietly. "I am not offended that you ask me this. When your country is at war, even if you are a sensitive artist, you will want to save it. But you must ask him directly about what he thought. I cannot tell you what is in his mind. We Rwandans are careful about that."

There was a halt in the conversation. Bill watched carefully to see which way their host would move, and when it looked as if he were about to rise they all stood up at once, Afrika last.

Josefu's eyes were filled with tears when the visitors silently shook hands, loosely, with the former minister. Their host was saying, "Ah, our poor Africa, our poor continent." Perhaps it was that which touched a raw nerve.

"Our poor humanity," Josefu finally responded, in a whisper.

When they came out and walked towards their vehicles, he felt the first strong stomach cramps which were to plague him for days to come.

17.

"Afrika, help me, I must find a toilet!" Josefu murmured. It was too embarrassing to go back into the former minister's house. As sweat poured down his brow, Josefu suddenly glimpsed through some trees a view of the lake, which was pale and incredibly still. "It's so flat, so wide and flat," he said, shaking his head. "Without turmoil, so indifferent, that lake's so wide and flat."

"Flat? I do not understand you," said Afrika softly.

"Later, later," Josefu replied.

Gesturing to Celestin to wait, they crossed the road towards a group of shacks nearby, with Josefu stooping in pain as he walked. Afrika spoke in Swahili, which Josefu recognised, to a girl of about seventeen with very short hair and to an elderly woman who may well have been her grandmother. They laughed a little, which Africa half-heartedly joined in, as other children appeared from nowhere. They pointed out a far direction and, with a small boy leading the way, they all followed.

In the dark latrine, Josefu began to sob as he relieved himself. He descended into hell, mingling with the heavy smells and seeking to find words that would burn out his tongue. So he would never talk again… "Mama," he cried, but he didn't know whether it was for Rosemary, too shapely and delicate to the touch, or for some strong-breasted dragon from the middle of the earth, who would rise and rescue him. "Block that man out, get him away from me," he pleaded, using his arm to wipe spittle from his lips.

As he crouched, he saw the former minister again, just his head moving on its own towards him, and who said, "Why do you blame me? I am human like you; I acted because I was faced with the opportunity of being part of world history, for Rwanda is indeed the centre of all the world. Our very beautiful Rwanda."

"Go away," Josefu screamed in his head, while clutching his stomach. "Wait! Did you really believe in what you did, in what you said?"

"I believed that for me it was right," the other answered.

"Self interest?"

"Not exactly. Yes, I participated in making large-scale plans with my colleagues for many months before the events. It gave my body a feeling of well being, to be able to take such strong decisions of such consequence; it filled my heart with the good warmth that such power gives you. And there was just a small tremor of doubt, like a mild indigestion," and he licked his lips with his kitten-like tongue. "You already recognise we are all alike. But whereas who knows what perhaps other human beings perhaps could have done, and what you yourself could have done perhaps? In contrast, I have done it, that's all; no perhaps—I did it!" and he moved his tongue across his lips one last time.

Josefu shook his head to dispel the image before him and lingered a while, crouching over the hole in the latrine, until he was calmer. Then he resignedly, slowly, tore out some pages of the small note pad in his shirt pocket and hoped he might find somewhere to wash his hands. When he emerged into the light, he saw Afrika surrounded by barefoot children to whom he was distributing his small change in Rwandan francs. The sky was turning an urgent, thick grey and it was a relief to know that soon there would be several showers of rain, probably starting within the hour.

⋮

Josefu is surprised to find himself standing upright, with his back pressed against the thick curtains drawn across his hotel window. He dimly sees 'Imperial' written on the door. There is hardly any light in the room, which looks stark with its standard furnishings and present emptiness. He worries that he has no recollection of moving from his bed to this erect stance, in which he feels a strong and reverberating sense of desolation.

Fearful of his sinking mood, unthinkingly he runs out of his room, letting the door slam behind him without taking the key, and wearing only his vest and boxer shorts. He races down the corridor, bangs on the gates of the lift and goes past them, looking for stairs. "I can't escape that pollution; I am part of it, because I'm human," he mutters, puzzled by what he has just said. Soon finding himself in a cold sweat, standing in front of several receptionists who were in the process of changing shifts, he says in his clearest tone, "So it is morning and breakfast time." He becomes increasingly more aware now of his surroundings, he tries to cough. Nobody seems to notice him, so engrossed are the staff in their conversation. He neatly tucks his vest inside his shorts and takes a few barefoot steps forward, more embarrassed than ever. "I got lost, you know, I apologise for this. I have lost my key too, my pass card."

"Pardon me?" says a receptionist with her hair tidily pulled back into a ponytail, and wearing large glasses, "Your room number?"

He pauses for a moment, looking at her glasses, and then answers, "I forgot."

"Are you staying in this hotel, Sir?" she asks slightly menacingly.

"Yes, my name is Josefu Mutesa. I'm sorry. I've been on a rather long journey."

"Your accent!" she booms. "My God, you're not from here! Okay, what's your name again? With an 'M'?"

Not wanting to be observed for longer than necessary, he runs back to the stairs with the spare pass instead of waiting for the lift. Mumbling repeatedly the words, "Bad news," he climbs up to reach what he correctly guesses is the right floor and, once back inside his room, he leans hard against the door he let slam closed.

With increasing anguish, he tries to recollect what his memories had just brought him. It was as if he were participating in a discussion he couldn't really hear.

It comes back to him at last and he begins nodding his head, "The other side's story, where you have to ignore the surrounding odour when they speak," he says aloud, "Otherwise known as listening to their subjective truth."

A band of heat out of nowhere is slapped on to his brow. It sweeps around his head and holds him in a tight grip. The stitches near his temple are still taut. Once again, he feels that a conversation is being had which fades whenever he tries to listen. His toes twitch.

Going into the bathroom he sees the large potted plant and falls on his knees to hold its branches, looking for refuge. He kisses some of the thick green leaves with tender passion, one by one, almost licking them, as he seeks relief from ice-cold solitude. Hand inside his boxer shorts, he find no movement and draws it away in resigned silence. Then, leaning both elbows on the edge of the bath, he glances across at the shining, panelled mirror. But what he half sees now is a surface appearing so full of cracks, reflecting a fragmented image so confusedly, that he forgets to breathe for several moments.

Rising, he returns to his room and goes dutifully to the small chair by a desk, on which he rests his arms. Eyes closed, he bows down, as if he were to be beheaded. Asked for one last wish—it is for fellowship, not to go alone. Wish granted instantly, a rain-starved, flat field appears before him, and at the edge, in the pale light, walks Père Ambroise dragging a large wooden pole, yet with his head held high. Behind him limps a haggard General Dallaire, who detaches one last brass button from his ragged clothes and throws it over his shoulder. A passing cloud, fast moving in the wind, speaks the words with gentle simplicity, "Always in that order: the Rwandans' own sorrow first, and the pain of outsiders can only follow behind it, several respectful steps back." Suitably humbled and, at last with some company, Josefu clears his throat and waits again, eyes still shut, ignoring the hungry rumblings in his belly.

⋮

In New York, Josefu once had hurried along the corridors, looking for Bill who at the time spent more time in the Security Council than in his office. He wanted him to see the missives from Dallaire protesting vigorously that his mandate had to be amended, so he could disable the Radio Mille Collines. That radio station screamed out against the Tutsis and even directed mobs to locations where they could find people to kill. Nothing like that, Josefu told him, should be tolerated on the planet after Hitler's war. But Dallaire was told—and it couldn't be changed—that to close the radio station would have been an aggressive act, which could not be sanctioned by the United Nations Organisation.

It was then that Josefu had toyed with the idea of illegally leaking to the media some of Dallaire's documents. When he decided not to, because at the time he cautiously thought the unknown consequences could be even more disastrous, it led to the worst falling out with Patricia he had ever experienced, seemingly the end of his marriage. From then onwards, more than ever, General Dallaire, with his clarion call for reason, but with a silhouette hardly clearer than Don Quixote's, stalked him daily into his bed, into his profession and later onto every hill in Rwanda where Josefu walked.

"What are you doing here, you fake?" Dallaire always seemed to whisper. The general himself was reluctant to join the ranks of failed dreamers caught in a spider's web of grandiose, but small-minded, institutions.

"Damn", says Josefu to himself, no longer aware he is alone in his hotel room, "I didn't budge, nothing moved. He couldn't even convince us in New York to do better next time round, when it was Tousignant's turn."

All of a sudden, Josefu perceives the bedrock of his UN mission in Rwanda: principled obstinacy. Its mandate in the aftermath of the genocide was regulated by the same high degree of principled obstinacy as before it had happened. Nothing changed, nothing at all.

The military on the ground had a different, more believable clarity of vision but that counted for nothing. Tousignant too, like his predecessor, had challenged the flat interpretation of the Charter of Universal Human Rights. The UN authorities had brandished it in front of him but, in the circumstances, they turned it into a nonsense. He had simply requested a scrambler, nothing more, for stopping inflammatory broadcasts—yet again—from the radio station now set up across the border in Zaire and being broadcast back into Rwanda.

Irritated as he remembers the incident now, Josefu scratches both his arms. "It was run by the genocidal government in exile—paid with diverted assets while their rank and file were fed by international charity."

Bill and Josefu both knew that the broadcasts sent acrid, fuming messages across to Rwanda, for the plans for the elimination of Tutsis to be completed. Tousignant had told Bill that some were translated into English for the UN headquarters, especially passages where Tutsi humans were said not to be human, but it had changed nothing.

Josefu now shakes his head, hands gripping the hotel furniture.

He and Bill, his prudent superior, had stayed on regardless, since that was the usual way they worked.

'General Tousignant was told by New York that it was not his mandate to ask for funds for a scrambler, or to take any measures to stop access to that radio station, whatever its contents, because to do so was a violation against freedom of speech. It would have been against the UN Charter—against Human Rights, they added, to make it clearer.

'The Kinyarwanda language in Africa, regardless of its use, could be allowed more freedom than German or English in which the same offensive substance would have been banned in their own countries.' And Josefu remarks to himself: 'Such liberty also conveniently saves on budgets'.

"Never again, never again!" the world had said about the propaganda build-up to the Shoah in Germany. Yet in Rwanda, despite that experience and its promises, there was only a post-war exclamation of slight distaste.'

His eyes burn.

⋮

Josefu had not wanted to visit Goma market and sat alone with Jean Pierre by a shack that passed itself off as a café, with a waiter keeping a folded cloth over his arm in elegant fashion. The rain had been short lived but violent, almost as if the sky had let out a frightened scream.

"It is so terrible to be here, in this region, and be a Belgian," said Jean Pierre very solemnly.

"Collective guilt is yet another form of racism," said Josefu without hesitation, as if he had said it many times before. "Keep away from it."

"But when I'm here it is a physical thing. My grandparents lived in

Bukavu down the coast, self-righteous colonials, and my grandfather whipped his servants here. My father spent years here too, right near here. So they ate what came out of this soil here, and it means part of this soil is in my own body, you see. How do you get away from that?"

"Why your guilt, though? Did you whip anyone yourself?"

"You have this calm way of speaking; it's your Anglo-Saxon manner. But you know nothing about Belgium."

Josefu noticed that Jean Pierre gesticulated frequently with his distinguished-looking, agile hands, with fragile wrists.

"This changing weather isn't easy. One minute blinded by the sun, a minute later it pours with rain," Josefu sighed. "I once went to Brussels with my fiancée, as she was then," and Josefu wished he hadn't said it.

"I live in Brussels. I live with my partner, George, a chef, since we left school." Jean Pierre laughed, "But here I say nothing because the Rwandans consider gays to be ill. Their society is very rigid, very repressed, you know."

"And in your opinion does that explain anything, about their use of violence?"

"Who knows. Such theories are used only to excuse the killers, not to explain anything. I have written about it. And I used one of Bernard's photographs. Overpopulation, repressed sexuality, the fall of coffee prices, anything is used to explain savagery. Bernard's photo showed the savagery. Do you think we are being watched?" he asked, discreetly looking in the direction diagonally opposite where a couple of young men, with basketball caps worn back to front, immediately turned away.

"I have broken our regulations: we should have never left the group and our escort, but who cares," said Josefu, putting any qualms straight out of his mind.

"Okay." Jean Pierre continued, "Belgium. I was saying...We were the masters here, so we brought our own views and our own maladies. We had our own problems between French speaking Walloons and the Flemish speaking Flamands and so we wanted to recreate the same shit here, for us to feel at home. So the Tutsi and Hutu were divided by the Belgians to create the same Belgian shit."

"You feel very strongly about it," said Josefu, who saw him angrily pulling his shirt collar down.

He then noticed that the two men opposite had not moved away.

"Perhaps traditional Rwandan society under a strong monarchy was not completely ideal. But it had a way of avoiding cataclysmic violence, anyway. Belgium brought pollution. In Europe we demand that factories pay for the pollution they make, to clear up their mess. Here we Belgians brought our shit, our divisions, and we never paid for it. My parents still don't understand the extent of our arrogance; they never look at what we did, us and the Church. We are Catholics. I am still Catholic, although we gays do not have an easy time." His right eyebrow twitched and he rubbed his nose with the back of his hand.

Josefu had a surge of compassion for Jean Pierre at that moment, but was suddenly aware all his feelings were hazy, like those of a drunk. "Don't worry," he said at last, pouring coke into his glass and ordering two more bottles. He now felt, in the pit of his stomach, a certainty that the men across the road were watching them.

"Don't stop me," snapped Jean Pierre. "You work for the United Nations and you know nothing about Belgium." His cheeks were very red now." I was saying, oh I don't know where I was," he said, distressed.

"Don't worry, I tell you, we've got plenty of time," Josefu smiled benevolently, though somewhat falsely. He so hated being stuck waiting for the others to return.

"I know you can understand what happened because you were brought up in Europe. You say you were born there and you know about the yellow stars Hitler used for the Jews in the lands they conquered."

"Yes, I did Modern History as an option at school," Josefu said formally.

"The Belgians introduced an ethnic identity card, Hutu, Tutsi, Twa, for all Rwandans, though until then they were an undivided people under one monarch and speaking the same language. Only it was worse, the Belgians called it not 'ethnic' but 'race'. The worst shit in the world."

"Did the Germans or the Belgians bring it, I can't remember? Both had their turn as colonials here," said Josefu.

"The Belgians did, I tell you. My ancestors, my direct ancestors. If it weren't for George, my partner, I would have killed myself when the troubles took place in Rwanda. Of course, I have been visiting these parts for many years. I have been a specialist, ever since graduating from the Free University of Brussels. I have enemies at the university, enemies I am proud to have."

"That's good," said Josefu lamely, now looking around for signs of his other companions. The waiter poured their drinks with a flourish. He had obviously seen better times. Paying him, Josefu asked, "Is this your own place, Monsieur?"

"My café-bar, it is my café-bar in the open air. I worked in Kinshasa and I have been to Israel."

"Israel? In the Holy Land?" said Josefu.

"No, not in the Holy Land. In a hotel there, to learn how my boss liked things to be in Kinshasa. An Israeli. But when I returned to Kinshasa there was so much jealousy from other Zairois, I had to leave my job and come home to Goma. It's like that in Africa, a lot of jealousy. There must be jealousy from where you come. You are not black American because you speak French. But you do not look like our confrères in the West of our continent, not Cameroon or Senegal and those parts."

"I was born in England and my parents came from Uganda but I studied in French speaking Switzerland. Does that satisfy you?" Josefu said to the waiter, now noticing that Jean Pierre was puce coloured with impatience. "I'm sorry, Monsieur," he added obsequiously, and yet the man moved away looking pleased.

Jean Pierre now felt the impact of Josefu's full attention.

"You have an intense gaze," he said.

"Do I? But I am waiting for you to continue what you had been saying," Josefu said, quickly glancing once again towards the road.

"So you really want to know my story?"

"Of course, I can learn from you."

Jean Pierre smiled innocently, gratified, and he began eagerly: "The Belgians decreed, with all their arrogance, who was to be Hutu and who Tutsi. As for the Twa, that was for anyone of abnormally short stature. And they decreed that the Hutu were those with less than ten cows and the Tutsi with more than ten cows. And they were called the three races of Rwanda. Listen to me well," he repeated. "It determined who was allowed to whip whom in the name of the Belgians. It permitted some to study and others to starve. It was all abominable. And the Church revelled in it, since being born into membership of one race or the other, they said, was an act of God. What shit!"

"They weren't alone," remarked Josefu.

"What? Are you looking for excuses for them? Signs of the times and all that?" said Jean Pierre angrily. "Don't you know how many Hutu have been killed just now, just in these past months, mistakenly, just because they were as tall as the Tutsi stereotype? But do you know that for most of them, the identity cards alone were used at the road blocks to decide whether you died on the spot or not?"

"Look, the Belgians switched sides. They started out by giving privileges for those they called Tutsi but towards the end of their rule they supported the Hutu," remarked Josefu.

"There was some Swiss shit too," Jean Pierre said knowingly. "Monsignor Perraudin was a prince of the church in Rwanda, with the Swiss fixation for cantons and separate languages and oh, God only knows, he had some of their strange mountain peasant ideas against monarchy or something like that. I don't understand the Swiss clergy very well. But this man was an influential churchman. And it was under his very own patronage, his misplaced Christian romanticism, yes, it is he who sponsored the writing of the famous "Manifesto of the Hutu People", in the late 1950's. There was a unitary Rwandan people, divided by the Belgians, and the church never denounced it, never pointed out the false science. Ah, such shit, such shit."

"I'm sorry," said Josefu. "Listen, Jean Pierre. I am grateful to you for telling me all this. It helps me reflect. Your point about responsibility here for clearing up the pollution of social thought is brilliant."

"Really?" Jean Pierre smiled like a schoolboy.

"But I'm worried now. I feel I must answer for your safety, and we are being watched, over there, and they may well be armed. All it takes is a passing motorcycle…"

Although he was of slight build, Jean Pierre straightened his back and said, "I try not to be afraid. I try to make it my business to record what I see. It is my profession. And to speak my mind."

At that moment, staggering under the weight of their plastic bags and other bundles, Afrika, Bill, Celestin and Bernard came towards them with smiles from ear to ear. But it began raining again and they all hurried in silence to the cars, followed by their similarly laden Senegalese and Canadian escorts. The self-appointed car attendant was given a large tip. Josefu only hoped Afrika had remembered to buy something for Marie Immaculée and her companion, as requested.

"You will like Ursule, whom we shall visit now," said Bernard, who had hidden his cameras from view while in the market. "You might not agree with her, but she is very sincere," he added.

"Very sincere," echoed Jean Pierre.

They were going to a Rwandan social worker, who had fled the country and was trying to organise women refugees into morale-raising collectives.

As they drove up, they heard some women screaming.

"Ah, that one's son has just been killed, here in the camps," said Afrika, "It happens every day. I am looking for my cousin's brother today—you remember his mother asked you. It's difficult. Look at those women, look how they are crying."

Josefu had not seen Rwandan women dressed in such rags before.

He remarked on it to Bill who replied, "Gabrielle will be coming to check up on things like that, a very useful job."

"We've not even been inside the actual camps yet; she won't be able to bear it, Bill!"

When they emerged from the car at Ursule's place, there was an embarrassingly subdued hush around them. A large group of women stared without a word, and there was utter silence except for two children who cried desperately, outdoing each other with their screams. It was obvious the women had little water to wash with. One seized the screaming children without a word and shook them, and instantly they too were silent. About ten paces away stood armed men, three of them, although it was impossible to know if they were Zairian troops or Rwandan exiled militia.

A woman came out of a lean-to built with plastic sheeting, by the wall of a low office building.

"It belongs to a church organisation," said Bernard. "But here comes Ursule," going up and kissing her on both cheeks.

She was of stocky build, late thirties perhaps, in a dark blue European dress, which had known better times and Josefu also saw her black leather, high heeled shoes. He noticed her round hands and that her decoratively plaited hair was dishevelled.

"Forgive us," she said, shaking hands with everyone, "We are going crazy here. We cannot get any accountability from anyone. Half these women's families have been affected by the cholera epidemic and they lived in such squalor that even though the relief services have improved things now, they have lost their will to survive. And every day someone is killed here and nobody can say anything. Just those of our self appointed authorities decide who can live or die, but if I say anything I can be killed too."

"Ursule, there are still four million Hutu in Rwanda," said Jean Pierre, as she invited them to lean against a tree. "Why did you have to come here? I still can't understand. You could try going back, couldn't you?"

"Where can we talk?" said Bill.

"I cannot invite you inside; there are two women lying down, one of them dying, my aunt, and one of them is my mother. Our life is a misery," said Ursule.

"So why did they all leave?"

"You have to understand our history," replied Ursule. "We suffered an unjust feudal system, we Hutu, and we were whipped by Tutsi princes."

"The Belgians got them to do it, don't you realise?" interrupted Jean Pierre. "My own grandfather said that when he got tired of punishing his lazy workers, as he called them, he made natives do it, here in the Congo. That is what they did in Rwanda too, the Belgians."

"If you know everything, Jean Pierre, go away and don't wait for me again. Not so fast! By the way, you know that article you wrote about me, after your last visit, well some woman in Belgium read it and sent me a message that in a week she is arriving with emergency supplies for these women and paper and crayons so we can start a school here, by this tree."

"Something achieved, the first I've heard of it," replied Jean Pierre modestly.

"We had our Social Revolution in 1959, when we overthrew the feudal power of the Tutsi." Ursule now talks with passion. "We have beautiful songs we sing to commemorate the Social Revolution. After that, we only let good Tutsi remain. They had been so arrogant before. They had not wanted to eat with us Hutu or to carry things if one of us Hutu could do it for them. Then we showed them what democracy was about, the power of a majority people. We had at last entered the modern world and left feudalism behind."

Josefu looked at this erudite woman standing against a large tree, her head leaning to one side, surrounded by half naked children and their destitute mothers, and she was speaking from the heart. About feudalism. About democracy. In language rapidly sinking into the sodden, clay-like ground. He could not help noticing a strong smell of excrement wafting in their direction.

"There were many injustices, though. I had many Tutsi friends and they should not have been treated the way they were," she added.

Everyone stood spellbound. Josefu wondered whether she knew Bernard was a Tutsi, but realised he could never ask her.

"Now you can understand," she continued, "That when we heard they, the Tutsis in Uganda, were returning with their armies, ready to massacre everybody they encountered, we had not enough courage to stay. They are being helped by Anglo-Saxons, we don't know exactly who, but in Uganda there are many. Even the Tutsis returning from Burundi are under the command of the RPF from Uganda. And the Burundi Tutsis kill everybody."

Josefu hoped she did not know where his parents came from. There was truth in what she said about some of the Burundi returnee soldiers. He had been told several times in Rwanda that the lack of discipline among a few of them, once they were incorporated into the new army, was turning into a real problem for the officers.

"Jean Pierre, you are a funny man," she said, looking at him saucily. "What if there are still four million of our people left behind? Don't you think that is merely one more indication of how much we are suffering? That we did not all have the power to leave? Everyone would have left if they could. There is another genocide going to take place where all those four million of our people will be killed. Only we here will survive and it will be the end of the Hutu people in Rwanda. You must help us. You must all help us. We are a dying people."

"What do you think of the elements of the old Rwandan Army who are regrouping here in Zaire? Is that happening?" said Bill in a whisper, and with his face almost as red as Jean Pierre's.

"Yes. They are taking away part of the donations we receive. Yes, they take away much of the distributed aid we would like to have had for ourselves, but they are our only hope for our people to survive and if they do not get us back into Rwanda soon, then we will all die, all the Hutu people."

Bill did not comment.

"Mind you, there are Hutu leaders whom I spit on, those in their big villas, with their cars. Some are here in Goma, but most of them are hiding in Bukavu. You know where it is: also on the shores of the lake. And we here are in this misery. If they, those rich leaders of ours, hadn't ruined our country with their greed, we would have been stronger to resist the RPF invaders. All of them have sent their wives and children to Paris, to Europe, to everywhere, and we are dying here, our women and children. Just look at them over there in the corner."

Josefu now was deeply horrified by the sullen looks of the women standing in silence. 'People's lives, bought and sold for a lie,' he thought to himself, but said nothing.

"I will fight till the end," said Ursule, "To give these women some hope. To give the children some schooling, some future."

Suddenly Josefu noticed Afrika, his hands behind his back, staring at his feet.

"You know, Bill," Josefu said in English, "You can write up the report yourself on this incident." Then turning to Ursule, he said in French, "You are approaching all the right organisations I hope, like UNICEF?"

"UNICEF have their own people among the Rwandans to whom they delegate their work, and because I am open and try to help everybody, those Rwandans don't let me come near them. Do you understand what I am saying?"

"I am sorry you have that impression," said Bill.

"You mean 'that experience'," Josefu corrected him in hushed voice. Then turning to Ursule he said, "My colleague and I, we both hope it will change." He knew Bill could detect some sarcasm in his tone.

"I don't know who you represent," said Ursule. "Those cars are of UNAMIR. They are our enemies. But I know Bernard and Jean Pierre and they would not have brought me enemies."

"We are not your enemies," Bill said promptly.

"We do not work for UNAMIR," Josefu said in a softer tone. "We only have them as a security escort because, as you will agree, we need it."

"But have you come here from Rwanda?" said Ursule, shocked and moving away.

"We come from New York," said Josefu swiftly, before Bill could speak. "And we are visiting everything we can."

"But Americans and Anglo-Saxons are our enemies, I already told you."

"I wouldn't say that. After all, as you can see from the sacks, you receive a lot of humanitarian aid from the United States," said Josefu, confirming her belief that he was American.

"It is France who helps us too," she replied. "But now we are without hope."

"While we were travelling here, Jean Pierre was telling us about the funding you need for your project. We'll look into it, won't we Bill?" said Josefu.

"Yes, definitely," he affirmed.

"We want to die, we just want to die," said Ursule, but she shook hands gaily with everybody present and waved as they left, telling the women to do likewise. Josefu could not bear to look back.

As they arrived at the main headquarters of the UN's refugee mission, he decided he would leave everything there to Bill. They had little to say. It was a short, formal call. The staff were so busy, and it was apparent Bill and he were not welcome.

Riding around Goma, Josefu was pained to see the proliferation of charity organisation offices, seemingly well equipped. Likewise, exiled leaders had cars, office support and communications, privileges which were very obvious, permitted happily and in some cases supplied by the so-called international agencies, who thought that it would promote local democracy. But Josefu said loudly to Afrika, in earshot of everyone else in their group, "The Minister of Justice of Rwanda, presiding now in a country that has witnessed the worst act of mass killings we can conceive of, sits in an office in Kigali without windowpanes. He has no typewriter, no telephone and he has to walk to the court and to the prison because he has no car."

"No, no, he is being lent a car by one of the donor countries," said Bernard. "I took a photograph of the car to give him and he was very pleased."

"I'm glad to hear it."

"Everything is going to be all right," said Bernard.

"Don't be so gloomy, Josefu," said Bill.

When they approached Lake Kivu, Josefu could not resist looking.

He reflected that its serenity had presided over so many versions of history and, on its shores, history was told in a different manner each time. Perhaps there was an older, more African version, perhaps even one of his own. For he knew that his own Kingdom of Buganda, to the east, had had conquest designs on Rwanda long ago, but had been roundly and thoroughly repulsed by incomparable, invincible warriors. Who can tell, though, if one of his ancestors had not tiptoed across the land, or crept up from another country, to this lake, on Rwanda's western border, and paid silent homage?

'There had been other times', he thought quietly, 'whose chronicles should be bound in golden volumes. The Kingdom of Rwanda was like no other.' Josefu pictured its shining pages. 'Importantly, no slave trade was ever permitted. Surely that deserved to be written down in careful lettering', he mused, reverently. 'Foreigners, until the Rwandans were humiliatingly conquered by gun-toting Europeans, were not allowed at all inside its jealously kept borders. And only select African neighbours, from the immediate vicinity, were admitted for brisk trading, then asked to leave again. And there was the King of Rwanda, in his capital, consecrated with his royal drum. At once divine and human, he held sway over all his people, all of them.' Josefu decided right then that a book should be made available with a footnote for later generations: *For early centralised government, see 'Rwanda.'*

'Take note,' he'd say if he were a teacher, reading carefully from the decorously bound, weighty book, 'In those days, the Tutsi, Hutu and Twa were parts of the same body. Then divisions were social and not racial, and passage between them was fluid.' Everyone would listen to him. 'And then the Twa, with song and poetry, pleased the

King. With the highest forms of art, they served him. Who, then, could challenge the Twa in the world order? And the politics then! So different then! Not all chiefs were Tutsi in those days. There were also Hutu chiefs in some regions, assigned by right, receiving both honour and authority.'

Josefu became even more melancholy, as he continued to ponder: 'But the Belgians came, replacing those Hutu chiefs of the north with their own Tutsi appointees. It was an asymmetry according to their own image.' Now Josefu knew it all. 'Later, all hell broke loose, and why should anyone be surprised anymore? Isn't that the way history, after the colonies, writes itself everywhere? Wrong was done then, with consequences. Yet who now pays the fines, the claimants' courts, and the advocates? Do even judges receive their due?'

With great force, Josefu felt he was being drawn back to face older pages, favoured ones with better treasures. He closed his eyes, knowing their written contents by memory, and he was overwhelmed with an imprecise yearning, as the words appeared in front of him:

> Before in Rwanda, in the times of the ancient kings, the Tutsi and the Hutu belonged to the same clans. The King stood above all differences, in those days, embodying Rwanda as a unity, unique like God the Trinity.

> And the lake sapped the freshness of the rivers and returned its water to the sky. And then it rained into the hillside streams and the fresh flow began again.

18.

"I'll come downstairs then," Josefu says on the telephone, for a hasty coffee from a machine and a muffin.

"So humbling. Such a leveller!" Josefu remarks amongst a gust of almost wordless, diverse reflections, 'Whether it's killer Interahamwe who stop for lunch between their working hours of nine till five, as they often did, or whether it's a priest whom crowds adore, or a provincial governor whom they fear, all of us need strategies to nibble food.'

First, though, he calls Gulshan's number from his room.

"I'm fine. I wondered whether we had anything in our literature on gastro-enteritis, or dysentery?"

"My God, what have you done?"

"I just want to understand what was wrong with me when I was sick in Rwanda."

Gulshan is silent to begin with. "Do those who wait for you in Winnipeg know about this?" she asks.

"It's only about what illness I had before, and nothing to do with now," he reassures her.

"You need some rice. You should stop driving and take an aeroplane. You've been too long without proper food." Her voice becomes smaller and smaller.

"I'll call you later, I promise," and he puts the receiver down and rises.

Having carried his simple breakfast upstairs, he pauses solemnly, sitting with his knees together at the small hotel room table. He feels like a fish with bait in his mouth, caught and ready for going into Gulshan's *balti* pot.

"I must leave Medicine Hat before it's too late, leave Alberta behind and reach Swift Current, and go right past it," he thinks aloud. He sits back in his chair, however, and smiles from ear to ear instead.

"Père Ambroise, how good of you to come to Kibuye," said Bill. "Let me introduce you to our colleague from the United States." He called out, "Gabrielle, it's the priest I told you about, he's here."

"Okay, Honey, I'm coming," she shouted, in her khaki knee-length shorts, adding more quietly, "Where's Josefu? He'll take the 'Honey' the wrong way."

Josefu burst out of the house, brushed past Gabrielle and hugged Père Ambroise, saying: "I've waited." They slapped each other on the back over and over again.

"I needed to see you," said Père Ambroise moving away.

Something had changed, Josefu noticed, in the way he looked. Suddenly he exclaimed: "Père Ambroise! You have new glasses! Hurrah!"

He grinned like a child. "They come from Kisangani, from the heart of Africa, although they must have been imported, I think from Italy."

"My father said that one day we'd produce those kinds of things in Africa and not have to import them," Josefu responded, suddenly noticing the youthful shape of the priest's cheeks, in contrast to his movements, which were elderly. A full gust of wind blew across the yard, giving some respite from the clinging heat. Josefu reflected that all would be well now, with Père Ambroise here.

"I have my new glasses but I'm not happy," the priest said, at the same time shaking hands with Gabrielle formally and quickly. Turning to Bill he added, "I thought that the Batutsi among us Rwandans would be different, that we would somehow break this cycle of vengeance, that we'd be the best in the world."

"What's happened?" said Bill, getting his turn to give Père Ambroise a bear hug.

"I'll tell you, I'll tell you. But later."

Josefu had learned that Rwandans have a great sense of timing for conversations and the slightest office boy would not report even the most trivial detail without first choosing his moment.

"Yes, of course," he said.

"So what will you show me today?" asked Père Ambroise.

"I was about to keep my rendezvous with a little girl who loves music, before I knew you would arrive," Josefu replied.

"Perfect. But where is Marie Immaculée?" Père Ambroise asked nervously.

"She doesn't live here," said Bill. "But I think she's on her way."

"It's not safe for her to live on her own," the priest said.

"Well, that's how the arrangement has been worked out," said Bill in a very positive voice. "If she had been alone it would have been different, but there are the two women and the three children. They found a hut to rent and we give them extra money, that's all,"

"I told you, Bill, we should think again," said Josefu.

"But that's the way it worked out," he repeated. "Security considerations are for us too—regulations issued by our Headquarters," Bill sighed.

Later, they strolled to the villa with the piano. "The girl is called Epiphanie," Josefu told Père Ambroise as they found her guarding the piano she had closed and locked.

The priest cajoled her in Kinyarwanda. "Ah, she's waiting for this nun who has returned to the safety of her Mother House. But what future does the girl have, with a father in prison? She says her mother wants them to move to a place where they can till the soil for food. So what can she take from Sister Geraldine but a clear conscience, perhaps?"

She cried when they left. Josefu came back for a moment and lamely gave her a sum of money. About a hundred dollars. They didn't see her again. It might have been the wrong amount.

⋮

That last visit to Epiphanie had been one more increasingly disconcerting experience in Kibuye. And the old man Josefu had met by the lake, Afrika said his body had been washed up, perhaps poisoned, he added. When asked why, he answered: "Perhaps, if the man lived on his own, it would be easy to take his property."

And then on a visit to Goma, Afrika had discovered that his young cousin had been murdered, on a whim, by his superiors who were the former government members he served. It had happened shortly after he reached the camp, only because he was overheard saying he preferred to return to Rwanda. His body had been placed with the cholera victims and dug into the ground with a bulldozer provided by the French army.

Josefu was thankful for Afrika's sake that now, at last, Père Ambroise had arrived so he could relate his loss. Père Ambroise, with him, bowed his head dejectedly. Josefu bowed his too, and lingered in the distance.

⋮

Saskatchewan, Land of the Living Skies, has an active road-building program. Josefu is on a stretch of a single lane highway now, but it could change by next year, it could improve.

The trips between Kibuye and Kigali had been made that much faster because they used part of the superior road surface built by the dead president and only partially destroyed by the fighting. He wonders if, these six years later, it had been fully restored and even extended.

Now he skirts Maple Creek and goes towards Swift Current, passing discarded tyres like so many dead bats on the road. He's glad they had not burst when he was following eighteen-wheeler trucks. He carefully keeps his distance from another lonely car that soon turns off and disappears from view. Josefu's driving is steady, as first he notices some clear green hills and then, without warning, flat land again as far as the eye can see. Soon after, he observes people playing a game of golf, in a prairie, with flags precisely marked, on a grass island with homely contours.

⋮

The rapidity of informal links across Lake Kivu astounded Josefu and Bill. Immediately after Père Ambroise's arrival in Kibuye, Bernard the photo-journalist, without ever saying how he knew, brought Jean Pierre unannounced to meet him, having travelled from Goma where both had stayed on indefinitely. Everyone sat together in the yard near a tree—which kind?—Josefu could not recall now. The conviviality was of a close kind, like when you share a small train carriage on a long journey. An absurd argument had developed amongst them over the names of Belgian beers, as to whether *Kriek* was a cherry beer and *Gueuze* a raspberry beer, or vice-versa.

Afrika joined in, saying that there are always problems when things have too many names. He explained, "We too, in Kinyarwanda, we have so many kinds of beans and people don't recognise their names, like *bahani mpubuke* or red ones called *magabali* and people want to call them 'Carolina' instead."

"Eeh," said Bernard approvingly, probably relieved not to be discussing the killings for once. Earlier on, after careful probing from Josefu, who was alarmed at his haggard looks, Bernard had admitted to being wearied by the intense pace of Jean Pierre's lugubrious deliberations.

"Bernard, he hasn't personally lost his own people in the killings, so he talks more than Rwandans would do about such things," Josefu had whispered discreetly. "He doesn't have to avoid remembering things; it's different for Jean Pierre than for you. But he has a sincerity that is worth knowing."

Later as they all sat together, Jean Pierre's voice started to rise above everyone else's. When he was sure they were all listening, he held his glass tightly with both hands. He declared that the potential for conflict within nations now could be accurately measured by using a mathematical formula, recently created by an Irishman for the purpose.

From then on, the evening conversation was like a wizard's lantern, which illuminated the surroundings in a way that proved difficult to believe was truthful.

⋮

Josefu is driving at maximum speed with new determination.

Granaries, painted white, in clusters of four or five, are huddled together like Arab tents. He knows where he is, though, since Herbert had been left behind, and the salt around Lake Chaplin, with the industry to secure it, has come into sight. Looking into the rear view mirror, the skies are dark volcanoes whereas ahead, glimmers of rising sun appear between the young clouds. Here the farmers had listened to national warnings, and revived sloughs for travelling geese and ducks to have water when they needed it; something Josefu already had read about, when alone in his house in Banff.

Never before now has that place in Buffalo Street seemed so distant. Here on either side of the highway there are ponds, and telephone wires in sets of three, where the lower ones in pairs are for electricity. Fields are not left fallow here, as far as he can tell, because there is only one planting season. He must find water for his plant in the back seat. The car windows are shut, to keep out the insects and the noise of the wind. He is 21 kilometres from Moose Jaw and extremely tired.

Stepping out to stretch and rest by the verge, Josefu sees General Dallaire walking towards him from the edge of the prairie, in full, spotless, military dress. Brass buttons shining on his sleeves, he is waving his arms with encouragement, as if Josefu had accomplished a job well done.

"But that's not right," replies Josefu to himself. "We did so little. In our last weeks in Rwanda we ran around taking evidence like demented scribes, Bill driven by mounting rage. Whereas I slowed down, insanely so; I couldn't jump the hurdles any more."

Josefu hugs his knees, surrounded by grass and thistles. But now he remembers having shouted out to Afrika, towards the end of their stay, "What's all that by the path leading to the ditch—wood chippings, or gravel, some kind of covering?"

⋮

They had been taken to a mass grave that day, filled with the remains of victims already killed well before 1994, but which could only be visited now, after the old government had gone. The whole surrounding area was empty, though, when Père Ambroise had shown them the recently discovered burial place. Next to it a new place was being prepared, though, by refugees returning from Tanzania. He was going to consecrate it.

Josefu repeated his question, "What are they?" pointing to the scattered chippings and saying they looked sinister. Afrika remained silent.

"Of course, nobody likes them. Don't you know what they are?" said Père Ambroise incredulously. "They are the shards which denote the presence of mass graves. They are the flakes from bones and skulls when too many of them are shoved together, even after the flesh all falls away. You have been here so long, and you still don't know things like that!"

"True," Josefu replied softly, "still so many things. And I regret it."

He'd avoid those shards, in future, that looked like gravel or wood chippings; he knew now what they were.

His mind, however, returns to the present, and the field before him is deserted and there is nobody to whom he can apologise for all his past ignorance.

⋮

Josefu stood back patiently, while Père Ambroise finished his conversation with Afrika who had waited so ardently for his arrival in Kibuye. They had been talking for a very long time.

Finally the priest turned, took off his new glasses and rubbed his eyes, saying, "It is terrible when you think of what people could have been if they had not become killers, like Afrika's young kinsman. If he hadn't chosen that path."

"When does it happen, that point of choice, Père Ambroise?"

"I often think there may be a small voice that whispers to you, urges you to waste your life and that of others'; we all hear it sometimes." Then the priest had smiled for a moment. "But that sounds like theology, a speculation, and it is unworthy of the suffering we witness here."

⋮

Here, alone by a flat and undemanding field, Josefu quietly weeps the world's losses, all of them! Slowly, though, he is becoming aware that the fences he had erected and tended so carefully, between his memories and his present travels, now are becoming windswept. In a small puddle close to him is the face of the girl he interviewed for evidence, who had been made to do gymnastics in the nude, before mocking crowds, in the courtyard of the prefecture right there in Kibuye. He turns away and catches his breath.

And now, sitting beside him in the field, Père Ambroise puts his arm around Josefu's aching shoulders and says, "Do you remember what I told you, that when men kill, they do it as a command, to put their finger upon world history—that's what they think they are doing. But the cruelty they do, they do it for themselves."

"What do you mean?"

"Many different things happen. Just a moment ago, you remembered my arrival for the last time in Kibuye, didn't you? And you recalled that when I arrived I was so troubled. It was acts of revenge which had caused my anger that day, the acts I had seen. Kagame punished some of his own troops for doing it, but many were out of control and they took revenge on Hutu villagers. Some took men and burned their private parts on slow, charcoal embers. And an entire village population was killed, one by one, just like the other side had done, in the name of revenge. In this incident I went to bury them myself; I was really surprised to be asked by the victims' surviving relatives. My grief was almost worse than theirs because of the shame I felt. You, Josefu, can understand that, you were always expert at that kind of thing," Père Ambroise says.

Josefu weeps.

Père Ambroise laughs lightly, though, and pats him on the arm. "Won't you let me finish my speech? You take it so much to heart, you prevent me from speaking and yet I want to finish what I began."

Josefu watches a flock of ducks swoop low along the flat horizon, towards a westward prairie. "Cruelty, you were explaining it," he says softly.

"So cruelty sometimes is practiced for revenge. Or, sometimes, it's as a lesson or a warning, of course. But mostly you do it for your own benefit, for yourself. I'll explain. When you've killed, you feel fear straight after. Then you go and inflict cruelty and it brings you not fear but a sense of your power. And so you can use that power to quench the thirst which fear had given you. So you do it, the cruelty, for your own sake. That is my explanation. Now I've finished my speech."

"But it so weighed on me, having to write it all down, especially by Lake Kivu," Josefu says. "I couldn't stop, it was my job, and day in and day out, writing down the cruelty. The child who was asked to eat a piece of his mother's breast before he was killed in turn. And the child who had his arms cut off and when I talked with him he told me he didn't cry because it would have pleased his enemies. *Write. Write.* Do you know, it was after hearing that boy without arms, when I really began to lose my bearings."

"You lost your sleep after that, you lost knowing which day it was, Monday or Tuesday. I know that well, ah Josefu, lying awake. The planet fell on you."

He can feel Père Ambroise rubbing him lightly on the back and lifting the soreness from between his shoulders.

"Do you know what it's like to be right here?" Josefu says, "And no longer be able to keep all the roads in separate places?"

"Don't worry, they will soon become distinct again," says Père Ambroise. "I missed you so much, Josefu, I wanted to sit with you. For that, it was necessary for your thoughts to blur a little, but I'll go now and it will be easier." He takes a long breath and says, "From now on, what you see will become so much clearer for you." His whole face lights up, but whether or not his eyes smile through his glasses, Josefu cannot tell.

"Père Ambroise," cries Josefu like a child, trying to turn and get closer, and see him better. At that moment, a large silver tanker goes by on the highway, and hoots its horn playfully. Josefu glances at the road behind him. He rises resignedly from the edge of the now empty field, and climbs back in his car.

At first he doesn't know where he is, as he drives ahead. At

Moosejaw, past the brown plastic sculpture of a moose, Josefu finds a gasoline station. Quietly, dutifully, he consumes a sandwich and a large carton-full of orange juice standing by his car, among the hubbub at the edge of the busy town, with agricultural machinery on display. It is good to be active.

He is reminded now of the list of activities drawn up for the torpid Kibuye prisoners. None were implemented, for lack of funds. The prisons were brought into service rapidly, everywhere, on the insistence of the young Procurator of the Republic of Rwanda. Josefu had really liked him when they met briefly, impressed by his courage and energy, none of which he had any longer himself. The Procurator said adamantly, that he had to get the killers into safety behind bars, so that they would face justice, rather than merely be slaughtered in vengeance.

⋮

Josefu recalls now that there was a woman accused of killing several villagers, who languished in a separate section of the jail in Kibuye he and Bill had visited regularly. She readily admitted to the crime, explaining that she had never liked those families anyway, and was glad of the chance to be rid of them. She said she hated being idle.

Then, to his astonishment, while he was visiting Marie Immaculée's tidy hut and pretty courtyard at the edge of Kibuye, and after Afrika recounted to her their morning in the prison, she offered to send some food to the woman prisoner. She had said it in a tired voice, devoid of feeling, but following a logic that few outsiders understood.

⋮

Shortly after that visit to Marie Immaculée, Josefu had gone on another trip to Goma. Bernard pointed out a couple of men, standing by an open lorry and checking a consignment of humanitarian rice. One looked briefly in their direction. Then Josefu was told he might be the Tharcisse whom they sought.

It was a real shock for Josefu to see the similarity with himself—same height, same age group, same bronze tinge to their black skin, same eyes shaped like almonds. But their jaws were different, and their lips; the other man's hung down like those of a sloppy predator. Josefu had blinked just once, then looked again. The men had completely disappeared. Cameras swinging on his chest, Bernard very forcefully prevented him from trying to follow and search. They were alone; Afrika and Bill were somewhere else. So Josefu stopped speaking.

It was only late at night, lying alone in his bed, that Josefu expressed in silence the pitiful questions he would have asked Tharcisse before killing him.

⋮

Entering Regina, Josefu heaves a sigh of relief. He sees a billboard with a sign for the place where he immediately decides to seek shelter: *Comfort Inn at Journey's End Regina*. He takes a room on the ground floor and is allowed to park his vehicle in front of it.

At about one o'clock in the morning, a night watchman knocks on the car window and says, "Hey, what are you doing there?"

Josefu jumps and apologises, grabbing his overnight bag and the large potted plant. He enters his room and sits on a chair, only slowly moving to the bed and lying down with his shoes on.

The next morning when he leaves, he sees high school students, wearing orange covers with yellow crosses on them, picking up garbage on the roads and meadows of their community. They fill black plastic sacks. Josefu shivers, remembering the similar Rwandan tradition of community effort. The same name, 'community effort', was given to the killings too. The name 'Interahamwe' meant 'working together' or 'aiming together at the same goal.'

He rolls his shoulders, attempting to shrug off the impact of these out of place whisperings, the nagging commentary. As Josefu leaves Regina, the landscape narrows because of the trees planted on either side of the road. Then the expanse appears again, with signs that he is driving towards the edge of the province.

⋮

There had been some tourist brochures in the 'Comfort Inn at Journey's End Regina', including one mentioning the defeat of rebels in the Battle of Batoche. He notes, though, that the memorial place is too far from the Trans Canada Highway for him to get there quickly and pay his respects to the brave. The history of the nineteenth century, when the Battle of Batoche happened, had always interested him in school. One of his teachers especially made the pupils study rebellions of that period. Instead though, now Josefu recalls an important visit he made to a site close to Kibuye where he sought out the sole resistors who had really challenged the killers.

Josefu recollects, Bisesero was a name emblazoned in red in Rwanda. Bisesero was a place as unique as the ghetto in the Warsaw uprising in World War II, that had focused the few people who despised silence and who, defying reason, had refused to offer themselves up for slaughter without a fight. Josefu wanted everyone to know about Bisesero, and to distribute leaflets, multi-coloured, for a centre of world pilgrims.

Josefu wipes his brow with his hand, steering with the other.

These warriors were armed with sticks and stones alone, their women and children used rags in which to gather the stones. Against them, brought in by the regime's military—and with the help of the zealous director of a tea factory who contributed his lorries and employees—there were countless killers armed with powerful guns and shining new machetes. "What a terrifying sight the families of Bisesero had to face!" he remarks, as if preparing a text. "Worse still, these elite tea factory workers were joined by whole companies from the army ranks and by many bands of bussed-in Interahamwe, the best of Rwanda, their commanders riding around in smart Pajero jeeps."

"The warriors of Bisesero—amazing tactics—would run into the midst of the hordes of assailants and thus disorient them. It allowed the other Tutsis to live for another day."

"Some attackers turned and fled, only to be brought back with reinforcements."

"Eventually, out of more than fifty thousand on the Bisesero side, only some eleven hundred resistors survived. The women and children among them numbered less than half a dozen. An epic without compare, a battle to be remembered!" Josefu says aloud.

Those figures appear clearly before him. He rubs his eyes, not to see them, nor the festering wounds on the face of a Bisesero patrician he had spent a day with, respectfully recording what he said.

Josefu was told a few more might have lived, but French officers who found some of them huddled together, left them, just ordering them to wait for a couple of days for their return. It was hard to imagine what the French military believed would happen in those two days, Josefu had thought mockingly. Everyone has their reasons. By the time the reasons could be justified however, and the soldiers returned, those Bisesero survivors had been slaughtered.

The telling of this particular incident had saddened him inexorably. He had not wanted to hear it; he simply didn't want to know this about those Frenchmen who were there. He had always loved his mother's tales from French literature, learned in secret in her British colonial school in Uganda, which forbade French language. He was confused: the French forces saved lives, undoubtedly, somewhere in the region. He had the documentation somewhere too. Yet so many of their ideals had become absent, and with them his cherished images evaporated. So he had wanted to ignore it all. He repeated again: they had kept some Rwandans alive.

Yet how could he forget the words of the old survivor? According to him, those few remaining alive in Bisesero were finally rescued by French troops. The old man said he and his companions were relieved, but told the soldiers they did not want to remain in their uncertain hands, declaring that they preferred to be handed over to the arriving RPF rebel troops for protection instead. In response, they were left for a whole day without food and water.

There had been clarity, however, in the French thinking, Josefu conceded. For them, a semblance of order meant that the wishes of the previous government should never be excluded. That is how they had seen it. In their eyes, it had remained legitimate till its very last days, when the rump of the regime had fled to Goma. This was the logic, the consistency of the French here, he concluded grudgingly. For them, a mandate with clarity should never be overlooked, whatever the conditions or the morals on the ground. There was little else to say.

The debris of Josefu's thoughts are gathering into a storm, and he feels its best if they are pushed aside right now. He has to achieve clear concentration when driving very fast with both hands back on the wheel.

⋮

He is no Bisesero warrior, Josefu reflects, but he is getting to where he wants. Moosemin, daintier than other prairie towns, is near the province's border, and he definitely will stop to refuel. The place is bound to have a clean toilet too.

He washes his face and hands several times over. Outside, he sees the Dairy Queen place for good ice cream—soft or hard, with or without cones, and also banana splits—and when you sit down inside, next to you there are potted plants in a row. He looks behind him to see his children Alice and Patrick, then remembers where he is. It is not that easy to sit alone eating ice cream, he decides; better to do so standing.

Walking back to his car and looking up, he counts five small clouds stuck together in a weird procession. Time surely will tell if they continue like that across the sky's large expanse, though it is already crowded with other, larger and shapeless clouds.

He soon drives across the border into Manitoba, discreetly and in solitude. All he needs now is some persistence, to cross a lake-that one which he remembers—then to reach the far end of a prairie bathed in timid light.

VI   The Burning Hut

19

"Poor Ellie, why are you crying?" says Josefu, astounded. He stands at a garage telephone, somewhere between Elkhorn and Verdin, triumphantly and safely inside Manitoba Province. He hardly had time to say it was him, let alone to report his achievements.

"I wish we'd never phoned, Josefu, can't you hear me?"

"Something I've done wrong?"

"Yes, it would have been easier for me that way, if I'm going to lose them. Both breasts, perhaps both of them. Both breasts," she sobs.

Josefu looks out and the sky seems like a grey cathedral with dark grey stripes, tall and out of reach. He cannot answer her; she also is much too far out of reach.

"You don't understand. You probably think I'm mad, I actually dared dreaming, I mean one day, you'd see them. You've been calling me in this crazy way."

"You called me first," Josefu interrupts, as if defending himself.

She doesn't notice. "You know they changed after having the girls. Remember I was sort of flat, I mean I didn't always wear a bra, remember? Now it's always. You'd better go away. I'll put the phone down now."

"Please don't," Josefu booms out. "I so wanted to hear you! I'm just about hanging on out here; not much of me left. Are you sure it's definite they'll do that?"

"No, no, it's just the option, they said. It's another operation, though, as they didn't get it first time, it was a bleeding flop. And then there's this option they have to keep open, to save my life," she shouts. "I'm so tired. I don't know why I'm talking to you."

"Because we're friends, I hope," says Josefu politely.

"I bloody hope we're friends, some sort of friends," and Ellie starts to cry again.

"So it may not happen at all?"

"Shut up! You and reality!"

"But I think I've changed; I've had to accept plenty of reality since you knew me before. You can have counselling, Ellie, a strange procedure, but I saw it when I was in Ottawa, in hospital there."

"Counselling? What for?"

"Do you remember that green and gold Visitors Book in your parents' house? I see it in my dreams sometimes, worried that I don't know what to write in it."

"We still have it, Josefu! The same one in the same house! And I usually take the children there when it's my turn, because they live with their father and Veronica, that's his woman. But now I hate Martin because he took my breasts away—he saw them when they were nice."

"Can't you have any hope?"

"You sound like Father Christmas."

Josefu laughs. Before he replies, he looks out again and does not like the bleakness of the changing skyline. It's not to do with Ellie, he tells himself, not an omen. "We've got to fill up the empty spaces," he says into the phone, "Put nice things for you everywhere, fill your day with gifts, you know what I mean, Ellie, baskets of gifts. How long is your hair?"

"It's still the same colour. I let it grow long again."

"I see," he comments, aware he should be saying more, making better sense.

"Well, Josefu, perhaps I shouldn't expect the worst after all. Thank you for that." He knows she is waving with her hand while saying a quick goodbye down the telephone.

Josefu leaves, crestfallen. The thought of what might happen to her plagues him. He has seen so many women with their breasts cut off in hatred and insult. He knows what it could look like. Leaving his car he walks out into the open, scanning the surroundings with a hand over his brow. He doesn't want coffee anymore. He stands there, letting the prairie winds beat his cheeks.

Soon he puts his watch forward, then his car clock, by one hour, Manitoba time, and dutifully remembers the time difference between Rwanda and its eastwards neighbours. He decides to find an empty space in the prairies again so he can stop. From his car, he sees on one side of the highway a colourful little aircraft spraying crops and diving around like a bird. On the other side, in the distance, he can make out a large herd of cattle, at least a hundred head, probably Charlois, since they are almost white. But he senses he is losing a battle which making frequent observations of his surroundings will not save him from.

Parking to the side of the highway, he leans his head on the steering wheel, cowering under Ellie's blows. But then, even they are like nothing once the silver smoke, coming from behind his closed eyes, begins to fill the air and choke him.

⋮

Josefu stood contemplating the avocado tree in their Kibuye yard, which he raided for Marie Immaculée on a daily basis. Some branches she had pointed out to him were unattainable, he reckoned, and whose nubile fruit would never be consumed. Today was one of the clearest days he could remember since coming to the shores of Lake Kivu.

To one side he could hear the end of a conversation, about who would travel in which car, for Bill almost a point of military strategy. Josefu knew he should participate in these decisions, in order to protect Afrika and help him sit where he was most comfortable, but at present he did not have the necessary will to do so. Afrika, since hearing about his cousin's fate in Goma, seemed to have lost about four inches in height and looked frail and gaunt. Yet Josefu did not move. To his relief he heard Père Ambroise, who was still with them in Kibuye, adding to the discussion.

"I am going to travel with the young soldiers; these RPF lads say they are well seasoned and have seen everything, but that is just what they say. If what they want us to see it really is the way they describe it, then it's a scene which will shake even them, so I'll go with them. You follow in your car with Afrika and your escort in the third car can bring up the rear," he said pointing to the same sullen Senegalese trio and a Ghanaian, in blue helmets, who had accompanied them several times to Goma without hardly saying a word. Père Ambroise, though, sounded more like an army officer than a priest, and he had tied the bottom part of his cassock round his waist, revealing a plumpness Josefu hadn't noticed before.

"You shouldn't insist on coming," Bill said gently to Gabrielle.

"Fuck you, fuck you all. I haven't been anywhere except here and Goma, with your patronising attitude, all of you. Forget it, okay?" she answered spiritedly. "UNDP say it's all right. And I'm leaving soon. We're all going soon. Out of here."

"Now Gabrielle, you're being so… so unreasonable," Bill said, as if it were the strongest choice of vocabulary he could use.

Josefu decided he would stand by the tree till they were about to mount the jeep. Marie Immaculée came out and stood in the doorway and he caught her eye.

"Humura," she said, meaning 'Don't fear', with her usual, immovable face. But when she slightly raised her eyebrows for a moment, he almost detected a glimmer of affection being sent towards him.

His own fondness for her now was growing continuously. His own mother in her Ugandan pride expected so much of him, whereas he could love Marie Immaculée like a son without feeling his own failure. This aspect of his relationship was as clear to him as the Rwandan cloudless October sky above him. Its deep blue, though, appeared too pristine for his comfort.

If people were looking for an African landscape that concurred with their pre-set ideas, Rwanda was not the place for them. With its hills and mist, dense greenery and playfully clouded skies, it could not fulfil typecast expectations. This in itself had exhilarated Josefu at first. But now he was learning to read the signs; the sky became clear only better to provide unequivocal sightings of what had occurred in the hundred days of killings, or to warn against those further errors now being made so self-righteously. The sky was as judgemental as Josefu himself had become.

When they set off at last, he duly turned his head away from the lake, but still saw out of the corner of his eye its porcelain elegance today. He tapped Afrika on the arm reassuringly, something he had to do. Afrika dropped his head even further down.

They were going to visit a site that some soldiers had discovered. The interim préfet told Père Ambroise he was keen that foreigners should see it, because if there were ever a court of justice anywhere in the world, this evidence must be used. They travelled away from Kibuye, with their guides and their escort. Bill said he knew it was towards the edge of the former Zone Turquoise. The joyful green density of the banana plantations, followed by dainty hills of lush vegetation, ill prepared them for the next turning off the main road.

Celestin stopped the car and changed to four-wheel drive like the other two vehicles. The ground became stonier and slowly more barren as painfully, they advanced forwards. The shells of many burned out houses left their tell-tale histories behind. When the vehicles climbed even higher, Josefu felt as if thorns were attacking his feet inside his socks. The swaying of their car was so extreme, he struggled not to crush Afrika beside him. He could only see the back of Bill's head looking out of the other window and in front Gabrielle's hair, stubborn in its refusal to stay inside its elastic headband. Celestin held all their destinies in his hands at the wheel, something you could tell he was conscious of. Ahead, Josefu could not see Père Ambroise but knew he was in a front seat. He would be talking without stopping to the band of frightened young soldiers in his charge, building mental landmarks for them, or giving out hints as markers for the heart.

'I have no other world but this one,' said Josefu to himself, but as he surveyed the car ahead, his sense of distance from his surroundings grew acutely. He looked out at the sky again, in its cloudless solitude, keenly aware that there were to be no more diversions from his impending loneliness.

A good hour or so later, there was agitation in the front car. They had arrived and all piled out, four Rwandan soldiers and two Senegalese fanning out into position, with weapons ready. Excitedly talking to Père Ambroise, the others led the way as they all walked down a path, past a cluster of burned out huts, Josefu nearly walking on what he thought was a scorpion but on closer inspection were the remains of a baby's hand. He ran to catch up with the others, but Afrika had waited for him silently. The strong smell, which Josefu recognised so well, wafted up towards him, like a curse.

The soldiers said there were dead bodies there, but nothing more was translated from Kinyarwanda. It was, after all, their own story, their own looted heritage, and even their own serene sky above them, which disregarded all their words.

Along a narrow path behind some trees, shrubs and huts, there was a ramshackle but large barn. Père Ambroise stopped before the door, his clearer glasses revealing a haggard look. Once again, like at the entrance to the very first shed they had visited together, he turned and addressed all present in Kinyarwanda and in French.

"Brothers and my sister," he said, looking severely at Gabrielle while Bill whispered a translation to her, "In what we are about to see we must retain our humility; we are no better than either the victims or the perpetrators, I have nothing else to say."

Josefu thought Père Ambroise's was out of character in his brevity. 'But everyone changes, everyone' he said to himself.

Suddenly he felt Afrika's hand clasping his, with shyness, with innocence, questioningly. They stood still. Josefu was so acutely conscious of his inability to protect him, to reach outside the confines of his own concerns, that it marred the necessary silent moment. He put his arm around Afrika's shoulder though, stooping slightly to do so, until Afrika moved forward and entered into the dark.

Josefu heard Gabrielle, "Oh God, oh God," she groaned. Then he too went in.

"You see," said Père Ambroise, whispering, "They cut the Achilles tendons of these girls so they could not leave. You see they were already lying down like that, on their backs, ready to be ravished." He kneeled by a corner, "Ah look, they were used for that purpose for quite some time, kept alive with a little food and water, do you see in that corner, there. There. Over there?" Père Ambroise said, impatiently.

"How skilful," he remarked, lifting one girl's foot, an unusually long and thin one. He said, "See, how cleverly they made the incision, severing the tendons at the ankle, avoiding the main arteries and veins, inflicting pain but not death. Even these young Interahamwe, however drugged or drunk, still were not necrophiles," and he sighed. "How skilful," he repeated. "By the way, young girls aged between fourteen and twenty, I would say."

Josefu saw that two of them had been left fully naked, and another from the waist downwards, a detail of disregard, the coarseness of the damned.

An empty beer bottle, its frilly metal top nearby, lay between two corpses. Another pair had somehow linked arms in death. Quite a lot of light came in through the cracks in the walls and roof. A crumpled packet shone in the clear sun by one wall, Marlboro cigarettes, the end of a bygone evening. Nobody moved.

Père Ambroise spoke again, crisply. "You've counted them now, done your work. Some rats probably ate part of that body over there, but no large animals could attack them; they couldn't enter here."

He quickly glanced around, to ensure all were listening. "Now I'll explain," he continued. "Probably their tormentors were told to proceed to another area without warning, and so they never came back. These girls were unable to move and the door was bolted from the outside anyway. So they died alone, of fatigue, hunger, of silence. If it hadn't been for a trickle of blood that spread underneath the door, so some passers by noticed it, the bodies would never have been discovered. That's all."

Nobody spoke. Père Ambroise marched out. Josefu looked down at the carpet of disgrace beneath him, patterns tenderly shaped but the dye not evenly cast. How could part of the earth's surface be covered in this way? What human hands had woven it? He walked backwards, fleetingly blinded, holding his head with both hands.

⋮

Josefu jolts his steering wheel as he sits up, inadvertently hooting the horn. The stitches above his temple, because he has squeezed them, are stinging. He wonders whether they should be removed before reaching Winnipeg, not to dismay his hosts. Going beyond Virden, he passes a vintage car and tractor museum, then a cluster of granaries which he tries and fails to count. And, as his heart is pounding, he looks for somewhere to stop again, by rows of aspen trees that line both sides of the highway.

⋮

Josefu was about to make his way back to the jeep, but Père Ambroise told them all to follow him behind the barn and along a further path. Everyone had diminished in size: Gabrielle with Bill's arm around her was like a small hunchback, unrecognisable, and Bill looked older than his years. Celestin had kept his back straight yet trembled quietly, not aloof as usual though, but huddled up against the group of young soldiers who walked in close formation. It was Afrika whom Josefu nearly lost sight of, however, because he was doubled up and hardly walking at all. His eyes were furtive, lips twitching, minute beads of sweat trickling down his temples.

Josefu seethed with fury that there were still no clouds above them, that the sky was so implacably blue, so impervious to the crushed spectators making their way beneath it. A sudden movement might have been a snake. Josefu kicked a clump of rushes. They were skirting a village, deserted, most of its buildings burned. He knew it was useless telling Afrika he didn't have to come. Instead, to give himself willpower too, he squeezed Afrika's shoulder with encouragement.

And then, as they approached a clearing, like a dirge, Gabrielle intoned in a low voice, again and again, "No, oh no, no, noooooo." Like many women, she spoke for everyone.

Josefu saw that Afrika was crying and so was Père Ambroise, tears fast covering nose and cheeks. Bill too was weeping. He then saw that the soldiers, their real young age showing, cried like children and Celestin with them. He had not seen them like this ever before and like a boulder, a sudden fear crushed his chest.

"No, no," wept Gabrielle.

And as Josefu saw more clearly, he fell to his knees.

Nine women crucified, arms and legs tied wide apart, cloth skirts ripped or torn away, nine of God's ransacked cathedrals, each against a tree. One had her white head scarf still perfectly tied, traditional black stripe in place and judging from her age, might well have been the mother of girls they had just seen. Another was plump, come from a city, perhaps. Nine of them attached to trees, as closely as possible in half a circle.

Once their limbs were held securely back and taut, their heads and bodies had been abandoned to them. For pushed up high through each vagina with great force was a large and sharpened wooden stave, wider than a strong man's arm and longer still. In this way, their faces contorted in the agony of unfinished screams, which no one else could hear, they expired.

There was a stillness here, with life suspended. Only one bird made a timid sound and flew away. Slowly Père Ambroise followed Josefu and kneeled too and bowed his head. Soon the rest did the same, including one of the soldiers who was a Muslim, saying with simplicity 'Allahu akbar', his cheeks wet.

Josefu could see that Père Ambroise was struggling to say something in response. So he spoke for him, though cringing in his dread of being arrogant. "We are held to ransom, all humanity, by what we have seen here," he whispered, not really knowing if it made sense. It hadn't, because still nobody moved, and words could only fall away like aged leaves.

⋮

The small bird returned noiselessly this time and rested on a banana flower. One of the young soldiers cried more desperately than the others, who calmed him with their arms, and Père Ambroise turned his head towards him like an automaton. His glasses had fallen to the ground and he picked them up, slowly wiping them with his cassock and placed them back with gravity.

Still no clouds appeared in the sky and as he tentatively looked up, Josefu again accused it of being implacable. Nobody stirred, though, as if the women provided some protection, which would be lost when they left. But Josefu knew his thoughts were straying wildly now. He despised himself, for he wanted to succour Père Ambroise and couldn't, not even this once. Of course the priest, trained for the circumstance, finally took the initiative. But his wrath smouldered.

"You there, you *Muzungu*. You Bill, haven't you got your camera? Don't you see we have to remove and bury them immediately, but that we need a record first?" Père Ambroise grumbled in Kinyarwanda while Bill disentangled himself from Gabrielle.

"Yes, I've got a new film," he replied meekly. As he stood up and got ready, he said, "But I don't think I can do it, you know, I can't, not this time."

Josefu had not brought his own camera with him.

"There will never be justice, the kind these women ask of us, that's your opinion, so it isn't worth trying. Is that what you think?" said Père Ambroise impatiently.

"I can't focus," said Bill lamely.

Gabrielle had covered her face with her hands, not understanding the French anyway.

"Give it here," said Père Ambroise, snatching the camera from Bill. "How does it work?"

"Oh, it's simple, it's auto-focus, just look and press this grey button," Bill said.

"But I can't see," said Père Ambroise, "Don't you know? My glasses can't let me take photographs, you know that."

Bill didn't answer. He held the camera up, arm outstretched, but with his head down, waiting for takers. The Muslim soldier came and bowed before him. He spoke in French. "I took photographs in

Egypt," he said, "As did my father who taught me. We have travelled a lot before. Then I went to join the rebels in the bush." He offered this in way of explanation and Bill handed him the camera.

Père Ambroise jumped up and down round the young soldier, telling him what to photograph. It seemed to take an age. Although everyone had got to their feet, nobody moved from their place.

Afrika stood behind Josefu, still breathing heavily. Then he whispered, "It's our shame, you see. We Rwandans should not cry in front of anyone else."

"But it happens and who cares," said Josefu irritated. "Oh sorry, Afrika, I just don't know how to talk right now," he said more conciliatory. When Afrika held his arm, Josefu felt then that he could resist being drawn into a void.

Père Ambroise sent two soldiers to call the armed guards from the jeeps. They all came and in turn they froze at what they saw. The priest did not give them time to reflect, though, because he commanded that the bodies be brought down and since it was impossible to dig into the ground, he ordered that the corpses be placed in a row, to be covered with branches later.

He beckoned to Josefu once they were laid down, to pull the staves out. "You are big," he said.

Josefu's head spun, but like a surgeon, although with his eyes half closed, turning his face away when he could and groaning, he dragged one out. Everyone else moved back, realising he could do it and Josefu, almost blinded, pulled the staves out as if rowing a boat in Oxford, one by one, almost rhythmically. He sobbed as he did it and hated himself forever.

Somehow, the branches used to cover the corpses looked tidy and decorative. Père Ambroise shouted as he chanted prayers, raising his arms wildly in blessings, finally breaking into Latin, which Josefu joined in, at the end.

As they walked back towards the vehicles, Bill almost carrying Gabrielle as he dragged her along, Père Ambroise spat several times. Turning at last to Josefu, he said, "This is the end, this is as far as we can go, this is the last stop, this bus will go no further," he said, pointing to his cassock. "I cannot carry more."

"Be yourself," said Josefu.

"You speak rubbish," said Père Ambroise. "Sorry, I must not speak anymore."

⋮

Celestin and Afrika both sought permission to return for one night to Kigali. Celestin had a significant amount of merchandise from Goma he wanted to profit from in the capital, leaving it there with someone he trusted and returning to Kibuye immediately, he promised. Afrika had said he could not rest until he shared the terrible news about his cousin with his aunt and the rest of his family. And Père Ambroise would be grateful for the lift in Celestin's car back to the capital. On returning to their building, a flurry of arrangements were made and documents signed for them.

Although Josefu was certain he had seen the two men from Goma again walking near their Kibuye street, it was judged safe for Bill, Gabrielle and himself to stay alone for the night, with just one armed guard sitting at the gate.

⋮

Josefu woke to a loud commotion coming from Bill's room—yelling, it sounded like. Although he had struggled to go to sleep, despite his heightened emotions and compounded by hardly being able to eat the igitoke Marie Immaculée had prepared, he now sat up and listened. The shouting was so loud; he shook his head with disbelief. He rose in his boxer shorts and went slowly towards Bill's open door.

Gabrielle was screaming, heaving and screaming, "For God's sake, can't you go harder? Harder? Oh my God!" she shouted.

Josefu saw Bill who groaned with such a deep voice that the plastered walls trembled, as did the door against which Josefu leaned. Bill lay without clothes, on his narrow bed, pounding over Gabrielle and shouting wordless cries.

"Oh my God I hate it here, this damned place!" yelled Gabrielle, "I hate my life, I hate it. I wish I hadn't been born." She cried and sobbed, at the top of her voice, repeating it again, "I wish I had never been born."

Bill said nothing but bellowed inarticulately, tearfully.

Josefu stood in the doorway, excitement timidly creeping into him, but a deeper emotion grabbed his throat. He felt a massive betrayal, he couldn't explain why, but it was there, immense, as imposing as a skyscraper and as real.

At that moment they both saw him, but continued as before. Josefu knew that if he went and joined them, it would make no difference as far as they were concerned. He could not, though, overcome his more powerful feelings of isolation and outrage at Bill's breach of faith. Although his own penis was erect now, he was stupefied as he watched them and did not move.

They both continued shouting tearfully, and Josefu thought they were not going anywhere. Again, they met his gaze, both so helpless as they saw him. This time he said, "You didn't have to make all that noise."

His hand in front of the opening in his shorts, he moved backwards into his own room across the corridor and sat on the edge of his bed. At that moment he saw his wife Patricia and knew she had kept a secret from him. "Treachery!" he exclaimed, as he felt himself go limp. Now he lay flat on his stomach, holding his pillow possessively as he sobbed, knowing very well that his mind was leaving him, like a clever seagull leaves a ship which has no cargo.

20.

Everyone overslept the next day, the luxury of a job in the Third World where outsiders can behave as if they were self-employed. Marie Immaculée was already downstairs. She had made some coffee bought in Goma. When Josefu went to drink the rich, black brew she sat opposite him, watching.

"I'm calling my mother today on the telephone," he said in English.

"Eeeh," she said, as if she understood. "Humura, don't fear," she added.

He felt heavy, slightly nauseated, as if he had a temperature. Bill came in shortly afterwards without greeting anyone and said, "Josefu, how could you do it to her? Your Mother is going crazy not hearing from you and she called Mary from England. Yes, I've just spoken with her, with Mary, middle of the night out there, but she was waiting for me."

"Mary? You spoke to her?" hissed Josefu.

"Yes, I did," said Bill coldly.

Gabrielle was pale and unsmiling, her eyes still puffed from crying. She hardly acknowledged him or Bill and left for the UNDP's two-person office, without breakfast, dishevelled and withdrawn.

Josefu ignored Bill's listing of things to do and nursed his abdomen instead. He focused now on Marie Immaculée at the table. This was the first time they did not have Afrika to interpret. What Josefu knew of Luganda, the language of his ancestors, consisted mostly of the words of one children's song about a singing bird, in which a child's father and mother and grandmother beat him, for losing it.

Leaning forward, tapping a light rhythm with his hands, he sang: "*Ogenda wa*? And then, Marie Immaculée, it goes, *Taata nakuba nankubira ennyonyi muzinge*, and Maama and Jjajja too, because of the muzinge, you see."

His strong impulse was to clown around, at last to force a smile from her. It didn't come, but her absent look became less intense. His head was spinning as he ignored the increasing cramps.

"Be careful" said Bill, "Take it easy," he added, looking a little worriedly at Josefu. "I'm taking the bodyguard along with me to the préfet. I'm not waiting for you. Anyway, no need for you to go. That préfet, he said he had some more names of those missing, for starting a record of lost Tutsi villagers, and I want to discuss what we saw yesterday with him. Stay behind, no problem."

Josefu tapped on the table in silence, looking again into the eyes of Marie Immaculée. She didn't move. He still felt sick. Gesticulating, he asked after the children. She also used her hands to say they were fine. It was then he became aware of how much his stomach ached. By then Bill had gone and they were alone. Gesturing to her not to follow, he ran upstairs to the toilet and retched, vomiting bile and all he had eaten for the past day.

To his embarrassment, though, he had diarrhoea too and soiled himself simultaneously. There was no running water and none in the red, plastic bucket. Disgusted, he undressed and used his shorts to wipe himself. This was a bad day. He tiptoed to his room and found something to wear so as to collect water downstairs. There, in his bedroom, he vomited uncontrollably and again soiled his clean clothes with diarrhoea. He shook, his nose stuffed, tired tears rolling. His revulsion was growing, as he mopped the floor and himself, and changed once more. When he had come to the top of the stairs, carrying the empty bucket, it all started again and he fell on the floor, trying to smother the abhorrence he experienced. He raised himself on his hands and knees, vomiting loudly, then turned away to lie on the floor again, hoping to roll away from the mess. He told himself that as a grown man, he had never been so humiliated.

His loathing for the smell overwhelmed him. He closed his eyes and saw himself side-stepping a path covered in dark brown shards fallen from bones and skulls. He realised his sleeve had dipped into his vomit and he groaned. The cramps, too, were crippling him now and he moaned once more, this time loudly. He felt the heavens open and pour down scorn.

At first he couldn't really tell, but then he saw that Marie Immaculée had come silently and stood immobile and in shock. "Go away," he gesticulated waving his hand, "Go away, please, please," but she did not budge. He rose on his knees again, retching vehemently, the diarrhoea shooting copiously out of the other end. This time he sobbed, but still waved his hand, telling her to go.

Falling down flat, he momentarily blacked out. A sculptured gargoyle from St. Alban's cathedral came to life and opened its mouth to swallow him. Unclothed cadavers floated over him in gentle procession while Bach was played out of tune on his oboe. A gash in the red earth widened, ready to inter him. He called out to little Patrick, his son, being pulled away by Alice, his daughter, calling to them that he had the right to say goodbye. He called on the Commissioners of Human Rights and told them they were useless, shouting down a plastic pipe. His cramps made him curl and stretch, excrement swishing around his legs. He believed the house was about to cave in. Why had it happened so suddenly?

After a while, he realised Marie Immaculée had kneeled beside him on the floor, with a bowl of warm water and a rag, with which she smoothed his brow and the nape of his neck, saying very quietly, "Ihorere, Don't cry." He no longer told her to leave. There was a way here in which he had found what he was looking for, the first forgiveness, something at last he could accept.

A long time went by, perhaps an hour or more, he thought, without either of them moving. When he had the urge to retch, he lifted himself on to his elbows, but nothing happened anymore at either end. Marie Immaculée pulled at his collar, gesturing that he should try to rise now, wash and change and go to his bed. She left to fetch several buckets of water, after she chose for him a set of fresh clothes including socks and shoes. The way she did it revealeded an experienced sleight of hand, an echo of when she had a family with men in it, all her own. His grief, on her behalf, now masked his feelings of repulsion as he watched the soiled trail he left while rising to enter the bathroom. She had filled with water every basin and bucket in the house and they stood in a colourful row.

He tried to wash his own clothes too, but left them in a wet huddle. He explained as best he could that he would deal with them later and she showed a bowl for him to vomit by his bed. As he lay back quietly confused, she sat by the doorway, on an upright chair, keeping vigil.

His stomach had given up on him, he felt, and would no longer plague him for a while.

He woke to a vivid conversation in Kinyarwanda coming from downstairs. Celestin and Afrika had come back already, and Marie Immaculée was telling them about him. That evening, an English doctor from the mobile medical unit paid a call and said that, unless he was mistaken, Josefu had a bad bout of common gastro-enteritis which had swept through the region. There was absolutely nothing to worry about if the symptoms had subsided. He said he'd heard about him, born in Maidenhead and educated at Stowe, "And now this," the doctor added, looking around the room but really meaning here, on the edge of Rwanda's blighted fortune.

⋮

Josefu senses that he is coming to such a serious juncture that he best push on straight towards Winnipeg, before it becomes too late. What he has just remembered has him wondering if he could stay with Pamela instead of her parents, Bill and Mary. He repeats aloud Bill's telephone number, though, to make sure he memorises it, to call at the next convenient moment and say he is on his way.

He asks himself whether this time he could turn on the radio at last, to block out the macabre musical round, playing in his head, that accompanies both Ellie's anguish and his own foreboding. The sky, though, unhindered by buildings or trees now, is filled with Marie Immaculée's face and he shouts as he drives, "What now? What now?"

A voice, Joe Swift's, or Dave's or even Rosemary his mother's—he cannot tell—asks him to lay Marie Immaculée to rest at last. And then, "Remember me once and forever hold your peace," the Rwandan woman says herself, in some language he understands.

A long train rolls by parallel to the highway, with fifty coaches or it could be a hundred. He drives silently, green fields with yellow and gold patches on either side of the road. He glimpses a solitary farmer at the wheel of his tractor seeding a vast expanse. In Rwanda, he recalls, cultivators lifted their hoes, pulled every sinew of their body upwards and then they hit with all their human might, inch by inch, their own small parcel of the globe, to loosen it up.

Josefu is perspiring. He says, "Easy now, like the Canadians say, take it easy, why not leave out that bit?" And then, as he switches on the windscreen wipers to clear the drizzle, he adds, "If I don't remember that part, then I can leave Marie Immaculée as she was that day when I was sick. She had healing powers; she had something left despite her losses, after all. And I had great plans for her, like getting the visa and immigration department in New York to grant her a nanny's permit and then to find other Rwandan exiles to keep her company. I mean, please God, why can't I stop there? I've done all I can; I've tried to break out of Banff. And if I returned, I'd find a bison's head to match Dave's next door, to show my appreciation. Can't I have one day without bad news? Especially from Marie Immaculée?"

He passes a sign with 'Brandon, the Wheat City'. There is no time to lose, none at all. Josefu feels uneasy; he dislikes having to decide whether to die or not, whether or not to crash the car. He knows that if he ever gets to Winnipeg he will be asked what he wants to do with his life and he doesn't know. And that daft, sunken eyed, white head-scarved, robbed and battered, soul-shrivelled woman on a Rwandan hill, she holds the key. He breaks the Manitoba speed limit as if he were being chased. He shouts out her name and the car swerves twice.

How bleak. All it takes is to be truthful.

⋮

"Afrika, please, tell her I'm grateful for the clothes she washed. I wasn't expecting her to do it," said Josefu.

"She answers that nothing matters, that's what she says."

Bill arrived and interrupted. "I've just seen the préfet and I asked him when it happened, what we saw, what was done to those women. He said it happened recently, it was done as a warning to the advancing enemy, the other army." And then Bill sat down and said, "It was a tactical affair."

Josefu gasped and repeated it, "A tactical affair."

Nobody spoke for a while. Afrika then told them he had returned back to Kibuye quickly because he could not bear seeing his aunt cry when he was home in Kigali.

'That young boy's woeful life lost, a tactical affair as well', Josefu reflected.

"One more thing," said Bill. "Afrika, can you tell Marie Immaculée that the documentation on her village, about the massacre there, is already being compiled. News just in, from that young Procurator, you know. It's already partly covered by a private Human Rights report, written by one of those women who do it—by the way, Josefu, probably the one from 'Africa Rights'," Bill continued. "And you must try to explain it to her, you Afrika, about this report which is being written. Because she might not understand what that means. But tell her," and he paused to make sure Josefu was listening, "...that in all likelihood the idea is growing, of having an international criminal court. Then we can catch those people. You said the main assailant, the one she said had led the others, is now in Goma, didn't you say that? And she can be a protected witness."

"You mean, that name she says, that Tharcisse?" asked Afrika.

"Yes, yes, the one she asked to spare her remaining children because he knew them, remember? That's the kind they'll be looking for," answered Bill. It was all related to her in careful and solemn Kinyarwanda.

After a while, Afrika said, "Marie Immaculée tells me, she doesn't care about Tharcisse or anybody. You see, they know that it's too late now because her family is already gone, already killed, you understand her, that is how it is, you understand her."

"But justice must be done," said Bill.

"She wanted it before. Now she doesn't care."

"But other people must live, and they should be spared forever, always, from more of the inhuman, inhuman…whatever it is…. Oh my, I can't say it anymore," said Bill, looking away. He appeared to be thinking perhaps he shouldn't be so confident of his views after all.

"No more unfinished business. No more tactical affairs," said Josefu bitterly. He rose and went to test the electricity, to see if he could write a report on his laptop computer, or whether to write it by hand. He knew Marie Immaculée liked to see him busy, or he imagined it at least.

Then he never saw her, because after a while he sipped water to steady his bruised intestines, went upstairs and waited for a better day after the weekend.

⋮

'One more chance,' Josefu thinks to himself, 'One more, and I can return to Banff without Rwanda on my map of humankind.' But his mind is darkening as he enters Brandon.

⋮

It happened very rapidly. As Afrika and he were filling another kerosene lamp to pass the evening, there was loud banging on the gate. People from the makeshift Kibuye hospital said remnants of the old regime—who had been allowed to leave freely, they added as if better to explain—had made an incursion from Zaire, with a terrible attack on a nearby village. Some victims were still alive but the medical team had no transport to bring them to the hospital. Celestin refused to drive, citing too much beer as his reason, but the rest knew he, like Afrika, loathed the sight of blood. Afrika nevertheless immediately volunteered, in a quiet voice. But when Josefu suggested it might be better if he himself did not go with them, in order to leave more space in the vehicle, the others replied they would like him to see what had happened, because he was an outsider and he could write a report. The same words again... Besides, if there were very small children who were orphaned needing treatment, it was useful to have someone to hold them during transport. So he went with them.

It was quite close to Kibuye, an uncomfortable realisation. The village was in flames and automatic weapons had been used abundantly, an advance on the battles before July.

'These improvements in the fighting capacity of the exiled forces, they've only happened because we've fed them, protected them. Such bad news,' Josefu reflected anxiously. He muttered in the car, and Afrika said he didn't follow his reasoning.

"It's us, us the foreigners, we've helped these attackers," he said. "The people outside our gate said so."

"I cannot understand what you're saying?" even Afrika showed his annoyance with him this time.

There was little chance to survey the damage as they ran behind the paramedics. He'd bring Bill out here tomorrow, as it would be the freshest, the most immediate damage assessment they would be able to do since they had arrived. Josefu realised he was able to revert to professional conduct, some sort of relief to him. Soon he was carrying over his shoulder several injured men and women in turn, back to a truck and when it was full, to their own vehicle. As his car was driven away, he held two children on his lap, one of whom seemed to have lost or had a shattered half of her face. Both her parents were dead, their throats slit. The other child had lost a hand, but it was the right one and he was barely four or five.

The strike had taken place somewhere near Kibuye where Josefu and his team had never been. Afrika tried to get back to the makeshift hospital in town, following directions given by the nurse in the back of the vehicle, who headed the rescue team. The problem, though, was that she owed her position to having been a medical officer in the bush in Uganda, yet she was newly arrived in Rwanda and unsure of the way. One of the patients guided them better. Josefu hoped vital minutes were not lost. This spoke volumes about the national situation, he related soberly to Bill on his return, with the growing dominance of returnees over locals.

But then Josefu suggested they should both become ambulance drivers and throw their pens away. This debate did not last long because Gabrielle ran downstairs saying she had been woken up by distant screaming which sounded serious. She had hardly spoken when there was a flash of thunder. It was followed by another commotion in the street.

⋮

And then his living ended, as Josefu heard the knocking on the iron gate. One step forward, and he knew where he was heading. The metal rattled, as the night watchman unbolted the door. Josefu stepped out into the dawn. A man clasped his arm, then drew away, seeing the bloodstains still on his shirt. Four or five people, men and women, were talking at once. Afrika and Bill came out, while Josefu took a few steps sideways, to see through to the lake and to curse it. He knew it, he knew it already, what there was to know. He turned to walk towards the edge of the town and to pass the villa with the piano in it.

Afrika silently ran after him and pulled him back unceremoniously.

"G'd dammit," Bill shouted, "Josefu, what the hell are you doing?"

Afrika said that the UNAMIR people were already there and RPF troops, that there were some huts burning on the edge of Kibuye, and it was too late, and one of them was the hut where Marie Immaculée's and her friends were. And everything that Afrika said was just an echo, resonating feebly in the hollow of Josefu's chest.

"Get in the car," Bill told Josefu, "You're fucking useless."

Africa had the keys; Celestin was still fast asleep and there was no time to lose. Bill sat in front, with Josefu crowded in the back with three of the people who had come to the gate. He had lost his sense of smell; that he remembers now.

Dawn delicately opened up the skies, their stillness reflected in the empty roads. Josefu saw a pair of dogs, the first he had seen in a long time, settling down to sleep. In the crown of his head, he could hear voices relaying news from distant places, beyond his understanding. There were no traffic lights. Nothing was there to stop them driving forward, nothing was in the way. He knew it.

A lot of noise was made when they drew up, the jeep tilting sideways on the stony road. Two huts were burning, but everyone was round the back where the bodies were.

Josefu's ability to guess Kinyarwanda words was at an end. Anyway, he knew already. But he stopped to hear what the young Canadian Blue Helmet, whom he recognised, had to say while running up to Bill.

"They say it's your cook," he said in French.

Afrika joined in. "They say they got the others too."

"But who was in the other hut?" asked Bill.

"They were Hutus," said Afrika, his head down. Josefu could see deep embers reflected in his eyes, and the smoke that stung him.

"Why the Hutus?" asked the young soldier.

There was a silence. Josefu stood there, already knowing word for word what Afrika would reply: "So there would be no witnesses. Who cares if they are Hutus or Tutsis in such a case? Those people, that's how they think. Their plans are big."

"Who cares?" Josefu repeated to a shrub that had escaped annihilation, as he walked around to the back. He stood high up in the sky and gazed down on the figures lying still in the timid sun at daybreak. The legless little boy had his head cut off and placed beside him. Josefu looked again and saw that the other two children and their woman guardian were also beheaded in a clean swoop of death.

'Brand new knives,' he thought, 'Well sharpened on both edges, better than before, more rapid than machetes. Finely recorded details.' He swayed from side to side, suspended in the air, not even a branch to steady him. 'Come down,' he said to himself, 'People are trying to talk to you.'

Afrika held a piece of paper and was crying. "They left it here," he sobbed, "On top of Marie Immaculée. It's for you, for us. It's a message, that's what it is."

A tall Rwandan officer snatched it from him and read it out in Kinyarwanda.

"But that's only part of it," said Afrika, wiping his eyes and taking back the note. "It's a page torn out of a book and this is underlined. It's a very old proverb and I don't know it, that's what I don't know." The yard was still.

He cleared his throat. "I have to read it in Kinyarwanda first: *Kwi horera ku Umwami ni ukumushuka alica abatoni be.* 'To take revenge on a king, you have to get him to kill those he favours.' You understand, to trick him so that he himself kills those he loves."

Nobody moved, nobody spoke, not even the officer.

"Do you understand?" Afrika repeated, this time looking straight up at Josefu, who flinched. "There is also a message in French, with mistakes. 'Anglo-Saxons, Belgians and all Rwandans enemies of the Rwandan people,' and it says, ' Do not try, you, to take the innocent to the justice'." And Afrika handed the note back to the officer.

Marie Immaculée had not been beheaded. She lay at Josefu's feet now, on her back, both hands demurely at her side. And he, bearing the proverb on both his shoulders like a dismal cloak, leaned down and took her body in his arms. She had been shot in the head with a clean pistol. Even from across the border, bullets were precious, but she had been destined to have one saved for her alone. A very small trickle of blood ran out of her lips which he sealed closed, for rigor mortis was not complete, as he softly lifted her scarf to kiss her brow.

There was a hum of voices around him, fading slowly. For Josefu, there was no other world than this one, destroyed, held between his arms.

⋮

Since then, he never moved again. Although he had risen and walked behind the fence, past clumps of trees and bushes, along a fruit grove and a dense plantation, through a stream and up a stony slope on another hill—he was not found till the afternoon—Josefu had stopped right there in the yard, no further away, down on his knees, on soil with wasted leftovers.

VII   THE SHORT END

21.

Without colour, it is not a place he is in, nor a country. Josefu fights through thick, cold mist, attempting to struggle out of a tubular corridor, a journey seemingly without end. The slight tinge to a distant voice, which convinces Josefu it is Bill's, locates a point in his mind and acts as a magnet to draw him along. Until then, he has been wedged between layers of cotton, an unfeeling surface. But now he heaves and pulls.

"I wonder if I could get a little closer to him?" Bill says to the Brandon City Gaol official.

"Sure, go ahead, you say you know the guy. We've gotten nothing but nonsense from him; he hasn't even been to the bathroom, since he came here last night. Just sits there and stares."

"He had a major breakdown before, like I explained to your supervisor. It's not the first time I've seen him like that," Bill says.

"What the hell. But why don't you just go on in there? I'm right behind you."

"He's not violent," says Bill.

"He's been charged with disturbing the peace and destruction of private property," says the jailer, "We have to see the charges here, that's how we do it."

Bill doesn't answer.

"Overnight ones, we let them keep their own clothes. But we worried about this one, put him under close surveillance because of his mental problem maybe?" the jailer says. "Not on drugs, but they found a plant in the back seat of his car and we're looking into it," he adds with his uncommonly high, soft voice.

Bill peers through the small window in the gaol door. Josefu sits on a plain wooden chair, legs loosely apart, clothes dishevelled, leaning back, his mouth half open.

"Oh my, that vacant look, that vacant look," Bill says, apprehensively, "...after all we did in Banff, all those years! Poor Mary, Pamela, Martina, all those efforts and we are right back where we started."

He enters the cell slowly, the jailer behind him. Bill says to him, "I've noticed these mottled colour walls here, off-white; are they Tyndalstone? Do you know?"

"Bill, you're there! I'm trying to reach you," Josefu says in a hoarse voice.

"Good, Josefu, good. Talk to me, that's so good," Bill responds.

"But I know what you did!" Josefu suddenly shouts as if carried by a wave. "Gabrielle and you," he booms, without turning or opening his eyes, "...copulating out of self pity!"

The jailer runs up, saying hurriedly to Bill, "Are you all right, Sir? Do you want to stay?"

"Sunova bitch, Josefu! You can go to hell! It's so hard not to be mad at you." Bill raises both hands to his head. "I was woken at five this morning and drove two hours to get here. The police tracked your call to me in Winnipeg from a phone booth. Did you know that? And here you are, shifting blame, bringing up that thing, out of everything else. And we've all been hanging around at home all these past days, waiting. But no, I get to rush out and bail you out all over again. Can you hear me?"

"Marie Immaculée adored that avocado tree," whispers Josefu.

"Do you still want to stay?" says the jailer.

"Just like last time," Bill continues, "when we nearly made it to the end of our Rwanda mission, barely a week to go. Oh no, you had to screw up just before. And the same now, just missing Winnipeg.

And I come out here to Brandon thinking, 'Shall I hug him? Shall I say Take it easy, everything's going to be all right?' And you lay into me like this?" Bill sighs, "I don't know you anymore. And that's the truth."

"Hey you, take it easy" says the guard, coming closer to Josefu.

Bill laughs awkwardly and waits, but Josefu just sways silently from side to side. "Well, at least you did say something. You've been talking," Bill intervenes. "So it's better than last time round. Perhaps our efforts over six years have been good, after all."

"I'll ask him if he wants some water," says the jailer.

"Go ahead," Bill says, but Josefu does not answer.

"I'll stand right beside you, Sir," the jailer says to Bill.

"Josefu, do you know where you are now?" There is no reply. "Why did you go on this crazy journey just now? And you've driven Mary crazy, my wife," Bill says testily.

"So you know all about this guy?" asks the gaoler.

"You wouldn't talk to me when I said to get more guards," Josefu hisses. "And you didn't get somewhere safer for our staff to live and I couldn't ask, because I wasn't chief of mission."

Bill moves back, "I don't have to take this."

Josefu murmurs, "The lake didn't have a tide. The waves were small and polite."

Turning towards the jailer, Bill asks, "What are you going to do next?"

"We'll lock him up again. He's from out-of-province, so getting him bail will be difficult. You can leave him here."

Bill answers, "He's rotting in hell already. We're both kind of, out of the same hell."

"You tell that to my boss."

Josefu hears them moving away. Then, without leaving his chair, without turning his head, he starts to sink under a wave of muddied water. 'If I can't breathe, it will all be over.' But for him, dying is to enter a crowded place.

⋮

"Easy, easy, we're just taking a blood sample from your vein, just to make sure," says a small voice next to Josefu.

"Back in hospital, again? The pastel colours of no man's land, again?" he asks with great effort. "We must bury Marie Immaculée properly, in the ground," he adds, eyes shut.

Bill's voice says excitedly, "Is that progress, Doctor? We were dealing with Marie Immaculée, the first time when his illness began. So is it a good sign?"

"All you've told me is very useful, Mr. Macpherson. I wonder if he'll speak to me now, then we can set up a schedule."

"Doctor, I've waited years for this, for him to recall," Bill says.

"It's an emotional experience for you too. A group experience," the doctor remarks.

"Josefu, I'll tell you right now. Just a few hours before we left Rwanda, we buried her, next to her daughters and with the legless child, remember? We'd brought her body from Kibuye to Kigali and we went with a full escort to the place near the shed where we first met her, remember? Père Ambroise did it."

"Hi, Joseph, I'm a doctor. You're in the psychiatric unit of Brandon General Hospital. Can you look at me?"

Josefu murmurs, "Only a few dead were ever buried before nightfall with their names, you know it, Bill. So he did it, Père Ambroise? He got it for Marie Immaculée?" So you did it, did you? Did it?"

"Can you eat? Are you vegetarian?" asks the doctor.

"No, he's not," Bill replies for him. "Josefu, where are you right now?"

"Responsibilities, did he have them?" the doctor queries.

"Yes, Doctor. You, Josefu, listen! The report I had written was released last year, just last year. It had been kept classified all this time, like the piles of leaves kept in our Kibuye kitchen to use as wraps for steaming food, which you said were UN secret archives, remember?" And Bill laughs very softly.

"Handle emotions?" asks the doctor.

"Did you find Dallaire?" Josefu asks, suddenly with full voice. Falling back on his pillow, he adds, "You know, somewhere in Saskatchewan, just outside Regina, was the last time I saw him, Dallaire, wandering along a prairie field. So good looking still, his moustache like in the picture, the one I had." Josefu closes his eyes tightly.

"Now, that's a new dimension," says the doctor.

"I can explain everything," says Bill.

"No you can't," says Josefu sighing. "He reproached us, over each exploding mine and skulls scattered, oh…"

"I have a job to do," the doctor interrupts. "I've got your name here. Josefu Mutesa, you're on police bail. Outside in the hallway, there are two guys from Brandon City Police. They want to ask you some questions and I have to assess you first, to see if you are fit. We've asked for your records from Strathmore in Alberta because of those stitches on your head. Now, can you understand what I'm saying?"

"You never had my stomach bug, Bill. I was the African and it's I who got sick," he chuckles eerily.

"Do you want me to step outside, Josefu?" Bill asks.

Josefu laughs softly, calmly. "Stay. Always stay. They make people like you in this world, who can stay."

In their light blue shirts and dark trousers, the two policemen come into the ward and soon four chairs surround Josefu's bed.

"We have some notes here and we want to check them," says the older of the two policemen. "Do you agree that it was between 18:00 and 18:15, yesterday, that you parked your car and entered the Hi-Way Esso Family Restaurant? Is that correct?"

"I hated Lake Kivu sometimes," says Josefu faintly.

"This might not work," the doctor remarks.

"Do you recall that you made a call from the telephone in the entrance?"

"To me," says Bill.

"When you found nobody was home, you ripped the handset from its socket. You damaged the phone. And we reckon that it was with your right elbow that you smashed the glass in the doorway. Is that all correct?"

Bill urges him, "Josefu, say 'Correct', or we'll be here all night."

"We follow procedures here," says the policeman, "and we'll take all the time it takes."

"Correct," says Josefu. "But there was nobody left alive," tears welling into his eyes.

"Let's be careful," says the doctor.

"He's lost it again. That's back in Rwanda," Bill explains.

Josefu rises from the bed and everyone stands up with him.

"Easy now," say the two policemen simultaneously. "Doctor, is it okay he gets up?" asks one of them.

"So long as he stays in here," she replies, going to take Josefu's arm. "We want to help you here."

"You fell to the ground underneath the telephone, surrounded by broken glass, just in the entrance to the diner," says the elder policeman. "You were sobbing, crying like a Loonie. The owner called us. You were an embarrassment, right at his entrance. Nobody could get in or out. The police sent out a patrol car."

Josefu sits down on the edge of the bed. "I had nowhere to go anymore. Nothing in her hut to save," he explains.

Sitting down again like the others, the policeman says, turning to Bill, "Here was this really big crazy black guy—he was real scary.

Expensive clothes, could be a drugs dealer, could be something else, how were we to know?"

"I couldn't leave her," says Josefu.

"That's a different voice he's using, more composed," says the doctor.

"Our records say you resisted arrest, correct? You punched and kicked a policeman. Who is Tharcisse? You called the police officer 'Tharcisse'."

"I can explain," says Bill repeatedly.

"Yeah, right," says the senior policeman, "It's convenient he can't remember wrecking the restaurant, but he remembers every detail of strange names from God-knows-where. You expect me to buy that?"

"Bill, I'm sorry, and for your Mary," interrupts Josefu.

"Look," Bill says, "I didn't want to hide. Just we'll tell her together, Josefu. About Gabrielle. It's been a long day, a long life."

"This is baloney–I need a statement here, and we're getting nowhere. Mr. Macpherson, can you help us out here?" asks the policeman.

"Yes, out there, I said my name is Riveau Macpherson; my mother's Francophone. There were a lot of Francophones out there."

"Can we solve this matter of the damage done at the restaurant, a crime committed in Brandon and that this guy is on bail? What's he doing here anyway?"

"Why, I'd like to know too," the doctor says.

"Where do we begin, Josefu?" says Bill.

He does not smile back. "Kibuye? Kigali? What we saw first?" he replies.

Bill begins with Josefu's parents and reaching the point when he came to New York to work at the UN headquarters. Bill says, "We realised a storm was brewing in Rwanda. You know the Dallaire he mentions?"

"How do you spell that? We have something on that, a name he was calling, besides the other guy's," says the policeman. "This is all very interesting and it's been a while since we heard such a cockamamie story. But we must get to the point."

"The general, I've heard of him! I know whom he means now," says the other policeman. "I've seen him on TV–some kinda hero who's gone bananas now! One of Canada's finest, among Generals," he said.

"So this other guy's not a drug dealer or anything so we can cross him off," says the elder policeman who is taking notes.

Bill waits patiently. "Dallaire warned of a massacre in Rwanda, planned in advance. At the UN, where Josefu and I worked, nobody was willing to act. And afterwards, the perpetrators escaped as if they were refugees, the ones who had organised the massacres. And again the UN didn't check them, didn't stop them, but fed them like everyone else on the other side of the border, though they made raids back into Rwanda. That is what bugged Josefu, that's what drove him."

The senior policeman stops Bill again. "Look, I've got the picture. Before you go any further, I'll see if the restaurant will drop their complaint."

"He'll pay compensation for the damage. And he gives to charities, so a police charity perhaps?" says Bill.

"Hey, I'd be careful, if I were you. You may be from the big city, but out here that sounds like a bribe to me! We'll be back. Don't jump bail."

⋮

"Nobody would speak, Josefu, when we looked for you," says Bill. "Then you wouldn't talk when you were found. You had that diarrhoea again and no Marie Immaculée to help out, you were a mess, you stank."

"I'm sorry," says Josefu with a grave voice.

"You can say that again. But the worst was that you just stared. And wouldn't walk, even to the toilet. You peed and shat in your clothes. We were out of our minds. Gabrielle thought you had some catching, incurable disease and moved out to the Red Cross. If you want to know, that was almost the last I saw of her. She sent me an email later saying she had cancelled her UNDP contracts and wasn't returning to Haiti. When I replied the email returned as undelivered. Did you want to hear that? It's over. It always was."

"I hated you, though."

"Yes, Josefu. I'm not your Dad. That's what Gabrielle said to me. This is embarrassing," Bill adds, turning to the doctor who sits taking notes.

"Can we pause, now?" she says.

"In October it will be seven years," Josefu says to Bill.

"You're lucid. It's so strange, this mixture of lucidity and then not," he replies.

The doctor returns with a small, plump, black haired woman, also in civilian clothes, whose eyes sparkle and catch Josefu's attention immediately.

The doctor says, "Here is a colleague of mine from Assiniboine Community College. She specialises in mental health for Native Studies. We have, it is sad to say, several Aboriginals here in our unit."

Josefu says, "I have a friend in Banff, a Stoney, and he has helped me on my way here."

"So you weren't travelling alone?" asks Bill.

"I did. But his name is Joe Swift and he sometimes appeared as a voice, or a slight movement." Josefu closes his eyes. "He encouraged me."

"Did you see him?" the doctor asks slowly.

"I'm an African. We don't have to see everything, we just know."

"It's something I understand; we get a lot of this in Native Studies, in Minority Studies. We are thinking about forming our own ways of giving therapy. Like, we think there should be sweat lodges for our young Aboriginal men, here and in the prisons."

"Do you know where you are?" asks the doctor.

There is a long silence, and then he says, "About two hundred kilometres from Winnipeg. I saw Brandon on the map."

"You have complete recall, with no medication. Yet you still don't remember yesterday? This is confidential; there's no police here," the doctor adds.

"Afrika sat beside you day and night, you know," says Bill, interrupting. "He and I cleaned you as best we could. There was a brilliant Australian medical team, sent by Tousignant. The doctor poked around a bit. But one look and he said you had to be flown home." Turning to the two hospital staff, Bill adds, "I can tell you straight away, the diagnosis was 'severe post traumatic stress'. There's lots of kinds, they say, but he had his kind. Having him live in Banff, later, was as far as he could get away from reminders, for no African political exiles to bug him. Yeah, that's his diagnosis."

"Could be. Knowing people around here, Mr. Macpherson, don't quote me, but I suggest you go yourself and see if you can get the complaint dropped at the Hi-Way Esso Restaurant. I think we can confidently say there was no criminal intent. He ought to be out enjoying the sun," and the doctor waves her hand.

"There is one thing I cannot understand, never have," Bill continues after a pause, including the doctors into the conversation, "How was it that these local people, the Rwandans, with so much of their own sorrow, were so upset by your illness, Josefu? A mob of visitors! A few suspected murderers turned up too, of course. You know Kibuye. And prisoners sent messages of good hope. People you'd interviewed about whole family massacres, they came like ghosts, standing outside our office, asking Afrika about you. Weird!"

Bill sighs, then continues: "One of the Bisesero survivors came. They asked for nothing, just news, how were you? A woman brought a chicken for you. She knew Marie Immaculée. She said God had taken her, not that the enemy had finally got her. Do you hear, Josefu? It was so haunting afterwards. It tore all the heart out of me."

Josefu's eyes are burning. "Did I ever say it before, what I feared?" He takes a breath and says ponderously, "That our own outsiders' sorrow for the Rwandans would hide theirs? At best, we had the pain of the guilty."

"But they encourage us," says Bill, "giving more importance to our little ailments than to themselves. Who knows, it may be some form of escapism. I meet with Rwandans sometimes, in Toronto, in Montreal. I never told you, Josefu, because, well, when you were in Banff…. Well, you know why," Bill says, glancing at the two doctors.

"I suggest we get you down to emergency to have those stitches removed," offered the first doctor.

Josefu rises slowly and takes a step. "My clothes," he says, finally.

"The police have your belongings, but I'll see if Social Services can find you something," she says.

Alone with him, Bill tells Josefu, "You came here from the jail in an ambulance just now. But out there we took you in a wheelchair up to a helicopter, simplest way out of Kibuye. They fixed you some kind of diapers. And gave you earphones. You just had that vacant look, no response, and we spoon-fed you. You swallowed liquids but wouldn't chew. Food just fell out of your mouth. Real scary."

Josefu remains silent, so Bill continues: "In Kigali, the government knew, Kagame knew, your relative came the very next day from Uganda. Mary and he still write to each other. Never told you in Banff, didn't know how. But they write. And Afrika's Dad came to see you in Kigali. He gave you some herbal tea. I've never seen a man cry like Afrika. For that matter, Père Ambroise nearly lost his faith, the little he had left. His entire family were killed but he'd comforted people, he'd done a lot, he had pride in his work, but you, you kind of humiliated him because he found he wasn't able to help you. And he tried more than anyone else, more than your own mother tried. You scared her away, but not Père Ambroise. Yes, you made him feel helpless and it took away his pride," Bill repeats quietly. "There's something I have to tell you about Père Ambroise . . ."

"Get out! Get out!" Josefu shouts.

"I'll go and get some coffee," says Bill and he runs down the solid floored corridor.

The sun is rising over Marie Immaculée's adopted avocado tree. And she stands before the tree, between Josefu and the sun. And she shadows so carefully the sun's light and warmth and trembling, that it is kind to him and he bears its shining force assuredly. With each arm, he shows his mother and his father to her and they rise above the ground and all is well. His clothes are clean, his cheeks are smooth and though they move out of sight until the firmament is starred and dark, he does not feel abandoned. The peaks of all the green hills glow and grow more rounded. Here and there, they spread out and become prairies.

⋮

"What happened next?" Josefu asks.

The lenient psychiatrist has arranged permission for Josefu to stay with Bill at the Victoria Inn, while waiting for the police to drop the assault charge; the restaurant dropped theirs. Josefu's stitches—his crown of thorns as Bill put it—had been removed and they both are lying back on twin beds.

"You remember Operation Homeward, our big plan to bring the refugees home from Zaire? The UN didn't do it; the Rwandan new army did. And the war continues like you said it would. The whole region is unstable. Last year we saw in the new millennium, the year 2000. You probably know that, so why am I saying it? Oh my, the reports came in of massacres of humans, of cattle, the mindlessness on the Goma side of Lake Kivu. And now it's called the Democratic Republic of Congo," says Bill.

"What is? Zaire?" Josefu's eyes burn. "I've come back from the dead, haven't I?" Josefu closes his eyes tightly. "All these days while I was driving, I struggled to stop them, Hitler's year 1933, or Rwanda's 1994."

"Time ticks by anyway. There's a lot to do." Bill rises, opens a curtain to bring in the daylight.

"That's now, whatever year it is now. What about my leaving Rwanda? I don't know a thing. I didn't want to know, I suppose. But now it's over, my journey, I mean. So how did it end over there?"

"Never thought you'd ask."

"Neither did I - But I have to know."

Bill pauses for a long time before starting: "General Tousignant, remember, was the kind of guy who took every expatriate UN staff member as his personal responsibility. The problem was not medical or transport, but Canada. You've never asked me, why Canada?"

"Ellie asked me the same."

"Ellie? Another of your spirits?" says Bill.

"You were telling me about my leaving Rwanda."

"Yeah, I went to Tousignant, kind of Canadian to Canadian, to help us out. I told him how you never left Mary's side when our son Mark died. Mary was insistent you come to Canada and it would have broken her heart if it didn't happen. What could I explain to him except that we both knew what wives can say. Common sense is all that's needed."

"Common sense," Josefu repeats.

"So Tousignant pulled out all the stops. He had good relations in Nairobi with the Canadian High Commissioner and the roving Ambassador for the Great Lakes Region. The highest you could get, Josefu, all pleaded on your behalf. And wrapped in blankets, wheeled along the airport corridors, you got to Ottawa. That's when I really cried, that you couldn't see anything, the parliament and the pretty buildings."

Josefu looks at him quizzically.

"Yes, it was a crazy thought perhaps. But it mattered to me. I had held back when I left our friends in Rwanda. It was such a mess."

"Me?"

"Yes, you. But me too. All the way back on the different flights, I was talking to Père Ambroise in my head, you know the feeling? Not giving way?"

"To what?"

"God damn you, Josefu! It shouldn't have ended like that." Without looking at him he adds, "I shouldn't be telling you this. You'll get sick again." He pauses.

"Oh my. Well, now we do our bit with fund raising, see? You'll have to dip into your pocket now, I'll have you know."

Josefu assents with a nod. He says, "I wonder though, if there is still a stench out there in Rwanda, after seven years—the rainy season is over now. Are things growing on the hills again?"

Bill turns away from him.

22.

Josefu stands in a hall doorway and sighs.

On the top floor of the Hotel Mille Collines, he sees a large wedding is taking place beneath banners of Rwandan flags. Several hundred guests, mostly in elegant Western clothes, sit in tidy rows of wooden chairs as if in a concert hall. The lighting is dim but the bridal pair are behind a brightly lit table, up on a podium at the far end. They hardly move.

Below them, a tall master of ceremonies in a dark, buttoned suit talks agitatedly into a microphone, overriding the piped music that relays popular American songs. Josefu flinches whenever the sound system screeches, as attempts are made for it to become even louder. Some men and women stand up, to talk into their mobile phones near the aisle, but they move away when a tiered wedding cake is rolled by on a squeaking trolley. The guests are eating chicken legs and finger food from plastic plates. Josefu guesses the hosts were charged this Kigali hotel's lavish prices; the money has come from God knows where.

He is standing by the ballroom entrance with Ellie and Mary. They have wandered up after losing their way in the hotel. Now they quickly move back, not to appear to be intruders. They search silently for the lift and reach the foyer, busy with humanitarian aid officials wearing conference labels.

Ellie says she will sit for a moment and rest. Josefu goes to lean against the reception desk, which is the same as it had always been. Tapping it affectionately, he now anxiously looks out as cars draw up. Government officials alight from three black limousines and several soldiers salute them by the doors.

Afrika is coming any minute now with one of his brothers, the one who is a state employee and updates its official website on a daily basis. Josefu with Ellie and Mary had accompanied a cargo delivery from Bill's charity. It is for setting up an entire printing press, hopefully to make reading materials more accessible. There is only one paper manufacturer in the whole of East Africa, Bill remarked, and that's hardly conducive to building democracy, not when paper and printing ink have to be imported expensively from Italy or France. Josefu immediately offered to go.

Watching guests collecting messages from reception, he attempts to be reconciled to his heaviness of heart.

He has heard the news: Père Ambroise is dead.

Bill had said nothing and left it for Josefu to discover from Afrika who met them at the airport. The next morning Josefu cried into Ellie's lap, a new sensation, before facing a day in Kigali without the priest. Père Ambroise had stepped on a mine on his way to a burial site. Afrika explained that in Rwanda, though, nobody could really know what happened, whether he had been killed and then placed on a mine to blow up, or whether it was an accident. His three sisters, however, all live in Belgium and one is about to get Belgian nationality to compete in the Olympic games in future years.

Afrika and his brother collect their three visitors from the hotel. He has continued to work as an interpreter and rents out his taxi-cab. So now he drives them through the town in his own small car. They have to queue in the traffic, which surprises Josefu. But street children and beggars are swarming by like flocks of birds. Ellie touches his hand.

All the taxis are busy with guests, especially since part of a Festival of World Music is taking place right then in the capital. The town has grown, but so has its cemetery, Afrika tells them. The fight against aids and tuberculosis has got to continue unabated, he remarks. Josefu holds his head in both hands. Ellie anxiously puts her hand on his knee.

They have a full program, even though several people they hoped to visit are not there. Paul Kagame, the new President of Rwanda, is on an official state visit, so Josefu will not see him. Neither is Masisi, his relative, stationed across the border nearby, as he too is away on a military course for senior staff in the United States. War threatens to engulf the whole Great Lakes Region. New Rwanda is at the centre.

"O ye of little faith," Josefu mutters, but not knowing whom to address.

At the earliest opportunity, Afrika asks Josefu to arrange for his eldest son to study abroad. Perhaps Ellie can help too, he suggests. The son will soon be of an age when he will have to do military service, and half the country's resources are still being used, fighting in the Congo.

Josefu says he will first arrange for Afrika and his wife to come for a holiday in Banff, and then he will see what he can do. He will start the formalities for their visit immediately, at a reception for diplomats that very evening.

He has been invited there by Madame Dubois, who never left Rwanda. Her warmth was impressive when she greeted Josefu after all this time. He had remembered to bring her some leaflets on colitis. She gave him a photo of herself with General Tousignant.

Josefu put it in his wallet next to his small, autographed picture of General Romeo Dallaire, which he carries everywhere.

Afrika's car radio has a broadcast in French now. It announces that several detainees at the International Tribunal, top Rwandan former government officials accused of planning the genocide, have protested about the quality of the food the UN is giving them in their prison cells.

"It's embarrassing," says Afrika, "For me, a Rwandan, when I hear that, it's embarrassing, that's what it is. But you know me," he says to Josefu. "Tomorrow we shall see something beautiful," he adds, changing the subject.

If Ellie can manage it, they will visit Butare in one day, but not Kibuye, and Mary said it would be too painful anyway. They are only staying for a week but might come back another time, though, with more cargo. Bill is very active. It is a good place to give aid, really, Josefu repeats patiently.

He himself hopes to contribute funds to a centre for traumatised women, though few surmount their shyness and come for treatment. Some of the few surviving victims are being asked by the government, without support and comfort, to testify on their villages' grassy slopes at gachacha traditional courts. This new project will take thousands of the accused from their prisons to the villages, to be judged by local opinion. But Josefu finds he is unable to gauge if Gachacha will be a genuine 'Truth Commission' unique to Africa, since the people he meets will not debate its usefulness. So far, he notes that although there are some national monuments erected to honour those who suffered in 1994, seven years on, few people discuss what really happened in any depth.

Humans take a long time to speak about a genocide, he realises, perhaps more than a lifetime allows.

One evening Afrika and Josefu spend alone, on a hill, up a road past the mosque, drinking beer above the city, and they sit in a corner in the increasing darkness. And the deafening silence between them is merciful.

THE END

Acknowledgments

My thanks first and foremost go to both *Colleen Armstrong* and *Francois Bugingo*. This book could never have taken the form it has without the meticulous help of **Colleen Armstrong** of Winnipeg, whose generosity has been boundless. *Francois Bugingo*, Rwandan now in Montreal, provided constant encouragement, guidance, introductions and he patiently imparted knowledge right to the end and beyond.

I am deeply indebted to them.

I would also like to thank the following (in alphabetical order) and others not named here but who will know who they are:

Openycan Akwanya, Glenn Armstrong, the late Jim Armstrong and Kay Armstrong, Nicholas Avery, Jean Baptiste Barambwira, Franck Batimba, Richard Batsinduka, Hugh Beach, Xandra Bingley, Emmanuel Biziganyi, Carol Black, the late Paul Bowles, Dizzy Buckingham, Terence Buie, Jane Conway-Gordon, Alan Cooke, Hazel Dakers, the late Ivan Dragadze my brother, the late Peter Dragadze my brother, Yvonne Meyer Dragadze, Willy Fabre, Ruth Fainlight, Leila Farrah, Beatrice Fion, Janet Fyle, Jean Gahururu, Mourka Glogowski, Abbe Pierre Haba, Marie-I Ingabire, Yvonne Kleefield, Nicholas Kolarz, Ignatius Mugabo, Jackie Mugabo, Beatrice Mukansinga, Epiphanie Mukanyawaya, Vincent Ndacyayisenga, Vedaste Ngarambe, Charles Noble, Francois Xavier Nsanzuwera, Frances Ongeira, Sancto Ongena, Brian Patton in Canmore, Leslie Plommer, Christian Scherrer, Cherry Scott, Josias Semujanga, Servilien Sebasoni, late Alan Sillitoe, Sybille van der Sprenkel, John Thompson, Guy Tousignant, Alice Violini, Michael Walsh, late Shaun de Warren, Antoinette Wortmann, Joan Wyatt, Vivian Wyatt, the women of the Mgwira Ndumva Association, *my friends at* Hammersmith Quaker Meeting, *the* Rwandan diplomatic delegations *to the* UN, the UK and Belgium, *the* Georgia and Azerbaijan delegations *to the* UN, *the information offices of* Alberta and Saskatchewan Provinces *and my* publisher *Annemarie Skjold Jensen.*

I am grateful to my ballet teacher, **Josephine Bell** and to **Candace Wait** and staff at **Yaddo** and the staff at **Blue Mountain Centre**, *all thanks to whom I was able to continue writing.*

Tamara Dragadze

About the Author

Dr. Tamara Dragadze B.A. (Kent) D.Phil (Oxon)
b Oswestry, Welsh border, UK.
Third generation British, Dragadze's parental relatives are from Georgia; she spent her childhood in Paris and Tangier, returning to the UK to complete an Academic education.

As an accomplished researcher, scholar and writer with more than 50 academic publications, to her name, Dragadze is an anthropoligist and social critic of some reknown. She lives in London.

languages:

English, French, Spanish Italian, Russian, Georgian (learning Danish)

Published Fiction:
"Like Milk on the Fire" 1965, Chatto and Windus

Proposed Fiction 2014 -, Whyte Tracks
Bk II "Texan Dreams in Chechnya"
Bk III "The Many Thoughts of Jane Kingsley"
"The Great Work of a Summer Month"
"Going Higher With Alison"
"Remembering the Good"

Published

WhyteTracks

Mill House
Møllehavevej 11
3200 Helsinge
Denmark
www.whytetracks.eu.com

Lightning Source UK Ltd.
Milton Keynes UK
UKOW02f0207091014

239739UK00004B/62/P

9 788792 63239